HELLSING ⑤

ヘルシング

平野耕太
KOHTA HIRANO

translation
DUANE JOHNSON

lettering
WILBERT LACUNA

DARK
HORSE
MANGA

DMP
Digital Manga
Publishing

publishers
MIKE RICHARDSON and HIKARU SASAHARA

editors
TIM ERVIN and FRED LUI

collection designer
DAVID NESTELLE

English-language version produced by
DARK HORSE COMICS and DIGITAL MANGA PUBLISHING.

HELLSING VOL. 5

published by
Dark Horse Manga
a division of Dark Horse Comics, Inc.
10956 SE Main Street
Milwaukie, OR 97222

DarkHorse.com

Digital Manga Publishing
1487 W. 178th St. Ste. 300
Gardena, CA 90248

DMPBooks.com

To find a comics shop in your area, call the
Comic Shop Locator Service toll-free at 1-888-266-4226

First edition: November 2004
ISBN 978-1-59307-272-8

7 9 10 8 6

Printed at Lake Book Manufacturing, Inc., Melrose Park, IL, USA

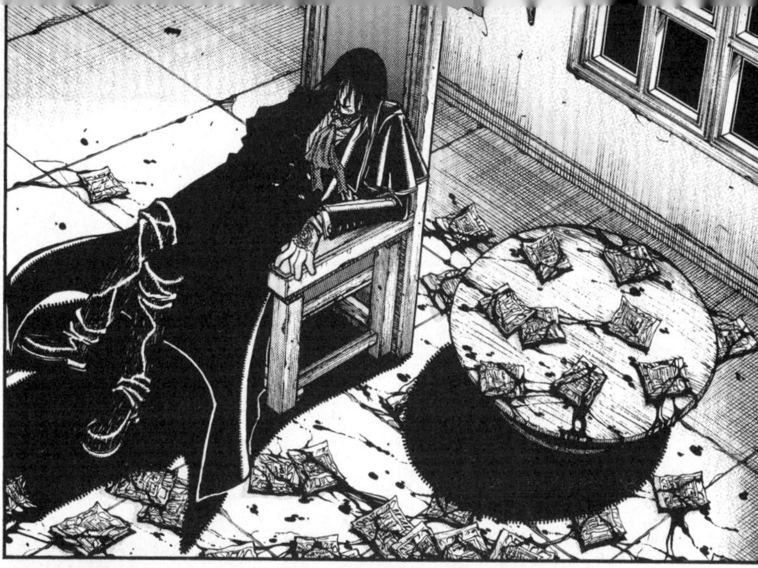

HELLSING

ヘルシング

平野耕太

ORDER 1 FLASH POINT

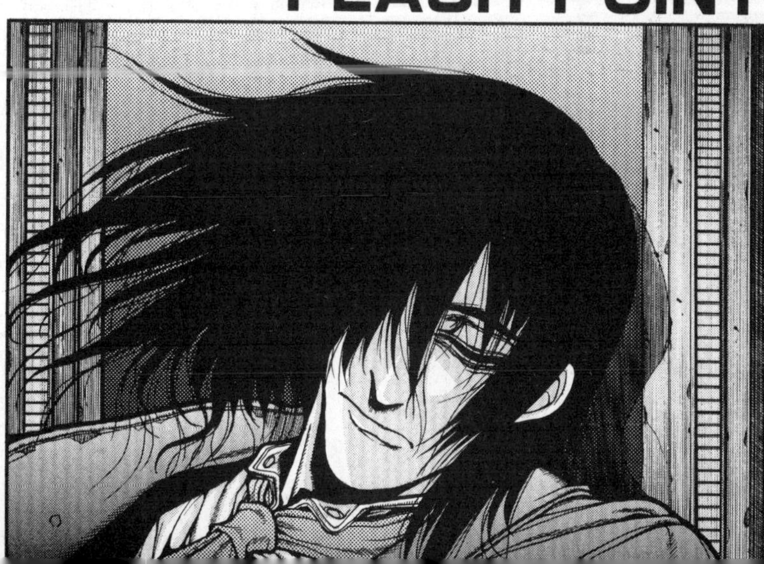

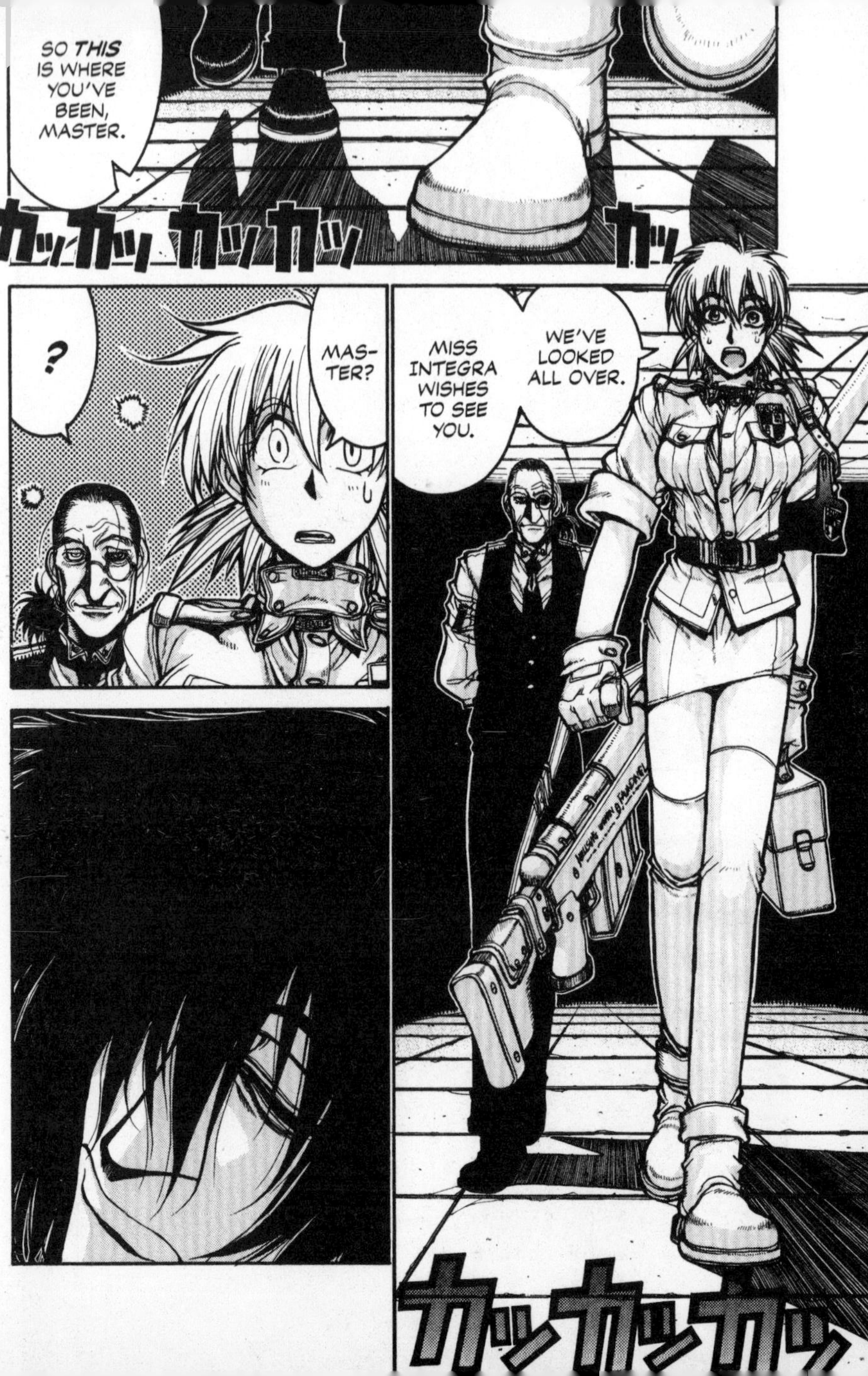
SO THIS IS WHERE YOU'VE BEEN, MASTER.
カッカッ カッカッ
カッ
WE'VE LOOKED ALL OVER.
MISS INTEGRA WISHES TO SEE YOU.
カッカッカッ
MAS-TER?
?

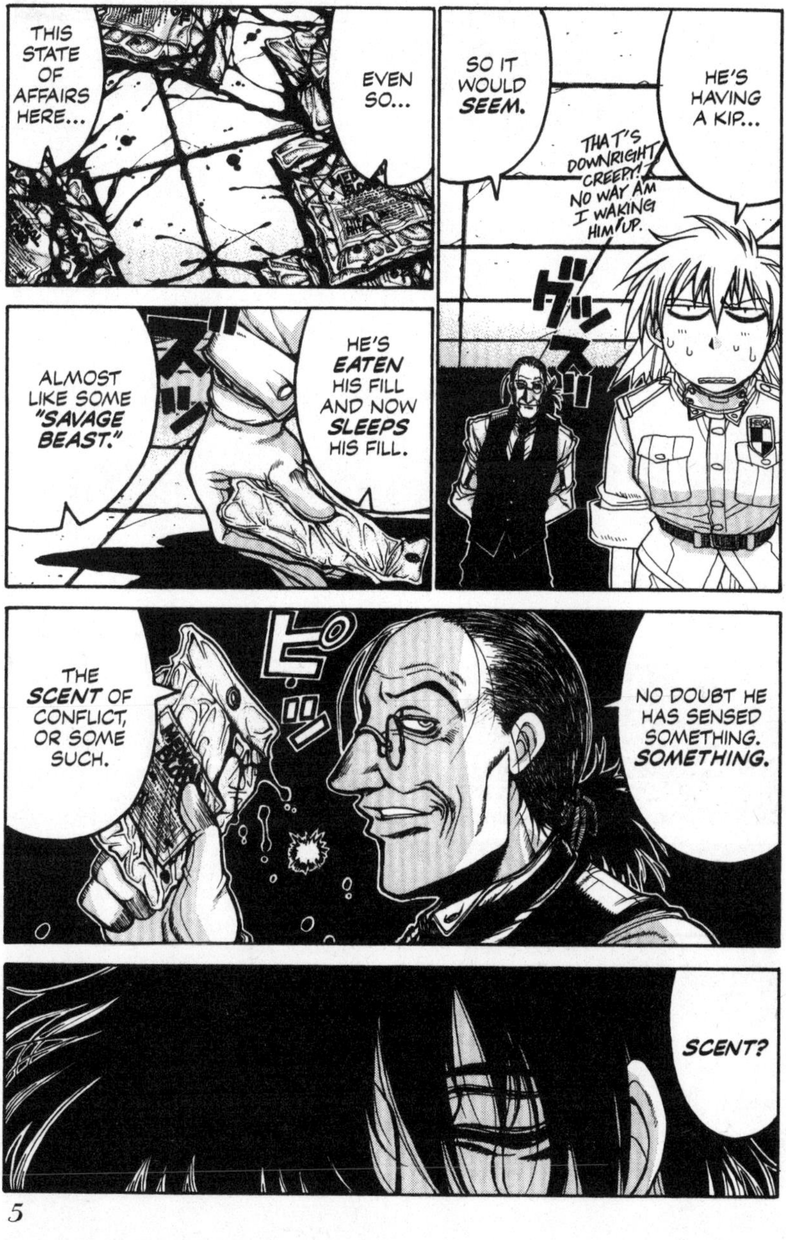
HE'S HAVING A KIP...
SO IT WOULD SEEM.
THAT'S DOWNRIGHT CREEPY!! NO WAY AM I WAKING HIM UP.
EVEN SO...
THIS STATE OF AFFAIRS HERE...
HE'S EATEN HIS FILL AND NOW SLEEPS HIS FILL.
ALMOST LIKE SOME "SAVAGE BEAST."
NO DOUBT HE HAS SENSED SOMETHING. SOMETHING.
THE SCENT OF CONFLICT, OR SOME SUCH.
SCENT?

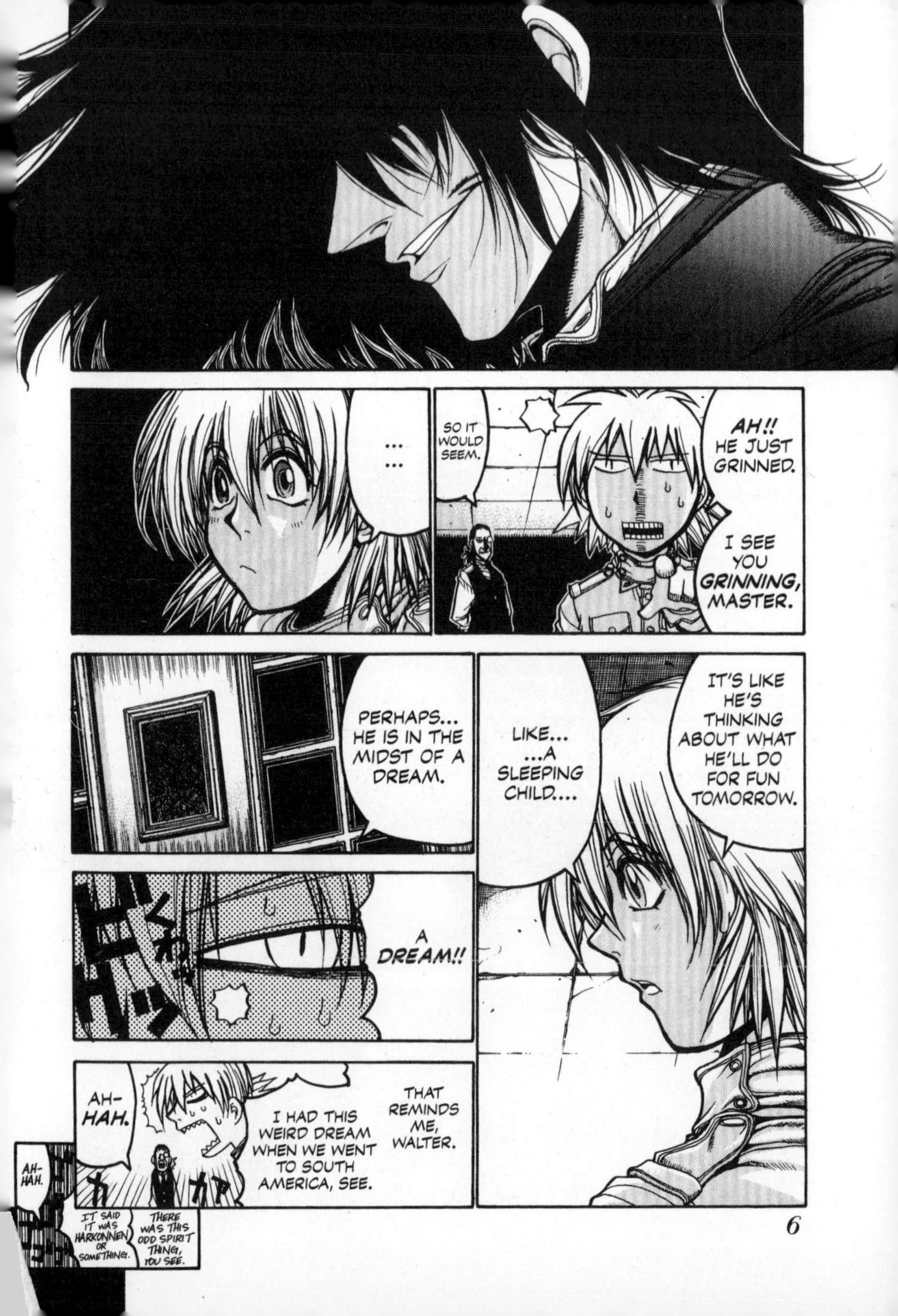

AH!! HE JUST GRINNED.
I SEE YOU GRINNING, MASTER.
SO IT WOULD SEEM.
... ...
IT'S LIKE HE'S THINKING ABOUT WHAT HE'LL DO FOR FUN TOMORROW.
LIKE... ...A SLEEPING CHILD....
PERHAPS... HE IS IN THE MIDST OF A DREAM.
A DREAM!!
THAT REMINDS ME, WALTER.
I HAD THIS WEIRD DREAM WHEN WE WENT TO SOUTH AMERICA, SEE.
AH-HAH.
THERE WAS THIS ODD SPIRIT THING, YOU SEE.
IT SAID IT WAS HARKONNEN OR SOMETHING.
AH-HAH.

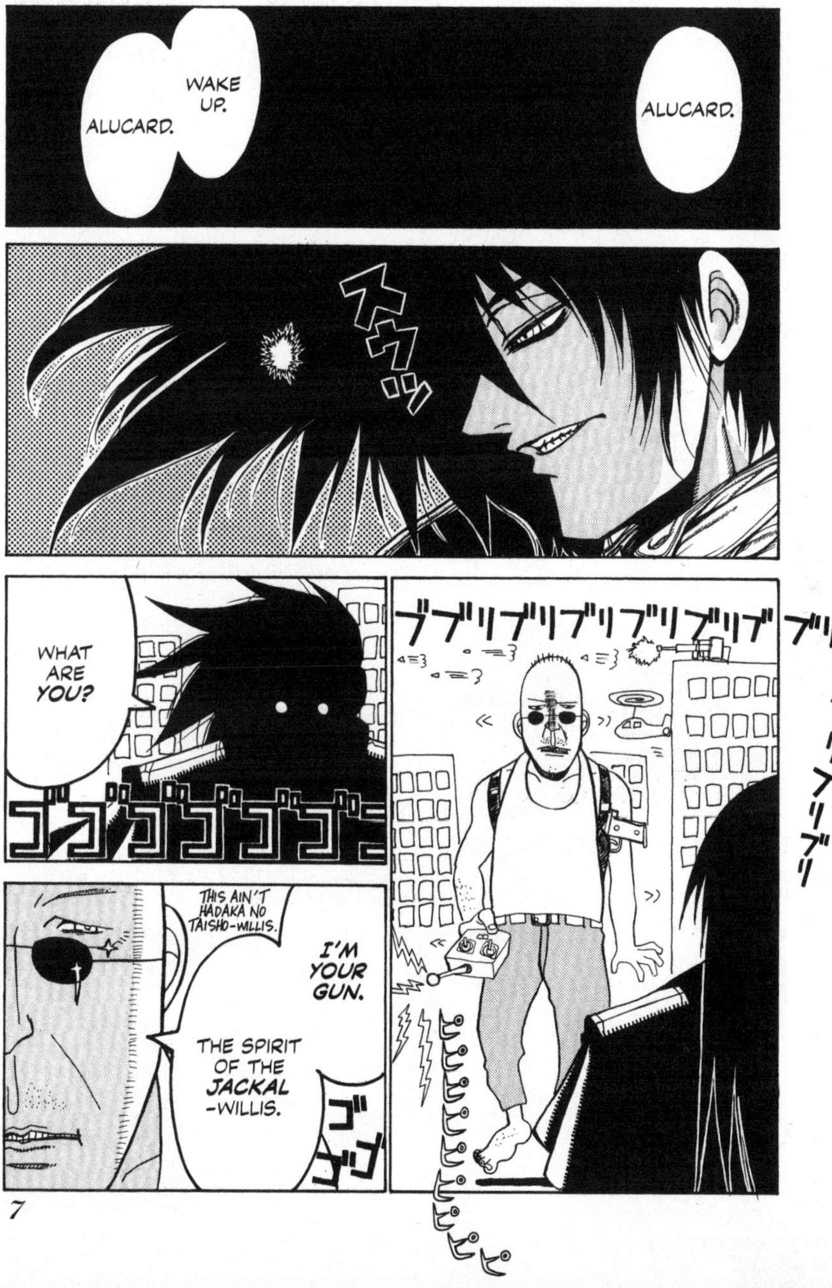
ALUCARD.
WAKE UP.
ALUCARD.
スゥッ
ブブリブリブリブリブリブ
WHAT ARE YOU?
ゴゴゴゴゴゴ
THIS AIN'T HADAKA NO TAISHO-WILLIS.
I'M YOUR GUN.
THE SPIRIT OF THE JACKAL-WILLIS.
ゴゴゴ

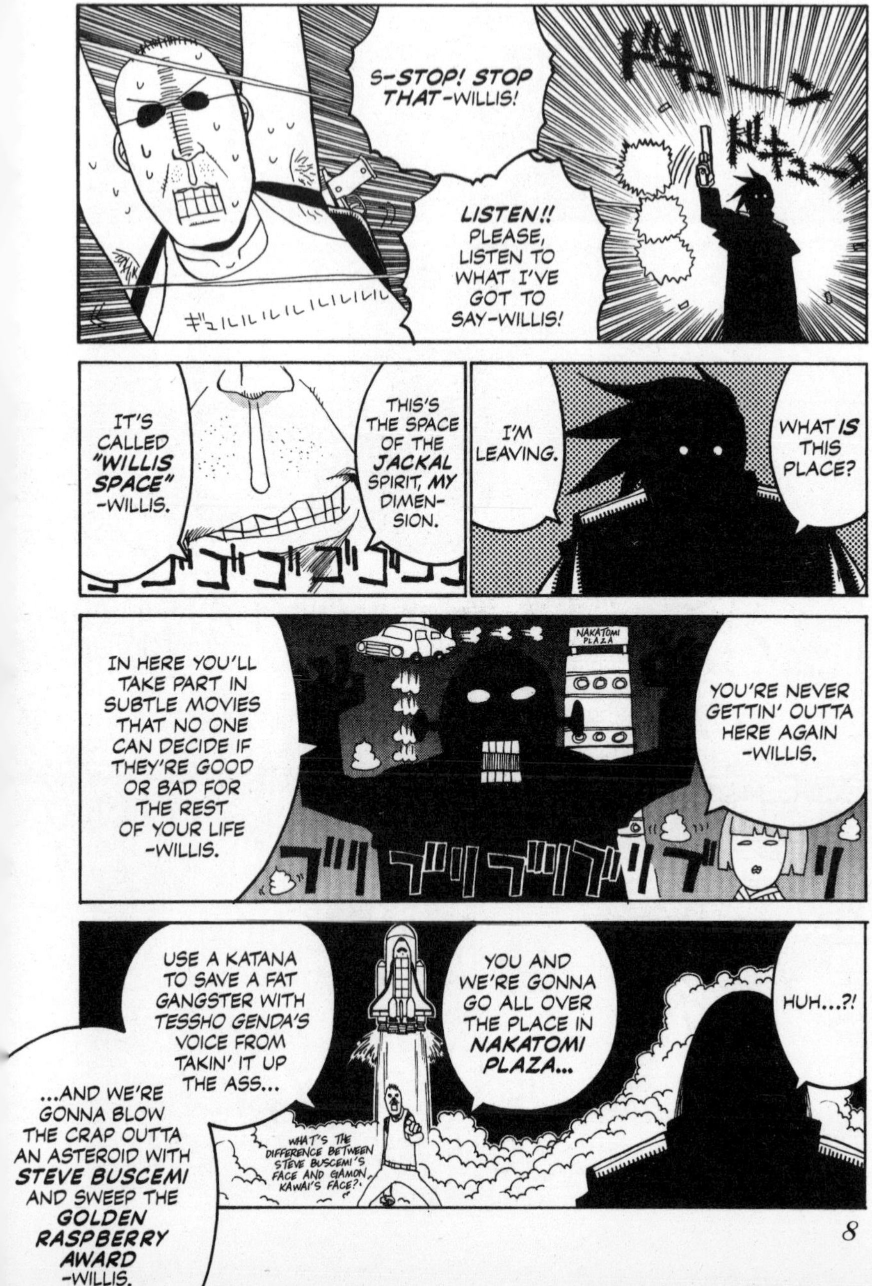
ドキューン
ドキューン
S-STOP! STOP THAT-WILLIS!
LISTEN!! PLEASE, LISTEN TO WHAT I'VE GOT TO SAY-WILLIS!
WHAT IS THIS PLACE?
I'M LEAVING.
THIS'S THE SPACE OF THE JACKAL SPIRIT, MY DIMENSION.
IT'S CALLED "WILLIS SPACE" -WILLIS.
YOU'RE NEVER GETTIN' OUTTA HERE AGAIN -WILLIS.
NAKATOMI PLAZA
IN HERE YOU'LL TAKE PART IN SUBTLE MOVIES THAT NO ONE CAN DECIDE IF THEY'RE GOOD OR BAD FOR THE REST OF YOUR LIFE -WILLIS.
HUH...?!
YOU AND WE'RE GONNA GO ALL OVER THE PLACE IN NAKATOMI PLAZA...
USE A KATANA TO SAVE A FAT GANGSTER WITH TESSHO GENDA'S VOICE FROM TAKIN' IT UP THE ASS...
WHAT'S THE DIFFERENCE BETWEEN STEVE BUSCEMI'S FACE AND GIAMON KAWAI'S FACE?
...AND WE'RE GONNA BLOW THE CRAP OUTTA AN ASTEROID WITH STEVE BUSCEMI AND SWEEP THE GOLDEN RASPBERRY AWARD -WILLIS.

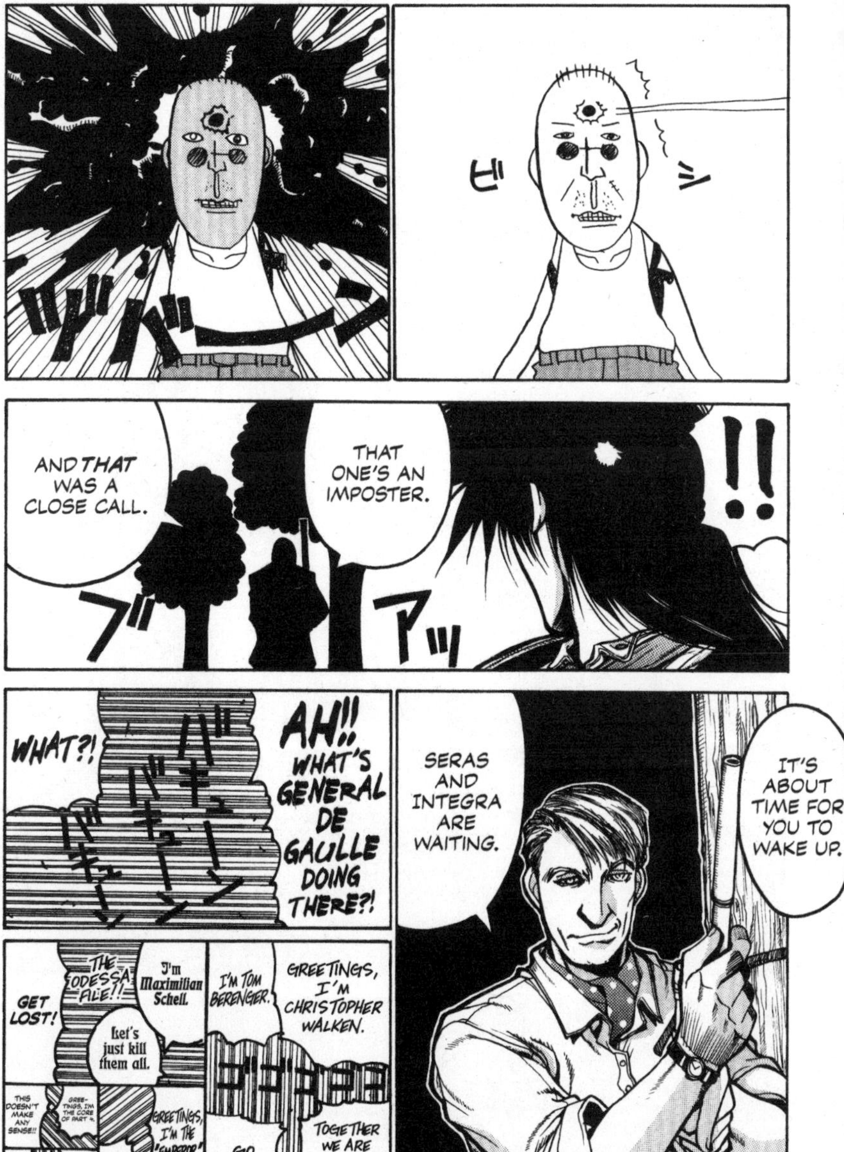

!!
THAT ONE'S AN IMPOSTER.
AND THAT WAS A CLOSE CALL.
IT'S ABOUT TIME FOR YOU TO WAKE UP.
SERAS AND INTEGRA ARE WAITING.
AH!! WHAT'S GENERAL DE GAULLE DOING THERE?!
WHAT?!
GREETINGS, I'M CHRISTOPHER WALKEN.
I'M TOM BERENGER.
TOGETHER WE ARE THE DOGS OF WAR. DEATH.
GO HOME.
I'm Maximilian Schell.
THE ODESSA FILE!!
GET LOST!
Let's just kill them all.
GREETINGS, I'M THE "EMPEROR."
WHO ARE YOU?!
GREETINGS, I'M THE CORE OF PART 4.
THIS DOESN'T MAKE ANY SENSE!!

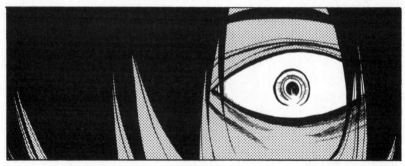

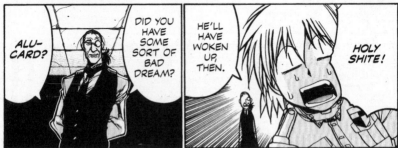

HOLY SHITE!
HE'LL HAVE WOKEN UP, THEN.
DID YOU HAVE SOME SORT OF BAD DREAM?
ALU-CARD?
NO.
IT'S NOTHING.
HMPH.
TO BE CONTINUED

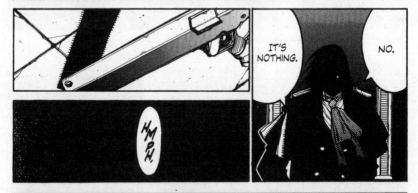

HELLSING ⑤

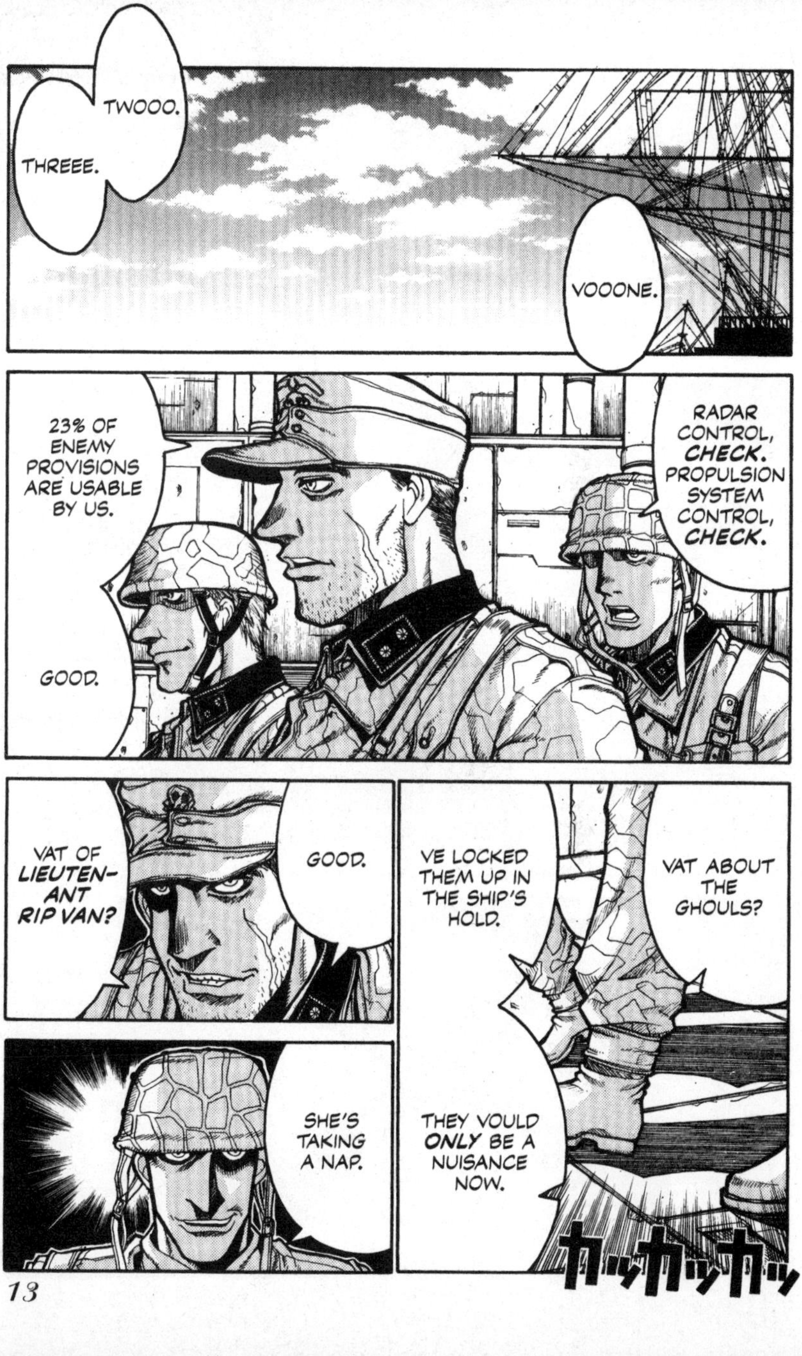
VOOONE.
TWOOO.
THREEE.
RADAR CONTROL, **CHECK.** PROPULSION SYSTEM CONTROL, **CHECK.**
23% OF ENEMY PROVISIONS ARE USABLE BY US.
GOOD.
VAT ABOUT THE GHOULS?
VE LOCKED THEM UP IN THE SHIP'S HOLD.
THEY VOULD **ONLY** BE A NUISANCE NOW.
カッカッカッ
GOOD.
VAT OF **LIEUTEN-ANT RIP VAN?**
SHE'S TAKING A NAP.

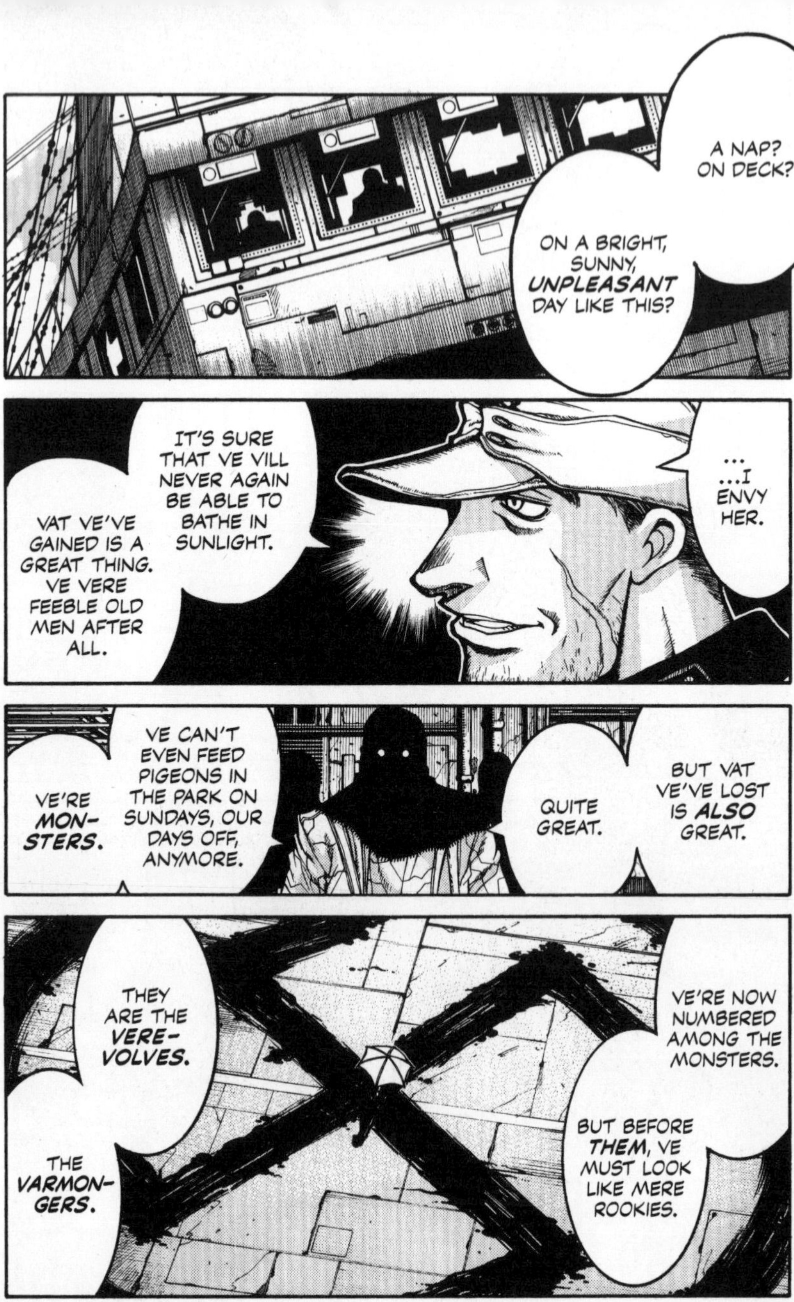
A NAP? ON DECK?
ON A BRIGHT, SUNNY, *UNPLEASANT* DAY LIKE THIS?
... ...I ENVY HER.
IT'S SURE THAT VE VILL NEVER AGAIN BE ABLE TO BATHE IN SUNLIGHT.
VAT VE'VE GAINED IS A GREAT THING. VE VERE FEEBLE OLD MEN AFTER ALL.
BUT VAT VE'VE LOST IS *ALSO* GREAT.
QUITE GREAT.
VE CAN'T EVEN FEED PIGEONS IN THE PARK ON SUNDAYS, OUR DAYS OFF, ANYMORE.
VE'RE *MONSTERS*.
VE'RE NOW NUMBERED AMONG THE MONSTERS.
BUT BEFORE *THEM*, VE MUST LOOK LIKE MERE ROOKIES.
THEY ARE THE *VEREVOLVES*.
THE *VARMONGERS*.

ORDER 2 D④

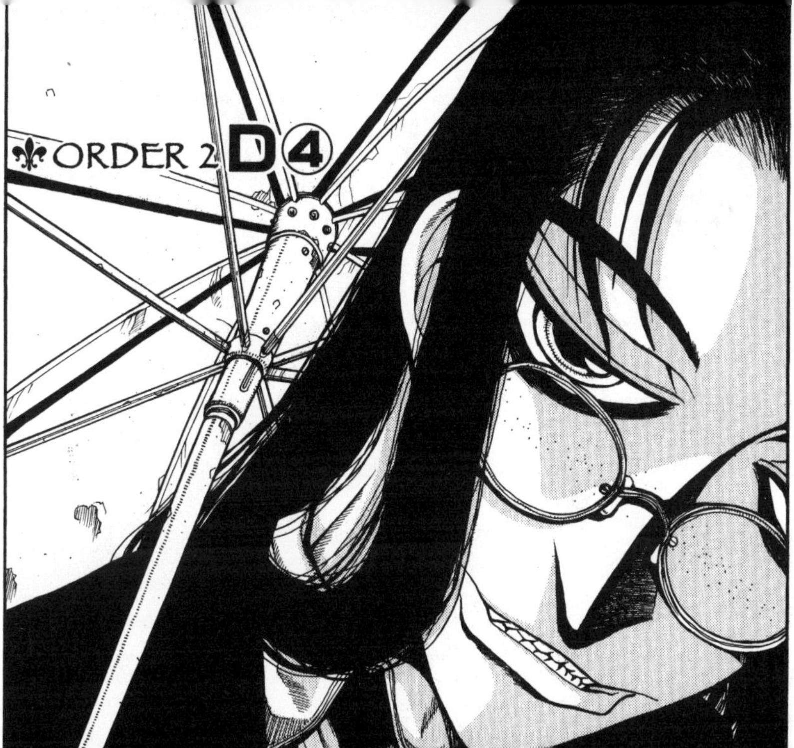

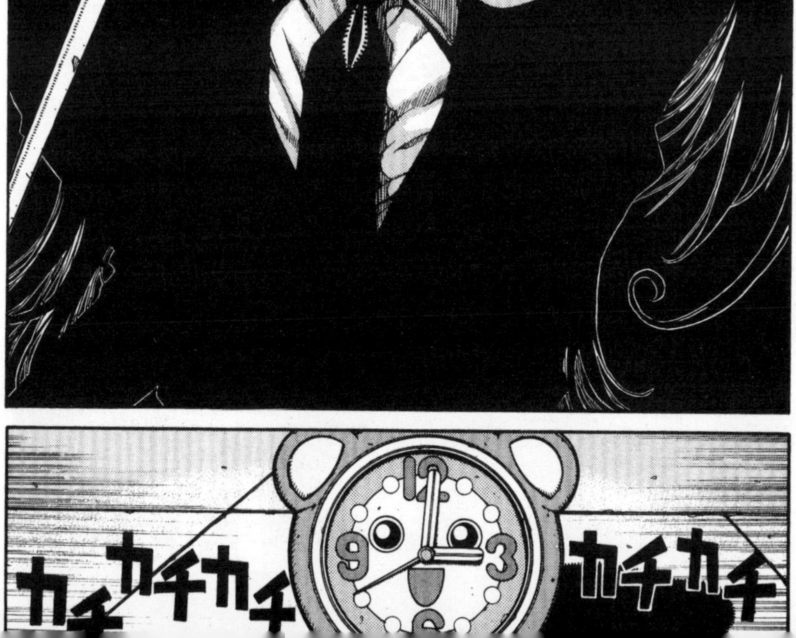
カチカチ
カチカチカチ

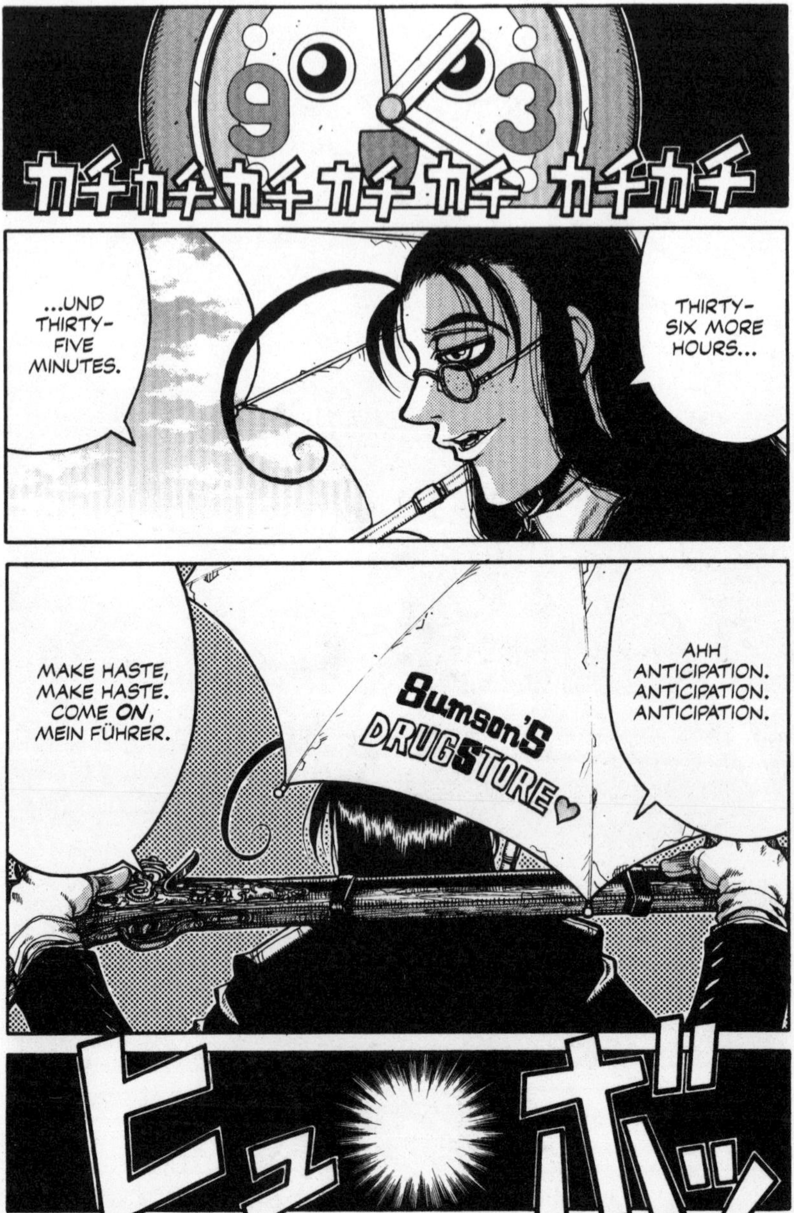
カチカチカチカチカチ カチカチ
THIRTY-SIX MORE HOURS...
...UND THIRTY-FIVE MINUTES.
AHH ANTICIPATION. ANTICIPATION. ANTICIPATION.
MAKE HASTE, MAKE HASTE. COME **ON**, MEIN FÜHRER.
Bumson'S DRUGSTORE
ヒュ
ボッ

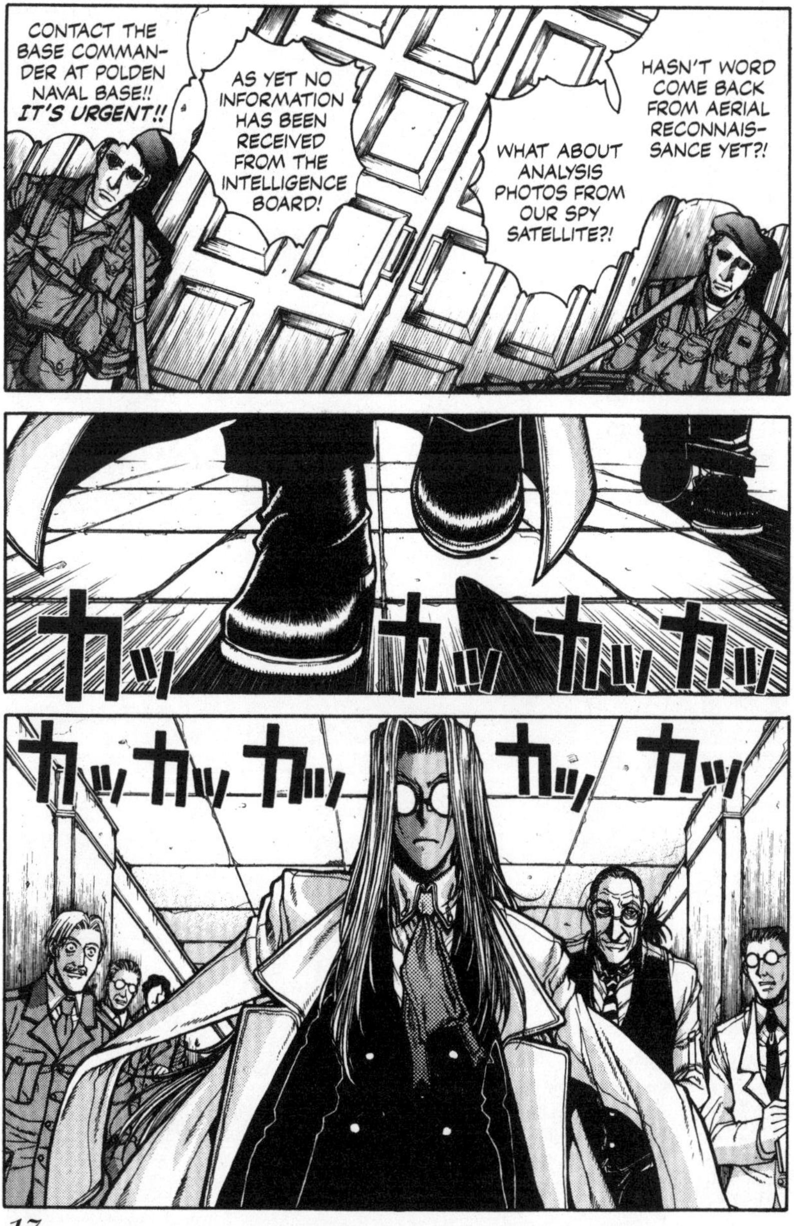

HASN'T WORD COME BACK FROM AERIAL RECONNAISSANCE YET?!
WHAT ABOUT ANALYSIS PHOTOS FROM OUR SPY SATELLITE?!
AS YET NO INFORMATION HAS BEEN RECEIVED FROM THE INTELLIGENCE BOARD!
CONTACT THE BASE COMMANDER AT POLDEN NAVAL BASE!! *IT'S URGENT!!*
カッ カッ カッ カッ
カッ カッ ガッ カッ カッ

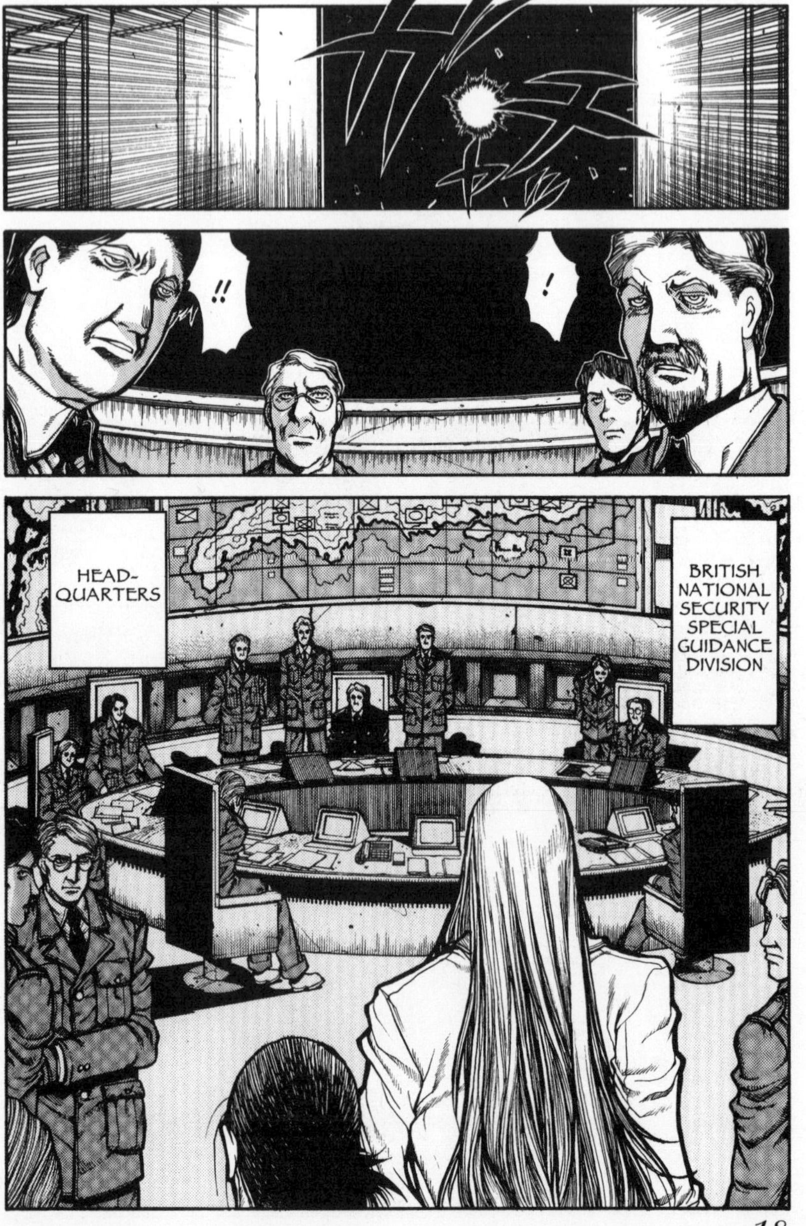
!
!!
BRITISH NATIONAL SECURITY SPECIAL GUIDANCE DIVISION
HEAD-QUARTERS

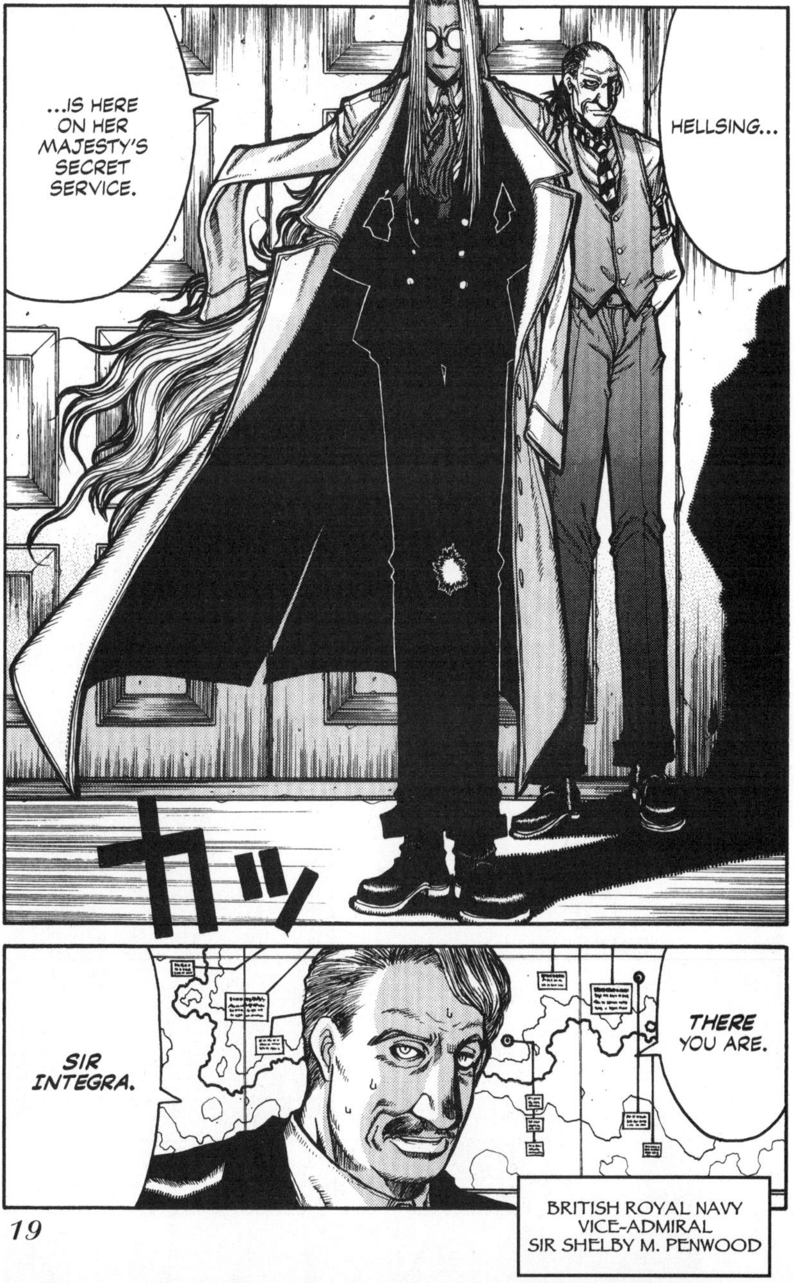
HELLSING...
...IS HERE ON HER MAJESTY'S SECRET SERVICE.
カッ
THERE YOU ARE.
SIR INTEGRA.
BRITISH ROYAL NAVY VICE-ADMIRAL SIR SHELBY M. PENWOOD

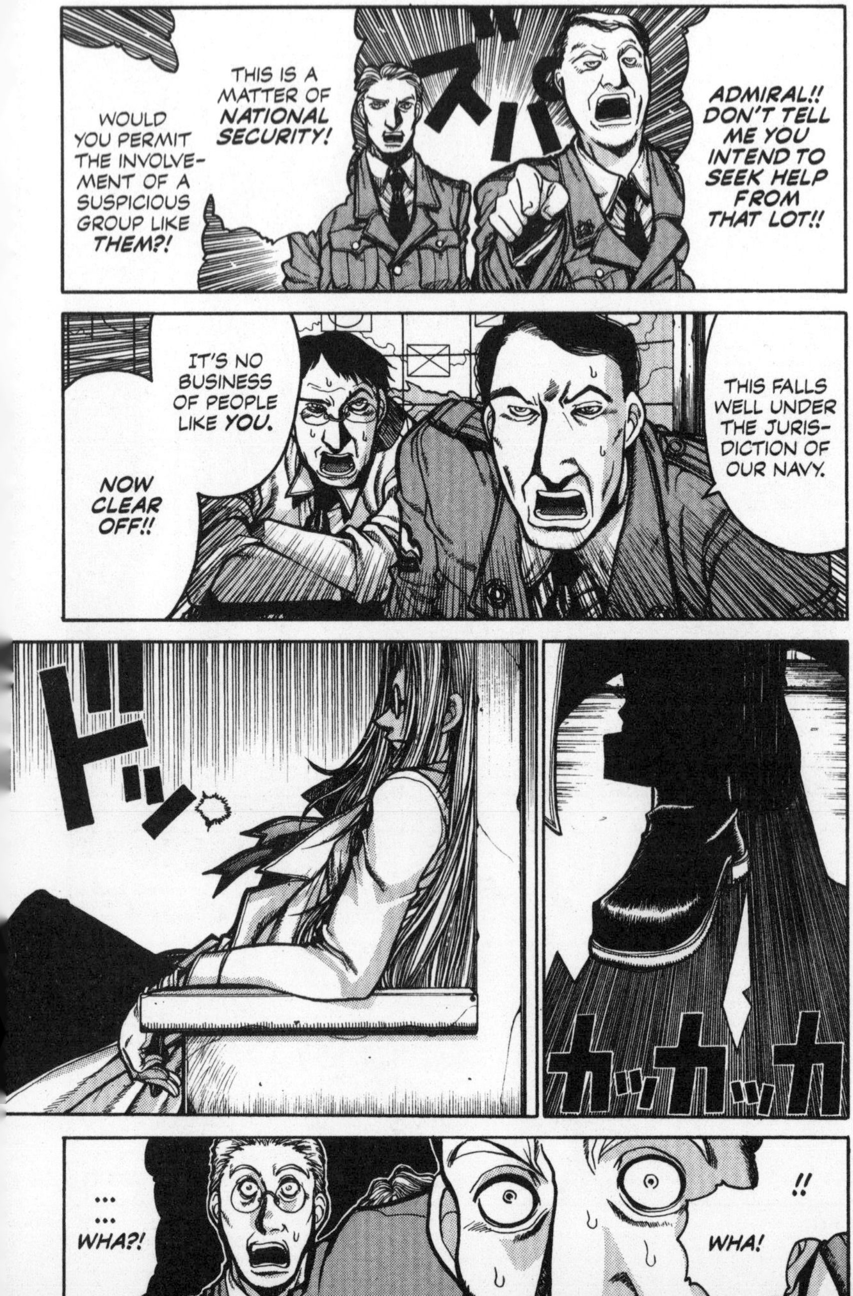
ADMIRAL!! DON'T TELL ME YOU INTEND TO SEEK HELP FROM THAT LOT!!
THIS IS A MATTER OF NATIONAL SECURITY!
WOULD YOU PERMIT THE INVOLVEMENT OF A SUSPICIOUS GROUP LIKE THEM?!
THIS FALLS WELL UNDER THE JURISDICTION OF OUR NAVY.
IT'S NO BUSINESS OF PEOPLE LIKE YOU.
NOW CLEAR OFF!!
カッカッカ
ドッ
!!
WHA!
...
...
WHA?!

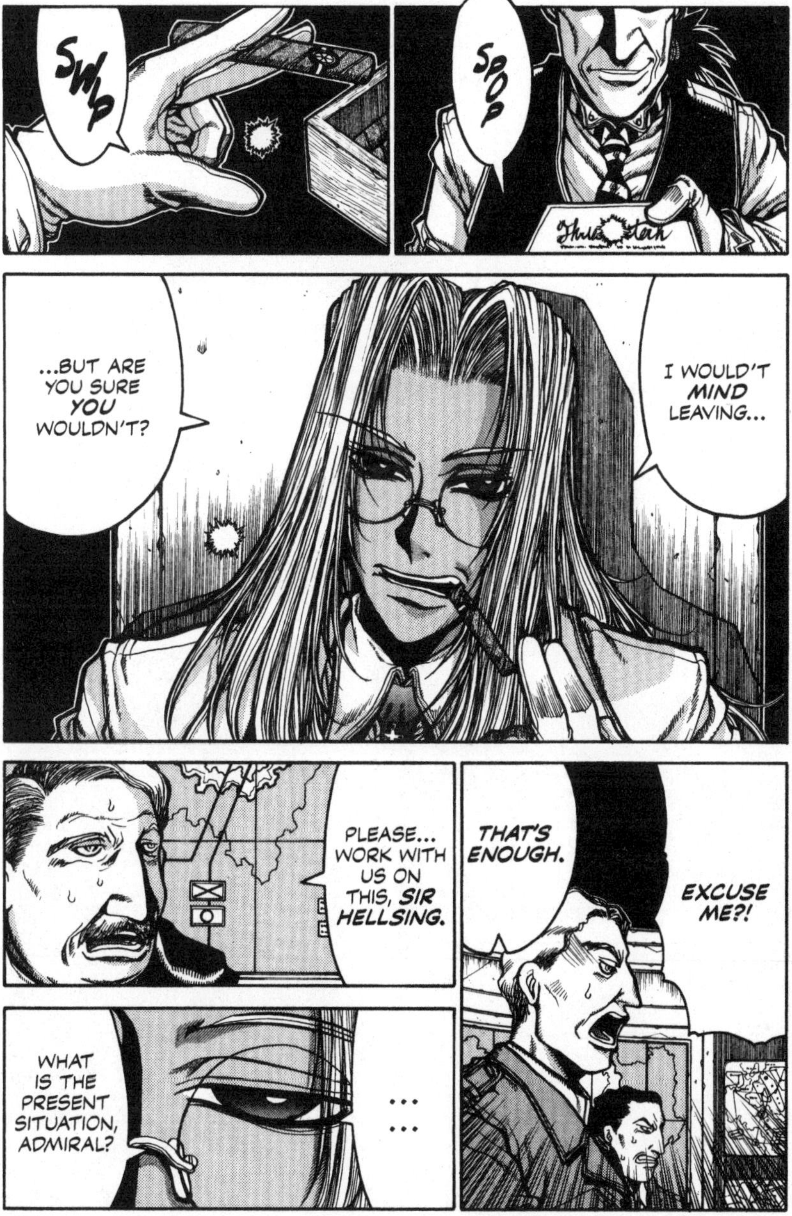
SPOP
SNIP
I WOULD'T MIND LEAVING...
...BUT ARE YOU SURE YOU WOULDN'T?
THAT'S ENOUGH.
EXCUSE ME?!
PLEASE... WORK WITH US ON THIS, SIR HELLSING.
...
...
WHAT IS THE PRESENT SITUATION, ADMIRAL?

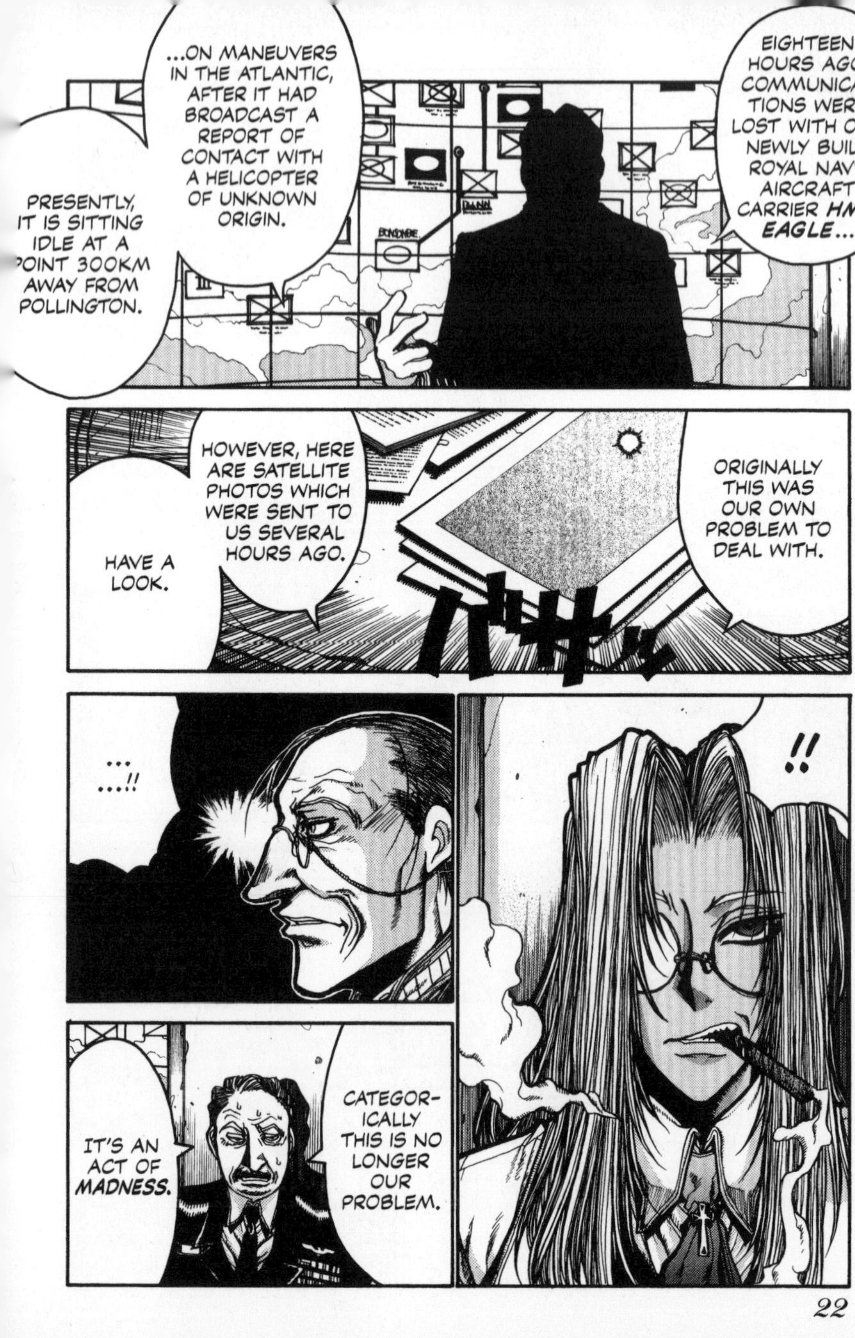
EIGHTEEN HOURS AGO, COMMUNICATIONS WERE LOST WITH OUR NEWLY BUILT ROYAL NAVY AIRCRAFT CARRIER ***HMS EAGLE***...
...ON MANEUVERS IN THE ATLANTIC, AFTER IT HAD BROADCAST A REPORT OF CONTACT WITH A HELICOPTER OF UNKNOWN ORIGIN.
PRESENTLY, IT IS SITTING IDLE AT A POINT 300KM AWAY FROM POLLINGTON.
ORIGINALLY THIS WAS OUR OWN PROBLEM TO DEAL WITH.
HOWEVER, HERE ARE SATELLITE PHOTOS WHICH WERE SENT TO US SEVERAL HOURS AGO.
HAVE A LOOK.
バサッ
!!
... ...!!
CATEGORICALLY THIS IS NO LONGER OUR PROBLEM.
IT'S AN ACT OF ***MADNESS.***

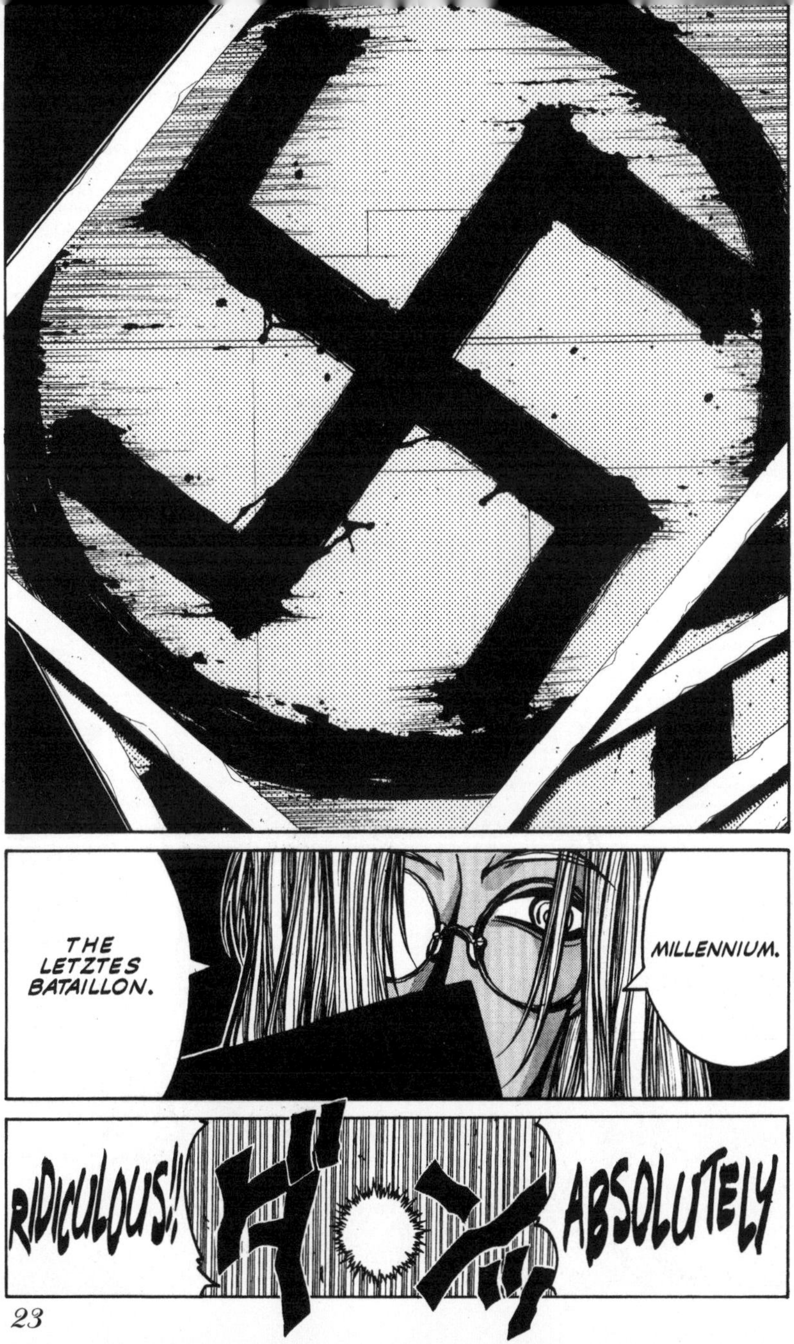
MILLENNIUM.
THE LETZTES BATAILLON.
ABSOLUTELY
RIDICULOUS!!

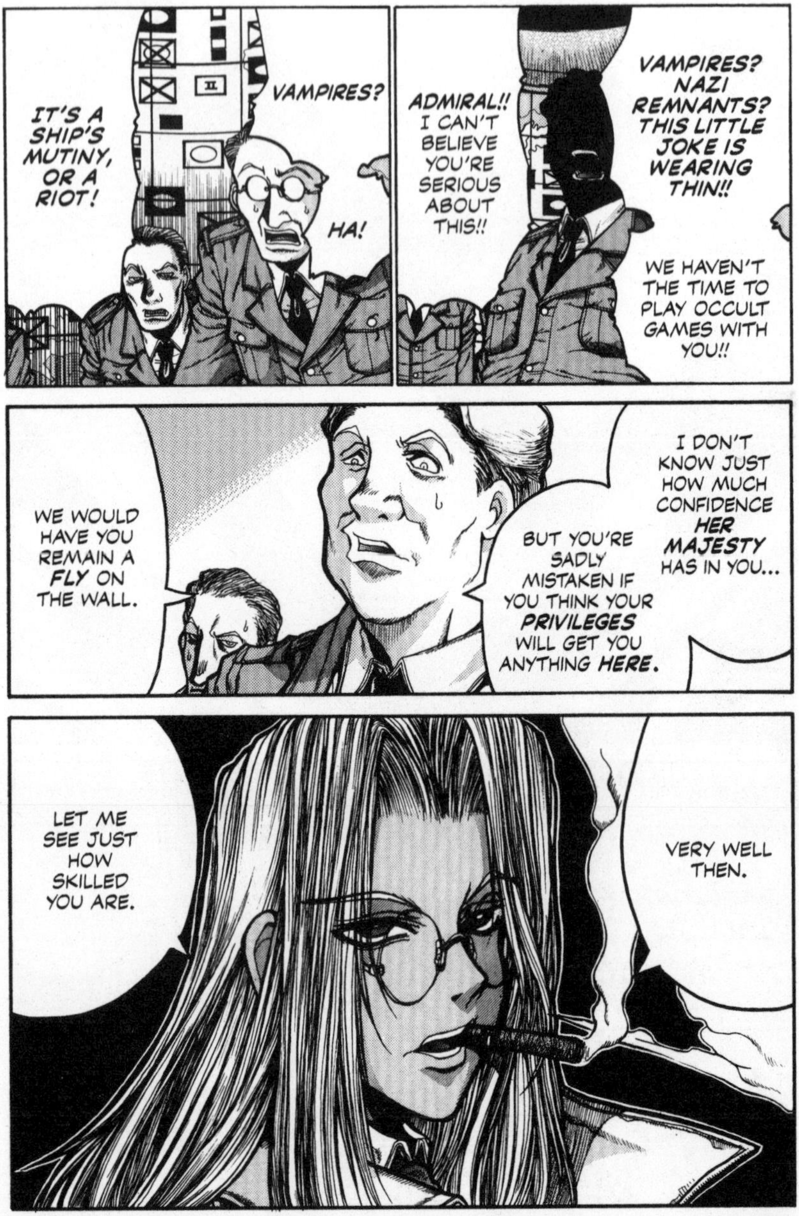
VAMPIRES? NAZI REMNANTS? THIS LITTLE JOKE IS WEARING THIN!!
WE HAVEN'T THE TIME TO PLAY OCCULT GAMES WITH YOU!!
ADMIRAL!! I CAN'T BELIEVE YOU'RE SERIOUS ABOUT THIS!!
VAMPIRES?
HA!
IT'S A SHIP'S MUTINY, OR A RIOT!
I DON'T KNOW JUST HOW MUCH CONFIDENCE HER MAJESTY HAS IN YOU...
BUT YOU'RE SADLY MISTAKEN IF YOU THINK YOUR PRIVILEGES WILL GET YOU ANYTHING HERE.
WE WOULD HAVE YOU REMAIN A FLY ON THE WALL.
VERY WELL THEN.
LET ME SEE JUST HOW SKILLED YOU ARE.

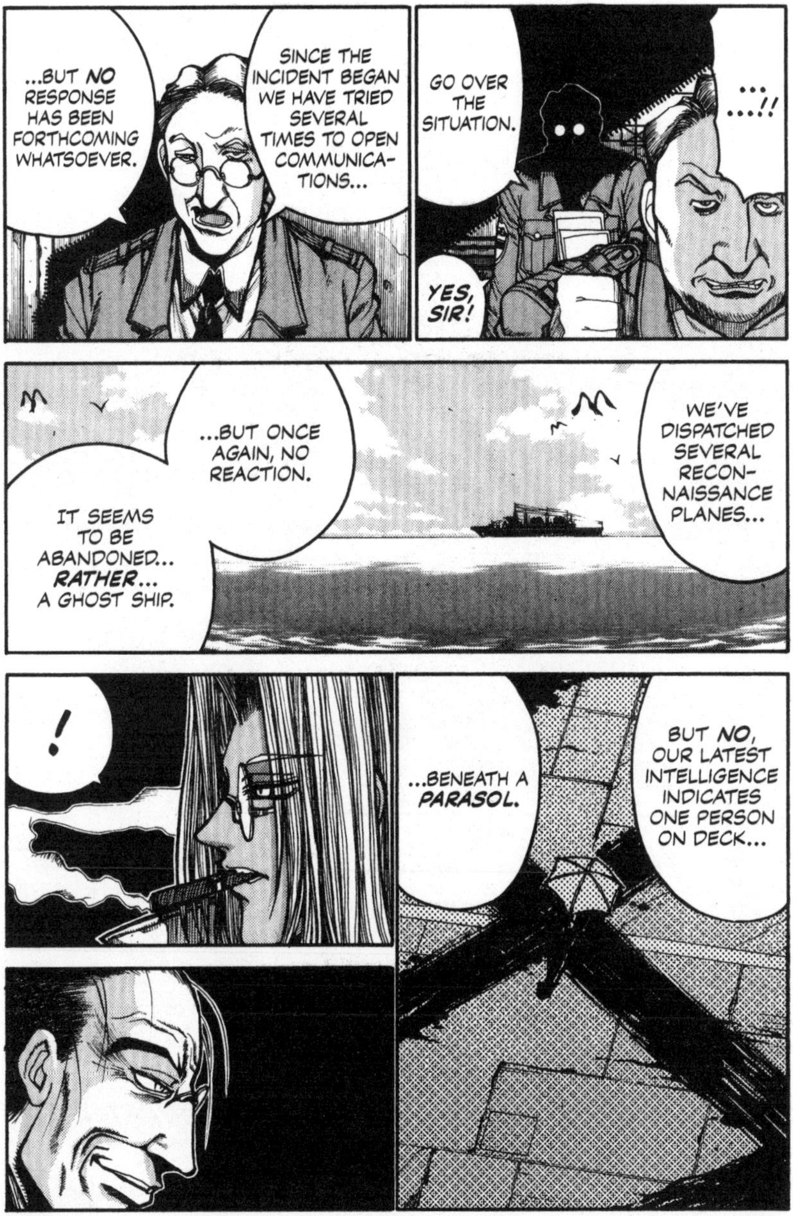
...
...!!
GO OVER THE SITUATION.
YES, SIR!
SINCE THE INCIDENT BEGAN WE HAVE TRIED SEVERAL TIMES TO OPEN COMMUNICATIONS...
...BUT NO RESPONSE HAS BEEN FORTHCOMING WHATSOEVER.
WE'VE DISPATCHED SEVERAL RECONNAISSANCE PLANES...
...BUT ONCE AGAIN, NO REACTION.
IT SEEMS TO BE ABANDONED... RATHER... A GHOST SHIP.
BUT NO, OUR LATEST INTELLIGENCE INDICATES ONE PERSON ON DECK...
...BENEATH A PARASOL.
!

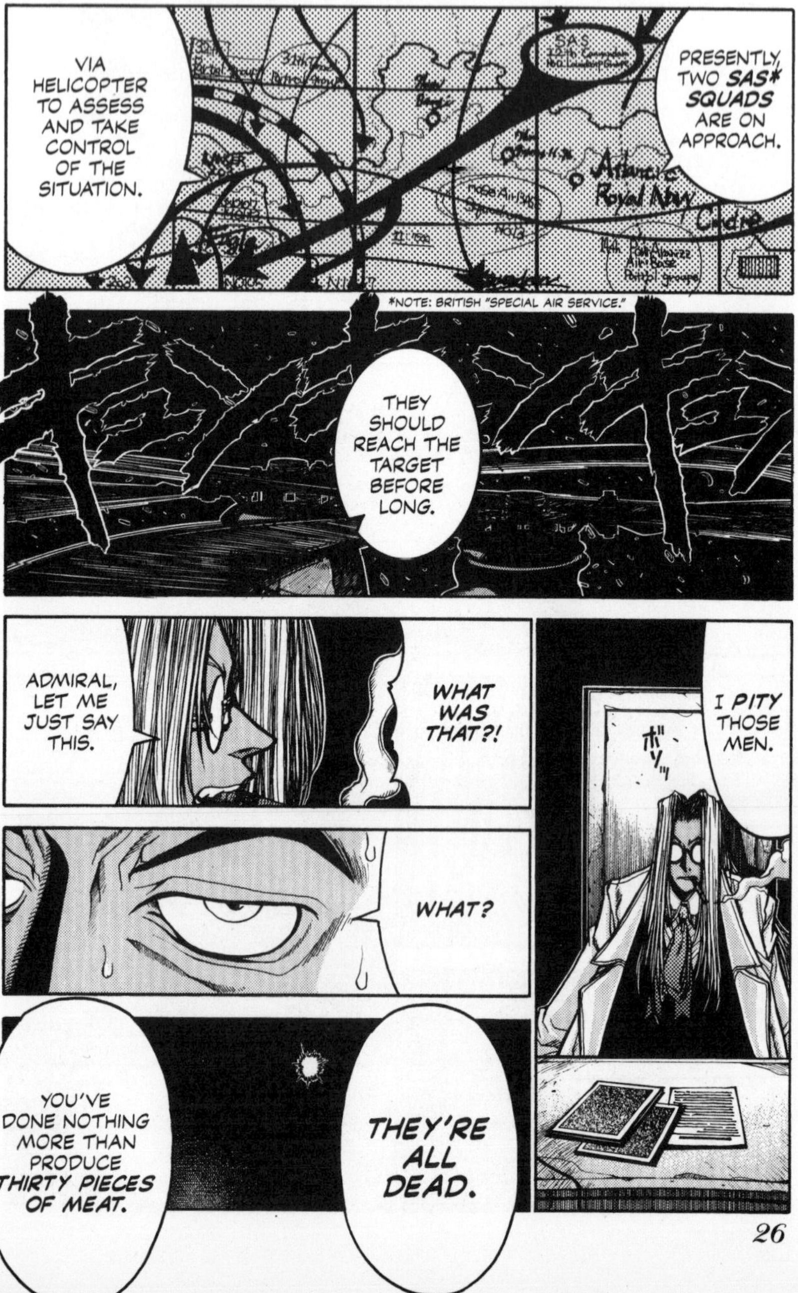
PRESENTLY, TWO SAS* SQUADS ARE ON APPROACH.
VIA HELICOPTER TO ASSESS AND TAKE CONTROL OF THE SITUATION.
SAS
*NOTE: BRITISH "SPECIAL AIR SERVICE."
THEY SHOULD REACH THE TARGET BEFORE LONG.
I PITY THOSE MEN.
ボソッ
WHAT WAS THAT?!
ADMIRAL, LET ME JUST SAY THIS.
WHAT?
THEY'RE ALL DEAD.
YOU'VE DONE NOTHING MORE THAN PRODUCE THIRTY PIECES OF MEAT.

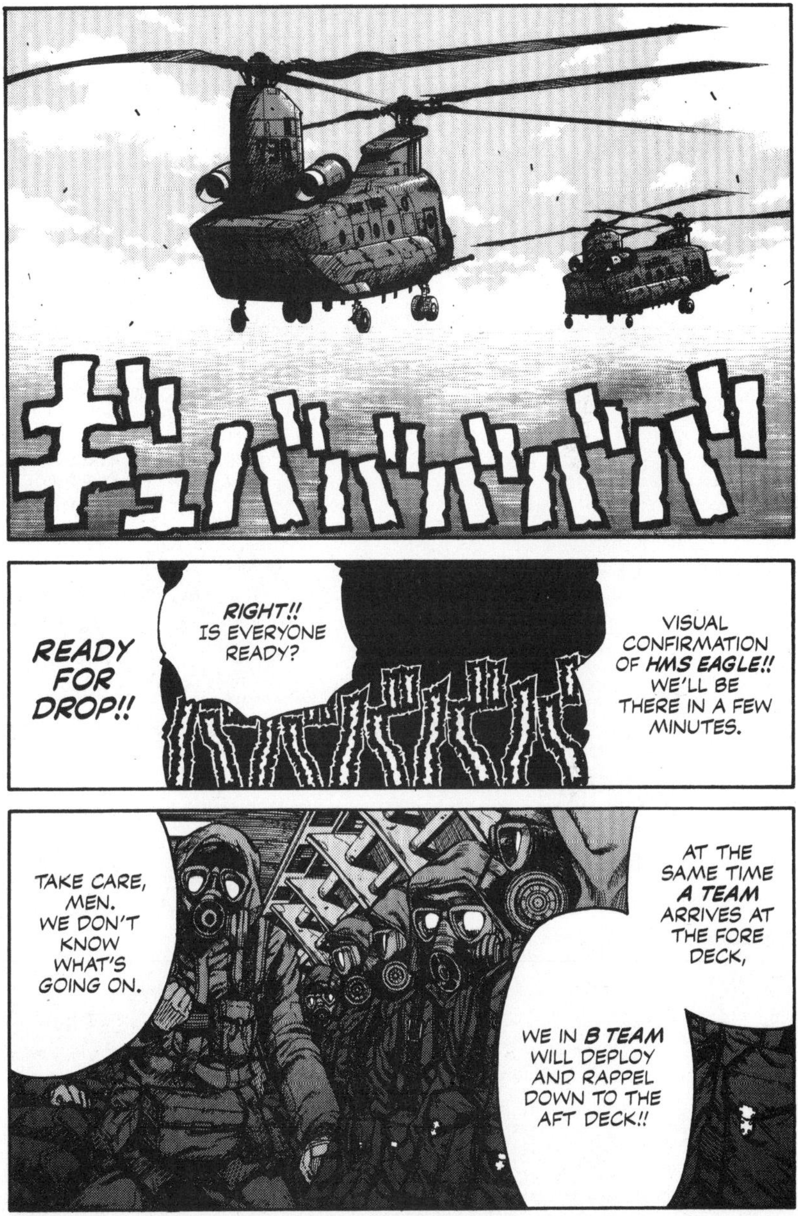
ギュバババババ
VISUAL CONFIRMATION OF **HMS EAGLE!!** WE'LL BE THERE IN A FEW MINUTES.
RIGHT!! IS EVERYONE READY?
READY FOR DROP!!
AT THE SAME TIME **A TEAM** ARRIVES AT THE FORE DECK,
WE IN **B TEAM** WILL DEPLOY AND RAPPEL DOWN TO THE AFT DECK!!
TAKE CARE, MEN. WE DON'T KNOW WHAT'S GOING ON.

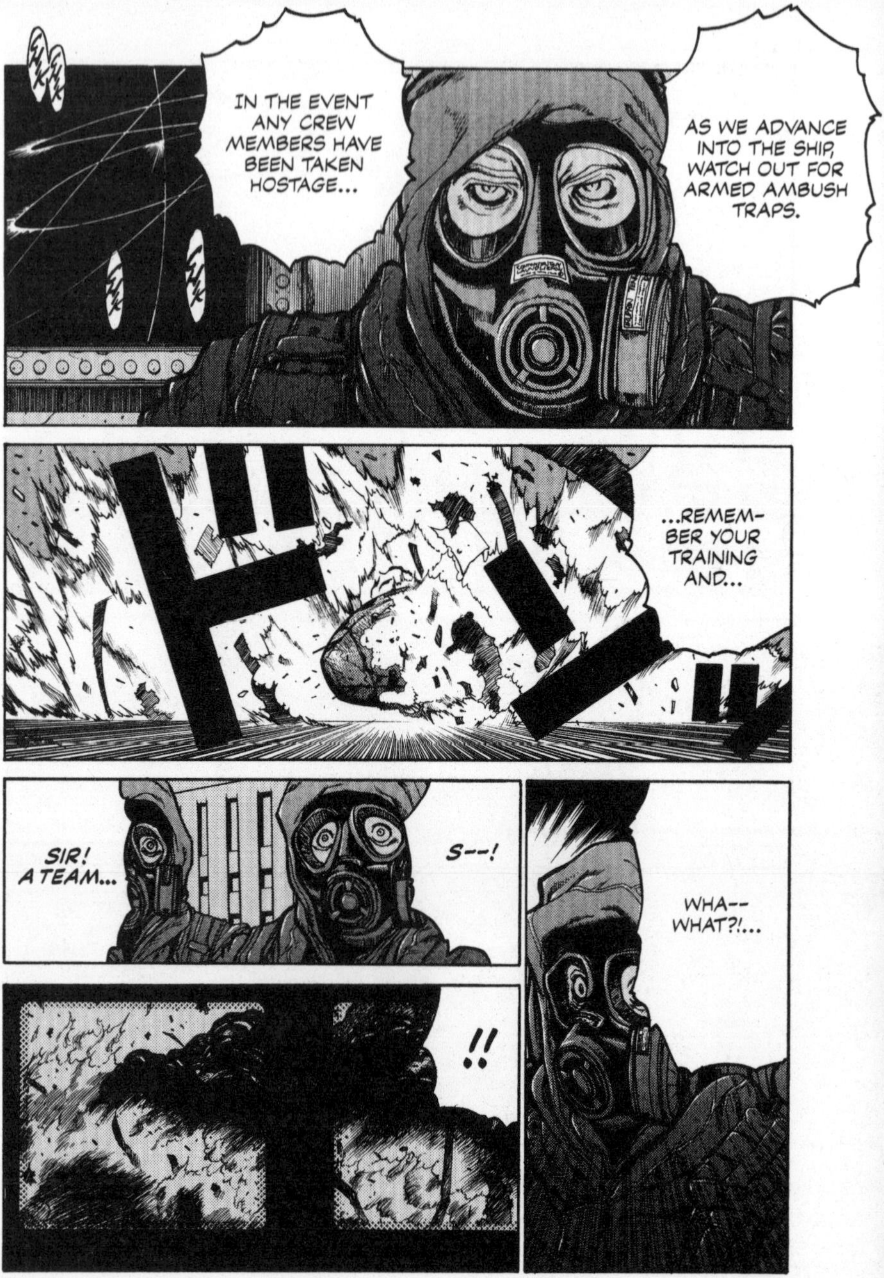
AS WE ADVANCE INTO THE SHIP, WATCH OUT FOR ARMED AMBUSH TRAPS.
IN THE EVENT ANY CREW MEMBERS HAVE BEEN TAKEN HOSTAGE...
...REMEM-BER YOUR TRAINING AND...
WHA-- WHAT?!...
S--!
SIR! A TEAM...
!!

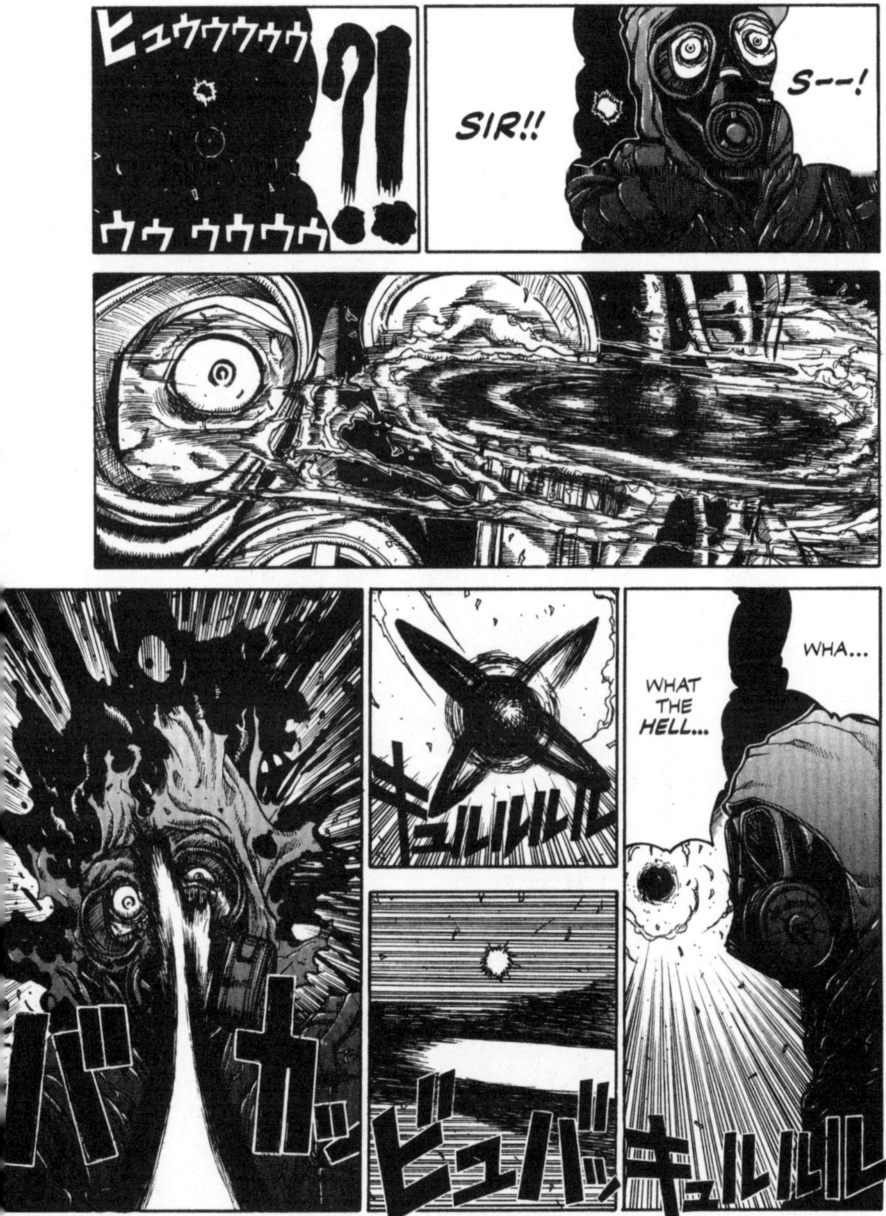
S--!
SIR!!
ヒュウウウウウ
ウウ ウウウウ
?!
WHA...
WHAT THE HELL...
キュルルルル
ビュバッキュルルルル
バカッ

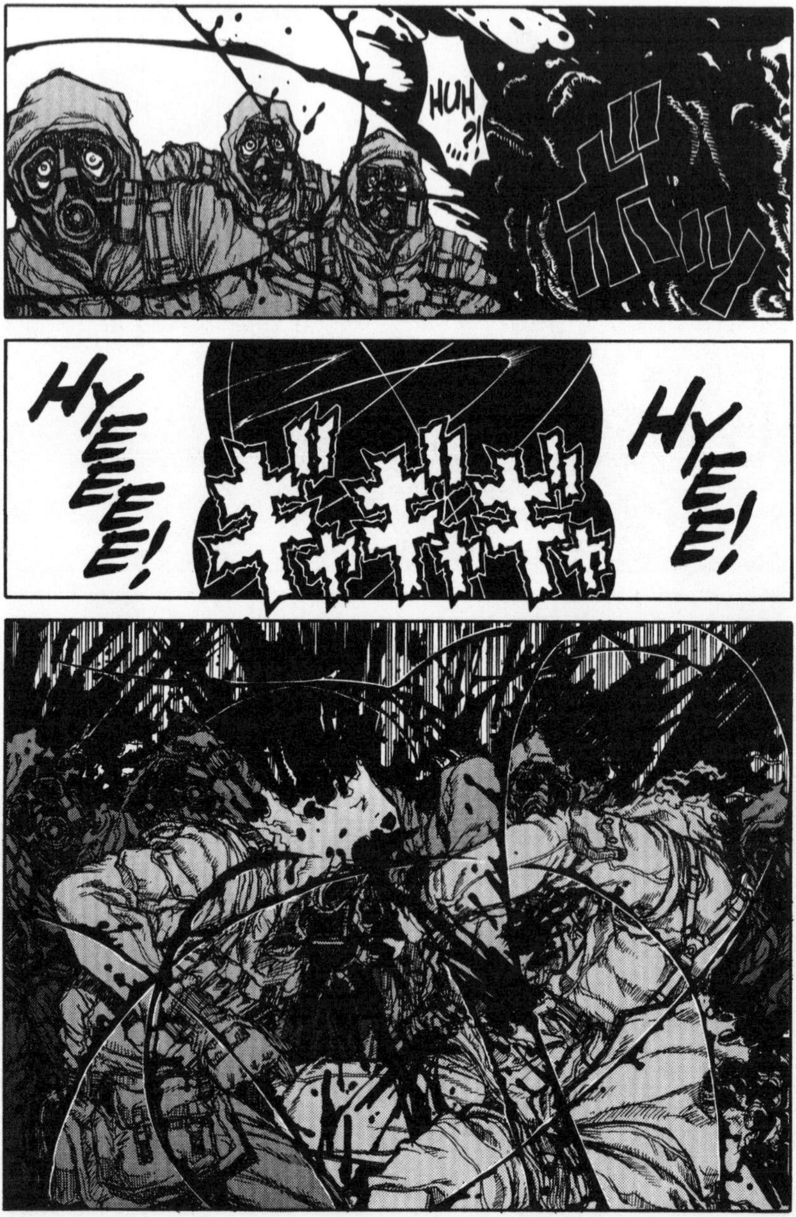
HUH ?! ....
HYEEE!
ギャギャギャ
HYEEEEE!

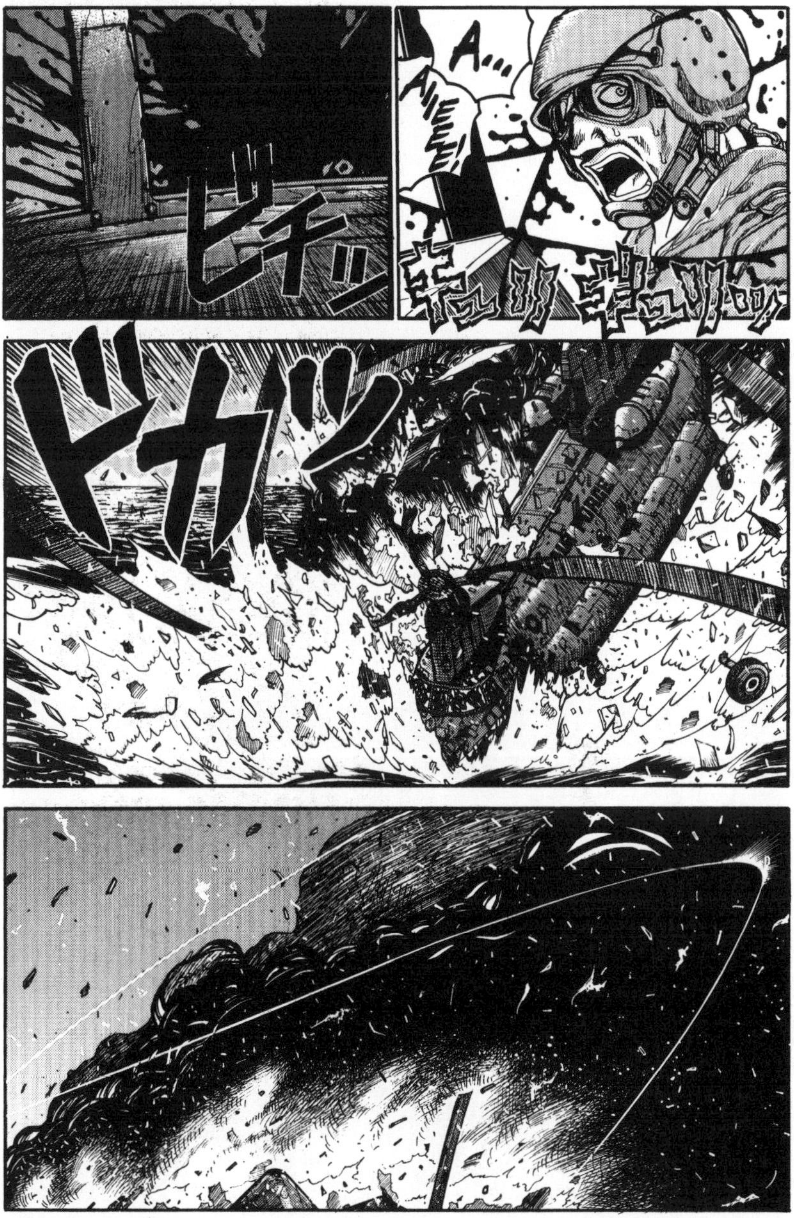
A....
AIEEEE!
ビチッ
ドガッ

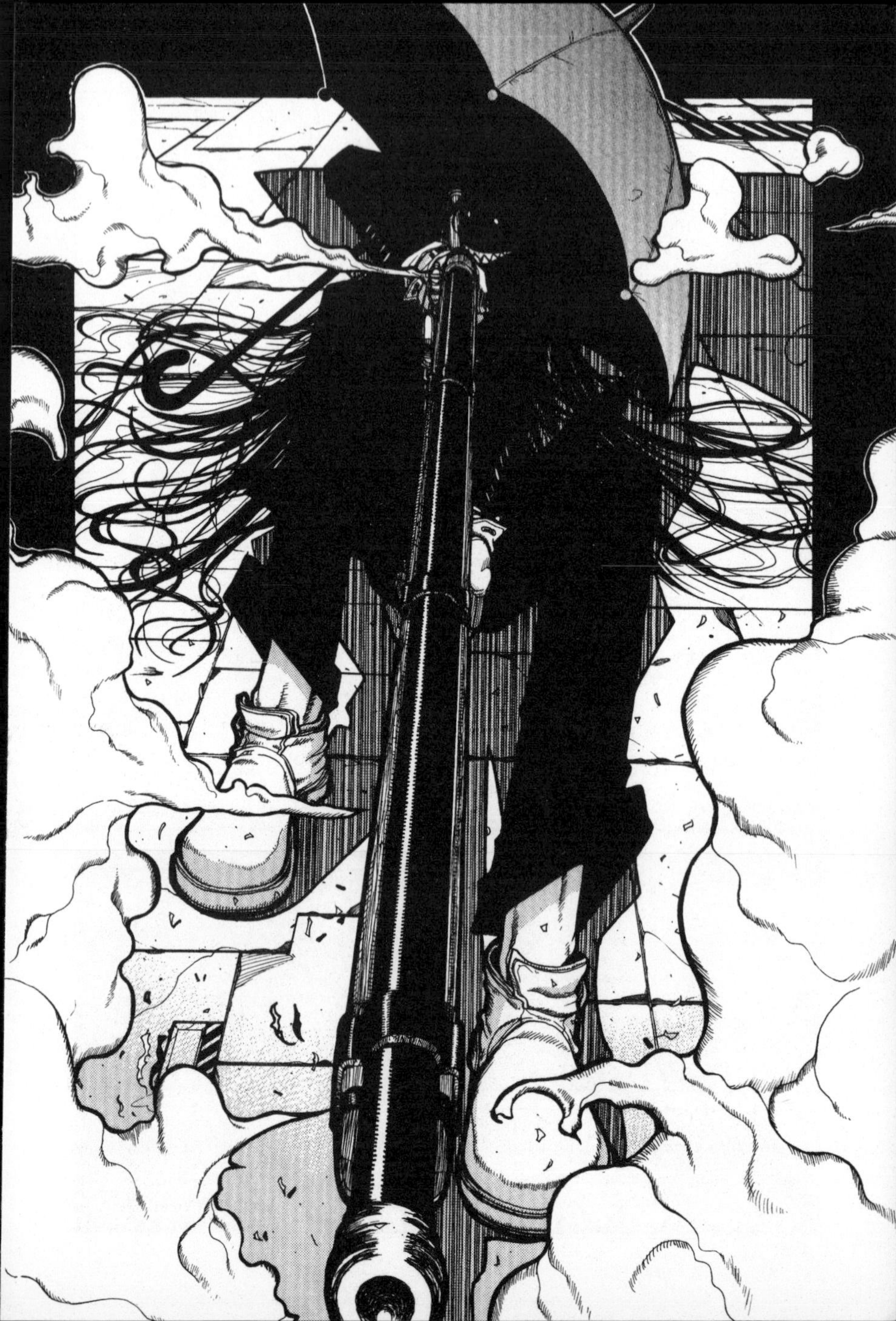

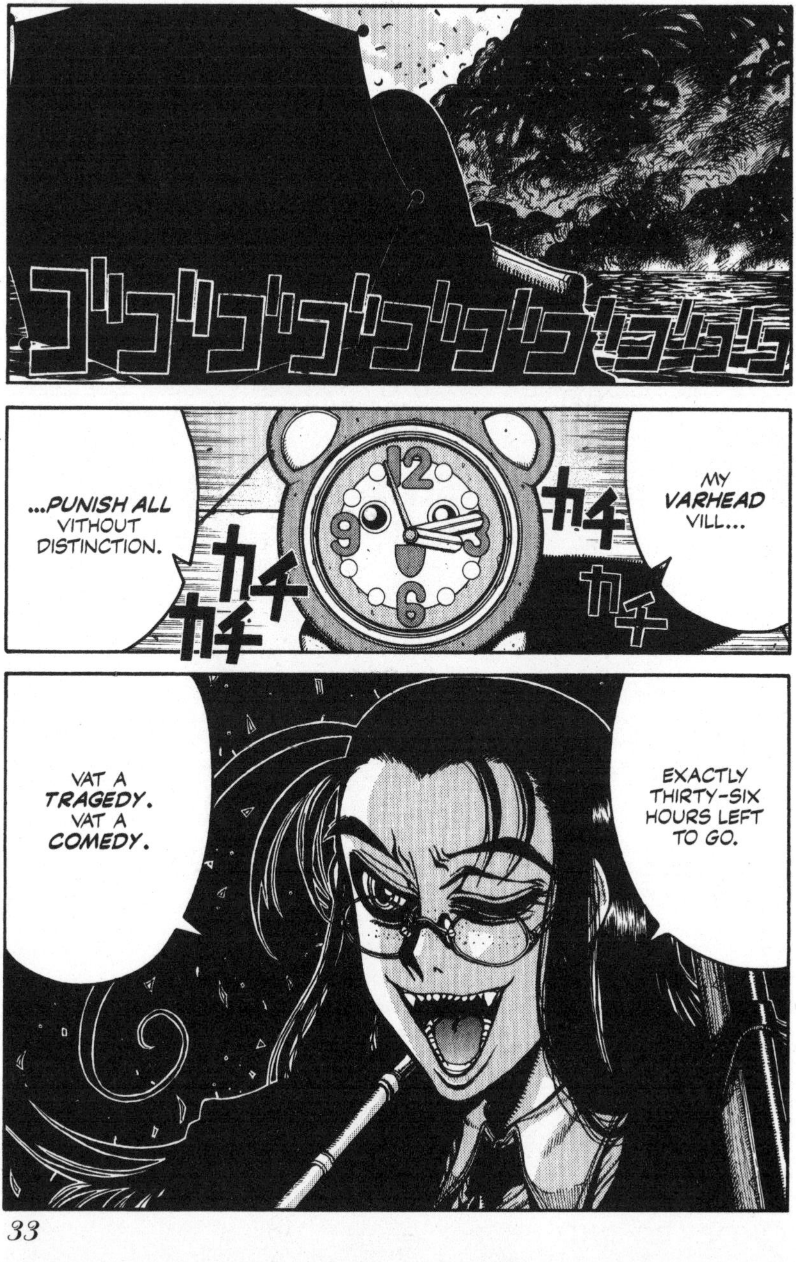
MY VARHEAD VILL...
...PUNISH ALL VITHOUT DISTINCTION.
カチ
カチ
カチ
カチ
EXACTLY THIRTY-SIX HOURS LEFT TO GO.
VAT A TRAGEDY. VAT A COMEDY.

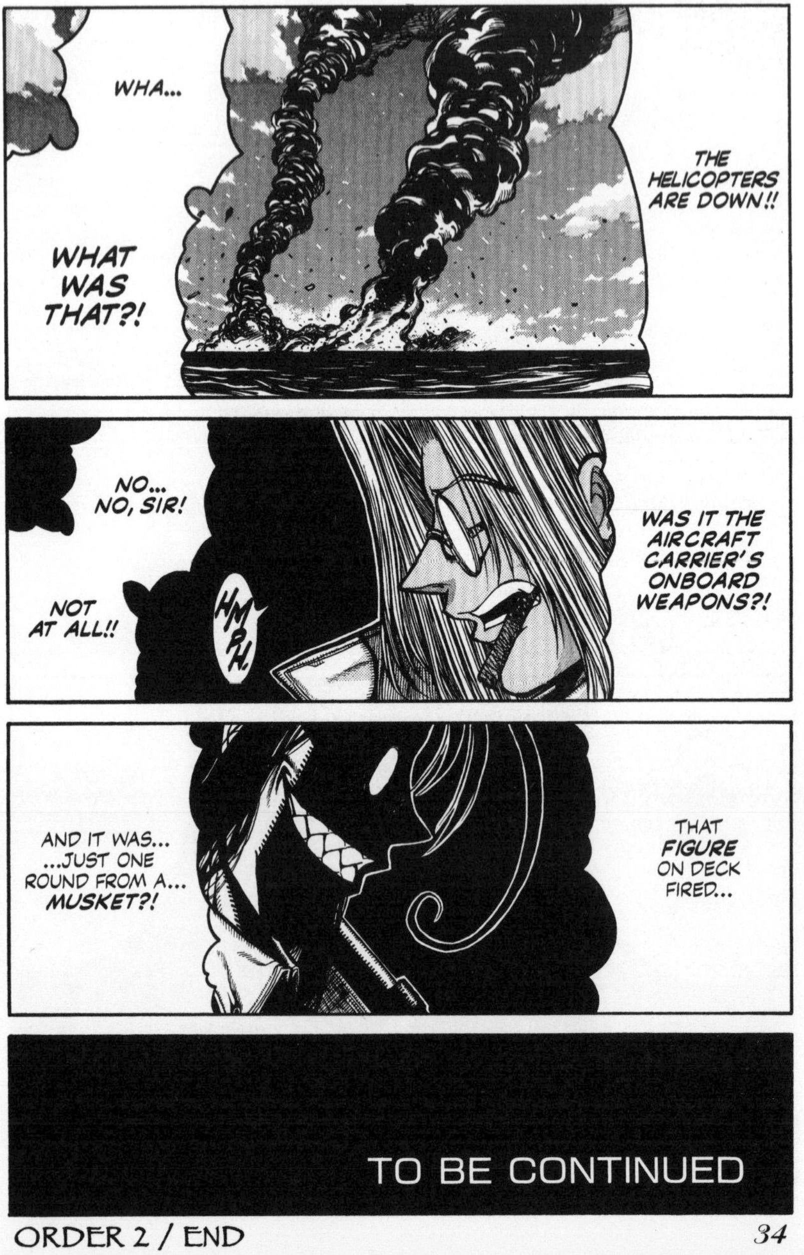
THE HELICOPTERS ARE DOWN!!
WHA...
WHAT WAS THAT?!
WAS IT THE AIRCRAFT CARRIER'S ONBOARD WEAPONS?!
HMPH.
NO... NO, SIR!
NOT AT ALL!!
THAT FIGURE ON DECK FIRED...
AND IT WAS... ...JUST ONE ROUND FROM A... MUSKET?!

TO BE CONTINUED

ORDER 2 / END

ORDER 3

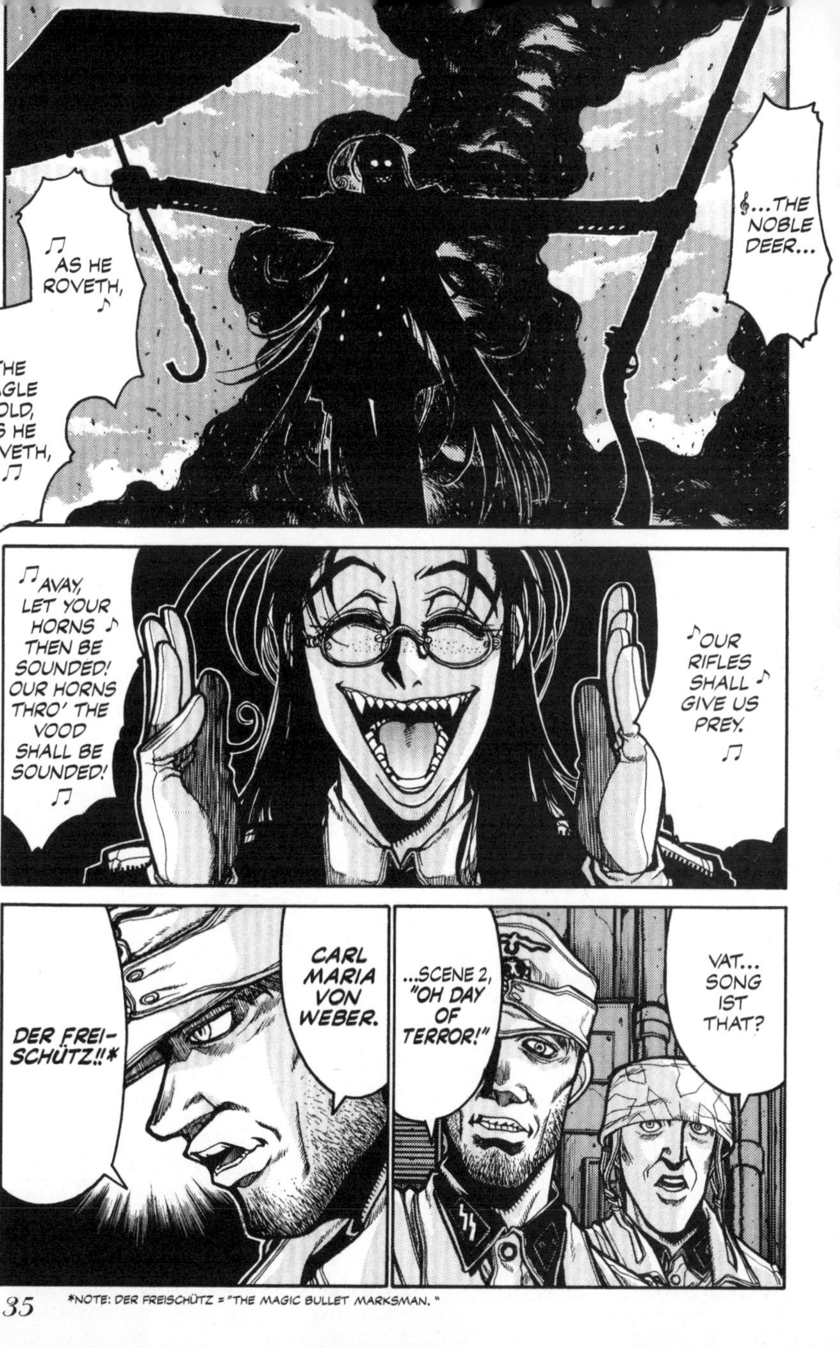

...THE NOBLE DEER...
AS HE ROVETH,
THE EAGLE BOLD, AS HE MOVETH,
OUR RIFLES SHALL GIVE US PREY.
AVAY, LET YOUR HORNS THEN BE SOUNDED! OUR HORNS THRO' THE VOOD SHALL BE SOUNDED!
VAT... SONG IST THAT?
...SCENE 2, "OH DAY OF TERROR!"
CARL MARIA VON WEBER.
DER FREISCHÜTZ!!*

*NOTE: DER FREISCHÜTZ = "THE MAGIC BULLET MARKSMAN."

ORDER 3
D⑤

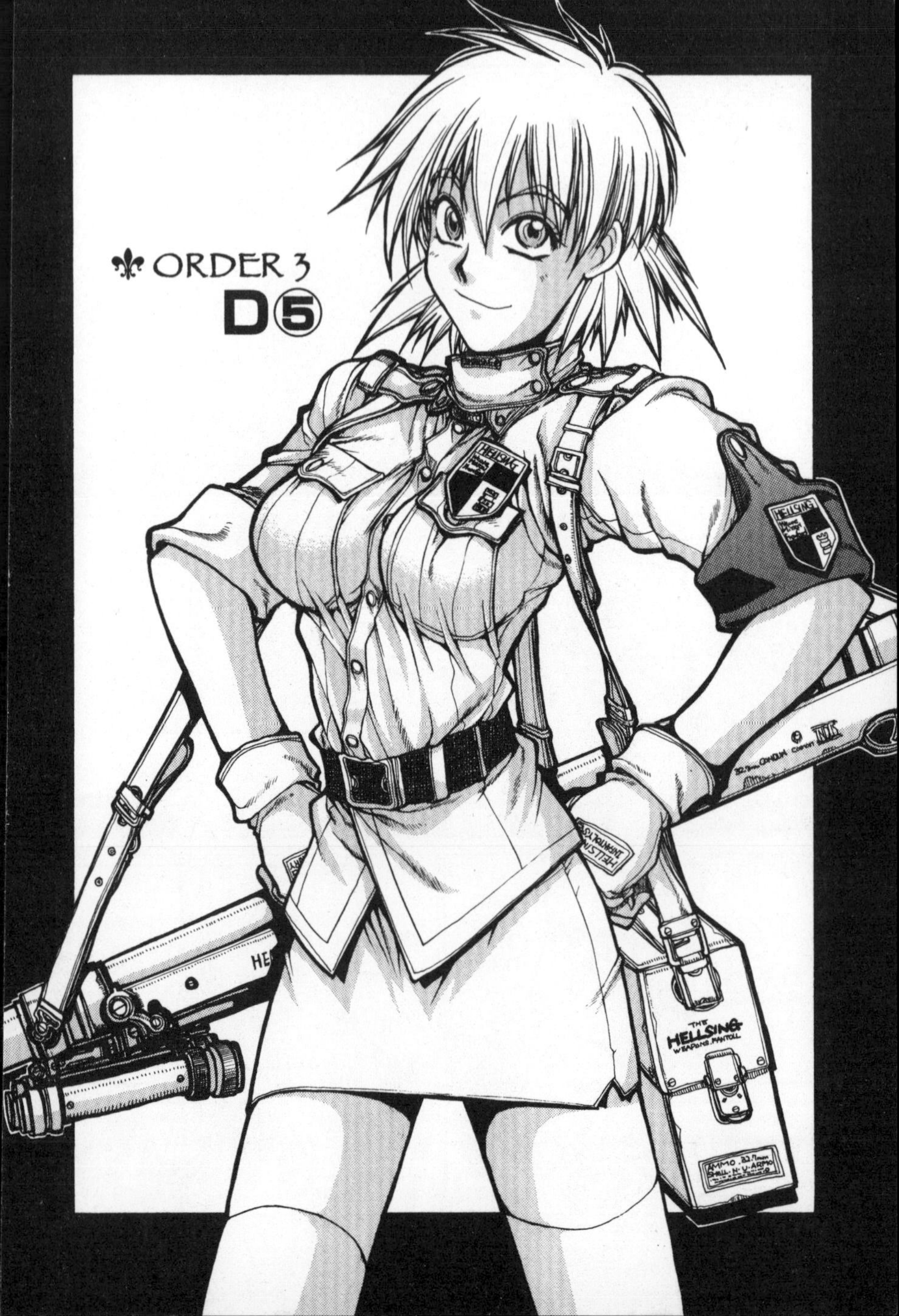

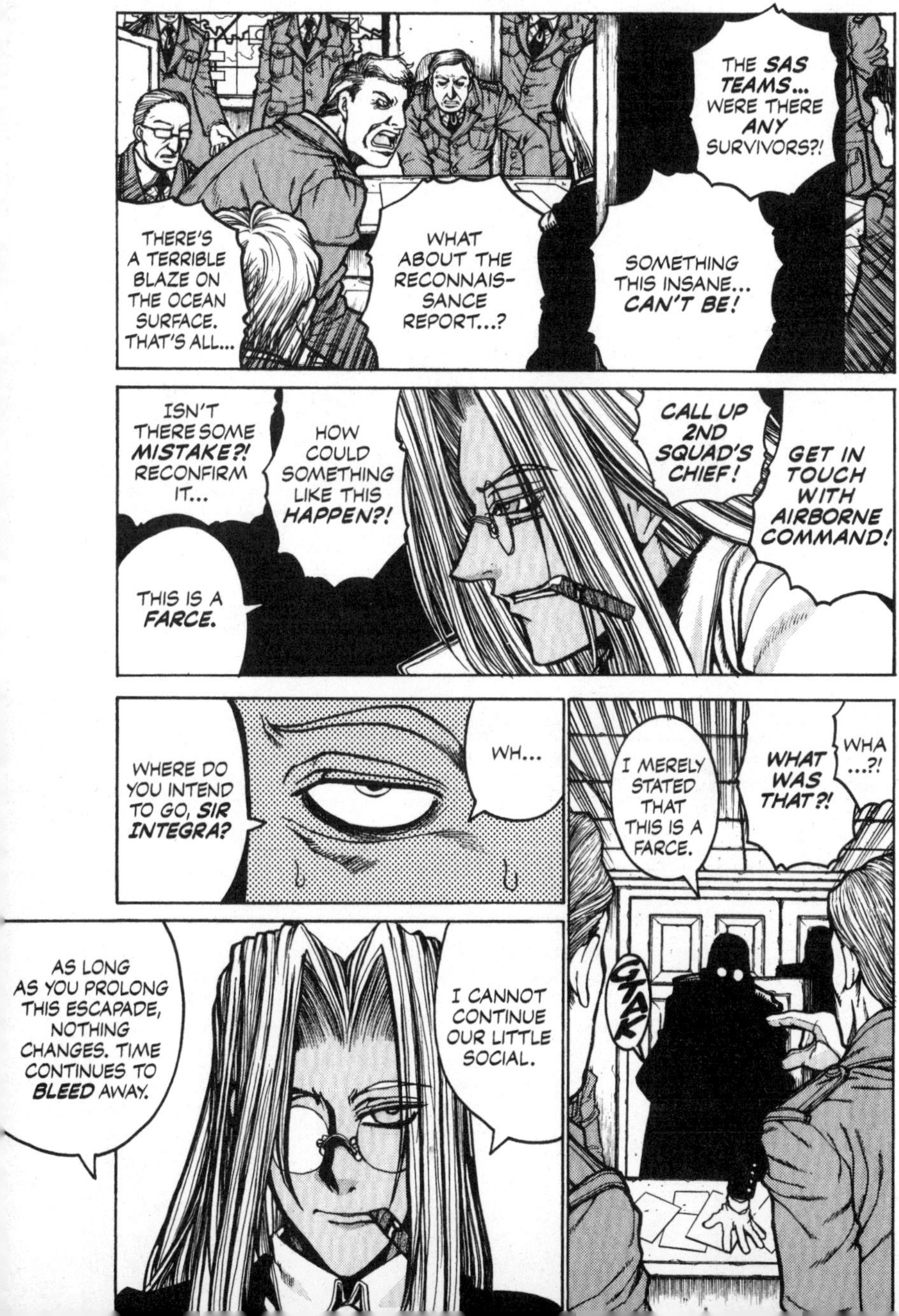
THE SAS TEAMS... WERE THERE ANY SURVIVORS?!
SOMETHING THIS INSANE... CAN'T BE!
WHAT ABOUT THE RECONNAIS-SANCE REPORT...?
THERE'S A TERRIBLE BLAZE ON THE OCEAN SURFACE. THAT'S ALL...
GET IN TOUCH WITH AIRBORNE COMMAND!
CALL UP 2ND SQUAD'S CHIEF!
HOW COULD SOMETHING LIKE THIS HAPPEN?!
ISN'T THERE SOME MISTAKE?! RECONFIRM IT...
THIS IS A FARCE.
WHA ...?!
WHAT WAS THAT?!
I MERELY STATED THAT THIS IS A FARCE.
GTAK
WH...
WHERE DO YOU INTEND TO GO, SIR INTEGRA?
I CANNOT CONTINUE OUR LITTLE SOCIAL.
AS LONG AS YOU PROLONG THIS ESCAPADE, NOTHING CHANGES. TIME CONTINUES TO BLEED AWAY.

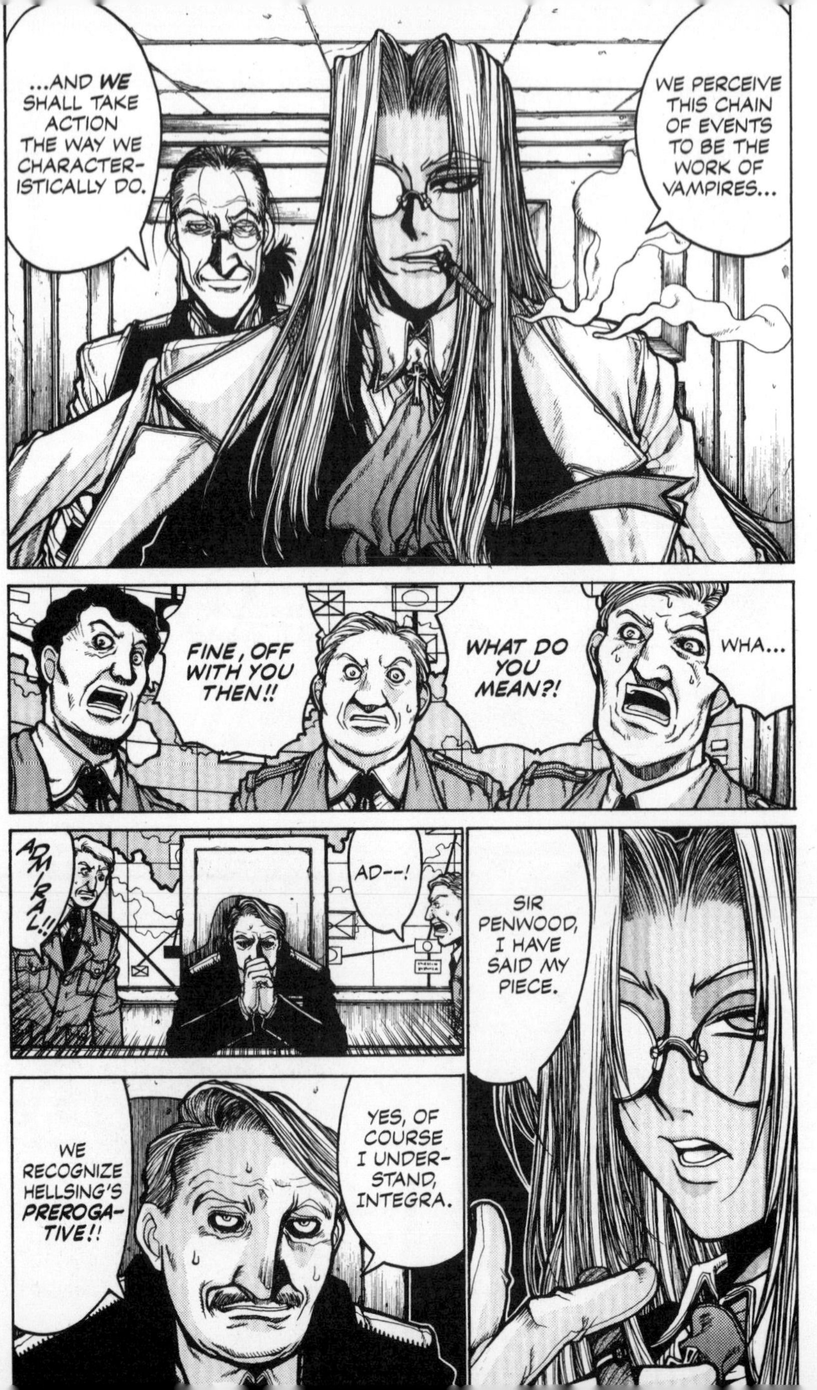
WE PERCEIVE THIS CHAIN OF EVENTS TO BE THE WORK OF VAMPIRES...
...AND WE SHALL TAKE ACTION THE WAY WE CHARACTERISTICALLY DO.
WHA...
WHAT DO YOU MEAN?!
FINE, OFF WITH YOU THEN!!
SIR PENWOOD, I HAVE SAID MY PIECE.
AD--!
ADMIRAL!!
YES, OF COURSE I UNDERSTAND, INTEGRA.
WE RECOGNIZE HELLSING'S PREROGATIVE!!

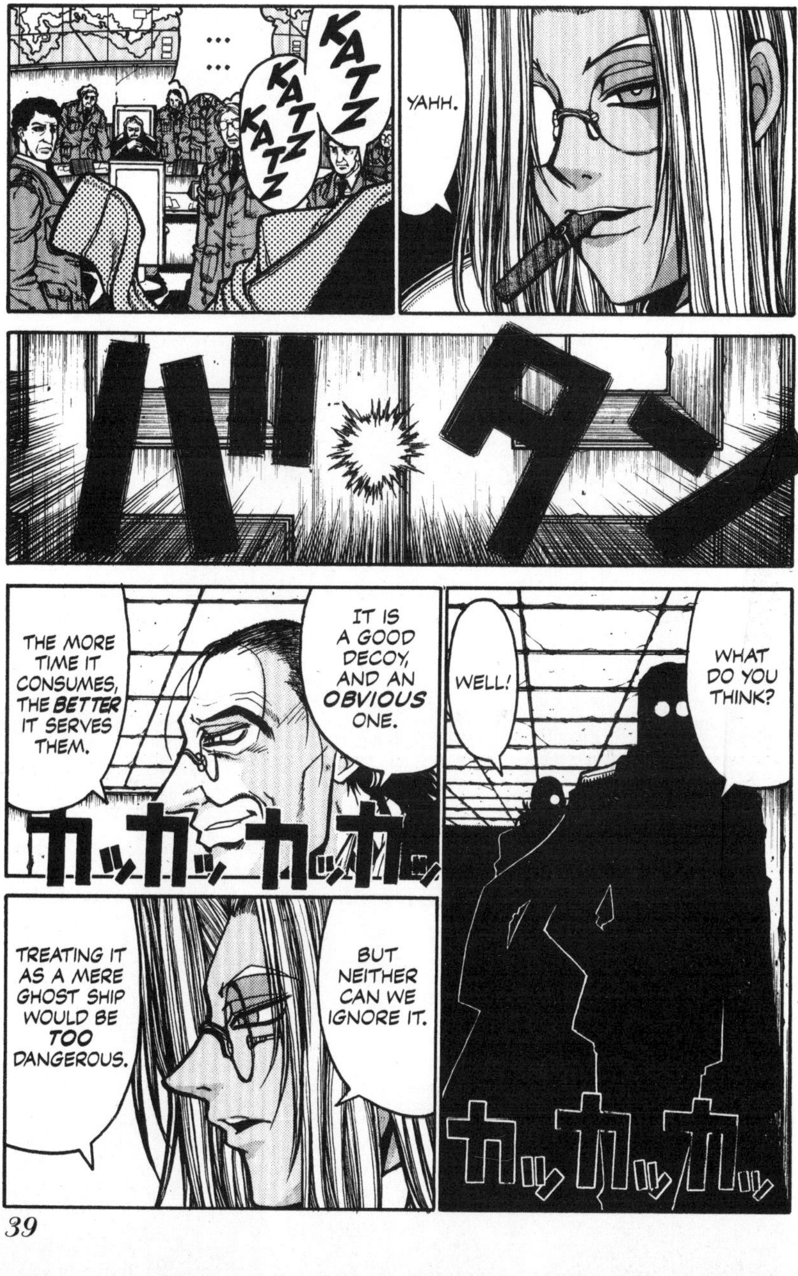
YAHH.
...
...
KATZ KATZ KATZ
WHAT DO YOU THINK?
WELL!
カッカッカッ
IT IS A GOOD DECOY, AND AN OBVIOUS ONE.
THE MORE TIME IT CONSUMES, THE BETTER IT SERVES THEM.
カッカッカッカッ
BUT NEITHER CAN WE IGNORE IT.
TREATING IT AS A MERE GHOST SHIP WOULD BE TOO DANGEROUS.

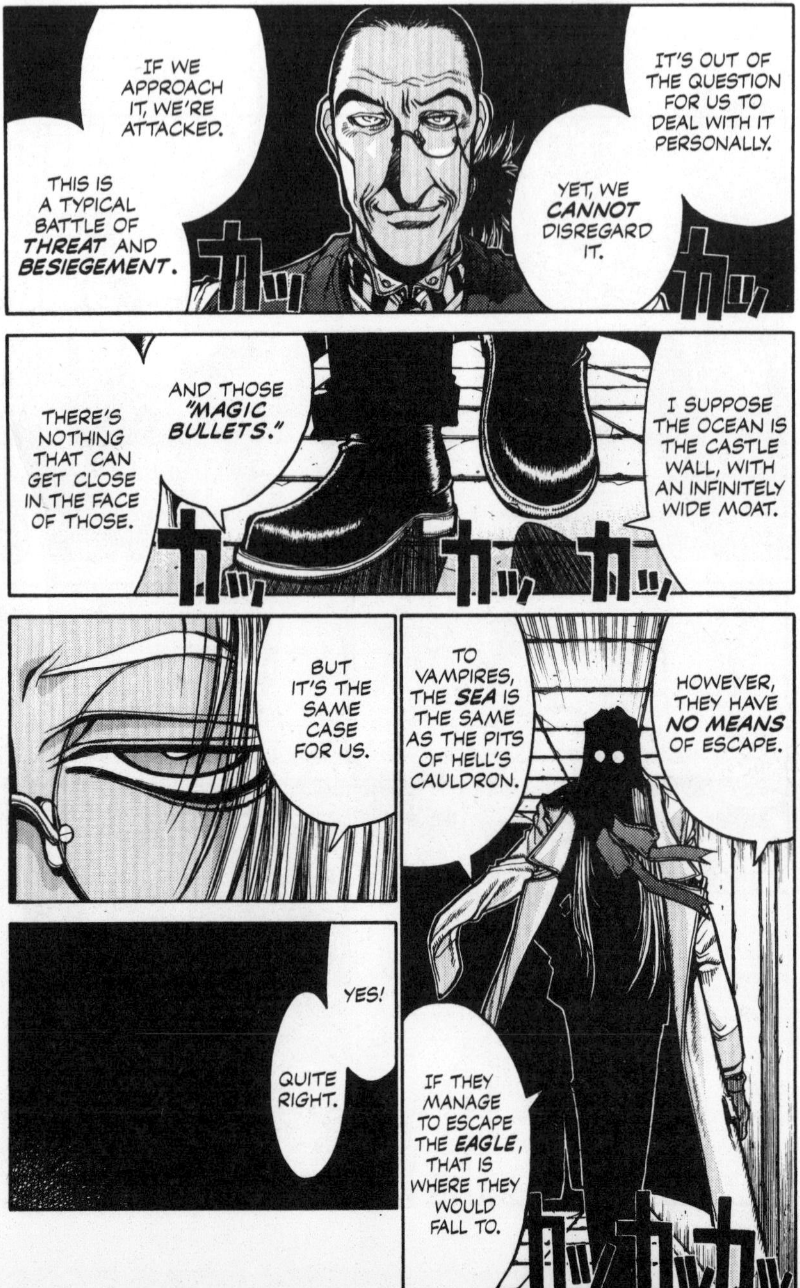
IT'S OUT OF THE QUESTION FOR US TO DEAL WITH IT PERSONALLY.
YET, WE CANNOT DISREGARD IT.
IF WE APPROACH IT, WE'RE ATTACKED.
THIS IS A TYPICAL BATTLE OF THREAT AND BESIEGEMENT.
カッ
カッ
I SUPPOSE THE OCEAN IS THE CASTLE WALL, WITH AN INFINITELY WIDE MOAT.
AND THOSE "MAGIC BULLETS."
THERE'S NOTHING THAT CAN GET CLOSE IN THE FACE OF THOSE.
カッ
カッ
カッ
HOWEVER, THEY HAVE NO MEANS OF ESCAPE.
TO VAMPIRES, THE SEA IS THE SAME AS THE PITS OF HELL'S CAULDRON.
IF THEY MANAGE TO ESCAPE THE EAGLE, THAT IS WHERE THEY WOULD FALL TO.
カッカッカッ
BUT IT'S THE SAME CASE FOR US.
YES!
QUITE RIGHT.

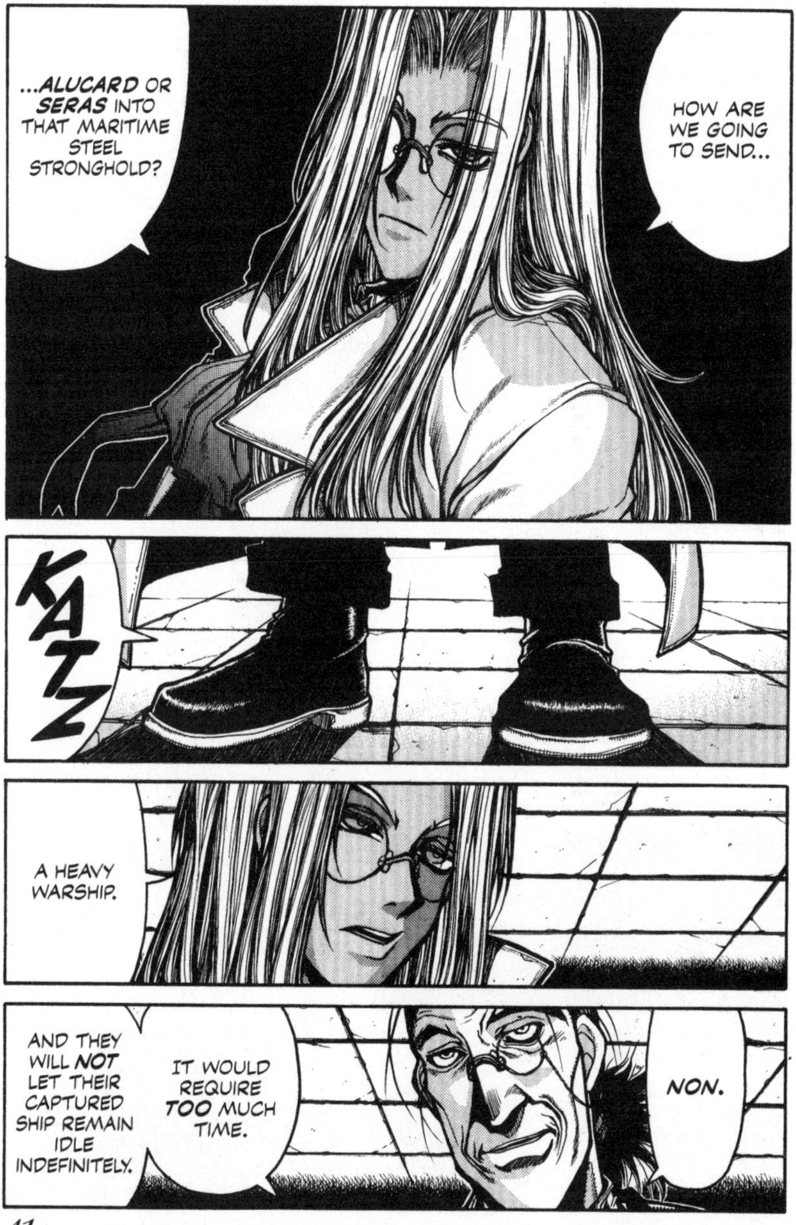
HOW ARE WE GOING TO SEND...
...ALUCARD OR SERAS INTO THAT MARITIME STEEL STRONGHOLD?
KATZ
A HEAVY WARSHIP.
NON.
IT WOULD REQUIRE TOO MUCH TIME.
AND THEY WILL NOT LET THEIR CAPTURED SHIP REMAIN IDLE INDEFINITELY.

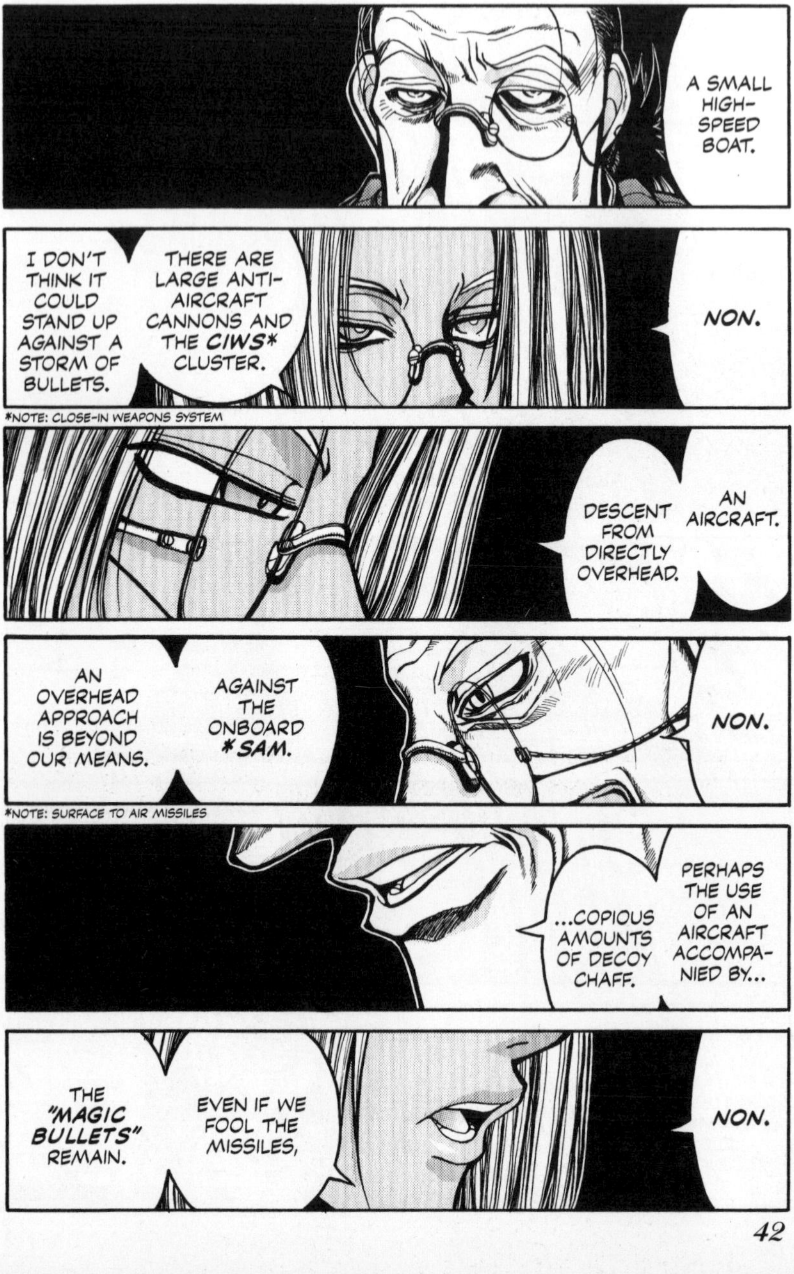
A SMALL HIGH-SPEED BOAT.
NON.
THERE ARE LARGE ANTI-AIRCRAFT CANNONS AND THE CIWS* CLUSTER.
I DON'T THINK IT COULD STAND UP AGAINST A STORM OF BULLETS.
*NOTE: CLOSE-IN WEAPONS SYSTEM
AN AIRCRAFT.
DESCENT FROM DIRECTLY OVERHEAD.
NON.
AGAINST THE ONBOARD *SAM.
AN OVERHEAD APPROACH IS BEYOND OUR MEANS.
*NOTE: SURFACE TO AIR MISSILES
PERHAPS THE USE OF AN AIRCRAFT ACCOMPANIED BY...
...COPIOUS AMOUNTS OF DECOY CHAFF.
NON.
EVEN IF WE FOOL THE MISSILES,
THE "MAGIC BULLETS" REMAIN.

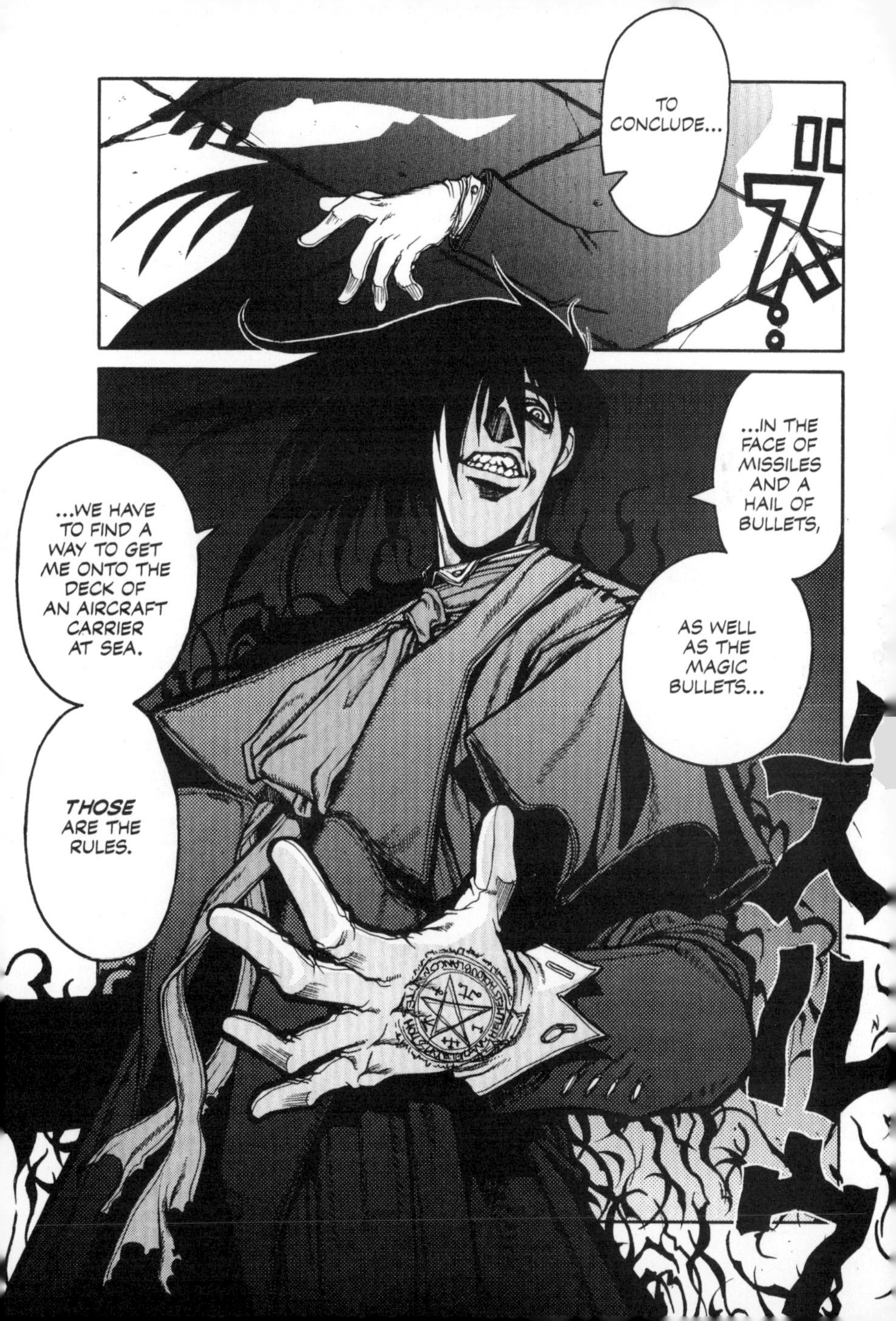
TO CONCLUDE...
...IN THE FACE OF MISSILES AND A HAIL OF BULLETS,
AS WELL AS THE MAGIC BULLETS...
...WE HAVE TO FIND A WAY TO GET ME ONTO THE DECK OF AN AIRCRAFT CARRIER AT SEA.
THOSE ARE THE RULES.

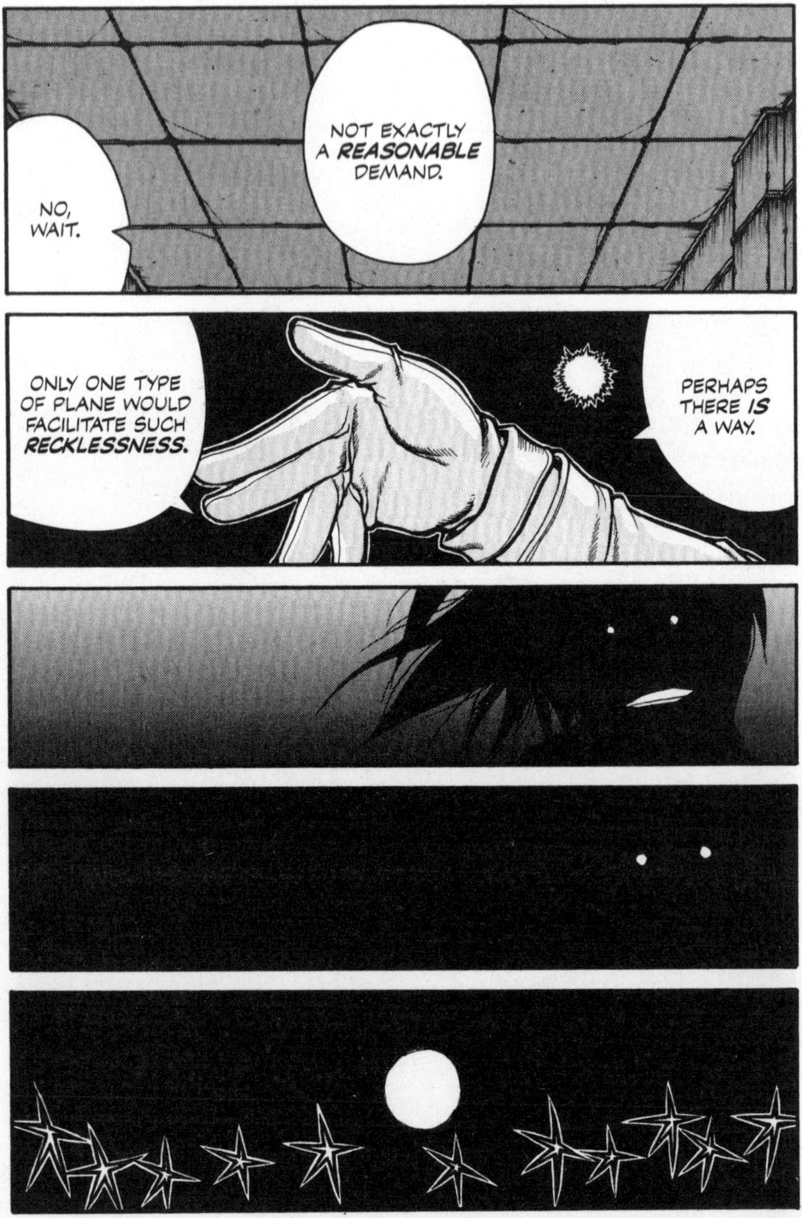
NOT EXACTLY A REASONABLE DEMAND.
NO, WAIT.
PERHAPS THERE IS A WAY.
ONLY ONE TYPE OF PLANE WOULD FACILITATE SUCH RECKLESSNESS.

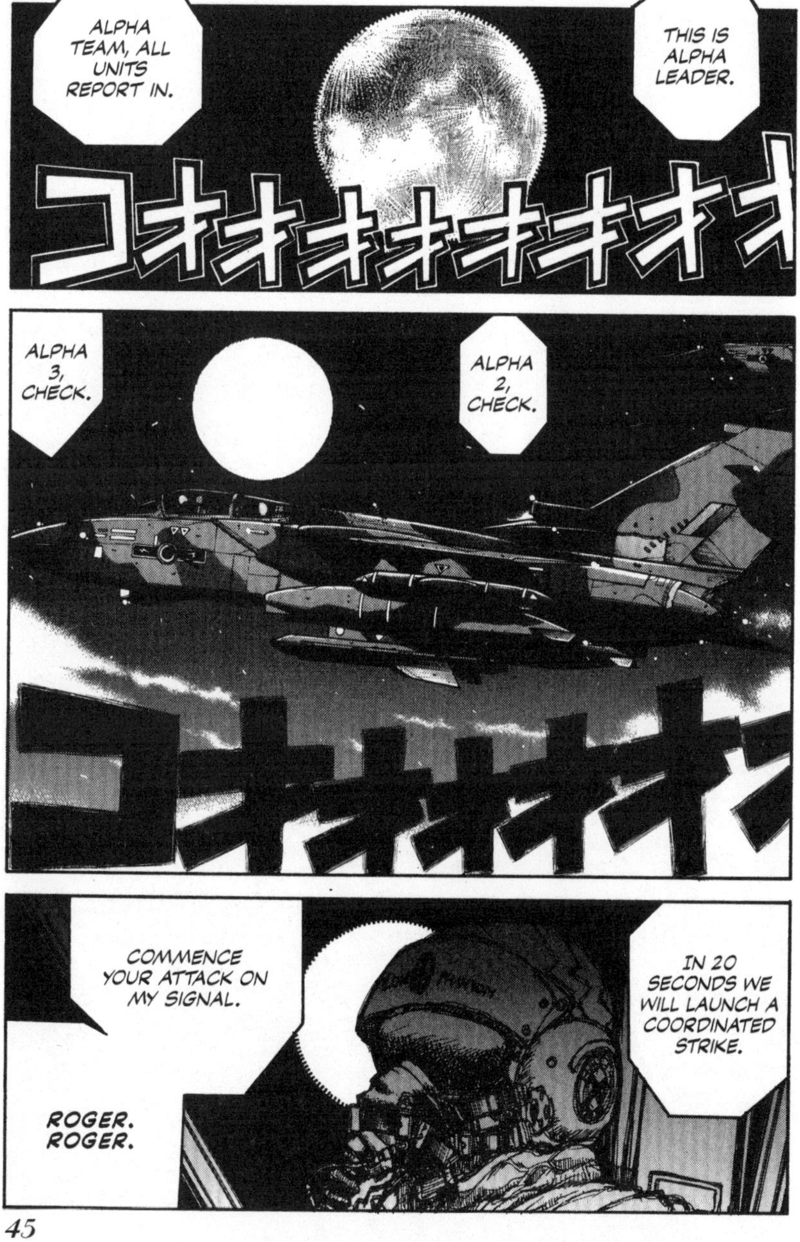
THIS IS ALPHA LEADER.
ALPHA TEAM, ALL UNITS REPORT IN.
コオオオオオオオ
ALPHA 2, CHECK.
ALPHA 3, CHECK.
コオオオオオ
IN 20 SECONDS WE WILL LAUNCH A COORDINATED STRIKE.
COMMENCE YOUR ATTACK ON MY SIGNAL.
ROGER. ROGER.

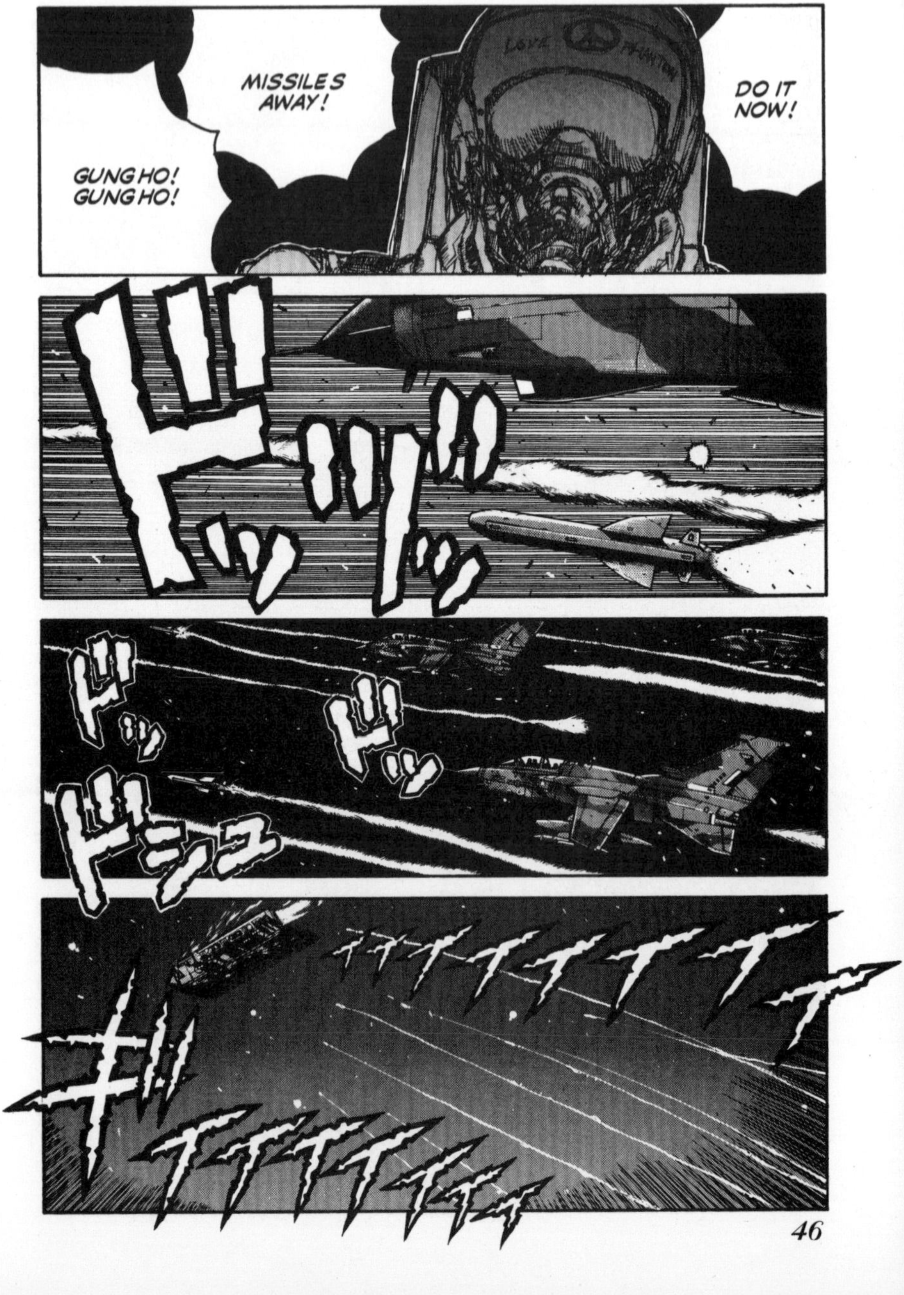
DO IT NOW!
MISSILES AWAY!
GUNG HO! GUNG HO!
ドッ
ドッ
ドッ
ドッ
ドシュ
キィィィィィィィィ

ガキュッ
ボッドッ
ボッ
ドドーン
ヒュ

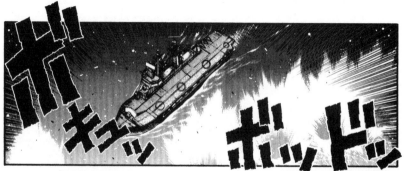

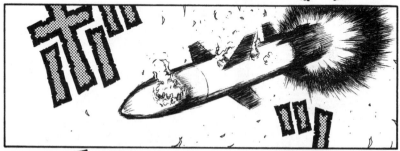

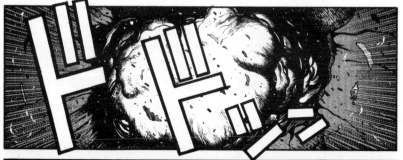

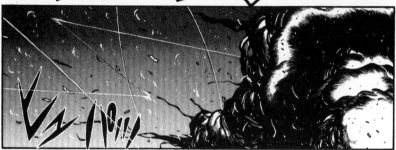

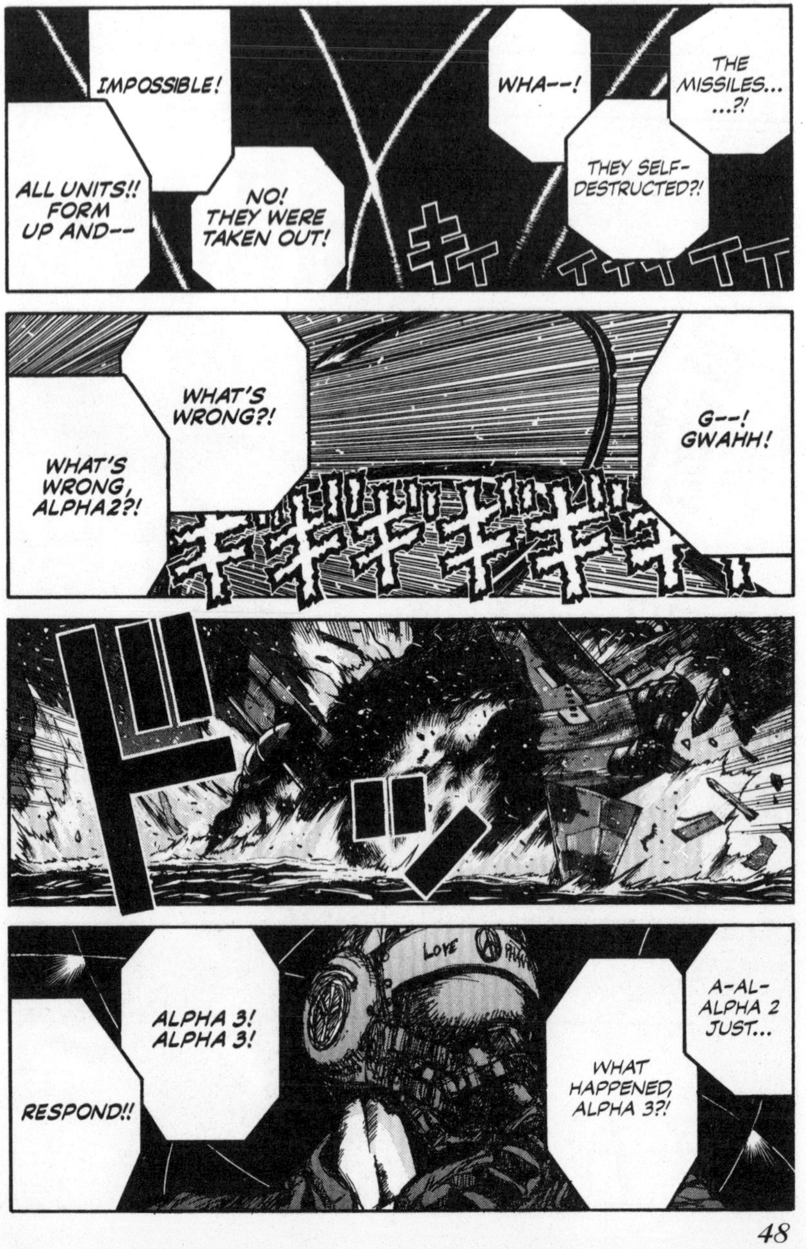
THE MISSILES... ...?!
WHA--!
THEY SELF-DESTRUCTED?!
IMPOSSIBLE!
NO! THEY WERE TAKEN OUT!
ALL UNITS!! FORM UP AND--
G--! GWAHH!
WHAT'S WRONG?!
WHAT'S WRONG, ALPHA2?!
A-AL- ALPHA 2 JUST...
WHAT HAPPENED, ALPHA 3?!
LOVE
ALPHA 3! ALPHA 3!
RESPOND!!

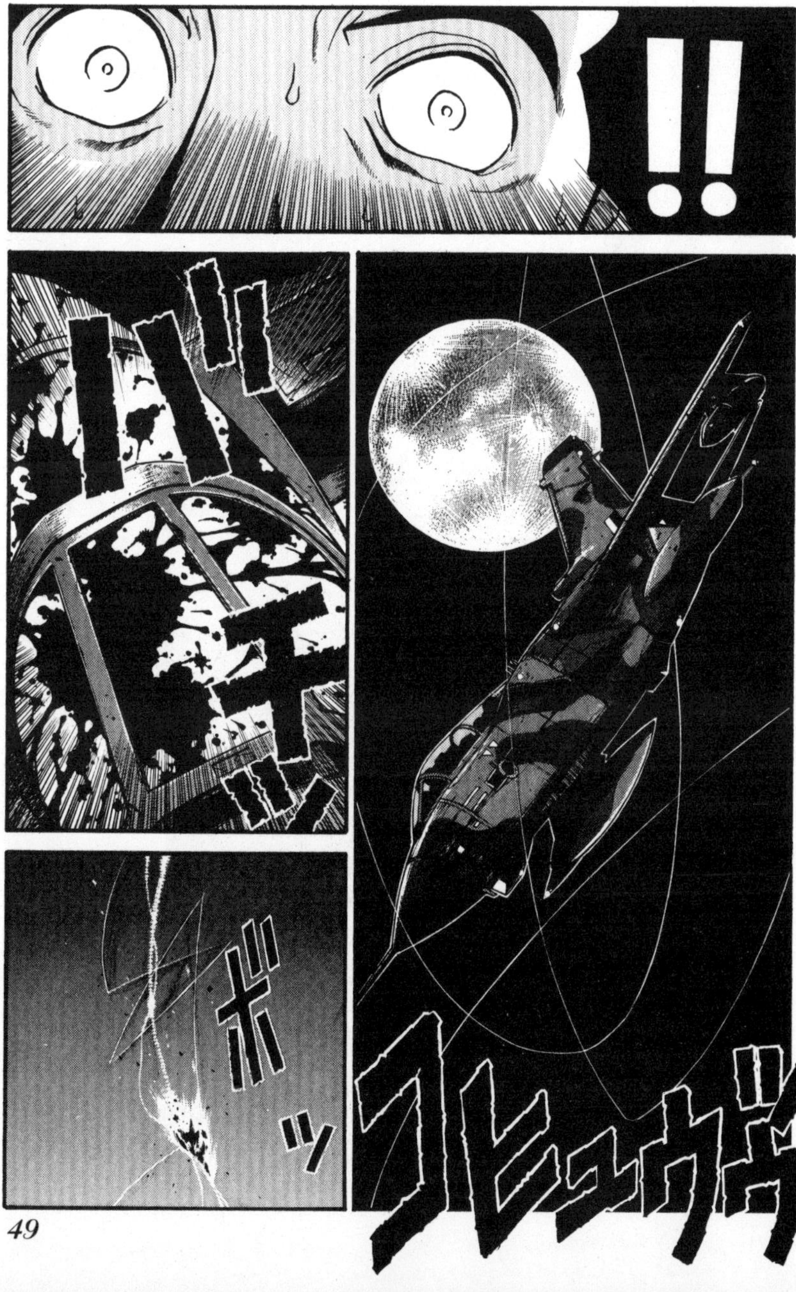
!!
バチッ
ボッ

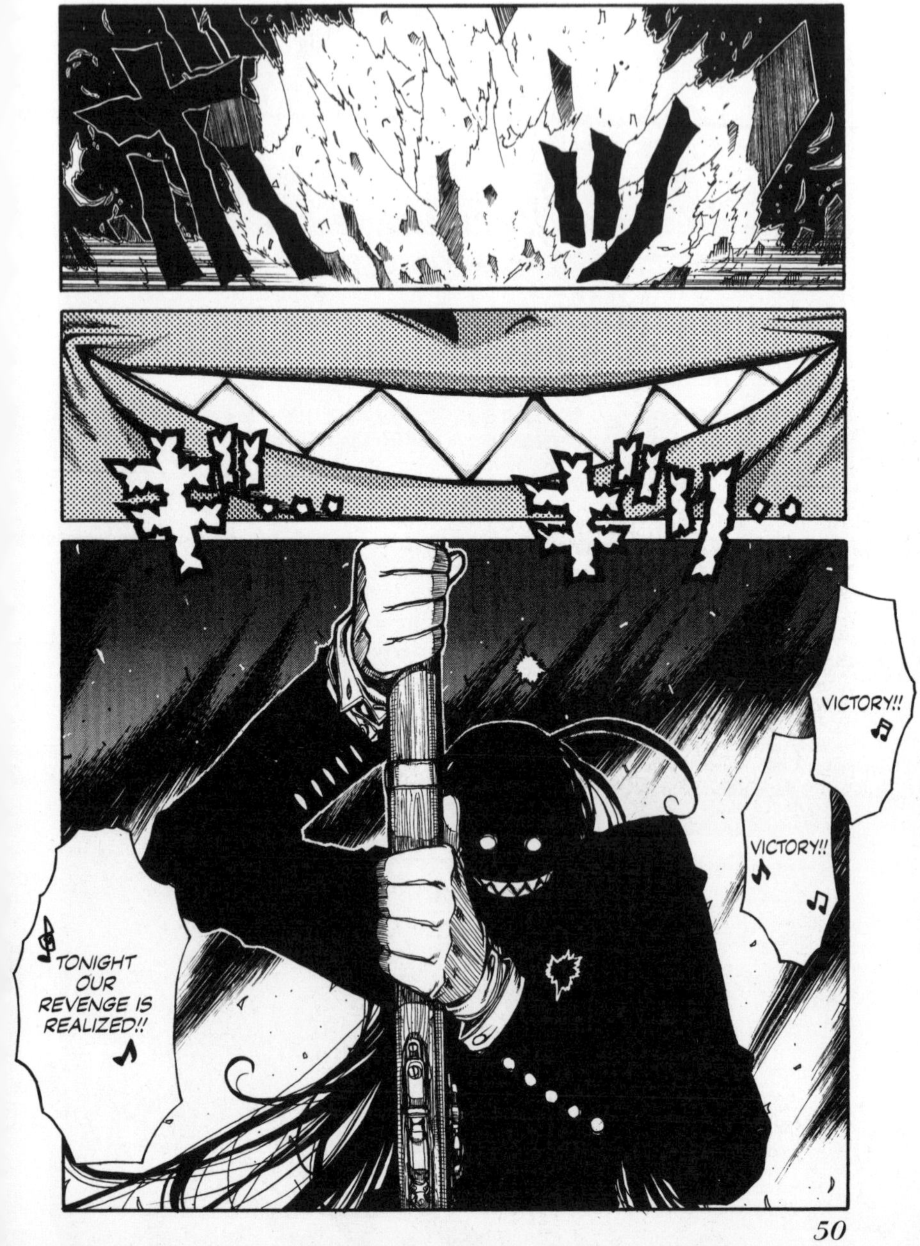
VICTORY!! ♫
VICTORY!! ♪ ♫
TONIGHT OUR REVENGE IS REALIZED!! ♪

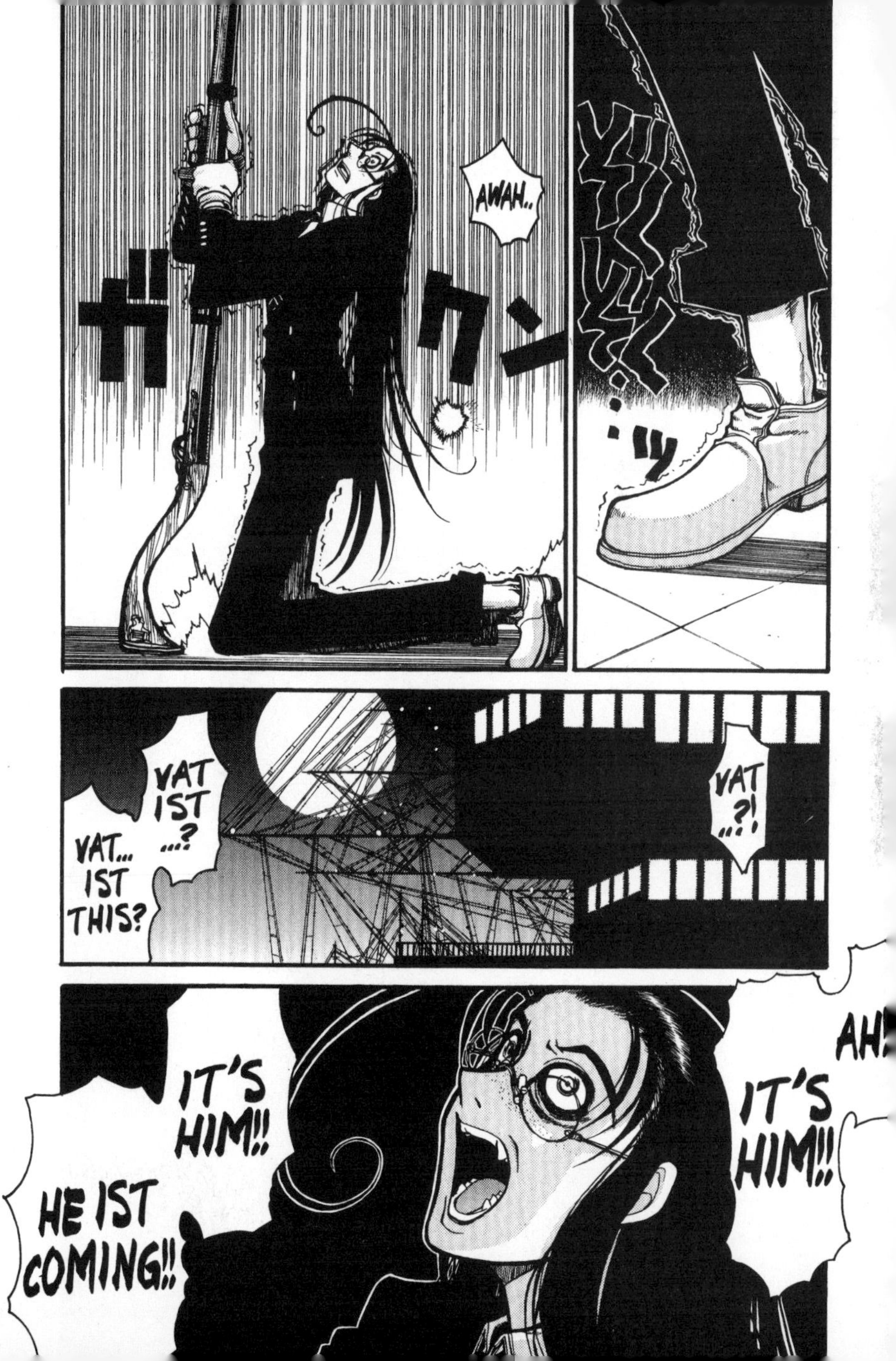
AWAH..
ガクン
VAT ?! ...
VAT IST ...?
VAT... IST THIS?
AH!
IT'S HIM!!
IT'S HIM!!
HE IST COMING!!

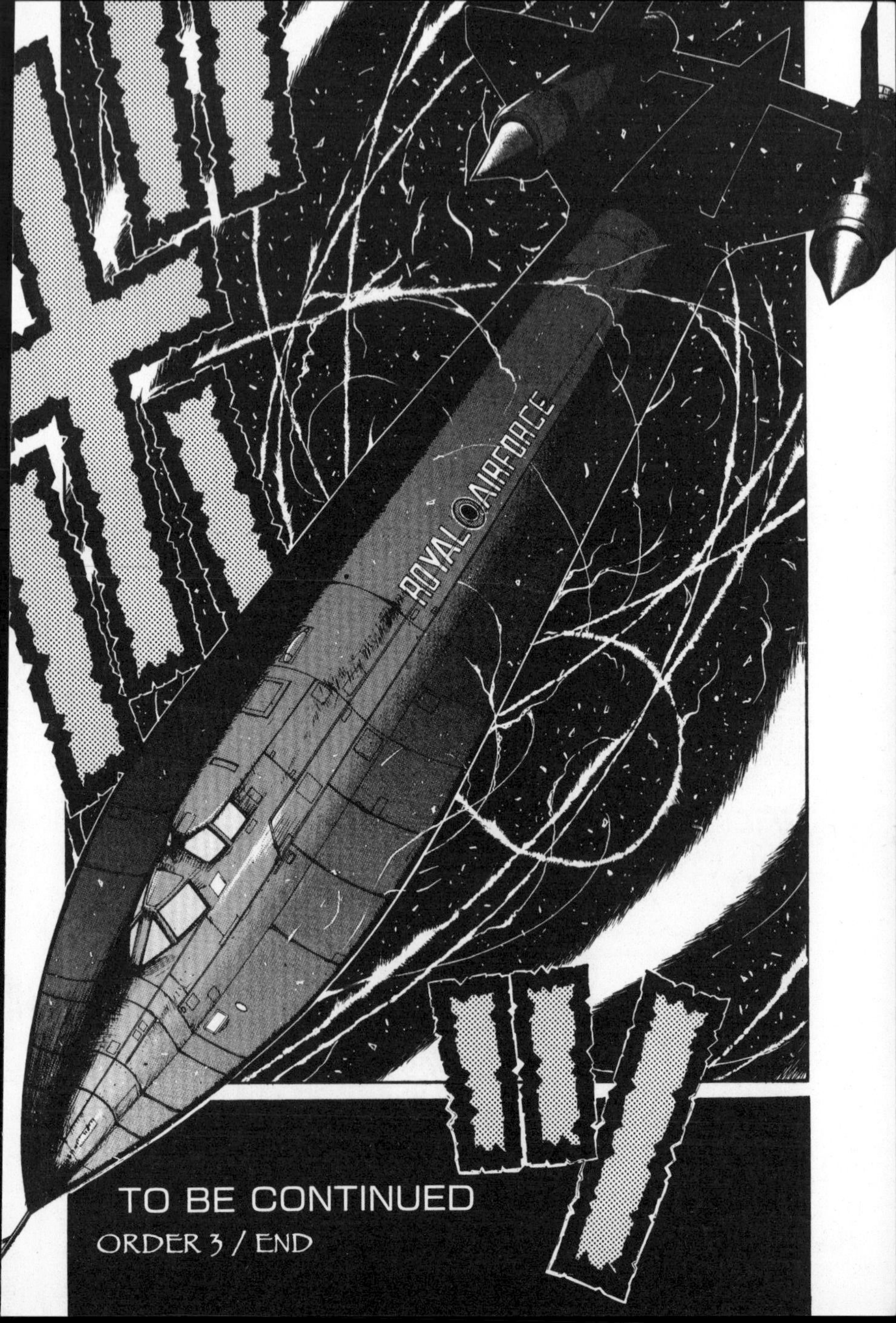
ROYAL AIRFORCE
TO BE CONTINUED
ORDER 3 / END

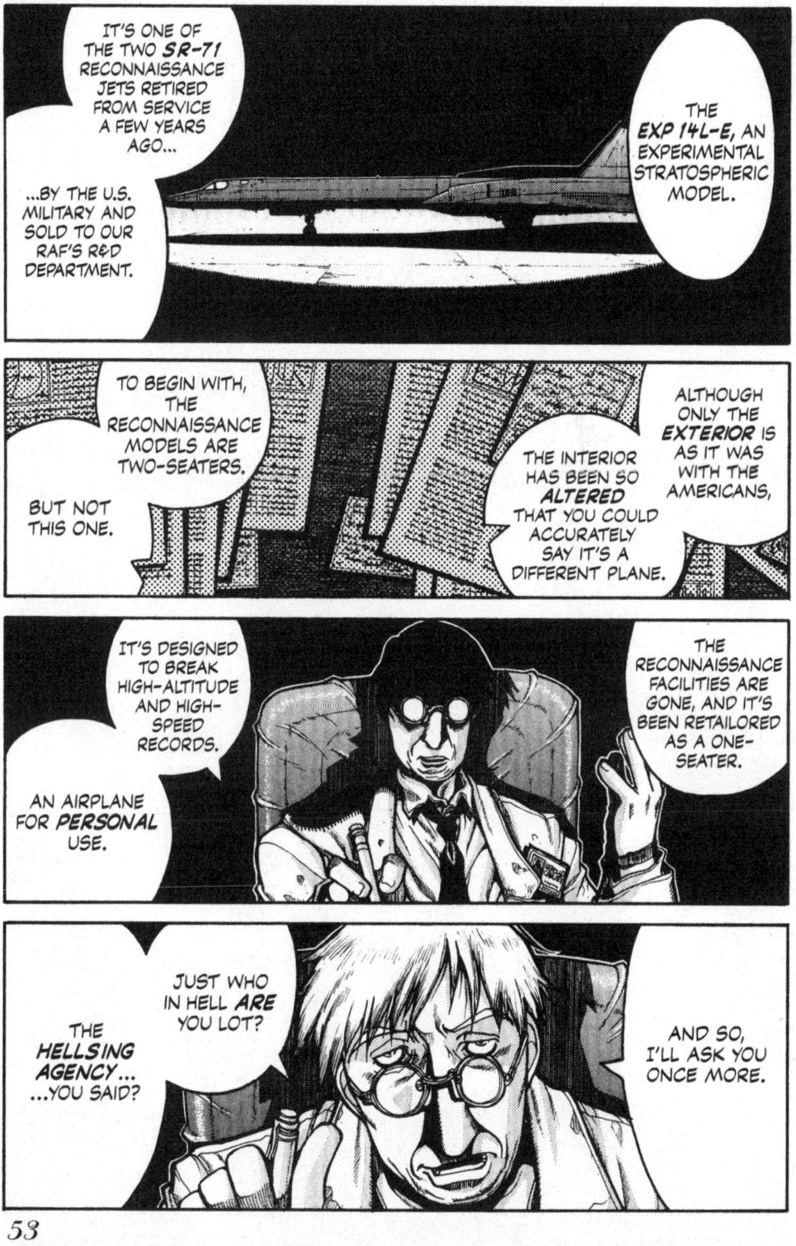
THE EXP 14L-E, AN EXPERIMENTAL STRATOSPHERIC MODEL.
IT'S ONE OF THE TWO SR-71 RECONNAISSANCE JETS RETIRED FROM SERVICE A FEW YEARS AGO...
...BY THE U.S. MILITARY AND SOLD TO OUR RAF'S R&D DEPARTMENT.
ALTHOUGH ONLY THE EXTERIOR IS AS IT WAS WITH THE AMERICANS,
THE INTERIOR HAS BEEN SO ALTERED THAT YOU COULD ACCURATELY SAY IT'S A DIFFERENT PLANE.
TO BEGIN WITH, THE RECONNAISSANCE MODELS ARE TWO-SEATERS.
BUT NOT THIS ONE.
THE RECONNAISSANCE FACILITIES ARE GONE, AND IT'S BEEN RETAILORED AS A ONE-SEATER.
IT'S DESIGNED TO BREAK HIGH-ALTITUDE AND HIGH-SPEED RECORDS.
AN AIRPLANE FOR PERSONAL USE.
AND SO, I'LL ASK YOU ONCE MORE.
JUST WHO IN HELL ARE YOU LOT?
THE HELLSING AGENCY... ...YOU SAID?

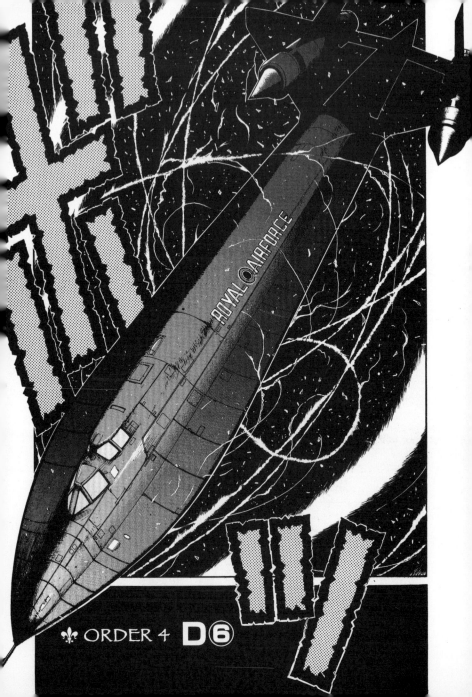

ROYAL❂AIRFORCE

⚜ ORDER 4 **D⑥**

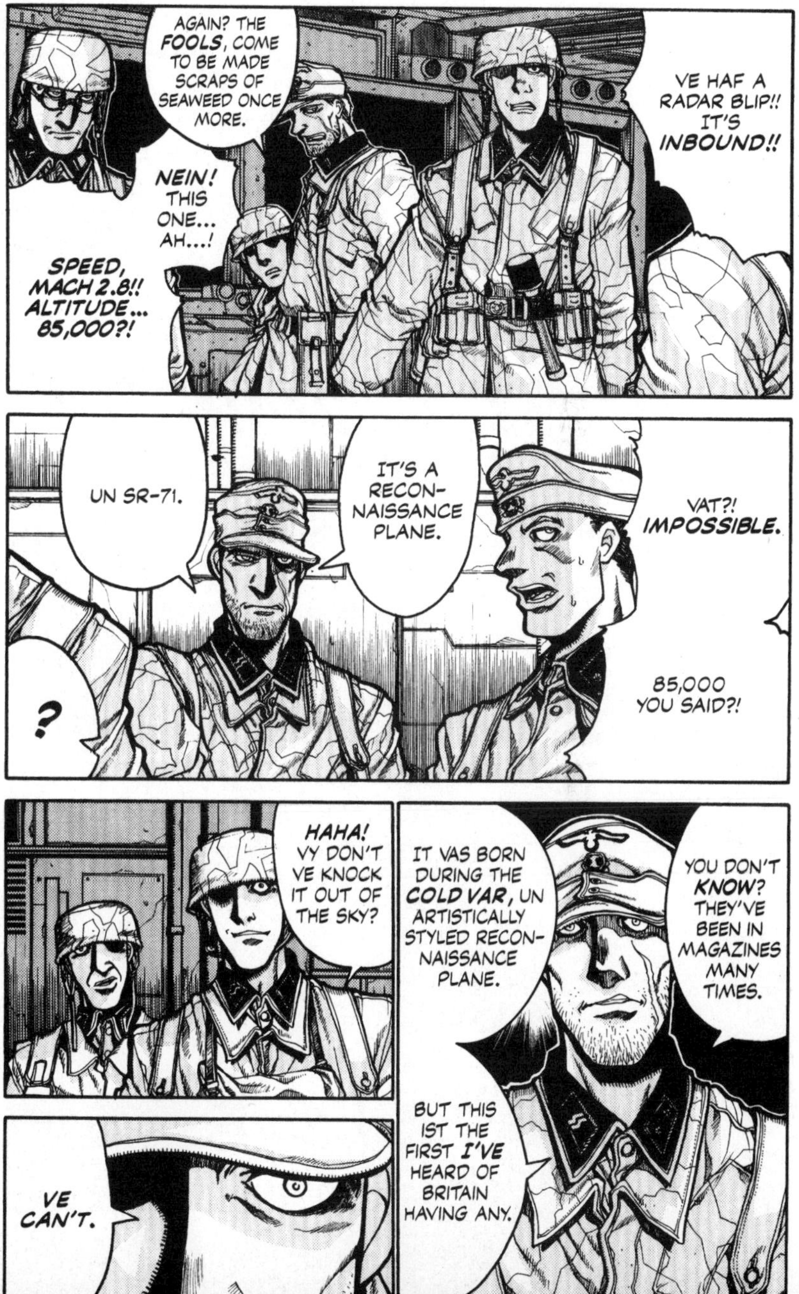
VE HAF A RADAR BLIP!! IT'S INBOUND!!
AGAIN? THE FOOLS, COME TO BE MADE SCRAPS OF SEAWEED ONCE MORE.
NEIN! THIS ONE... AH...!
SPEED, MACH 2.8!! ALTITUDE... 85,000?!
VAT?! IMPOSSIBLE.
IT'S A RECONNAISSANCE PLANE.
UN SR-71.
85,000 YOU SAID?!
?
YOU DON'T KNOW? THEY'VE BEEN IN MAGAZINES MANY TIMES.
IT VAS BORN DURING THE COLD VAR, UN ARTISTICALLY STYLED RECONNAISSANCE PLANE.
BUT THIS IST THE FIRST I'VE HEARD OF BRITAIN HAVING ANY.
HAHA! VY DON'T VE KNOCK IT OUT OF THE SKY?
VE CAN'T.

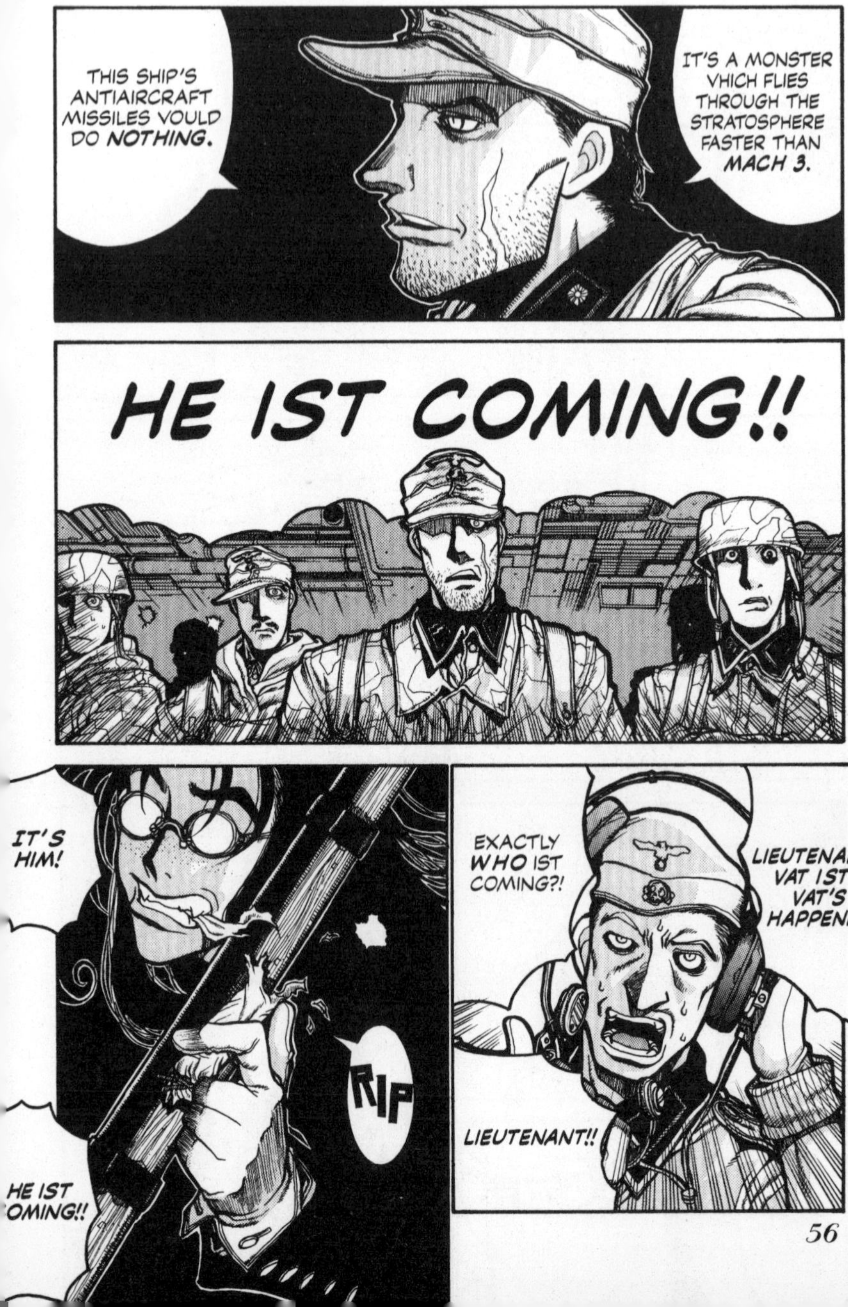
IT'S A MONSTER VHICH FLIES THROUGH THE STRATOSPHERE FASTER THAN MACH 3.
THIS SHIP'S ANTIAIRCRAFT MISSILES VOULD DO NOTHING.
HE IST COMING!!
LIEUTENANT!! VAT IST?! VAT'S HAPPENING?!
EXACTLY WHO IST COMING?!
LIEUTENANT!!
IT'S HIM!
RIP
HE IST OMING!!

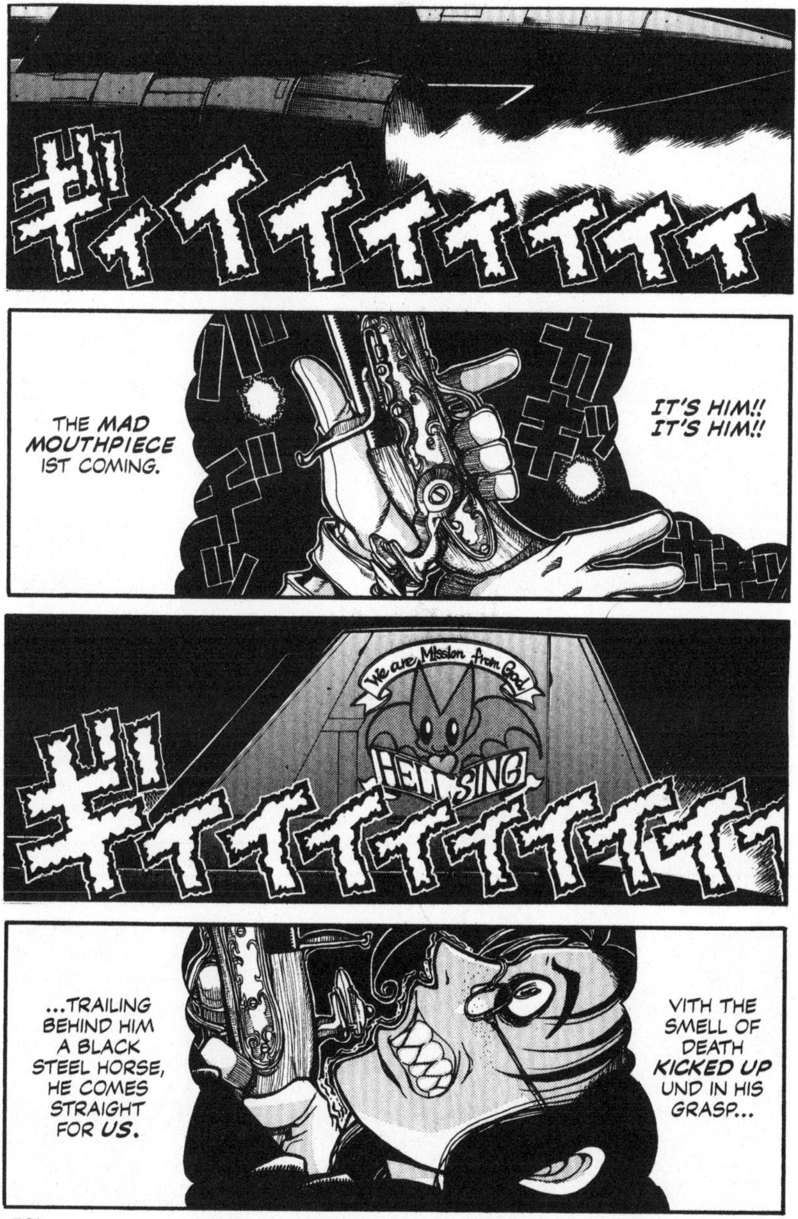
IT'S HIM!! IT'S HIM!!
THE MAD MOUTHPIECE IST COMING.
We are Mission from God
HELLSING
VITH THE SMELL OF DEATH KICKED UP UND IN HIS GRASP...
...TRAILING BEHIND HIM A BLACK STEEL HORSE, HE COMES STRAIGHT FOR US.

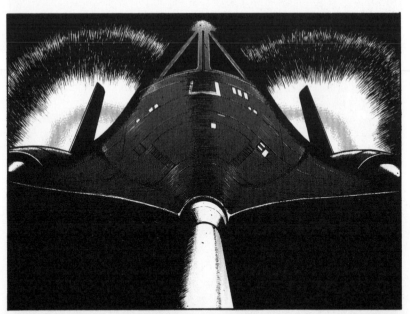

58

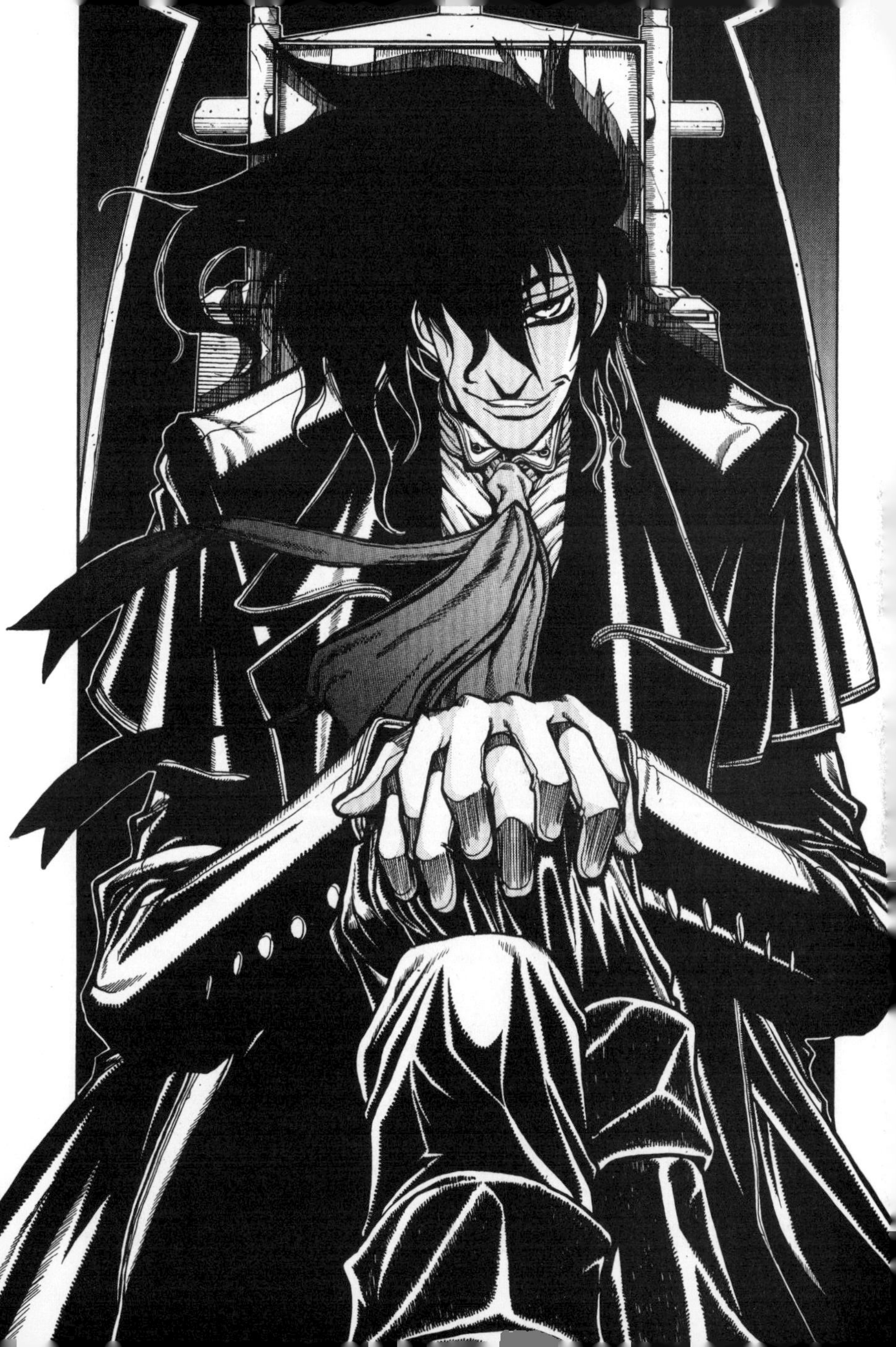

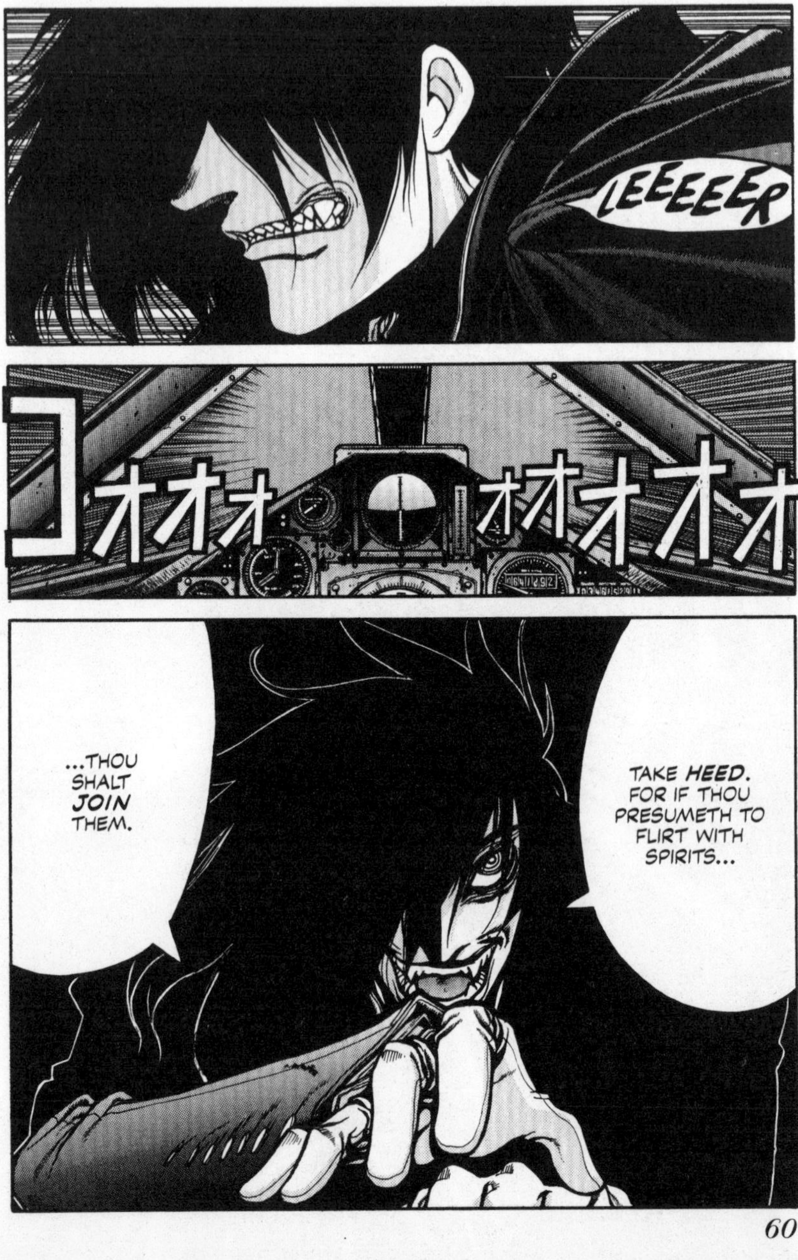
LEEEEEER
ゴオオオオオオオオオ
TAKE HEED. FOR IF THOU PRESUMETH TO FLIRT WITH SPIRITS...
...THOU SHALT JOIN THEM.

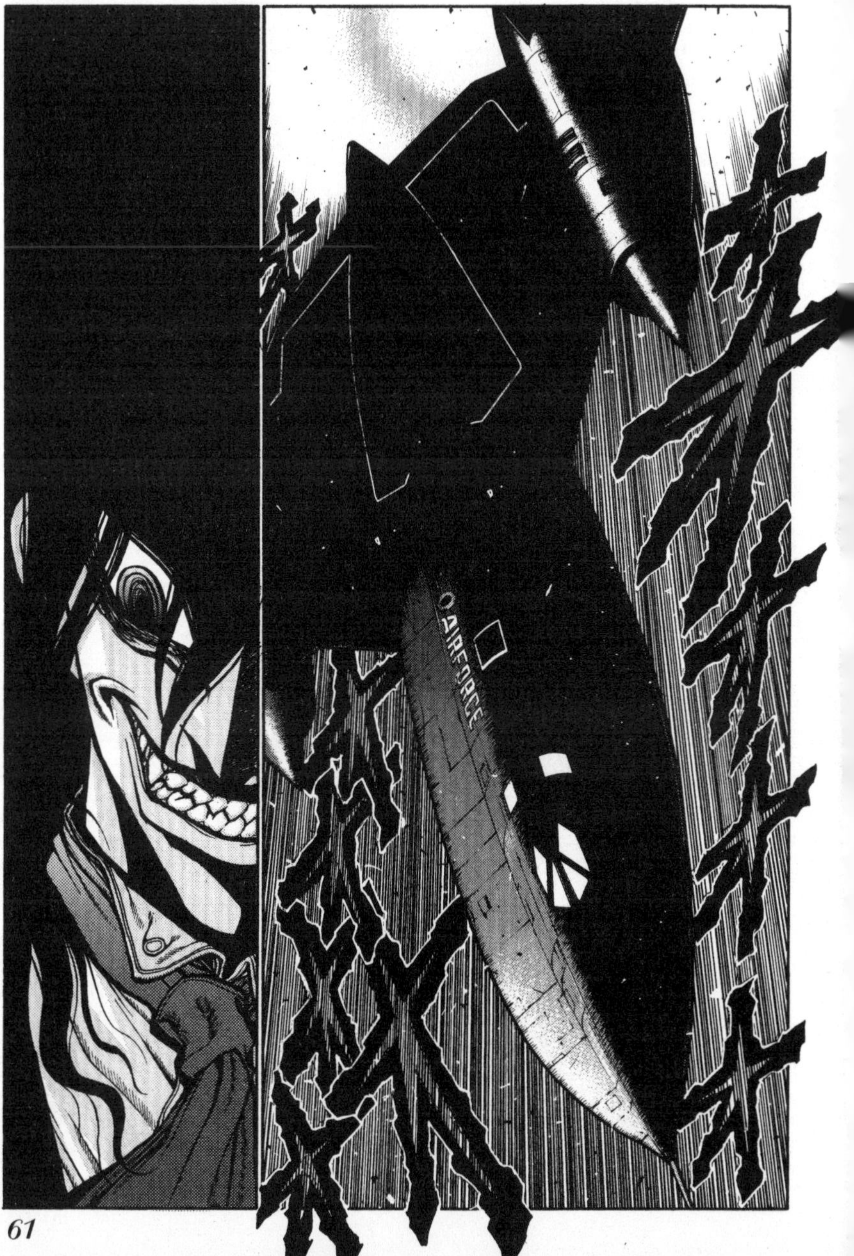
AIRFORCE

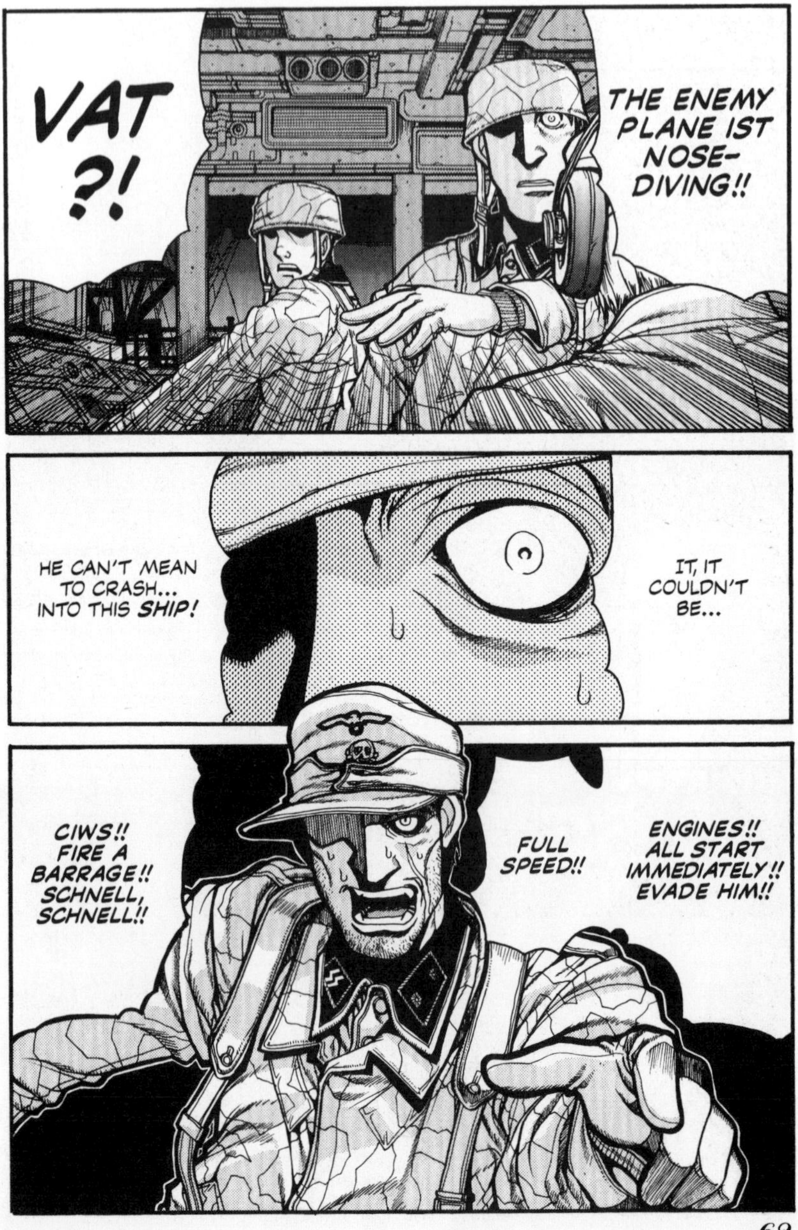
THE ENEMY PLANE IST NOSE-DIVING!!
VAT?!
IT, IT COULDN'T BE...
HE CAN'T MEAN TO CRASH... INTO THIS SHIP!
ENGINES!! ALL START IMMEDIATELY!! EVADE HIM!!
FULL SPEED!!
CIWS!! FIRE A BARRAGE!! SCHNELL, SCHNELL!!

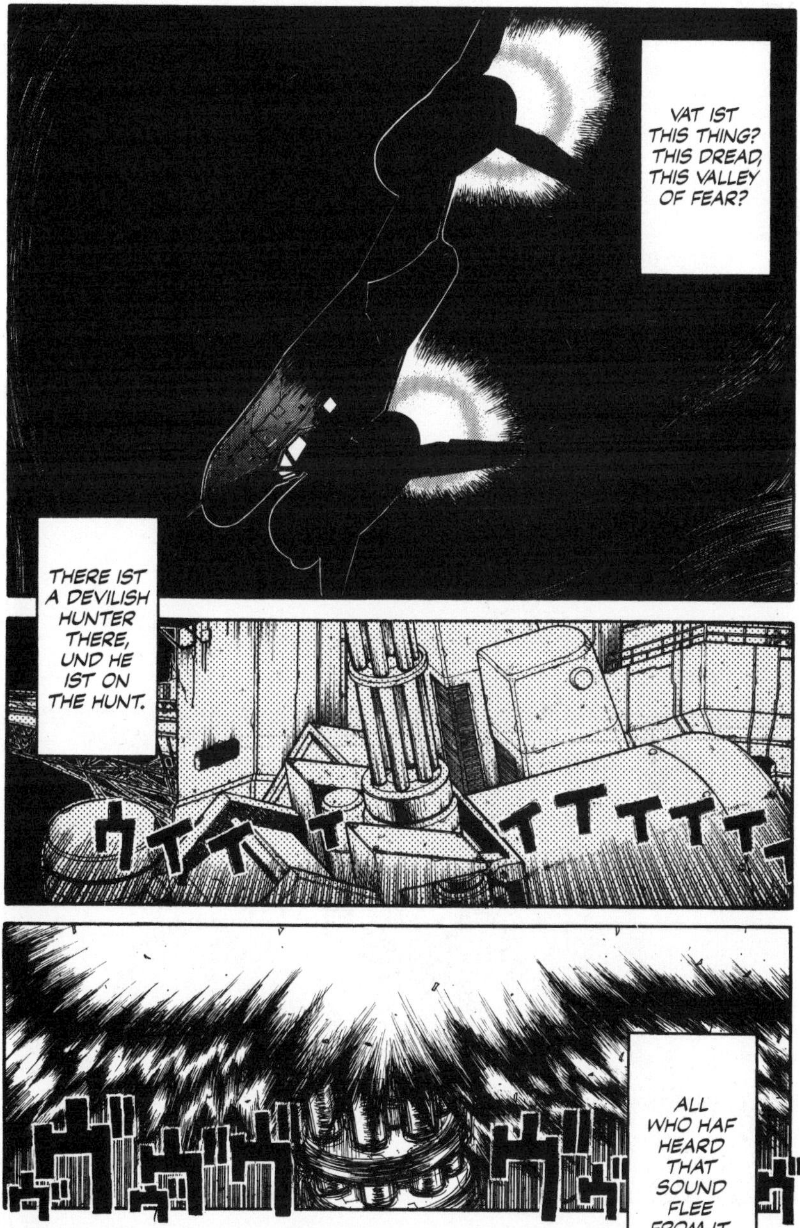
VAT IST THIS THING? THIS DREAD, THIS VALLEY OF FEAR?
THERE IST A DEVILISH HUNTER THERE, UND HE IST ON THE HUNT.
ALL WHO HAF HEARD THAT SOUND FLEE FROM IT.

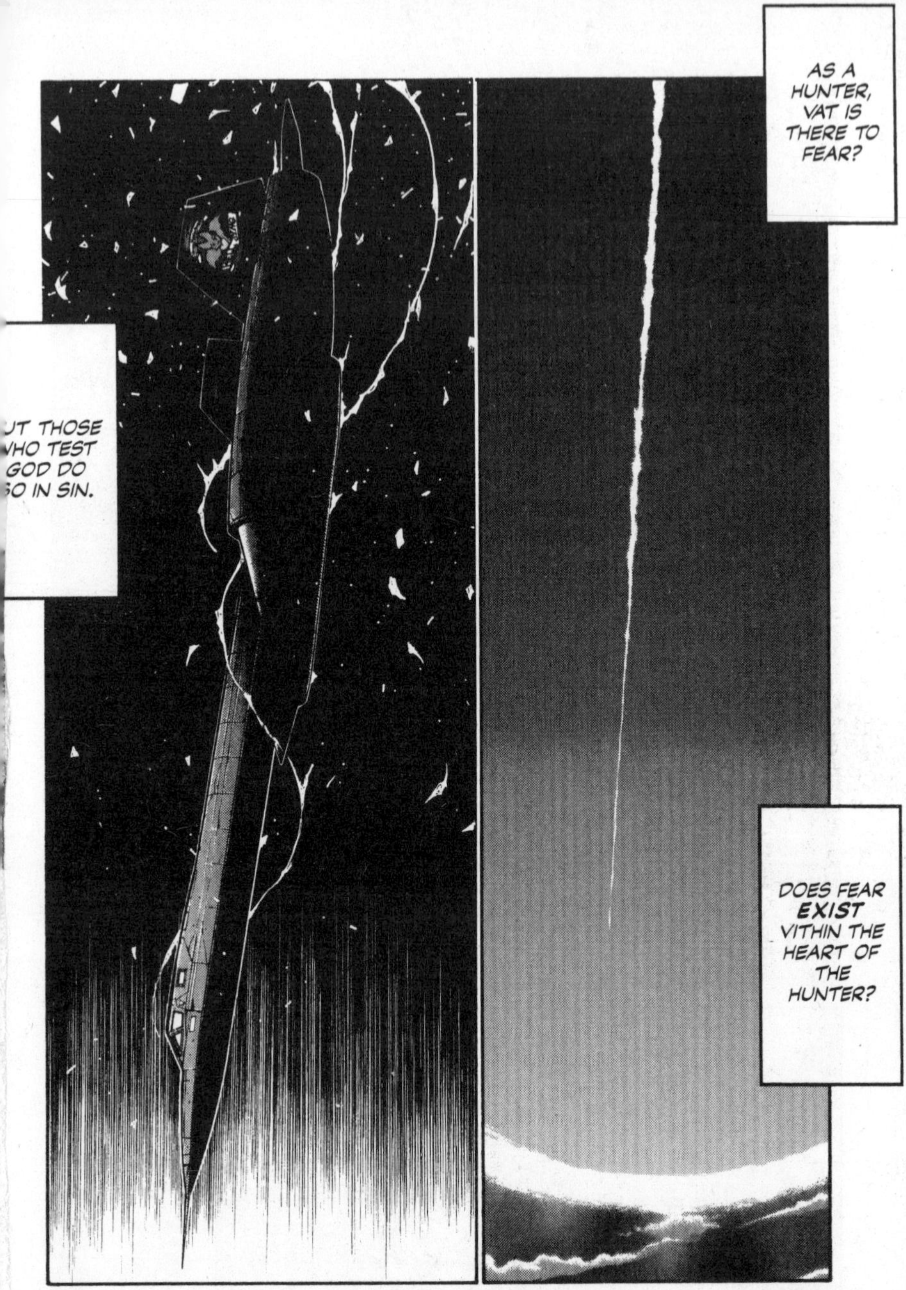
AS A HUNTER, VAT IS THERE TO FEAR?
DOES FEAR EXIST VITHIN THE HEART OF THE HUNTER?
UT THOSE HO TEST GOD DO O IN SIN.

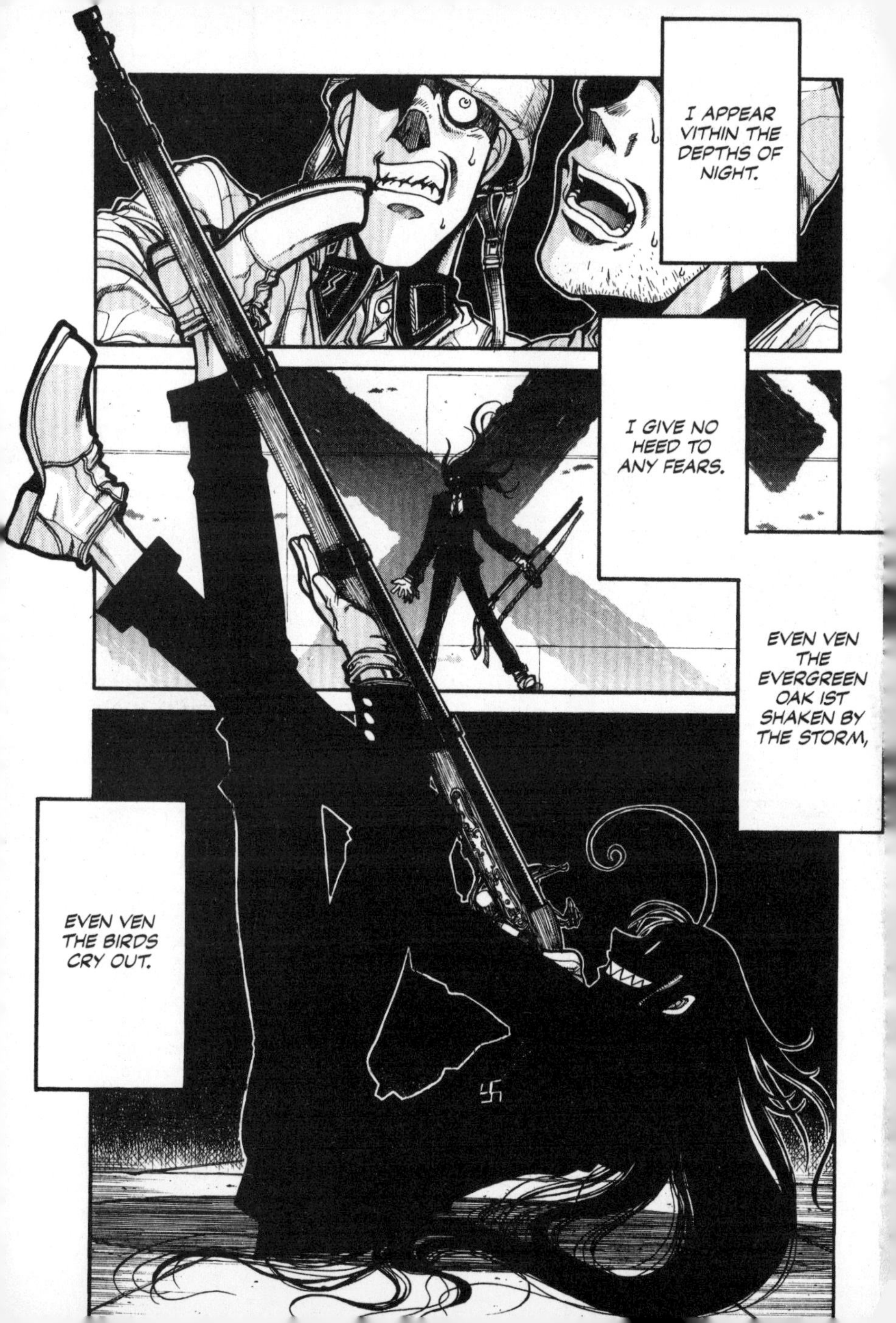
I APPEAR VITHIN THE DEPTHS OF NIGHT.
I GIVE NO HEED TO ANY FEARS.
EVEN VEN THE EVERGREEN OAK IST SHAKEN BY THE STORM,
EVEN VEN THE BIRDS CRY OUT.

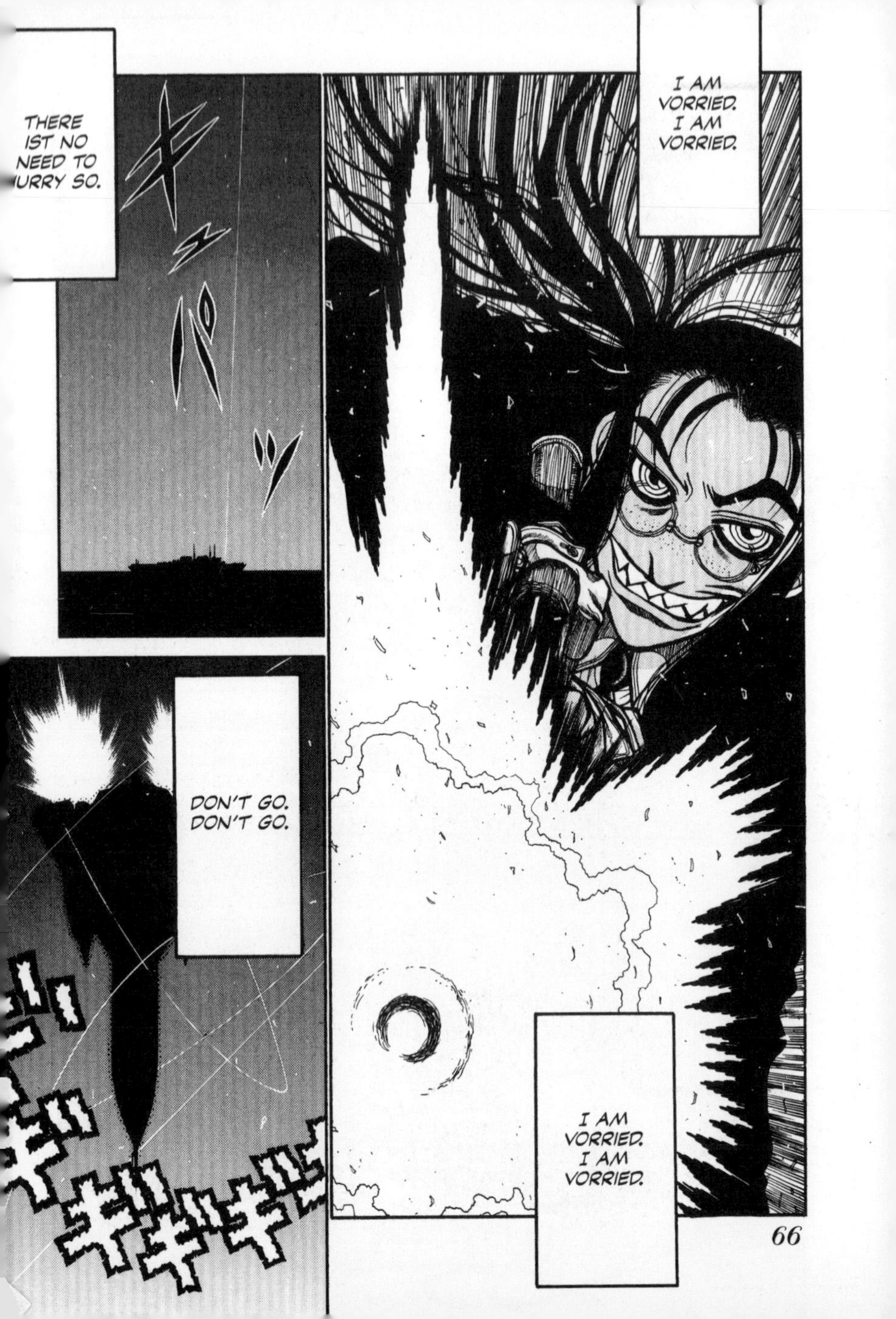
I AM VORRIED. I AM VORRIED.
I AM VORRIED. I AM VORRIED.
THERE IST NO NEED TO URRY SO.
DON'T GO. DON'T GO.

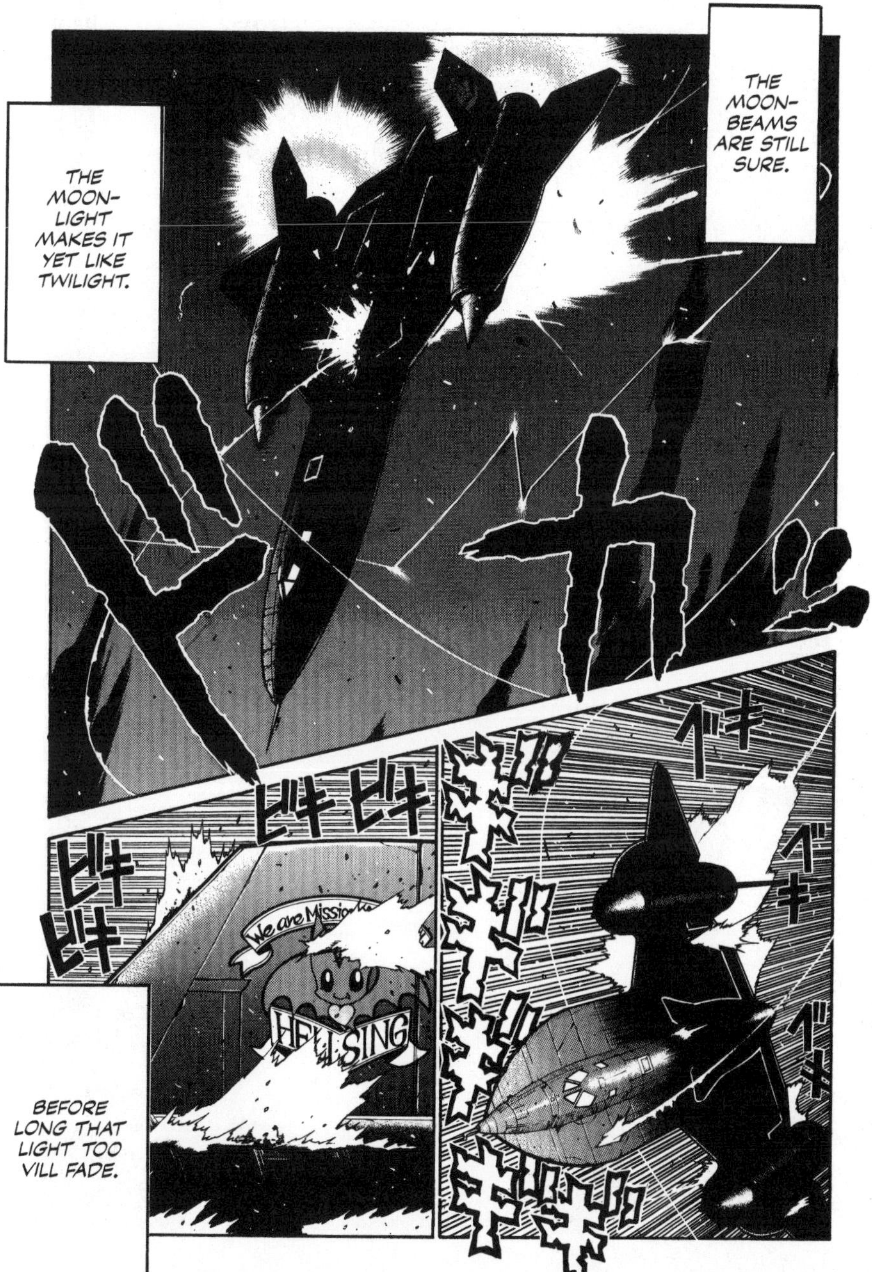
THE MOON-BEAMS ARE STILL SURE.
THE MOON-LIGHT MAKES IT YET LIKE TWILIGHT.
BEFORE LONG THAT LIGHT TOO VILL FADE.

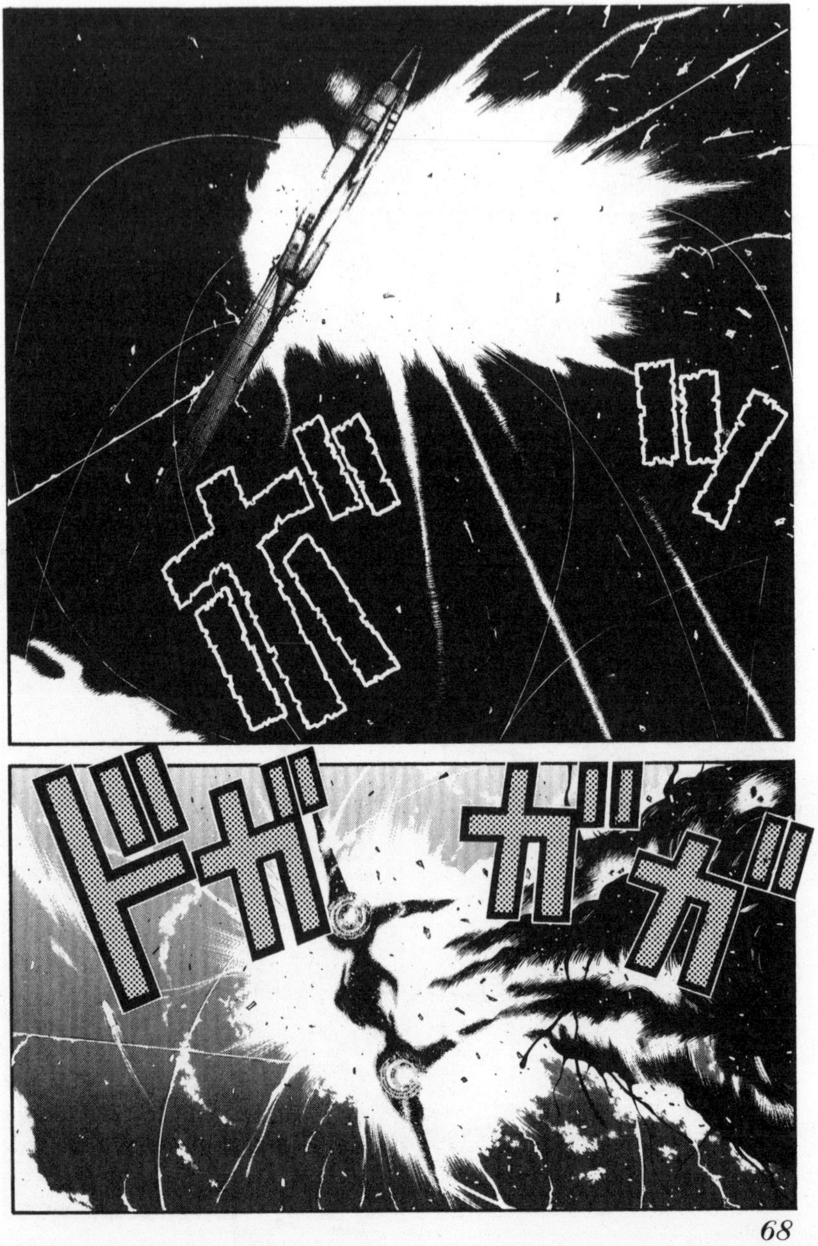
ガッ
ドガ ガガ

BRA AAAA VOO OO!!

A V-VOICE IST C-C-COMING FROM TH-THERE.

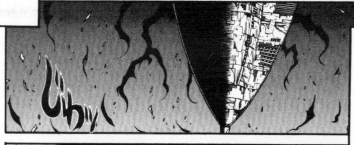

A-A V-V-VOICE TH-THAT IST C-C-CALLING T-TO M-ME.

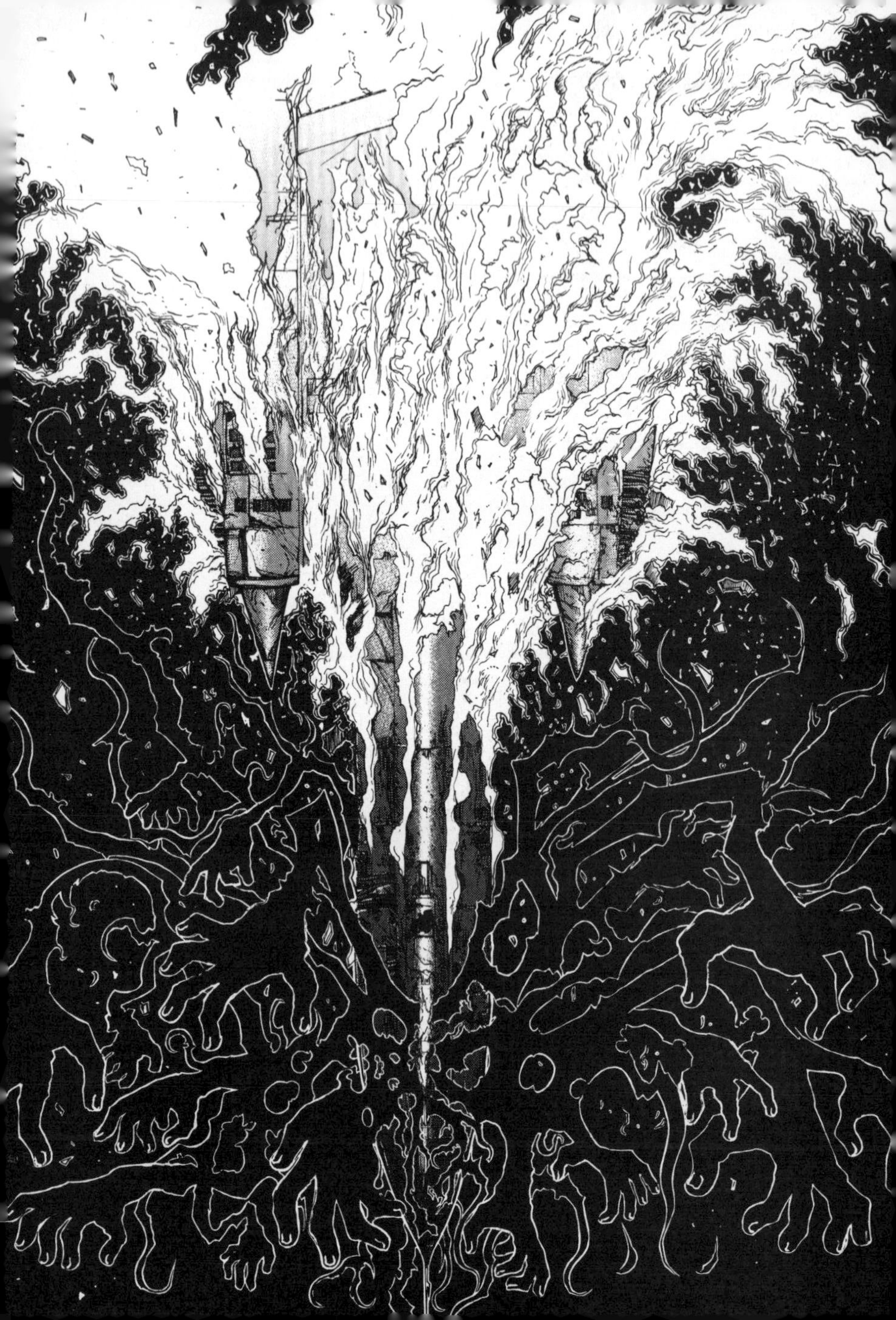

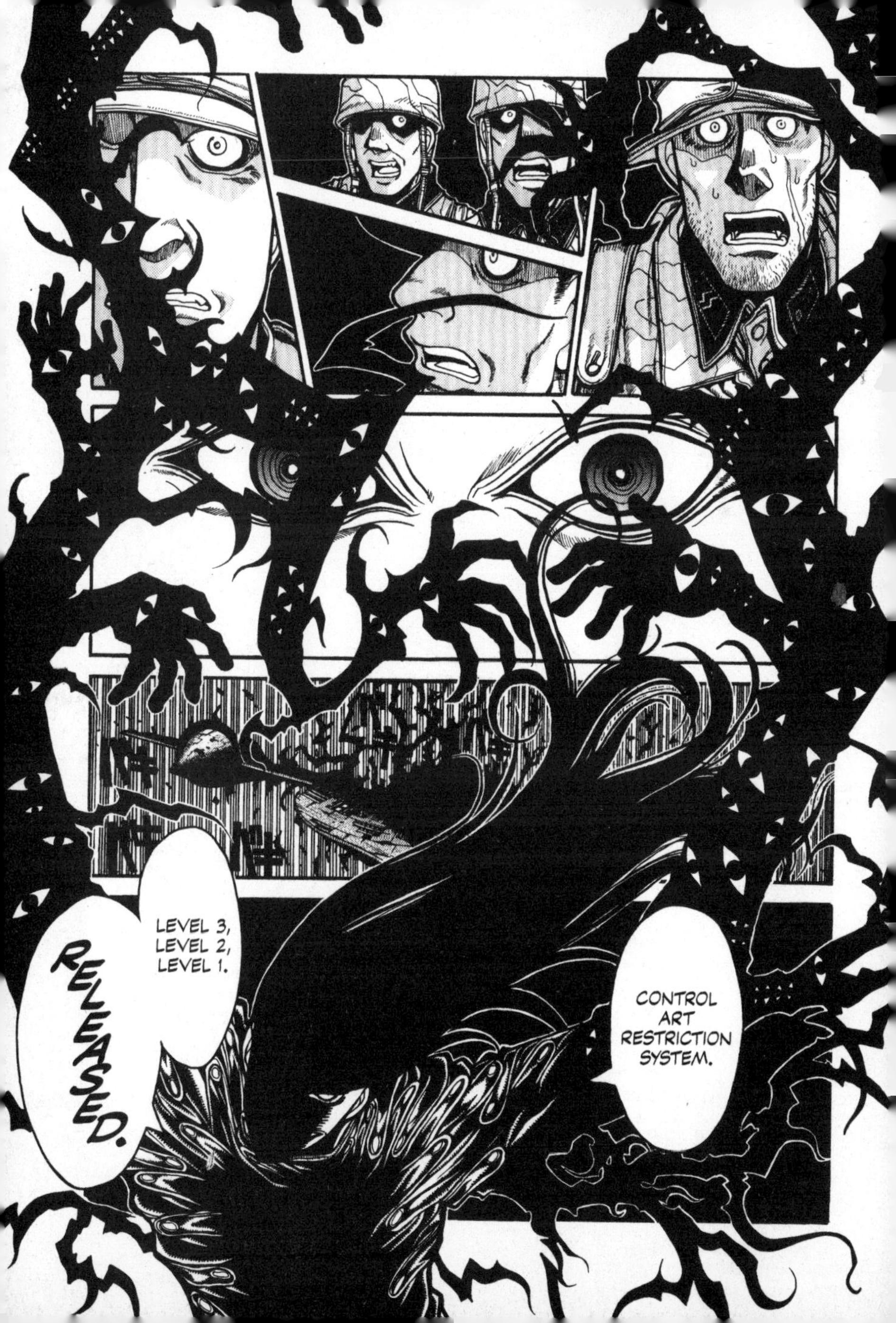
CONTROL ART RESTRICTION SYSTEM.
LEVEL 3, LEVEL 2, LEVEL 1.
RELEASED.

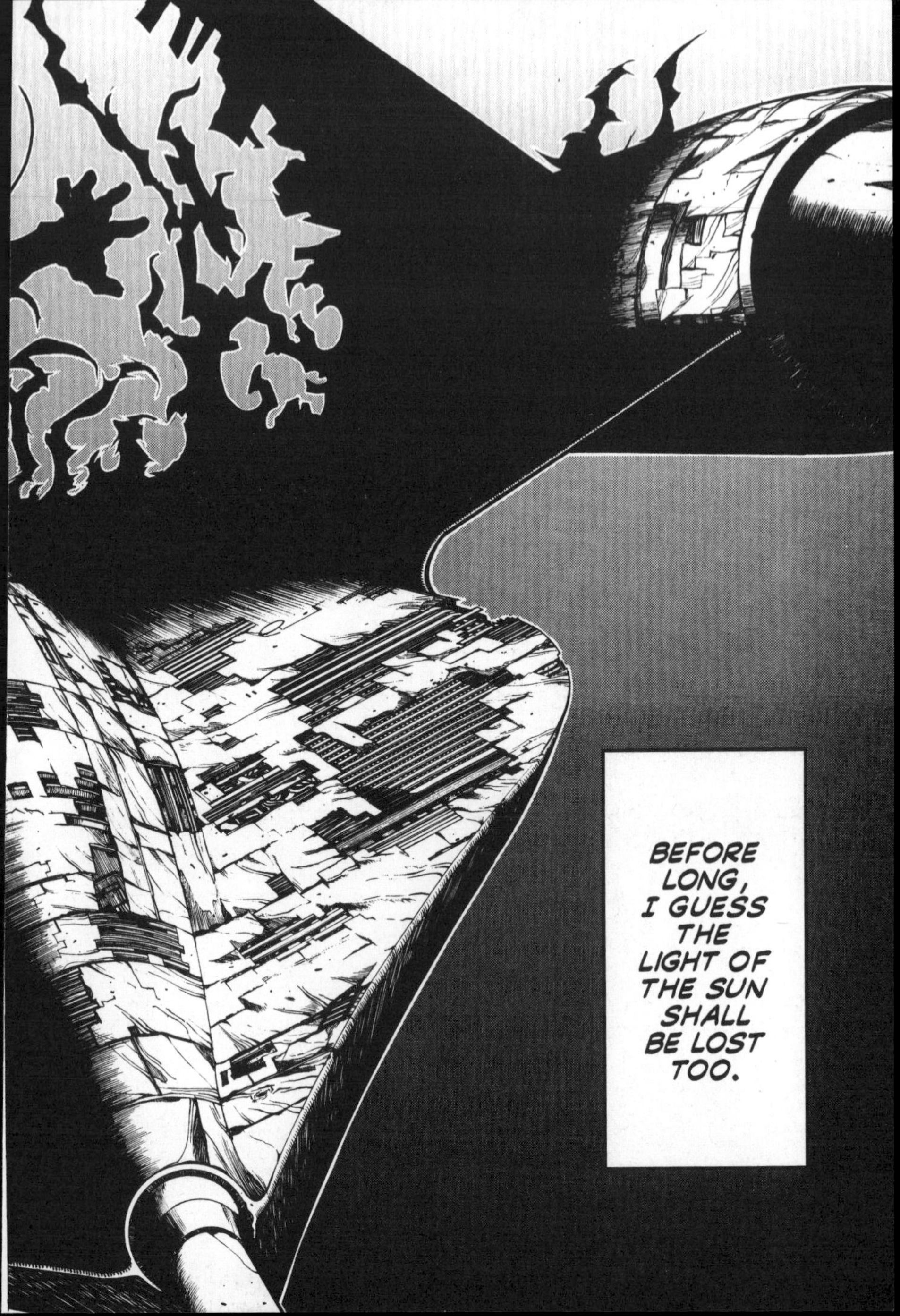
BEFORE LONG, I GUESS THE LIGHT OF THE SUN SHALL BE LOST TOO.

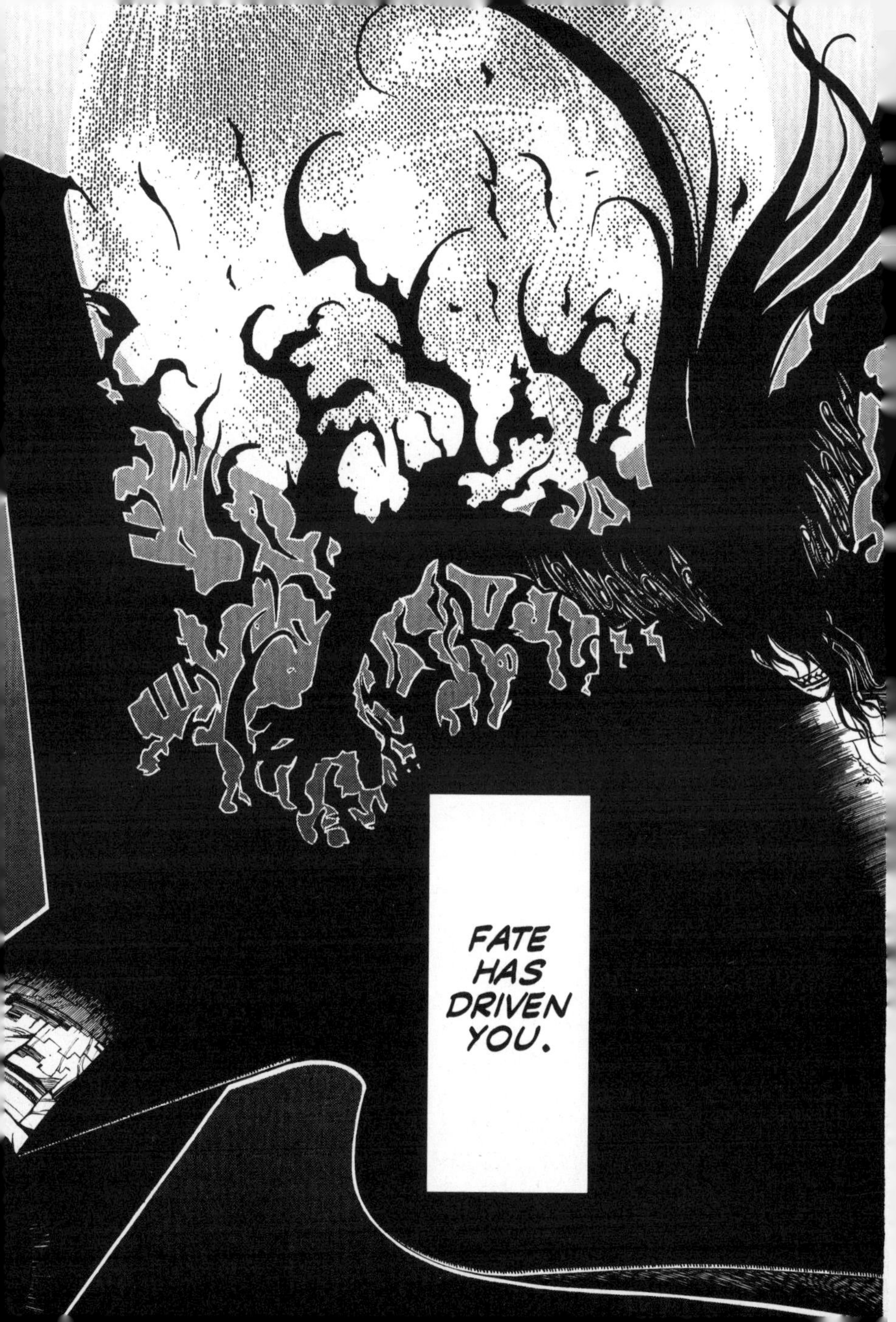
FATE HAS DRIVEN YOU.

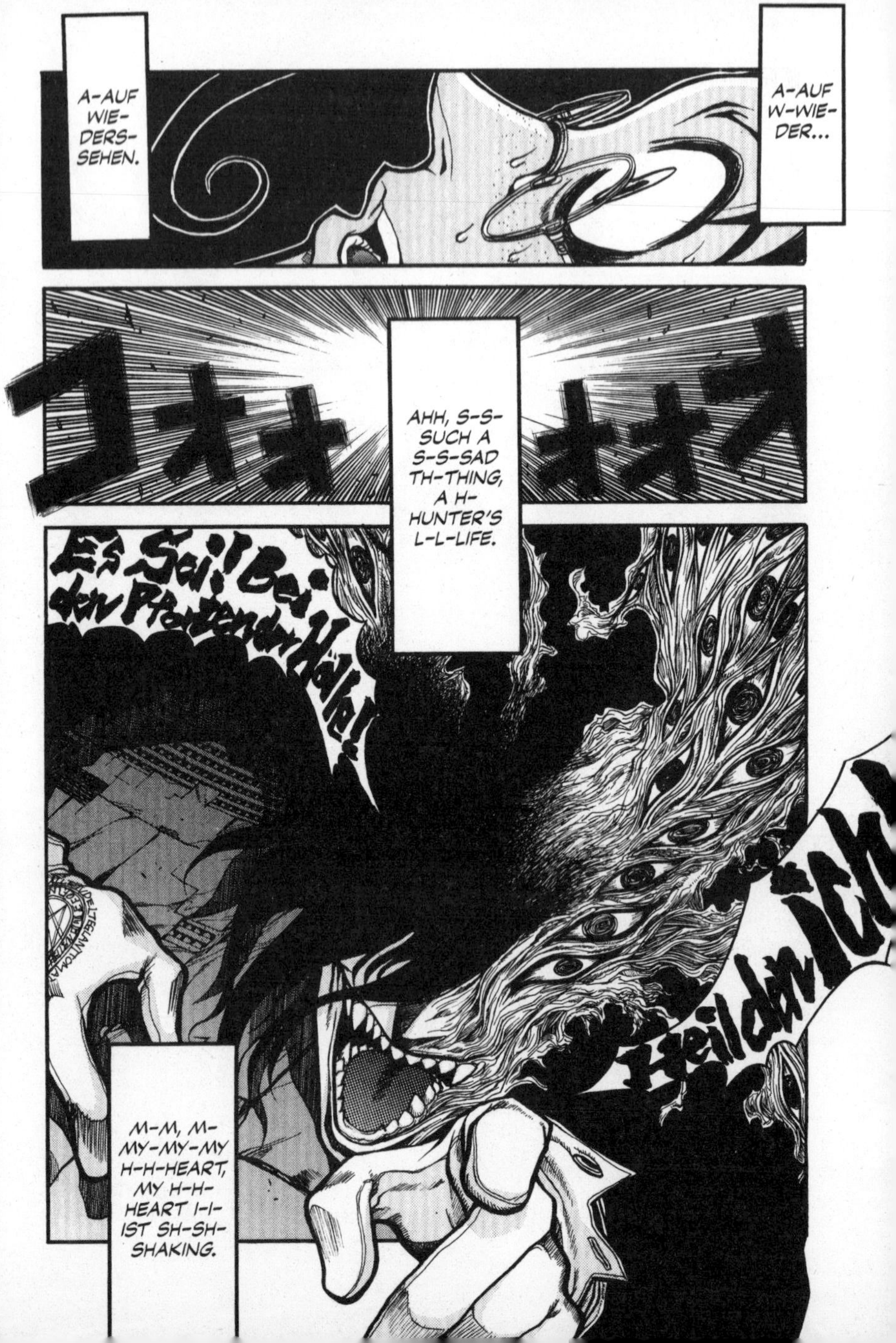
A-AUF W-WIE-DER...
A-AUF WIE-DERS-SEHEN.
AHH, S-S-SUCH A S-S-SAD TH-THING, A H-HUNTER'S L-L-LIFE.
Es Sei! Bei den Pforten der Hölle!!
M-M, M-MY-MY-MY H-H-HEART, MY H-H-HEART I-I-IST SH-SH-SHAKING.

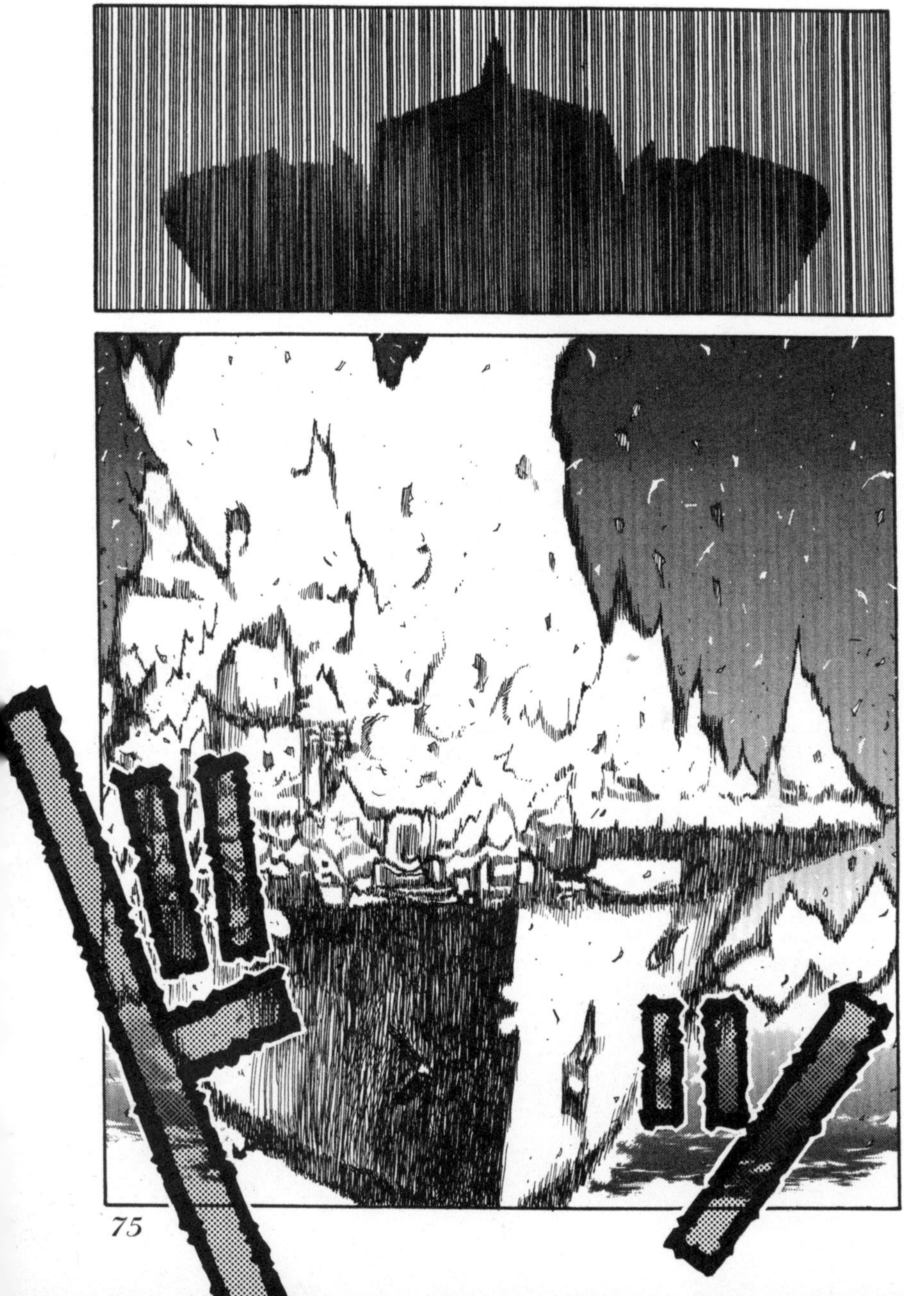

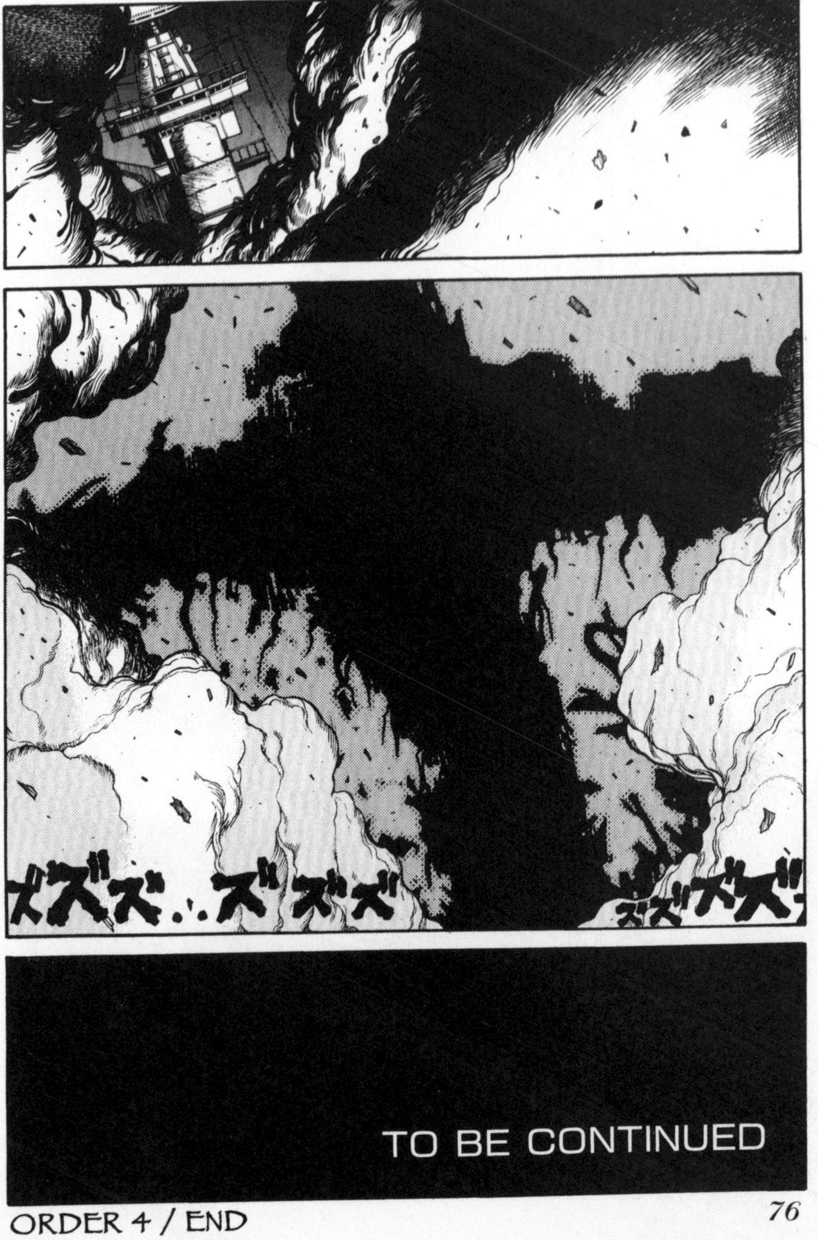
ズズズズ
ズズズ...ズズズ
TO BE CONTINUED

ORDER 5

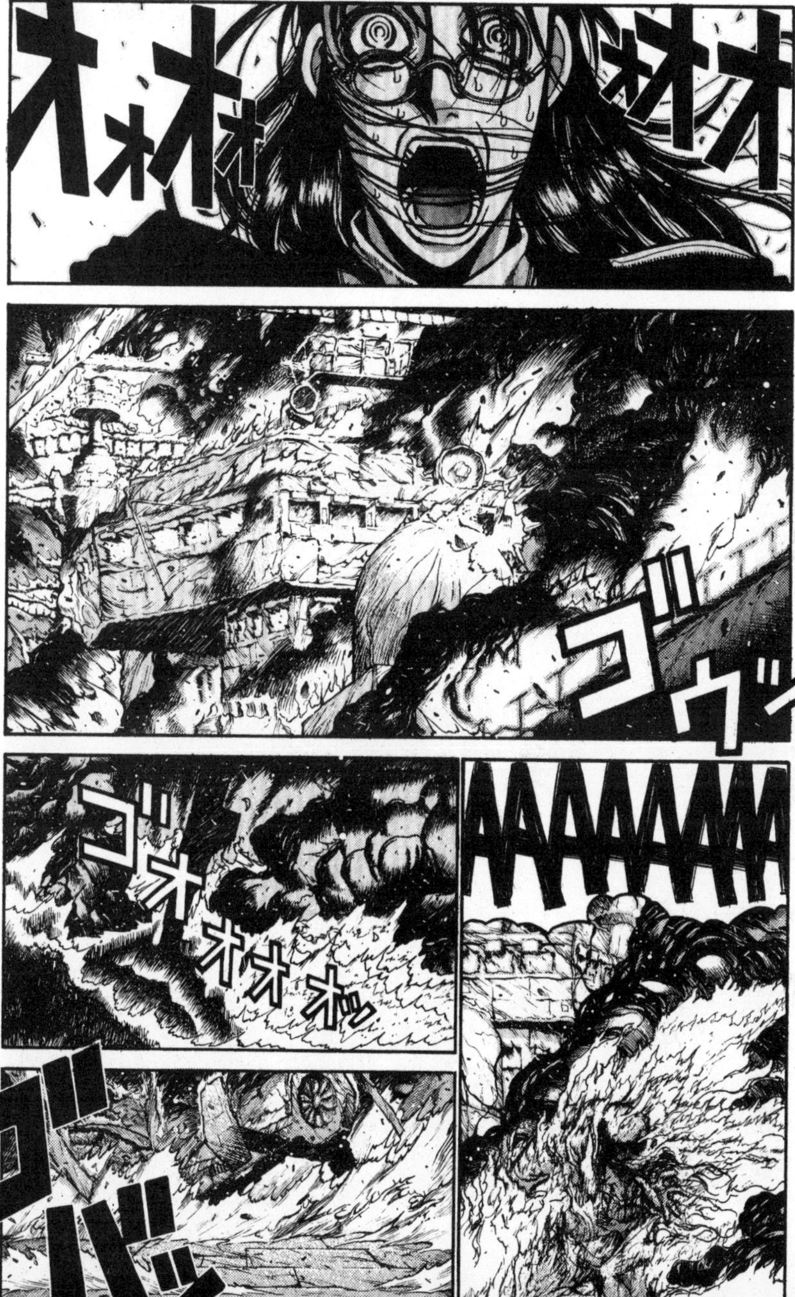
オォオォ
ォオオ
ゴヴー
AAAAAAAAA
ゴオオオオッ
ゴバ

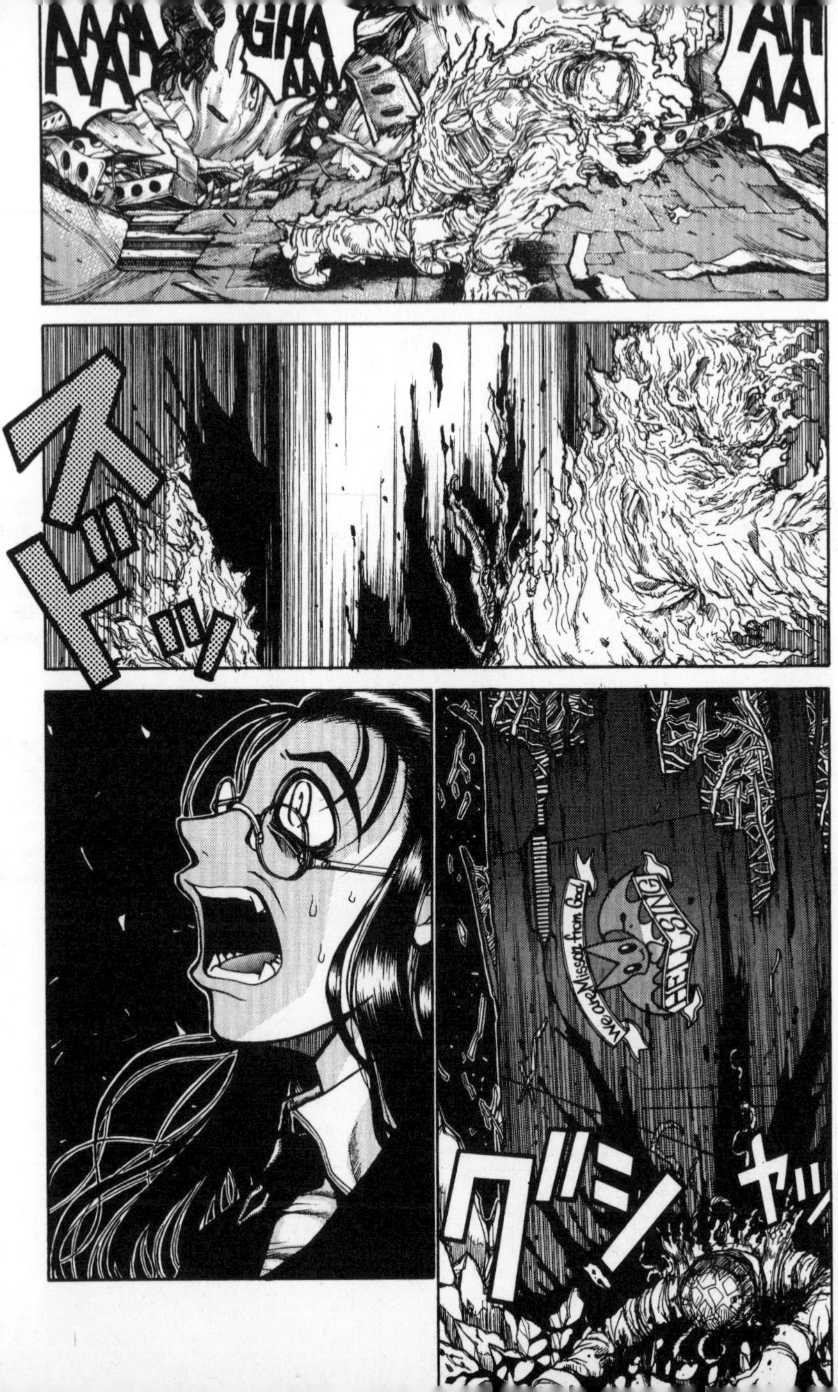
AHAAAA
GHAAAA
AAAAAA
ズドッ
HELLSING
We are Mission from God
グシャッ

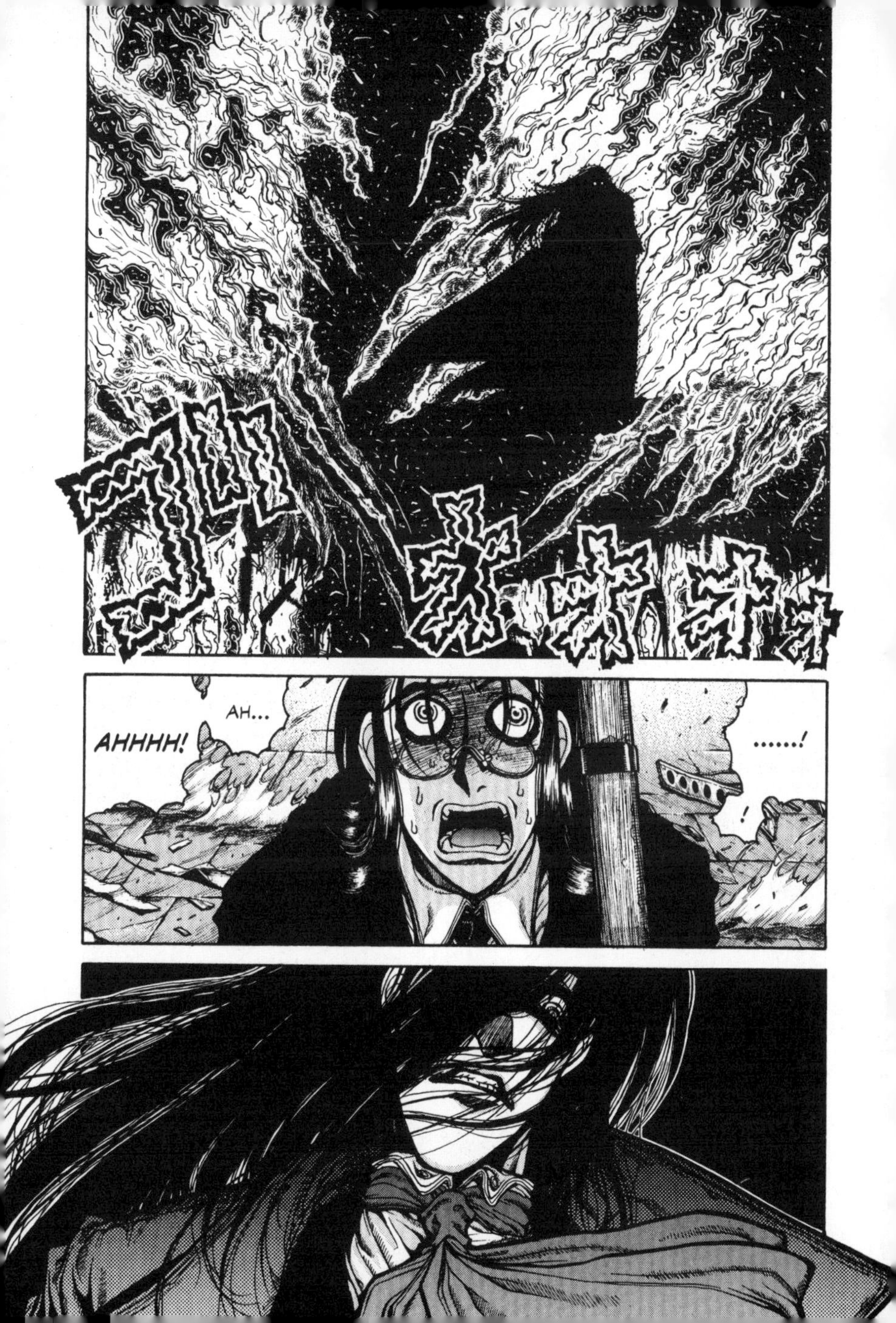

.......!
!
AH...
AHHHH!

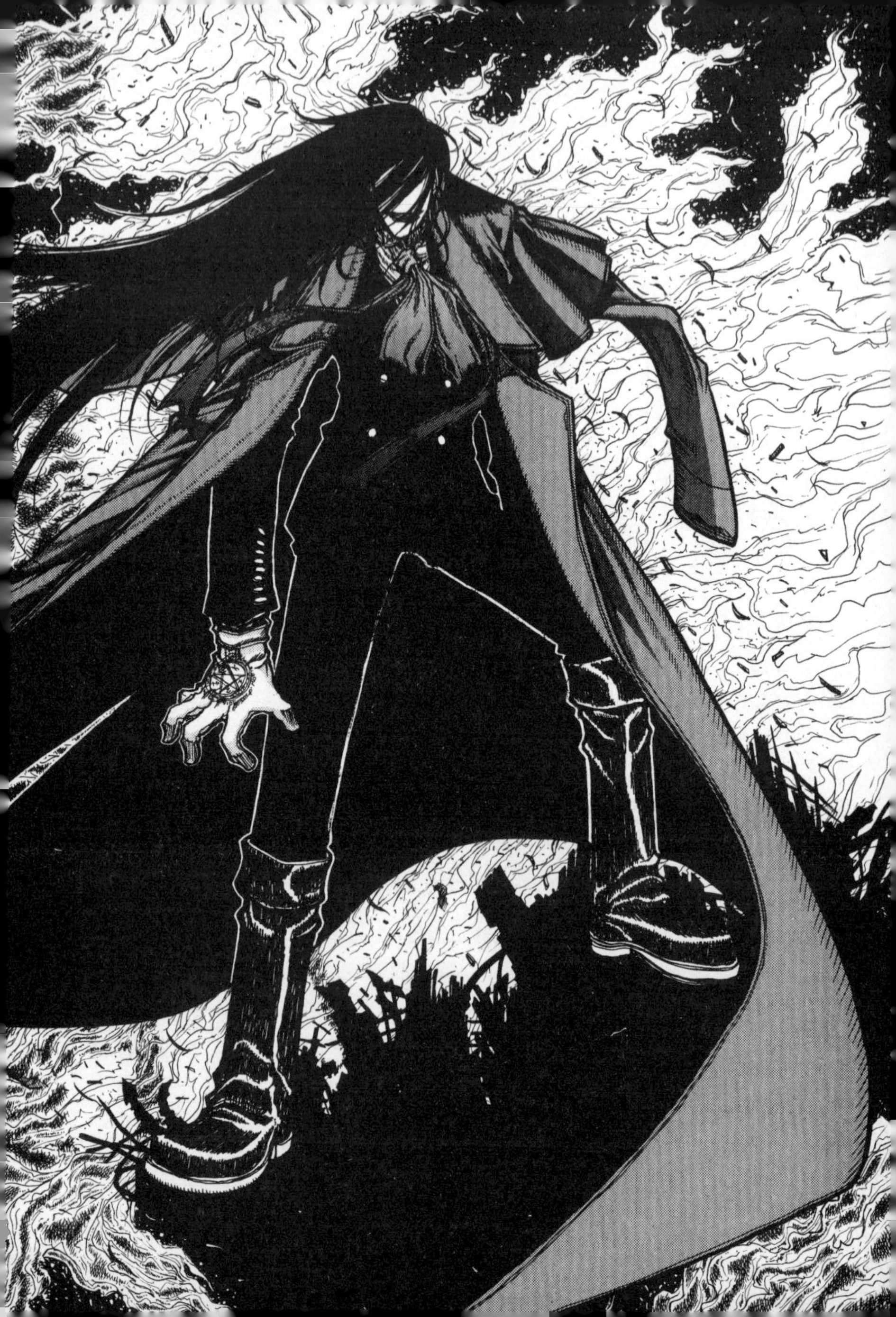

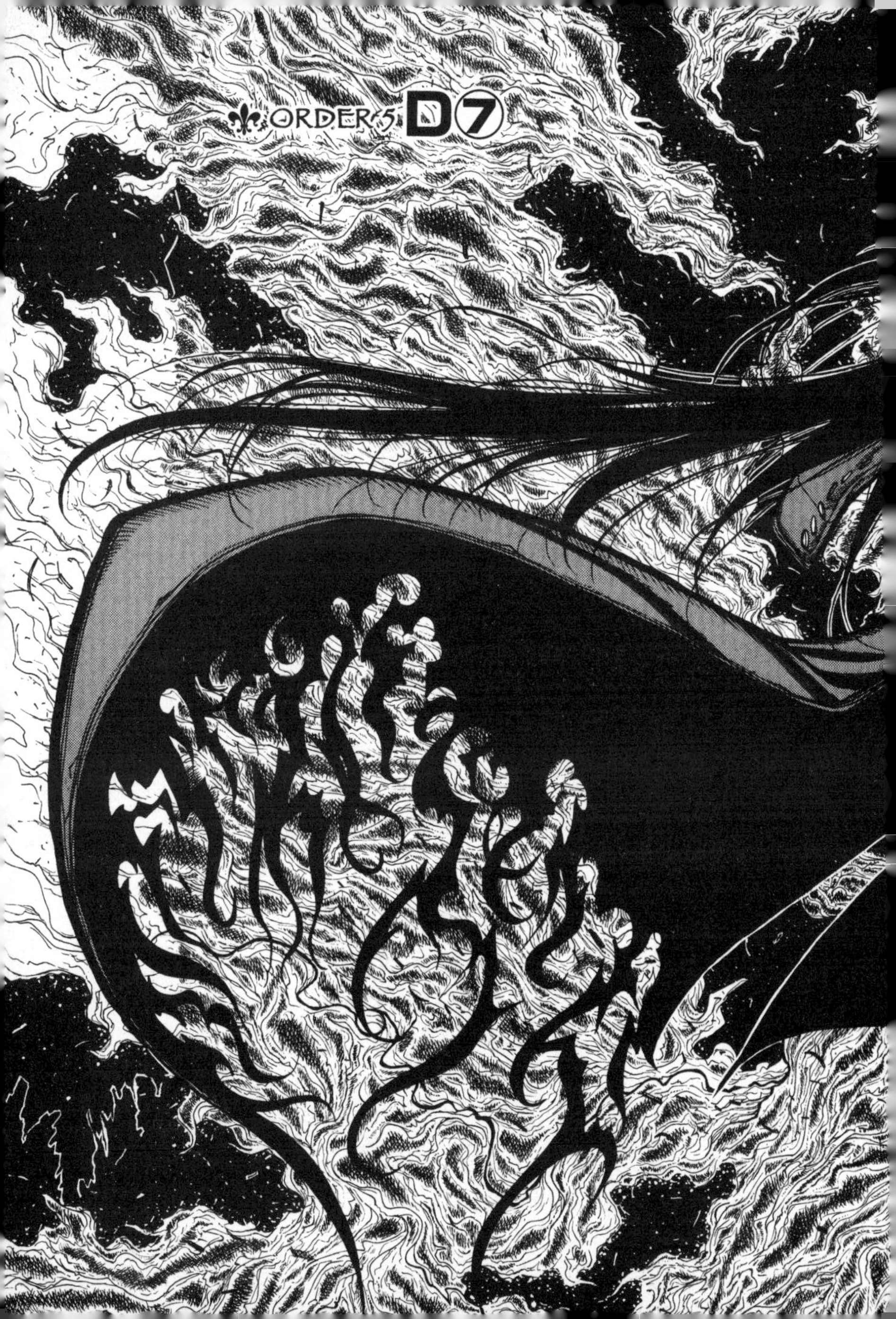
ORDER 5 D7

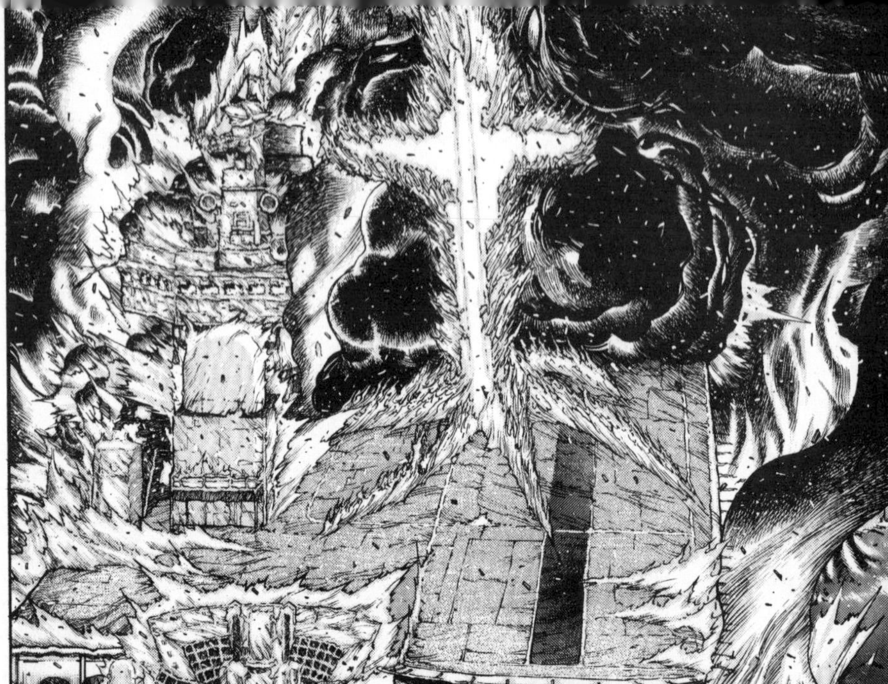

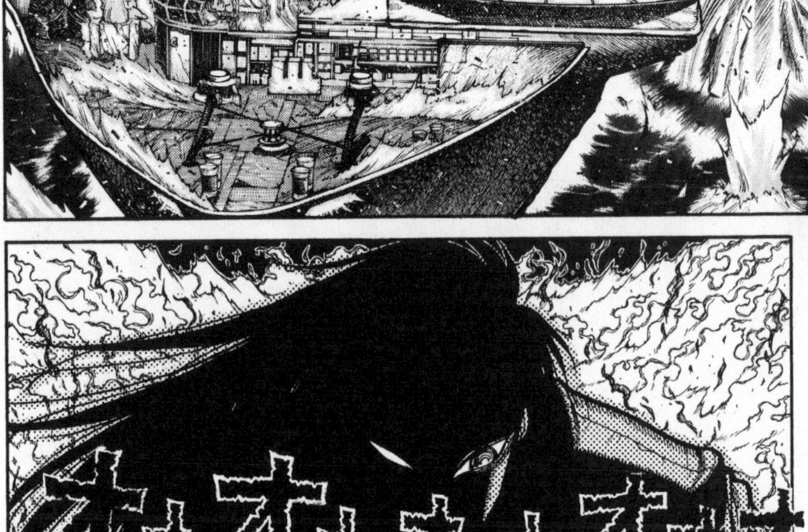
オォオォオォオォオ

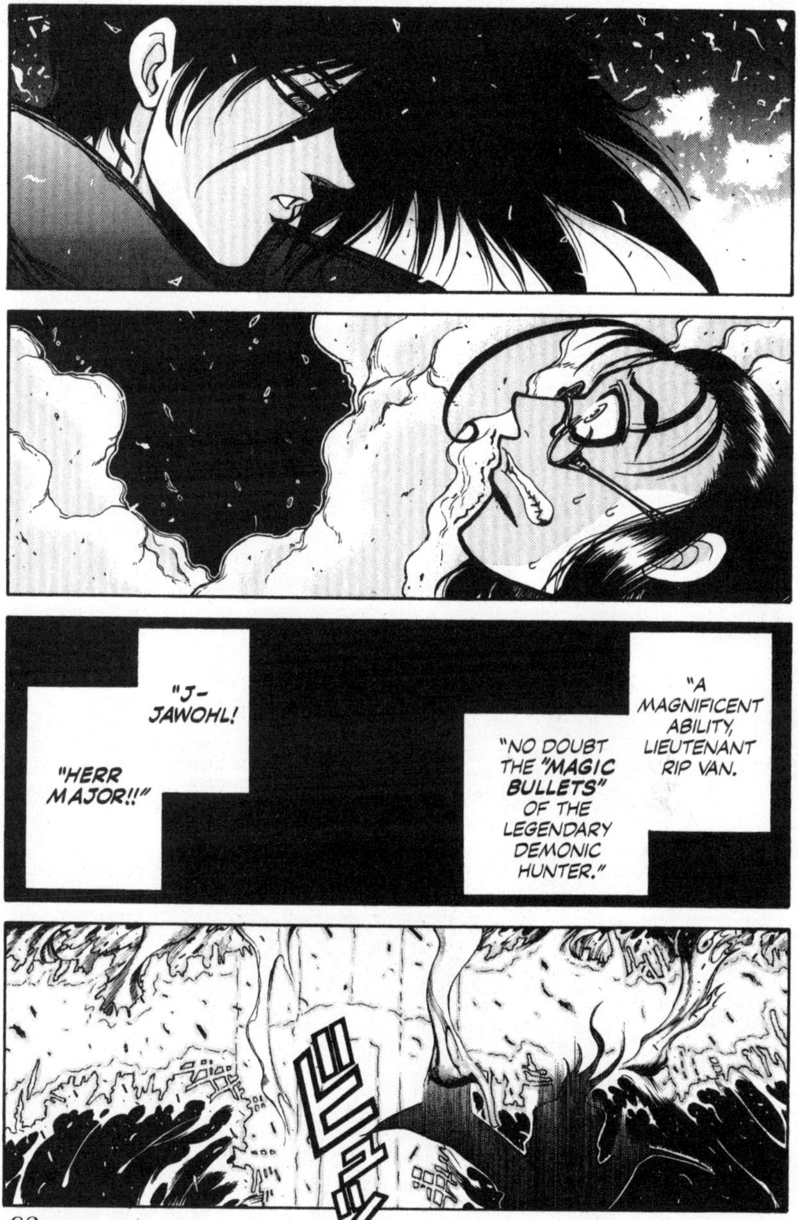
"A MAGNIFICENT ABILITY, LIEUTENANT RIP VAN.
"NO DOUBT THE "MAGIC BULLETS" OF THE LEGENDARY DEMONIC HUNTER."
"J-JAWOHL!
"HERR MAJOR!!"

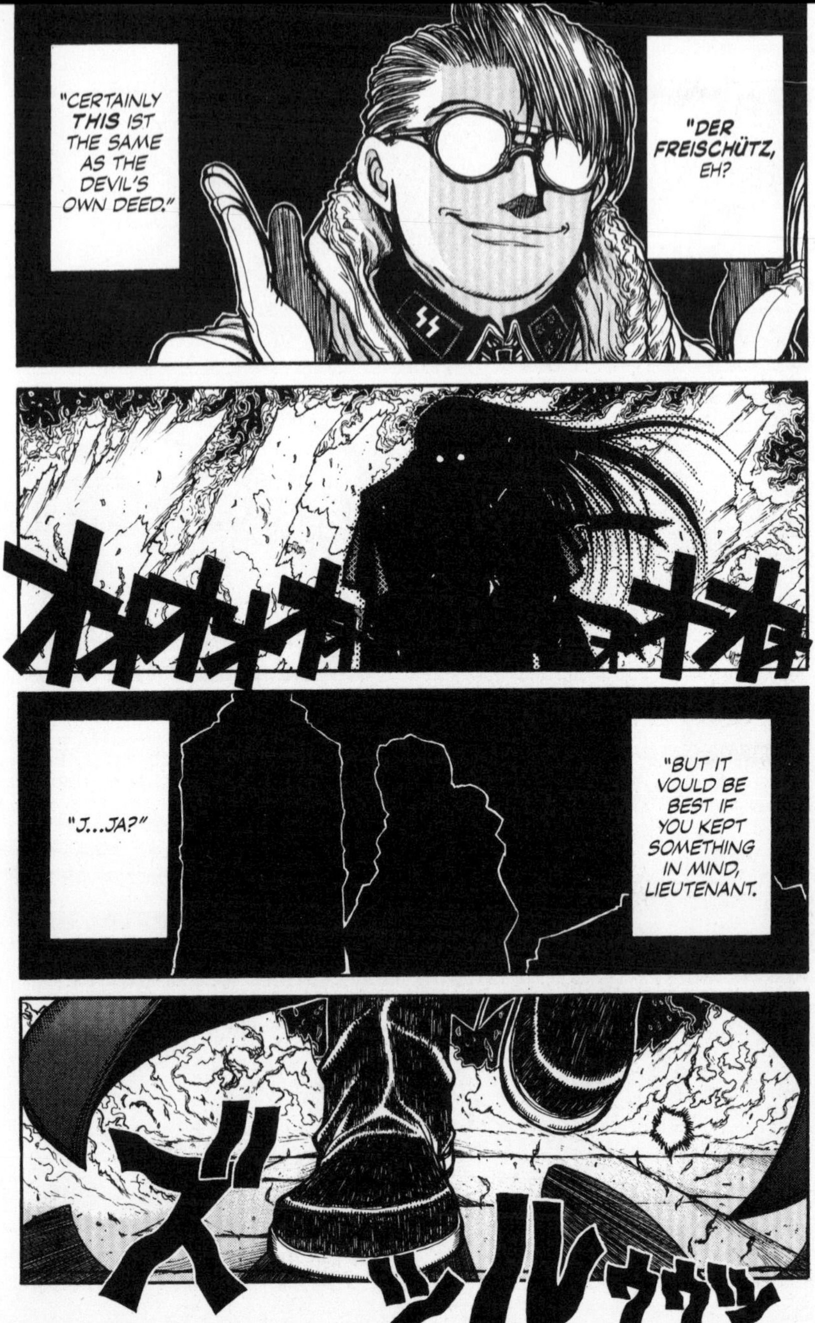
"DER FREISCHÜTZ, EH?
"CERTAINLY THIS IST THE SAME AS THE DEVIL'S OWN DEED."
"BUT IT VOULD BE BEST IF YOU KEPT SOMETHING IN MIND, LIEUTENANT.
"J...JA?"

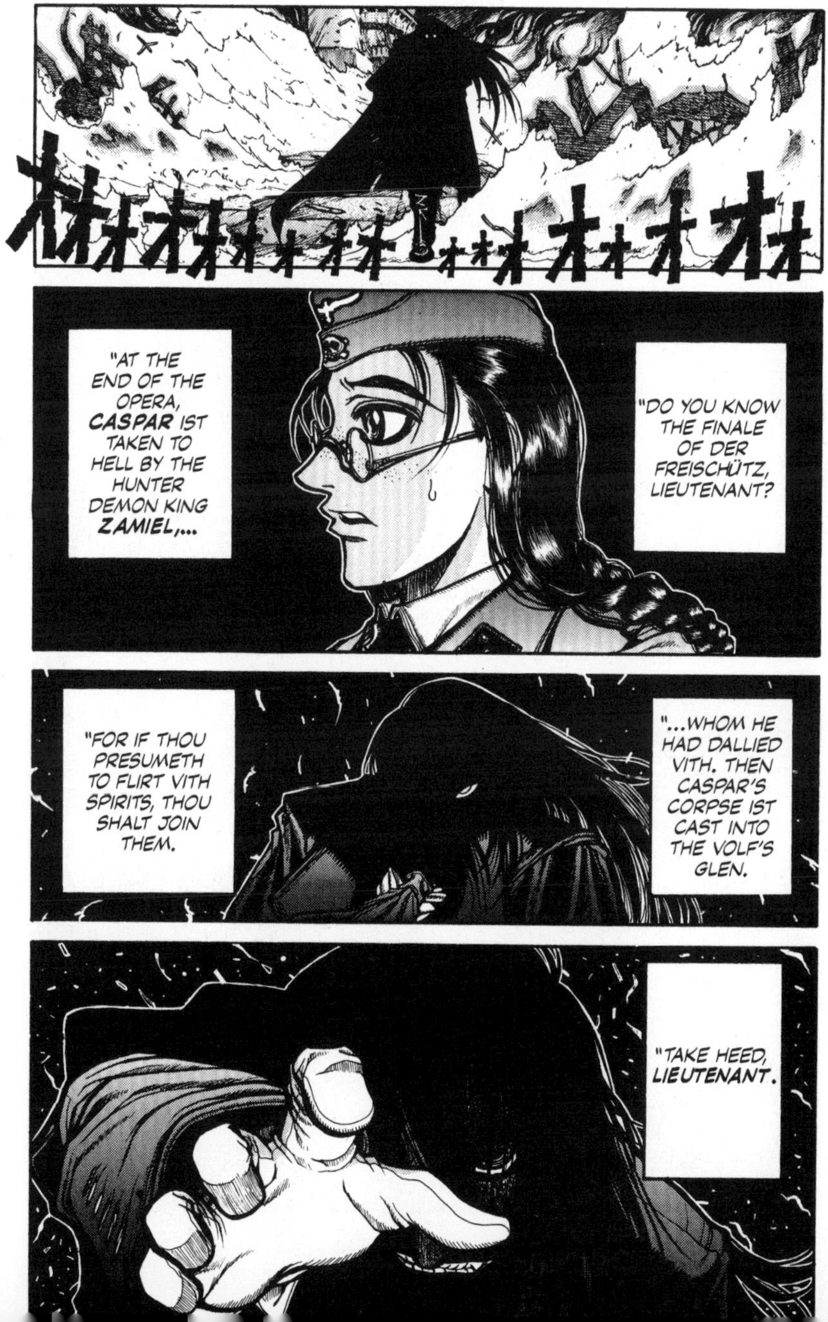
"DO YOU KNOW THE FINALE OF DER FREISCHÜTZ, LIEUTENANT?
"AT THE END OF THE OPERA, **CASPAR** IST TAKEN TO HELL BY THE HUNTER DEMON KING **ZAMIEL**,...
"...WHOM HE HAD DALLIED VITH. THEN CASPAR'S CORPSE IST CAST INTO THE VOLF'S GLEN.
"FOR IF THOU PRESUMETH TO FLIRT VITH SPIRITS, THOU SHALT JOIN THEM.
"TAKE HEED, **LIEUTENANT**.

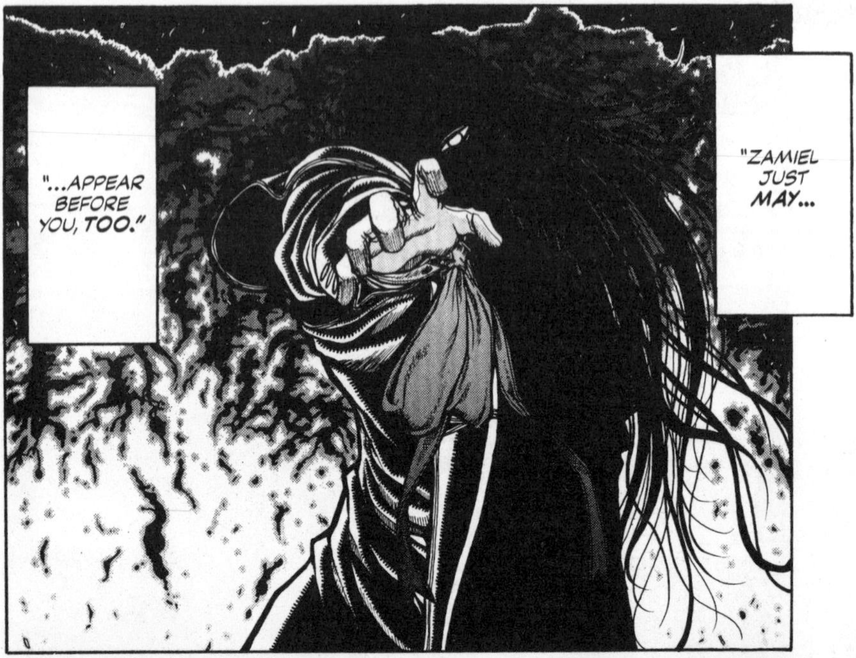
"ZAMIEL JUST MAY...
"...APPEAR BEFORE YOU, TOO."

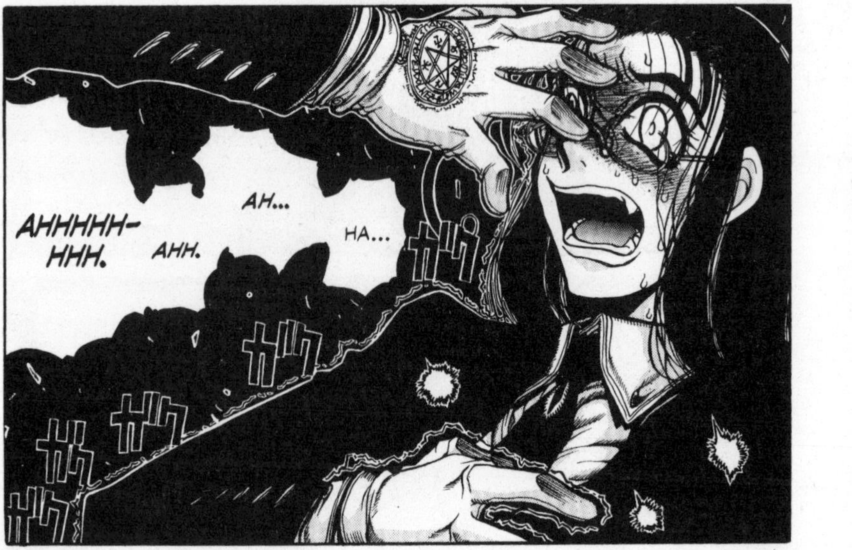
AH...
HA...
AHH.
AHHHHH-HHH.

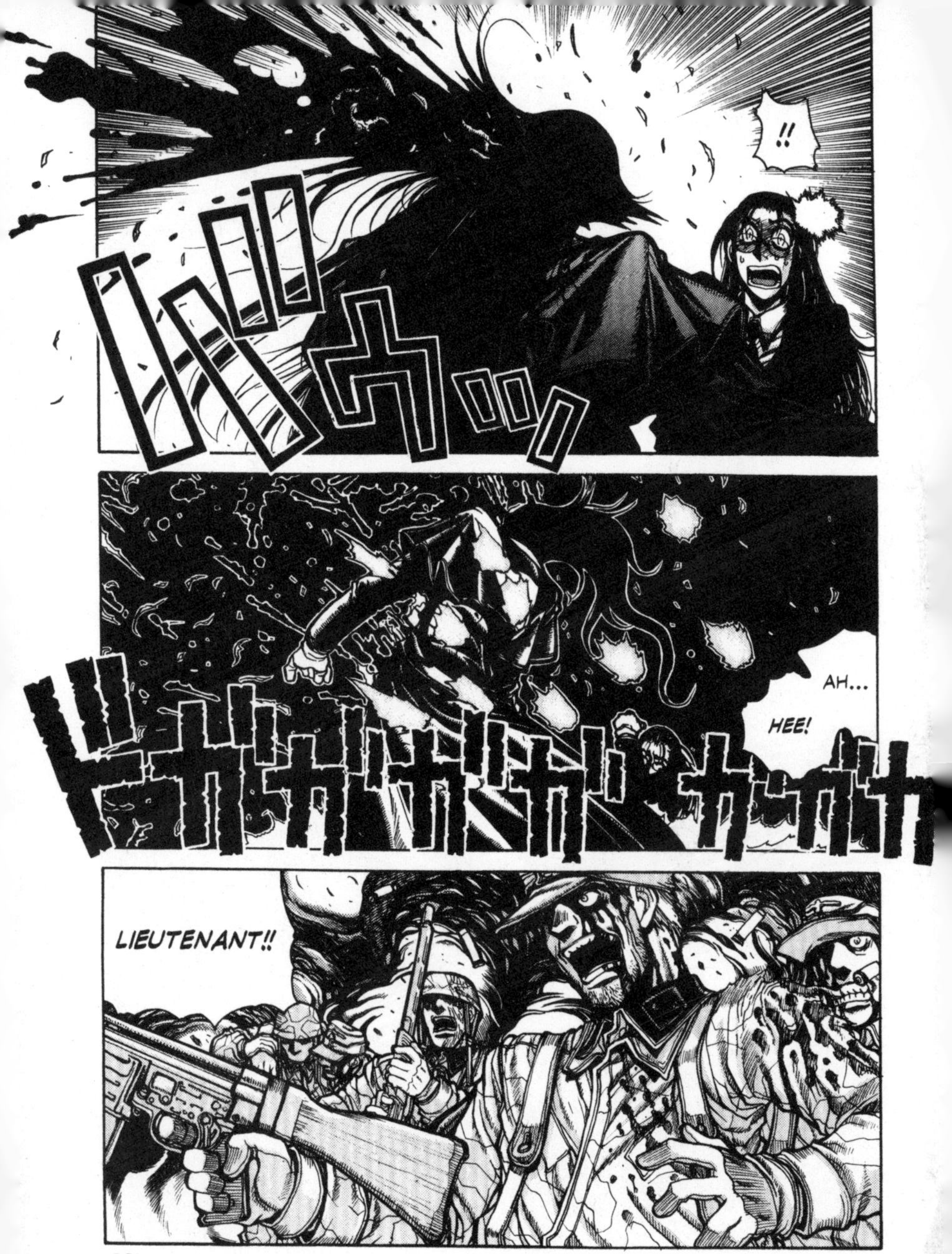
!!
AH...
HEE!
LIEUTENANT!!

AH...
AH
AHH...
ボビュ
ドカッ

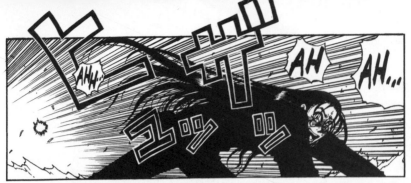

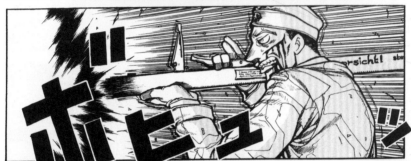

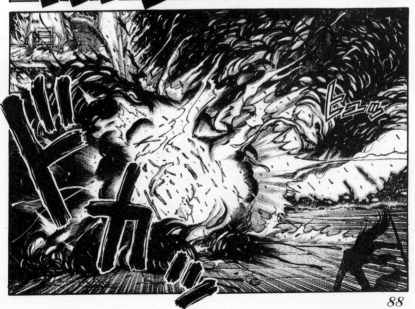

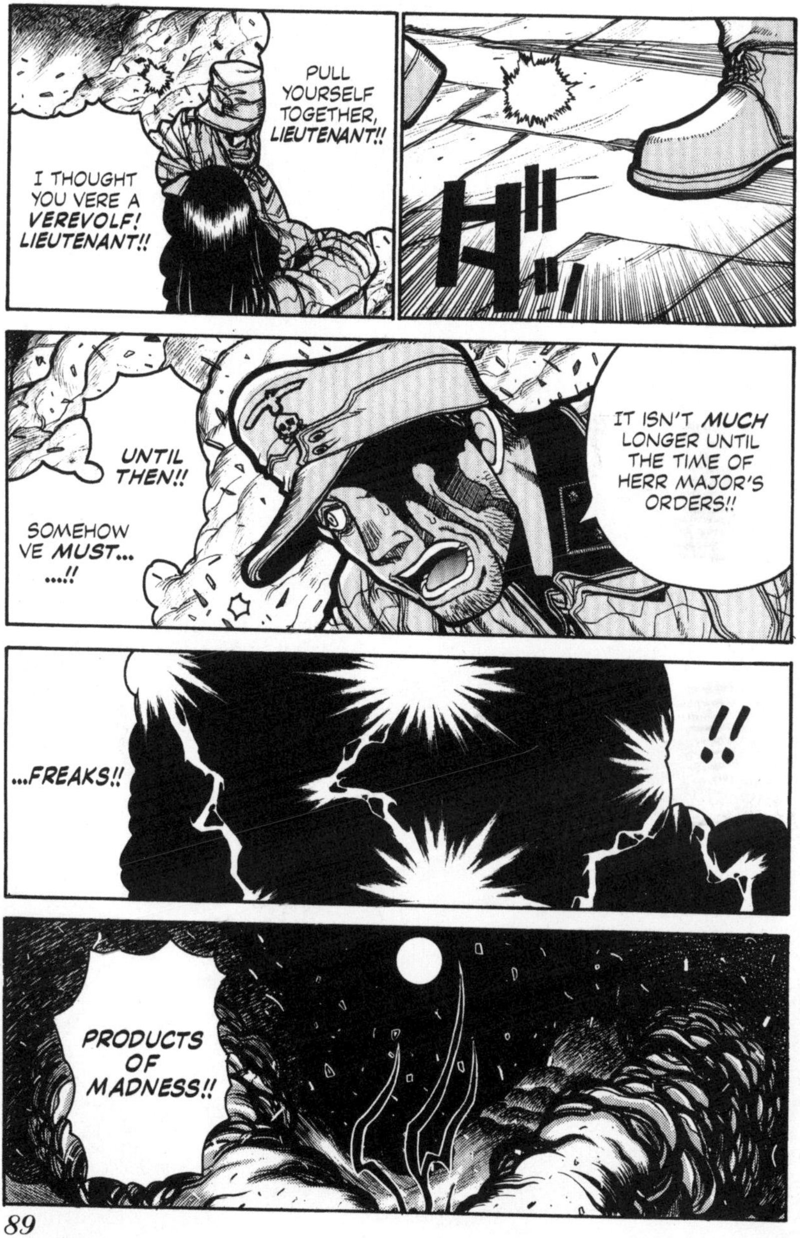
PULL YOURSELF TOGETHER, LIEUTENANT!!
I THOUGHT YOU VERE A VEREVOLF! LIEUTENANT!!
IT ISN'T MUCH LONGER UNTIL THE TIME OF HERR MAJOR'S ORDERS!!
UNTIL THEN!!
SOMEHOW VE MUST... ...!!
!!
...FREAKS!!
PRODUCTS OF MADNESS!!

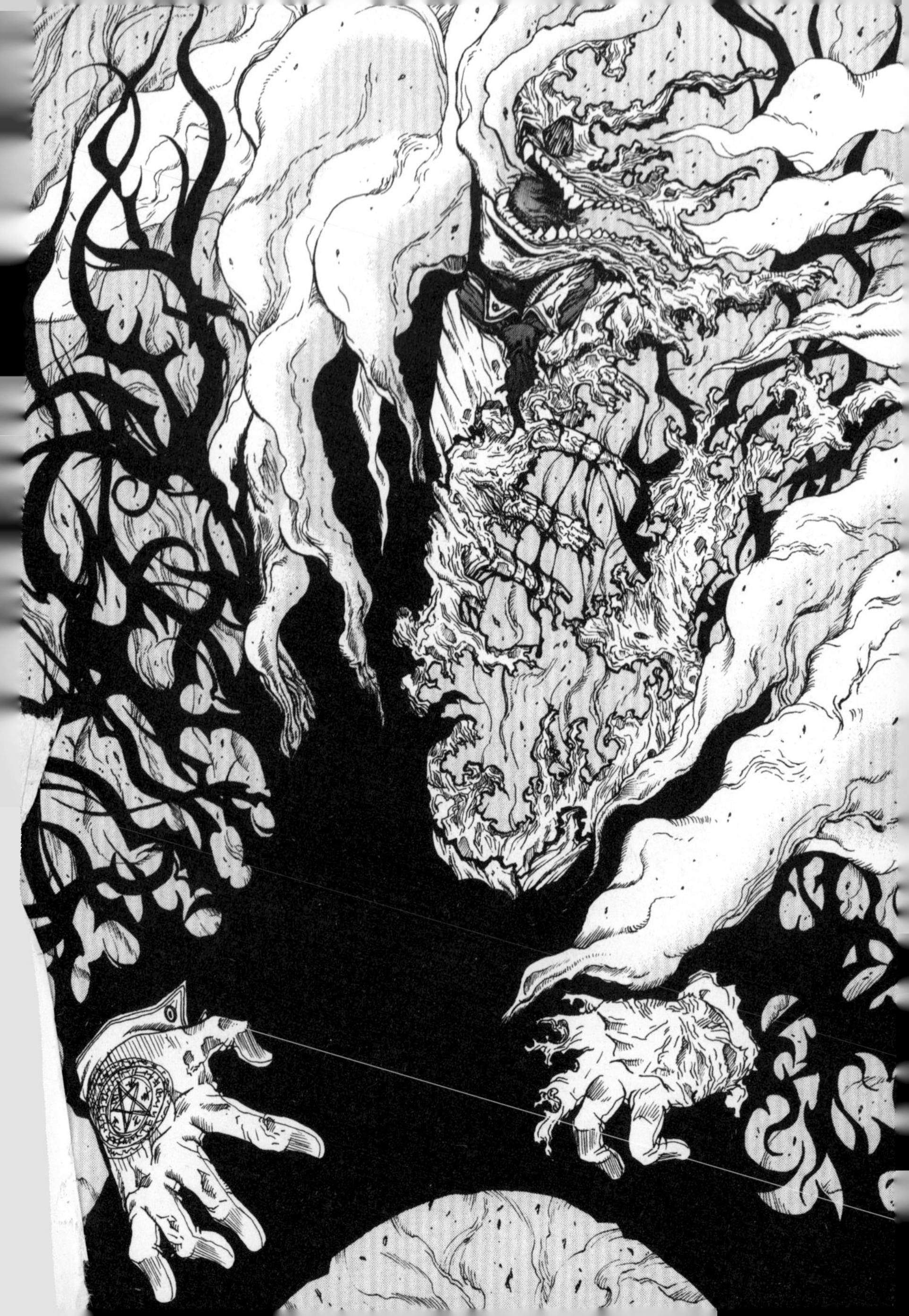

ギリ
ギリギリギリギリギリ
ギリ
CHK
CHNG
CHK
CHK
CHK
CHNG
CHK
CHK

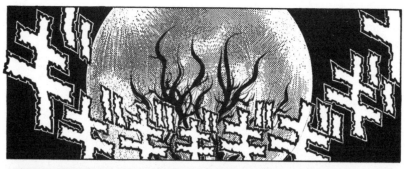

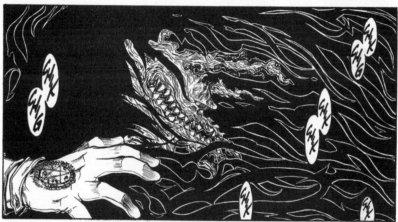

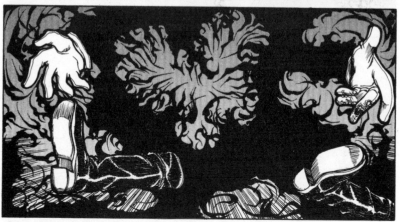

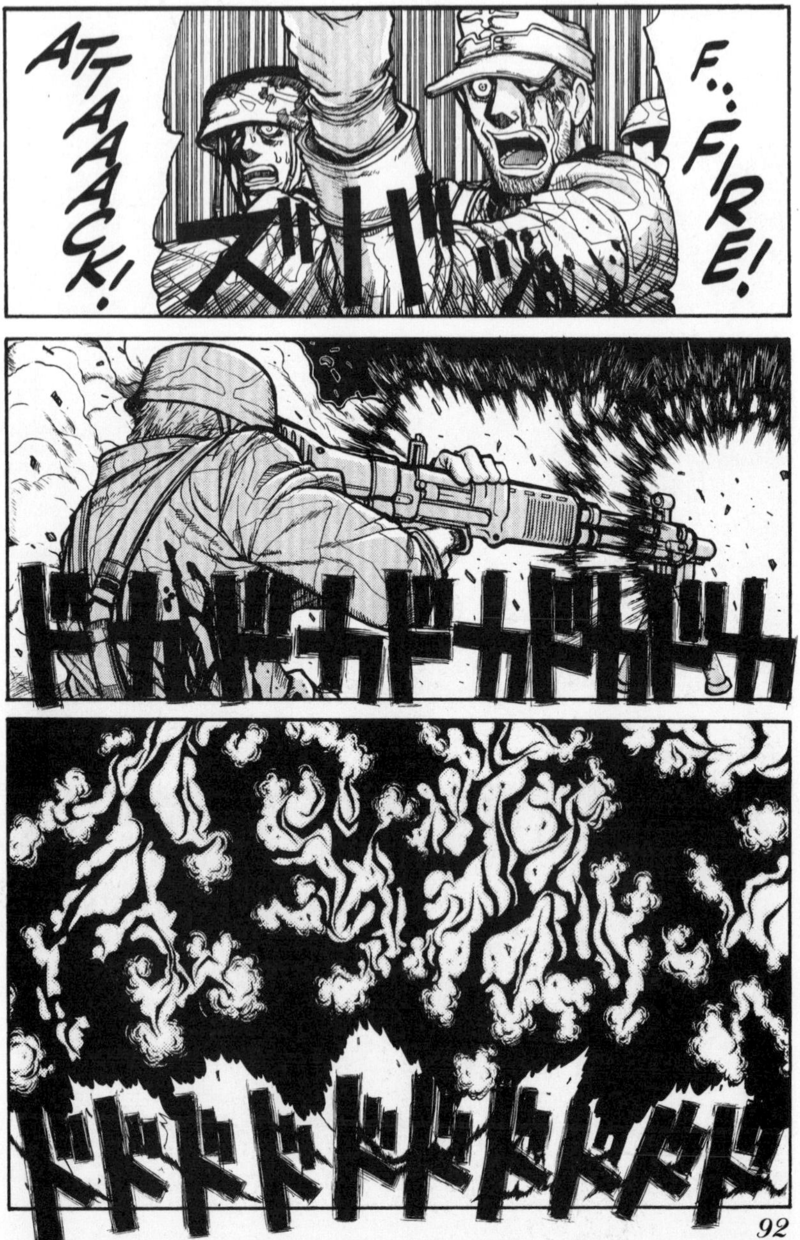
F...FIRE!
ATTAAACK!

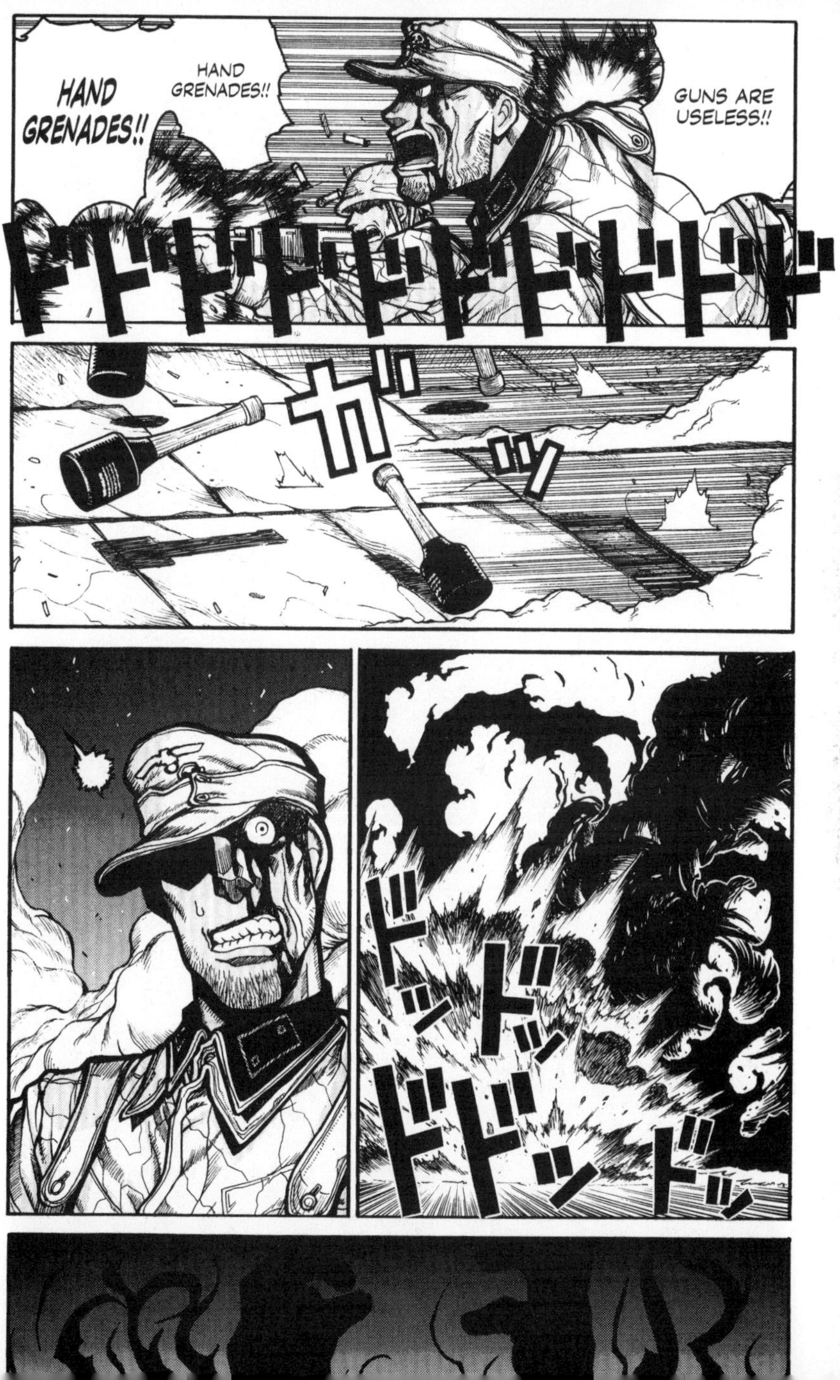
GUNS ARE USELESS!!
HAND GRENADES!!
HAND GRENADES!!

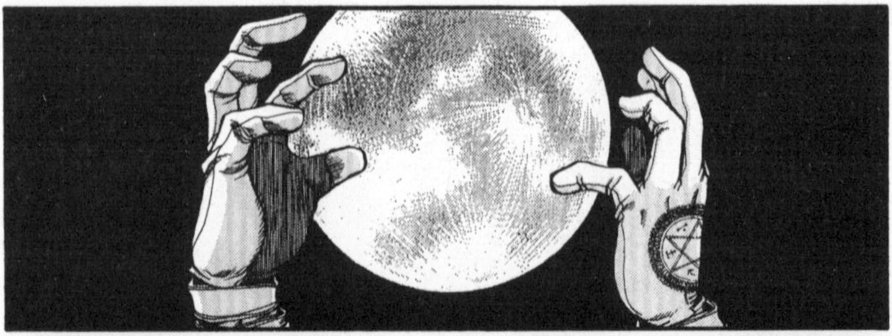
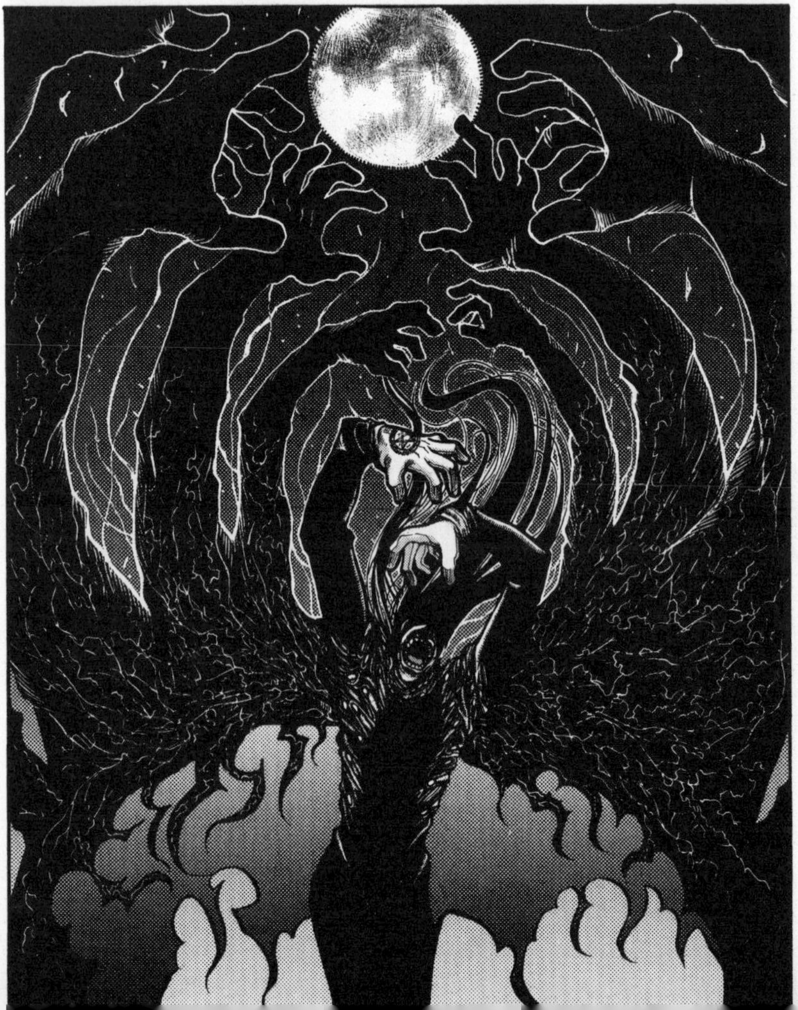

コリッ

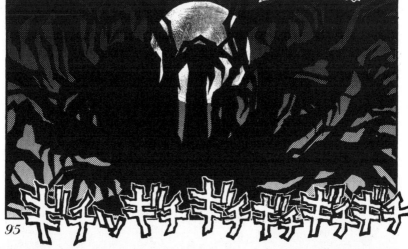

ギリギリギリギリギリギリギリ

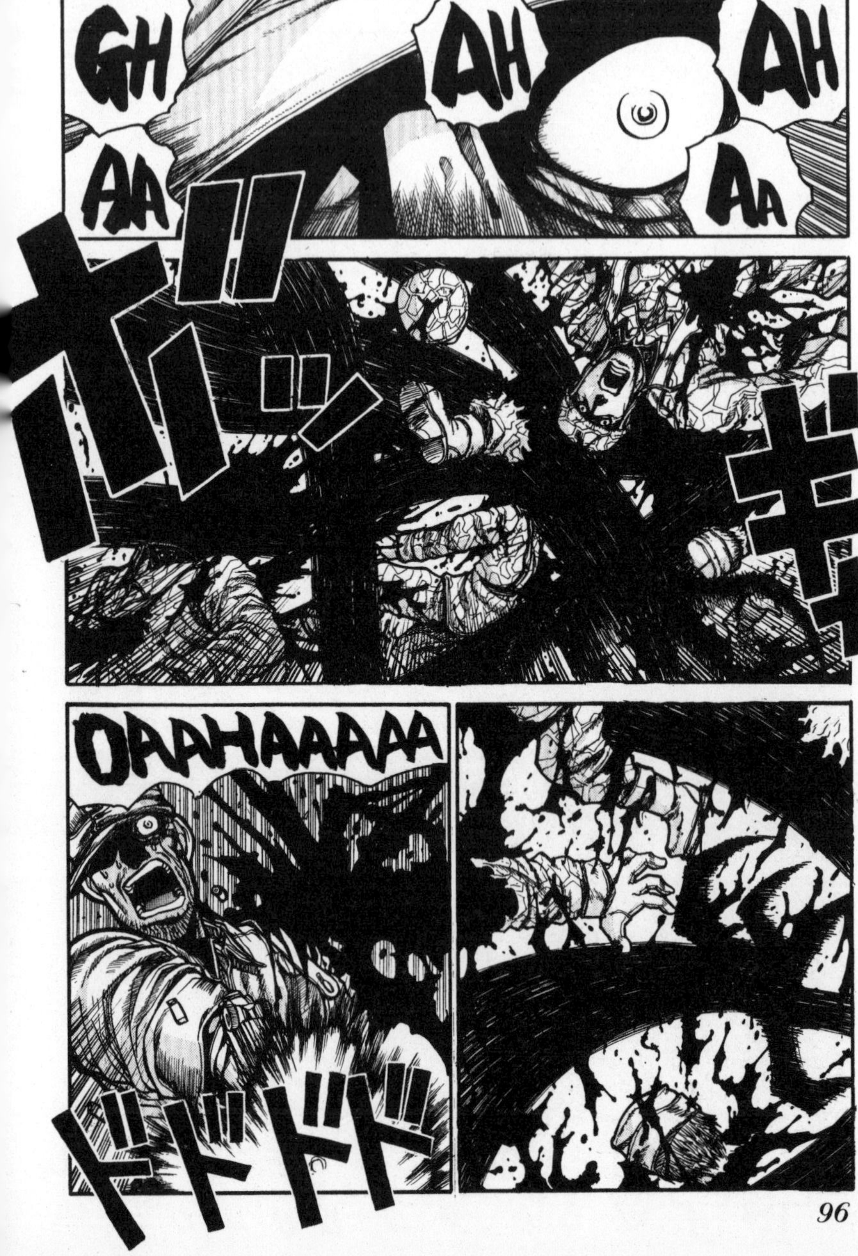
AH
AA
AH
GH
AA
OAAHAAAAA

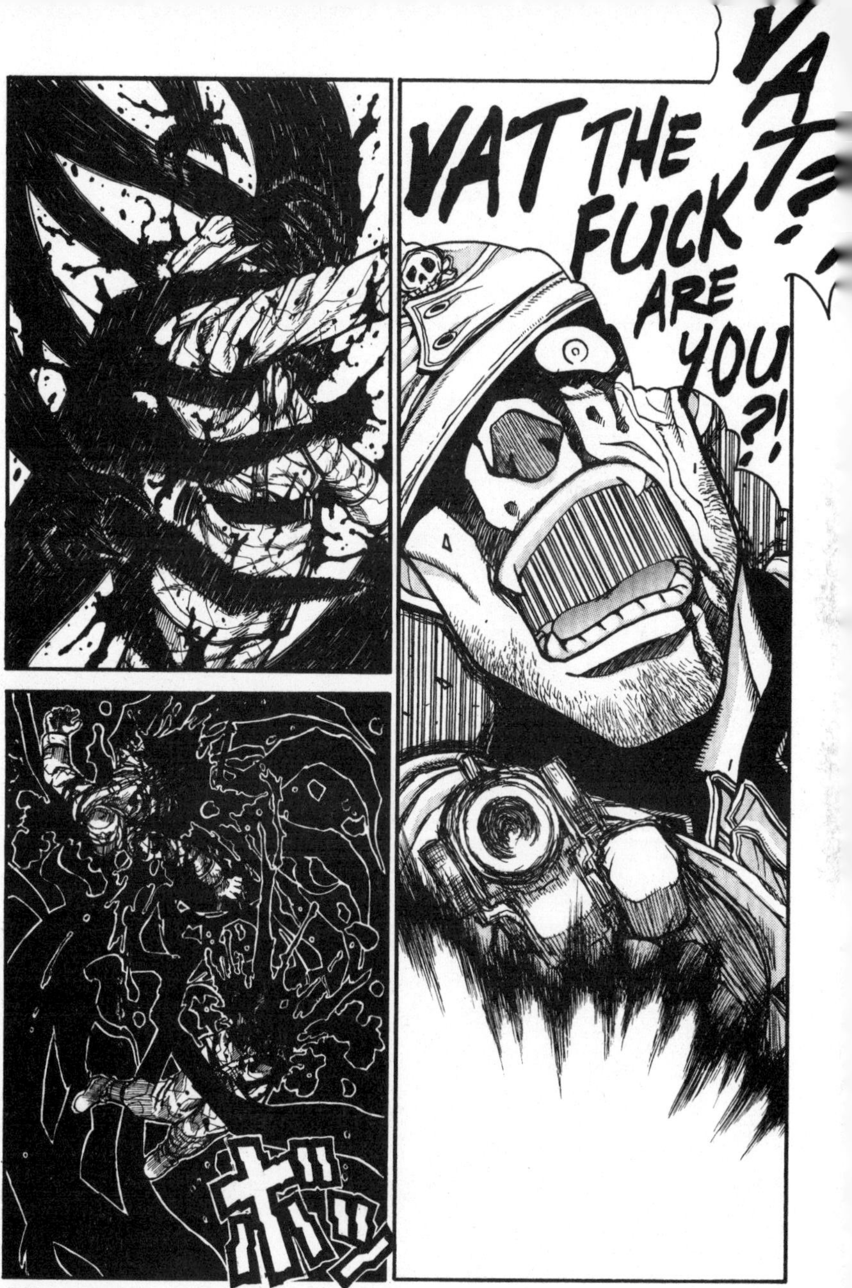
YAT?!
VAT THE FUCK ARE YOU?!
ボッ

オオオオオオオオオ

ゴッゴッゴリゴッゴッゴリ

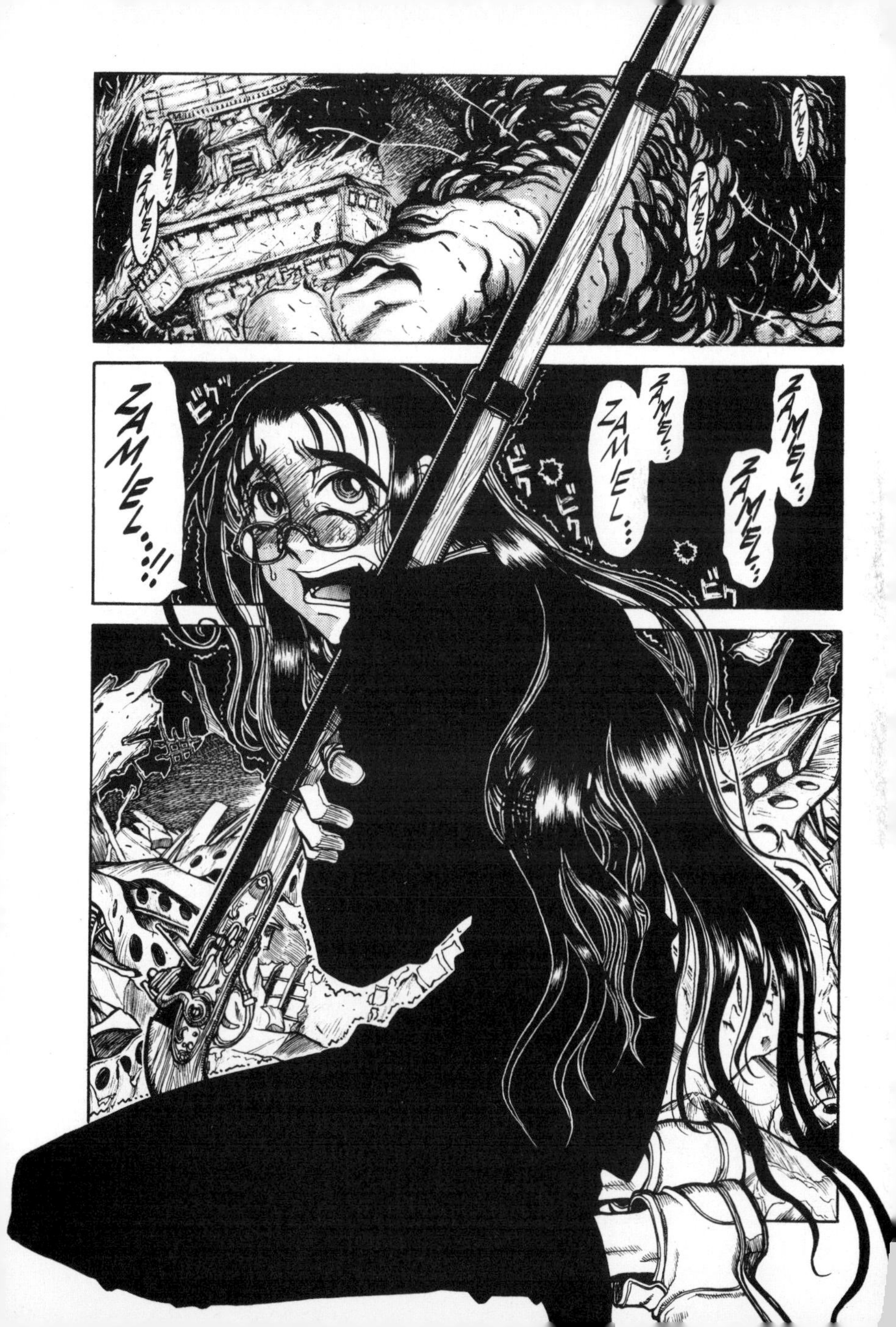
ZAMIEL...
ZAMIEL...
ZAMIEL...
ZAMIEL...
ZAMIEL...
ZAMIEL...
ZAMIEL...
ZAMIEL...
ビク
ビクッ
ビク
ビクッ
ZAMIEL...!!

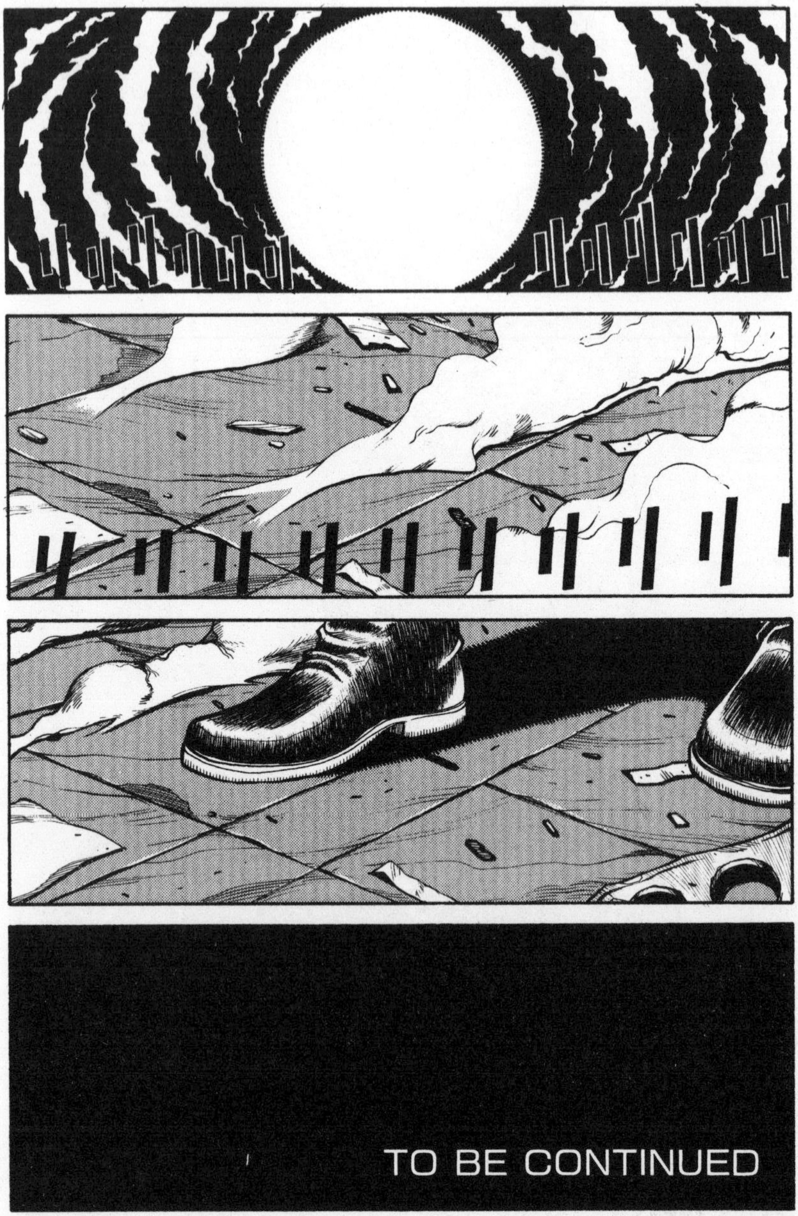
TO BE CONTINUED

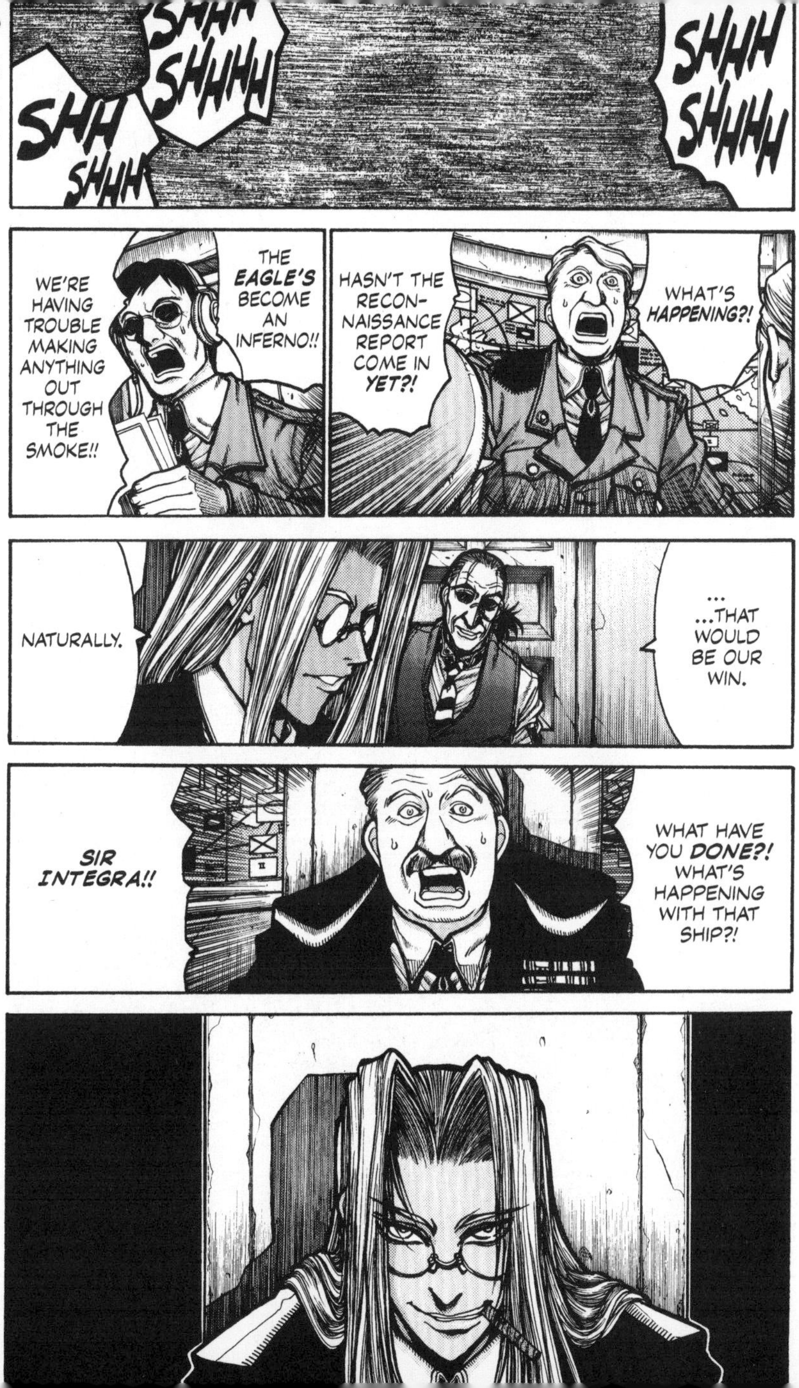
SHHH SHHHH
SHHH SHHHH
SHH SHHH
WHAT'S HAPPENING?!
HASN'T THE RECON-NAISSANCE REPORT COME IN YET?!
THE EAGLE'S BECOME AN INFERNO!!
WE'RE HAVING TROUBLE MAKING ANYTHING OUT THROUGH THE SMOKE!!
... ...THAT WOULD BE OUR WIN.
NATURALLY.
WHAT HAVE YOU DONE?! WHAT'S HAPPENING WITH THAT SHIP?!
SIR INTEGRA!!

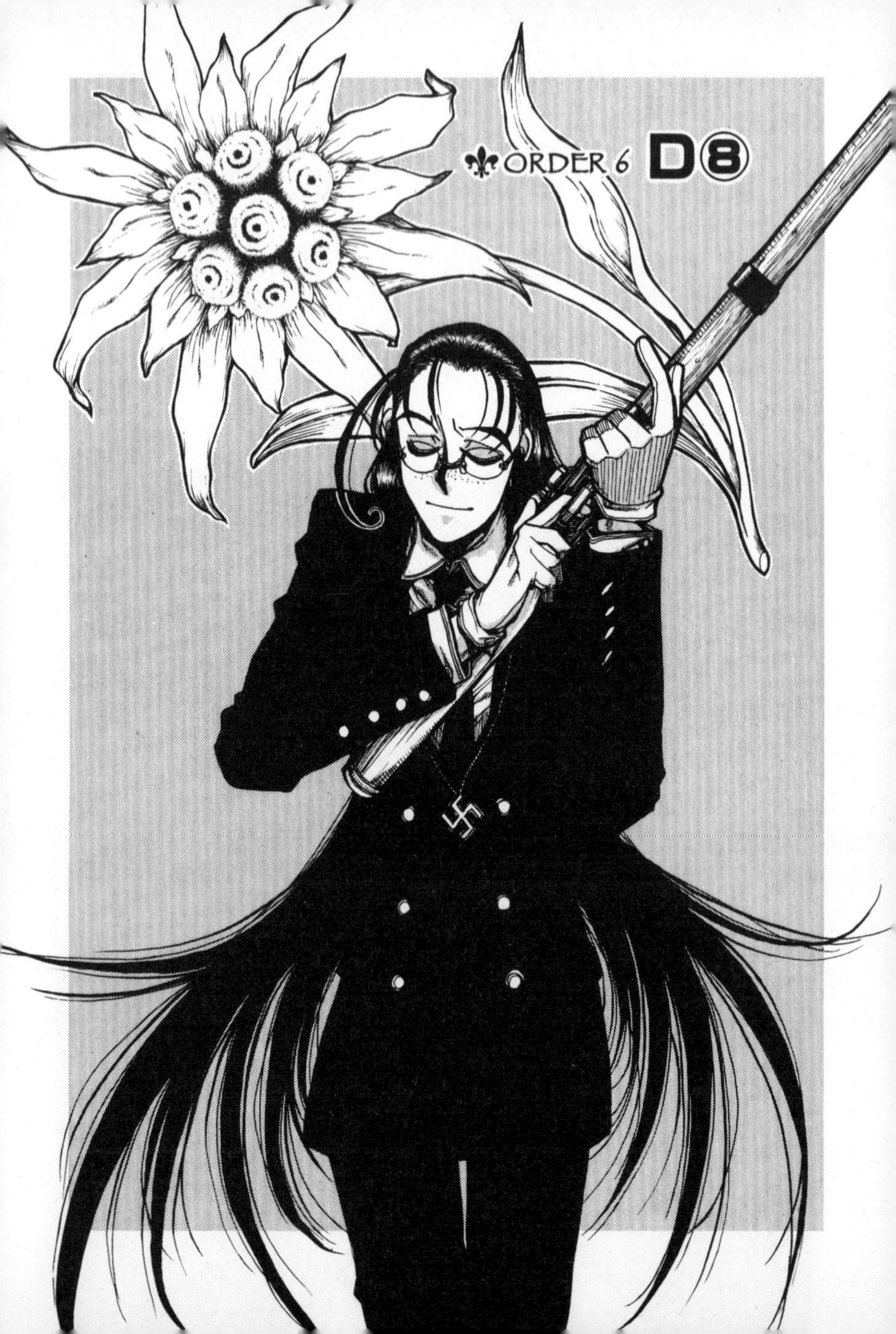
ORDER 6 D8

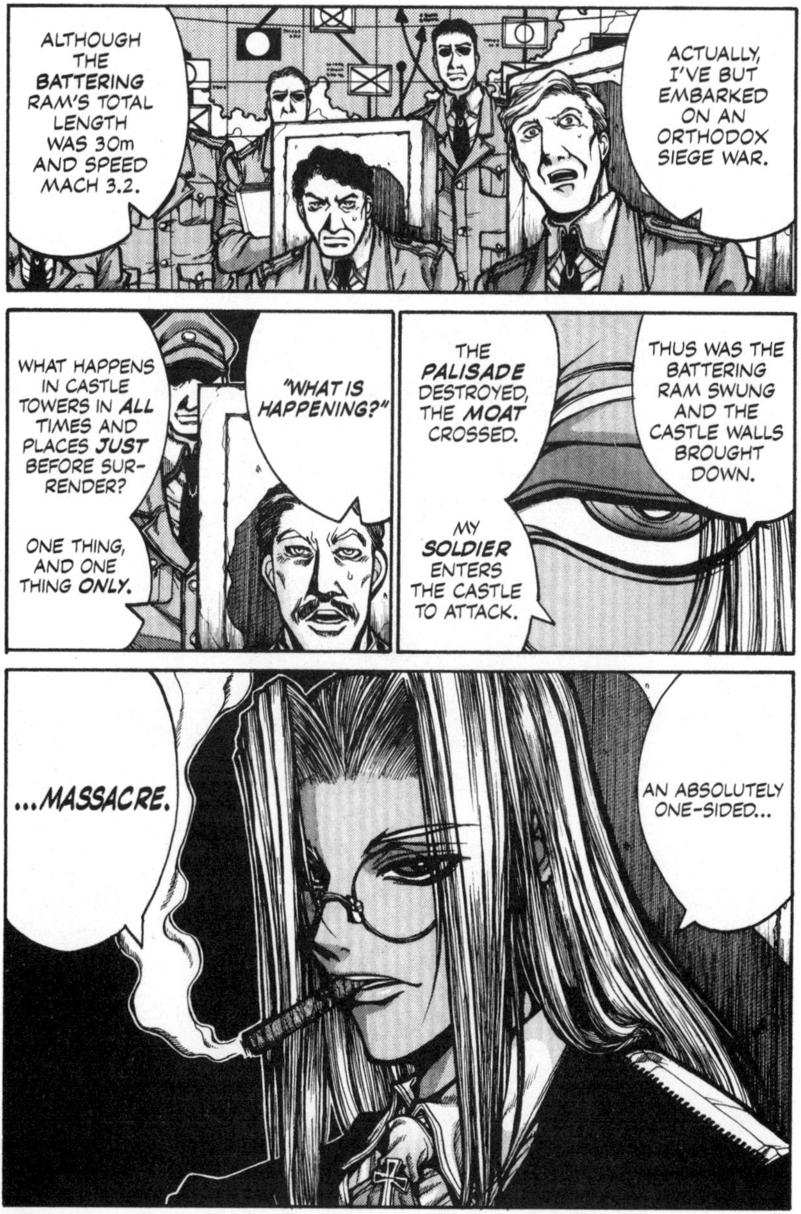
ACTUALLY, I'VE BUT EMBARKED ON AN ORTHODOX SIEGE WAR.
ALTHOUGH THE BATTERING RAM'S TOTAL LENGTH WAS 30m AND SPEED MACH 3.2.
THUS WAS THE BATTERING RAM SWUNG AND THE CASTLE WALLS BROUGHT DOWN.
THE PALISADE DESTROYED, THE MOAT CROSSED.
MY SOLDIER ENTERS THE CASTLE TO ATTACK.
"WHAT IS HAPPENING?"
WHAT HAPPENS IN CASTLE TOWERS IN ALL TIMES AND PLACES JUST BEFORE SUR-RENDER?
ONE THING, AND ONE THING ONLY.
AN ABSOLUTELY ONE-SIDED...
...MASSACRE.

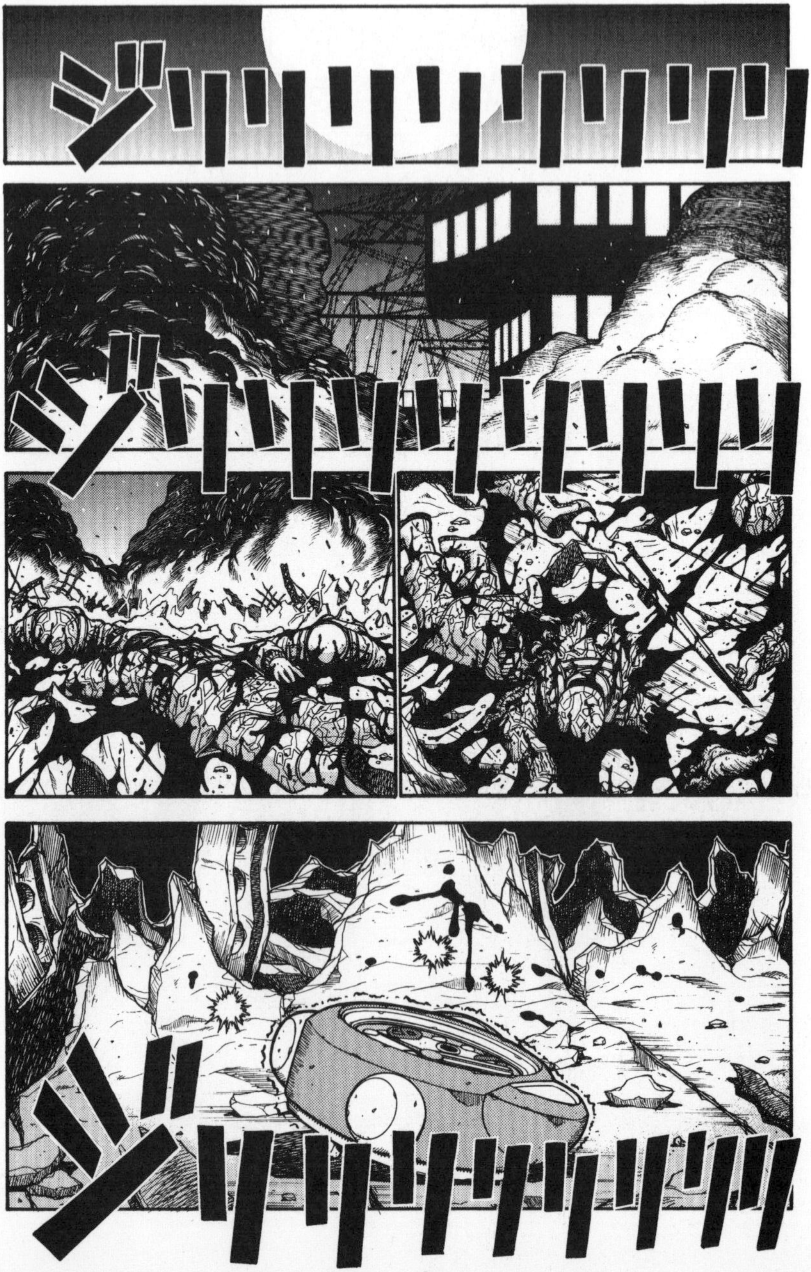
ジリリリリリリリリリ
ジリリリリリリリリリ
ジリリリリリリリリリ

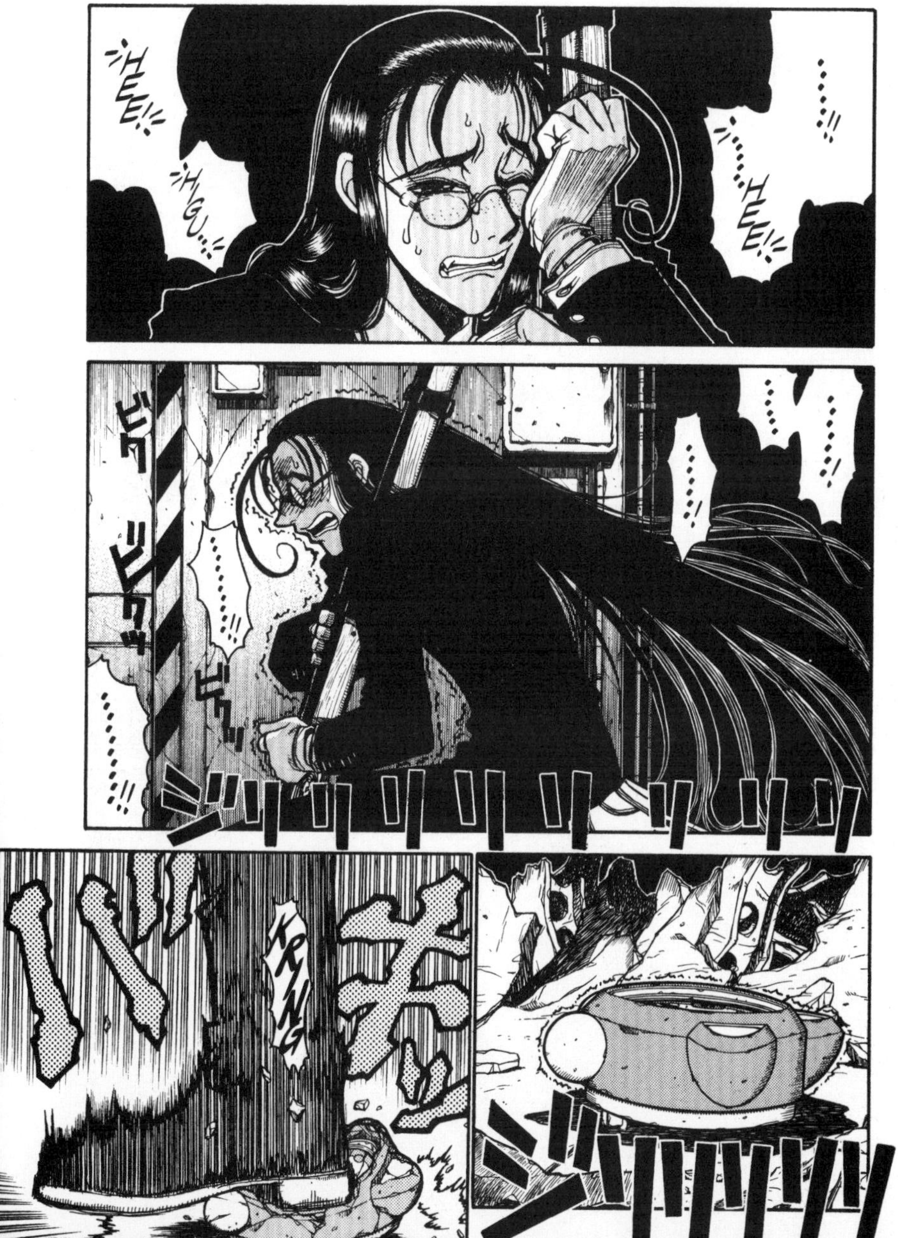

......!!
......HEE!!
HEE!!
HIGU...!
......
......
......!!
......!!
KRING

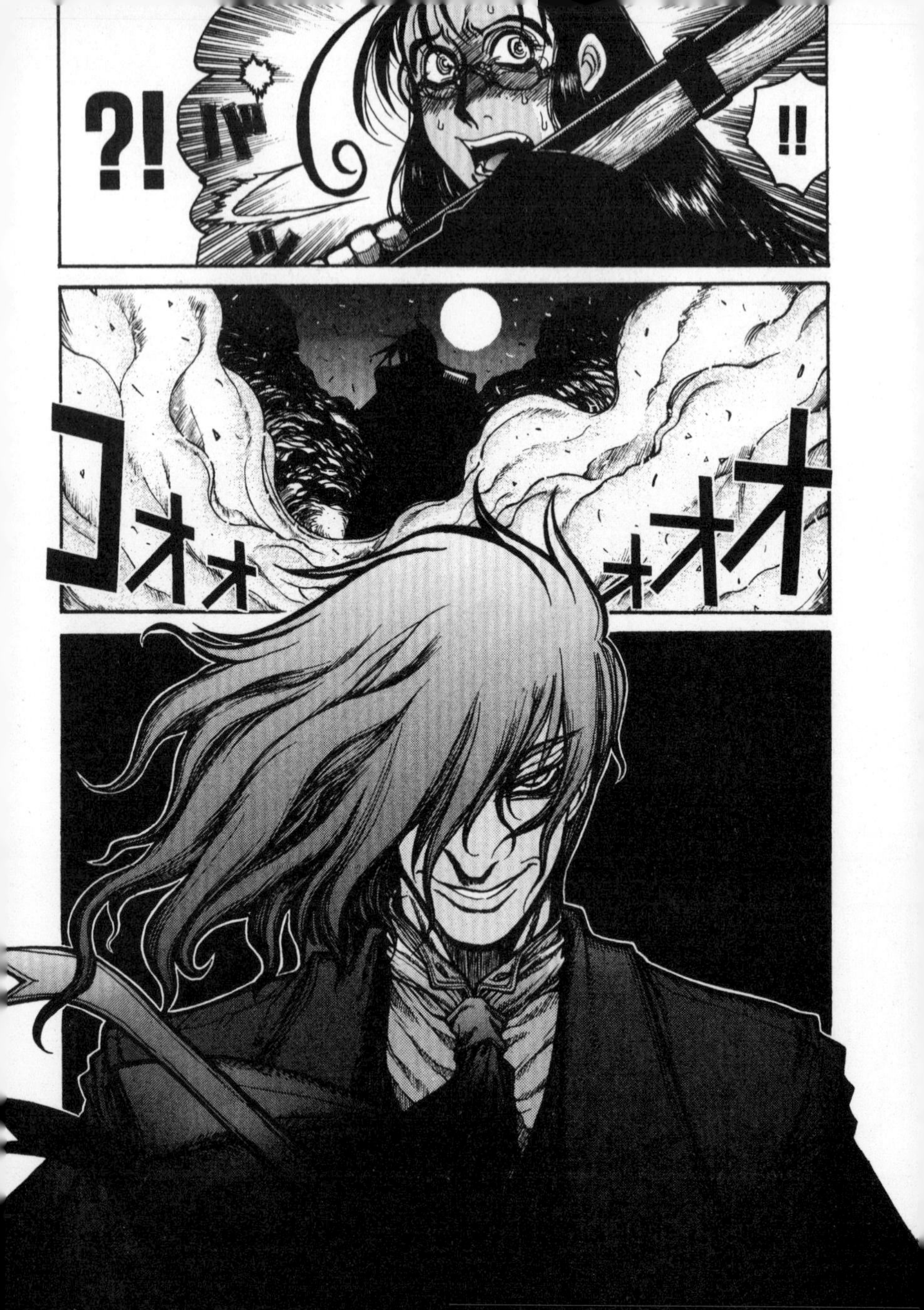
!!
?!
コオォォォオオ

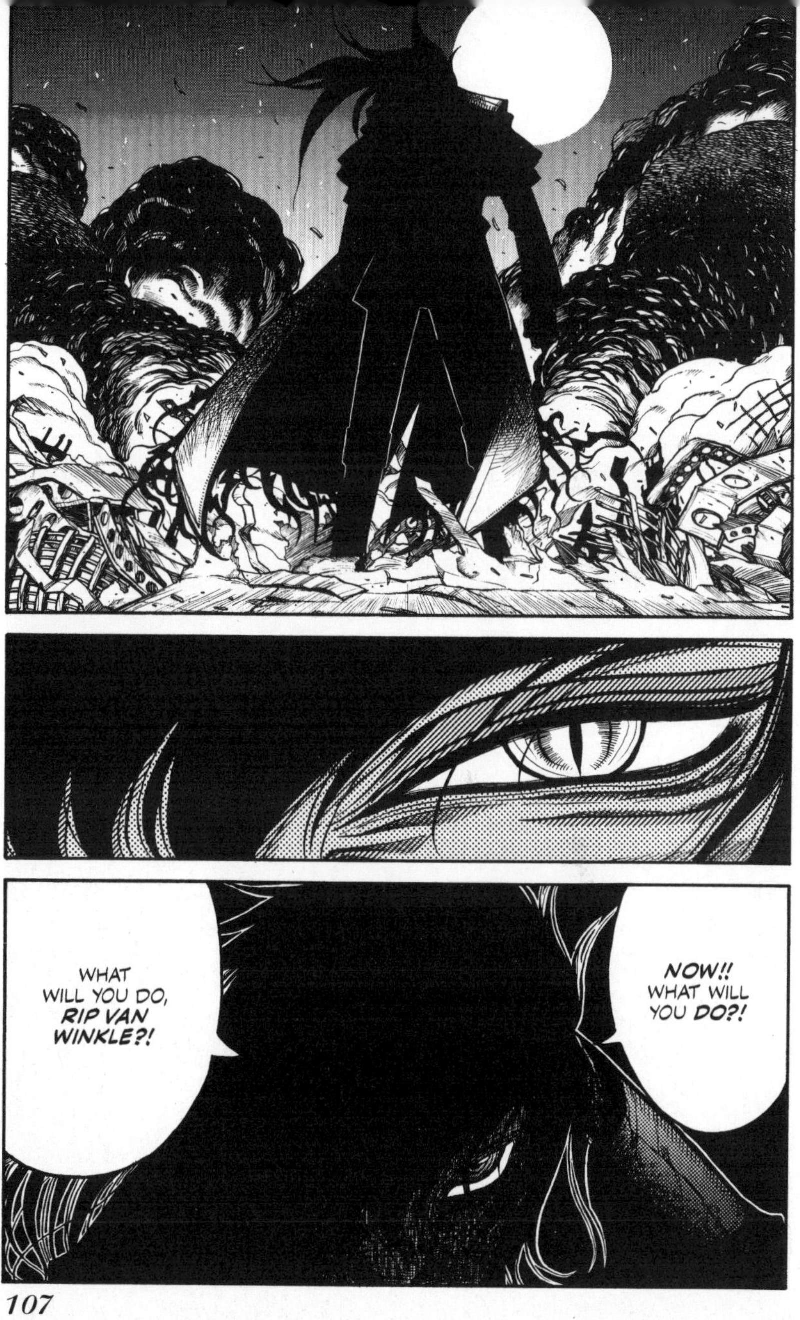
NOW!! WHAT WILL YOU DO?!
WHAT WILL YOU DO, RIP VAN WINKLE?!

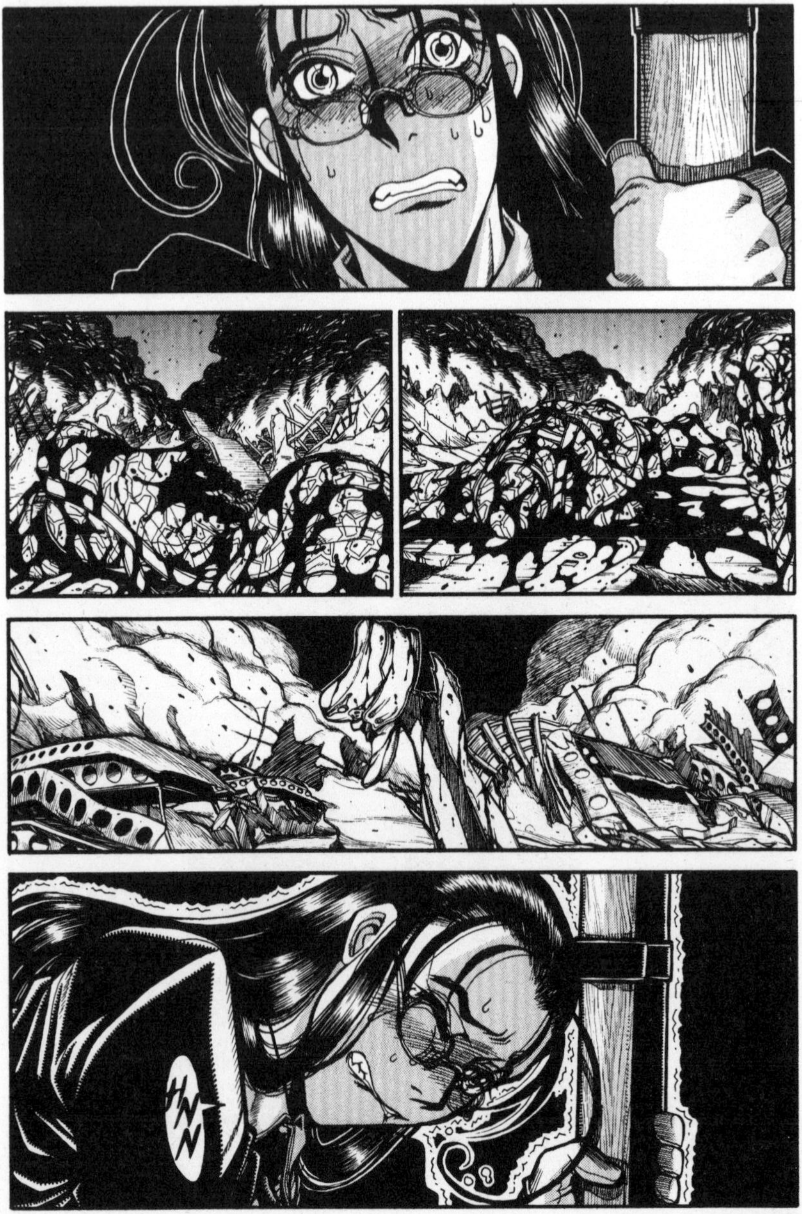
HNN

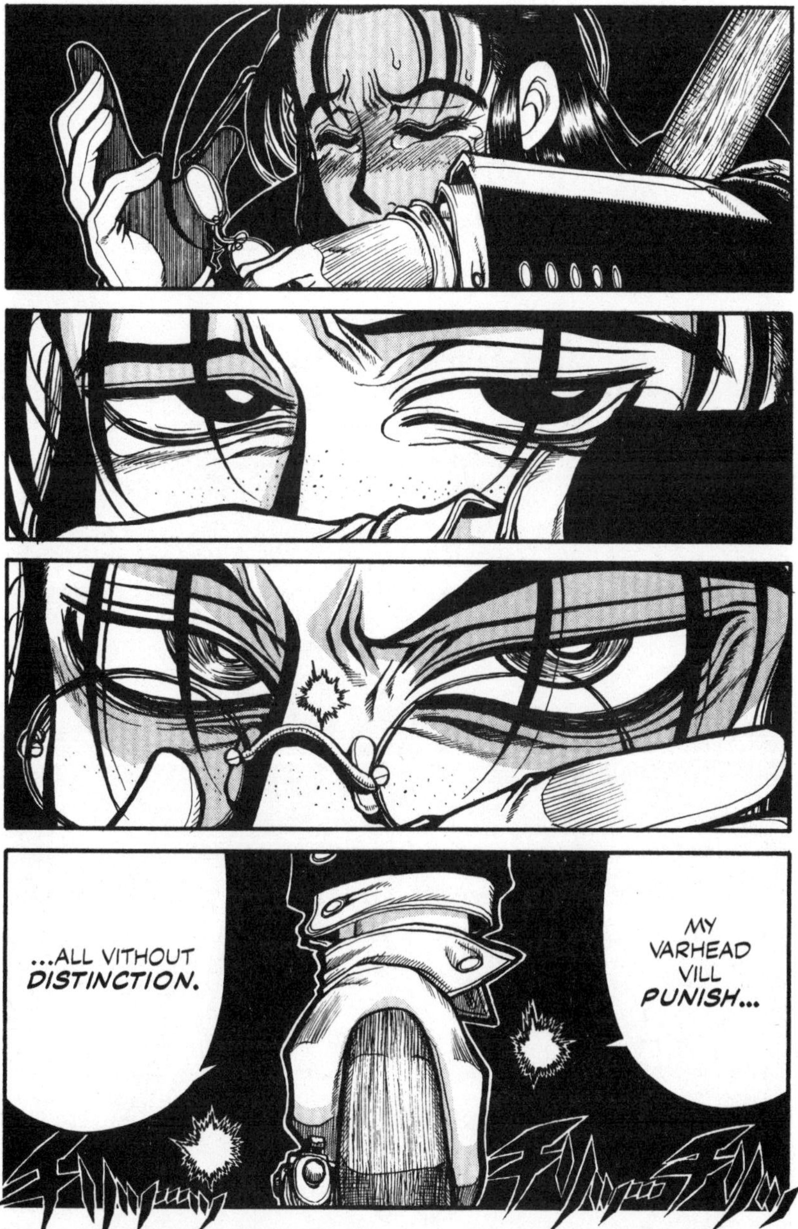
MY VARHEAD VILL PUNISH...
...ALL VITHOUT DISTINCTION.

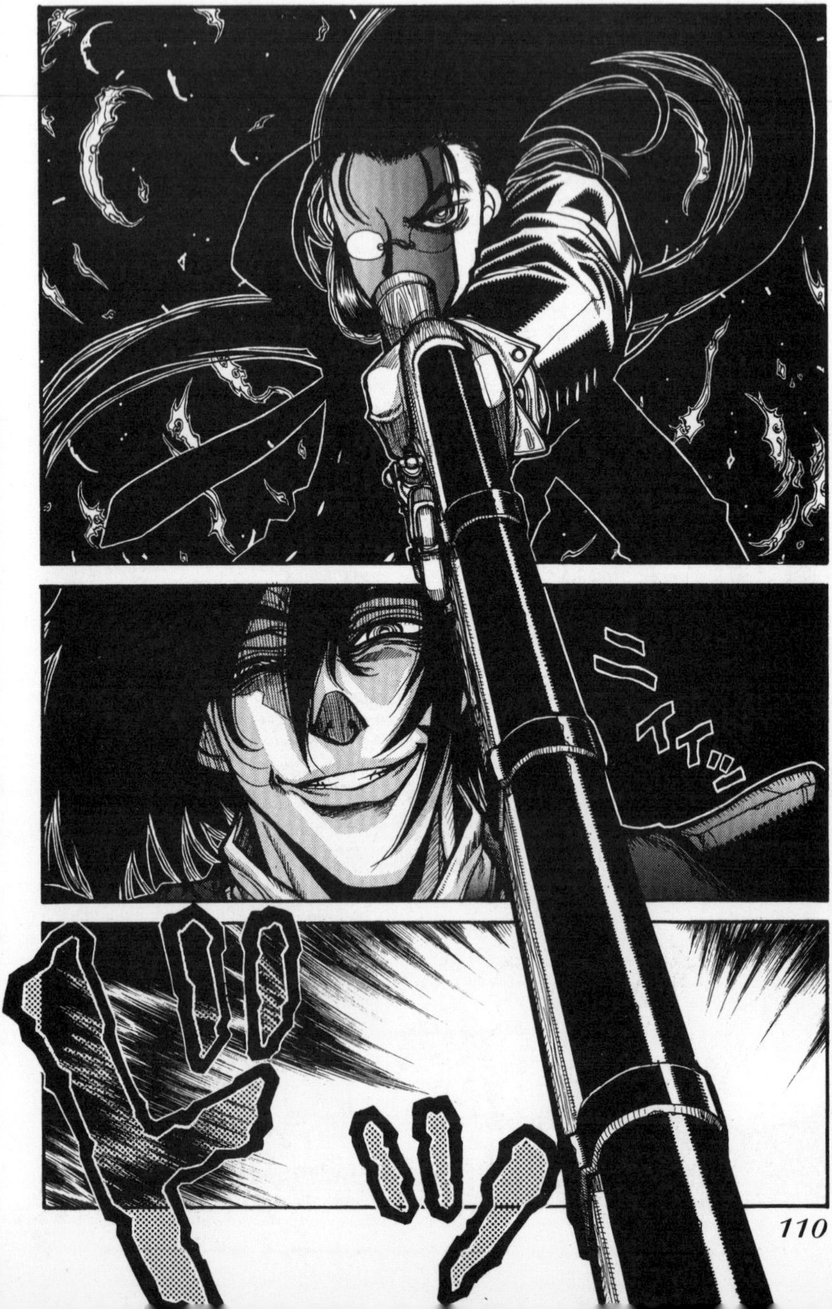
ニイィッ

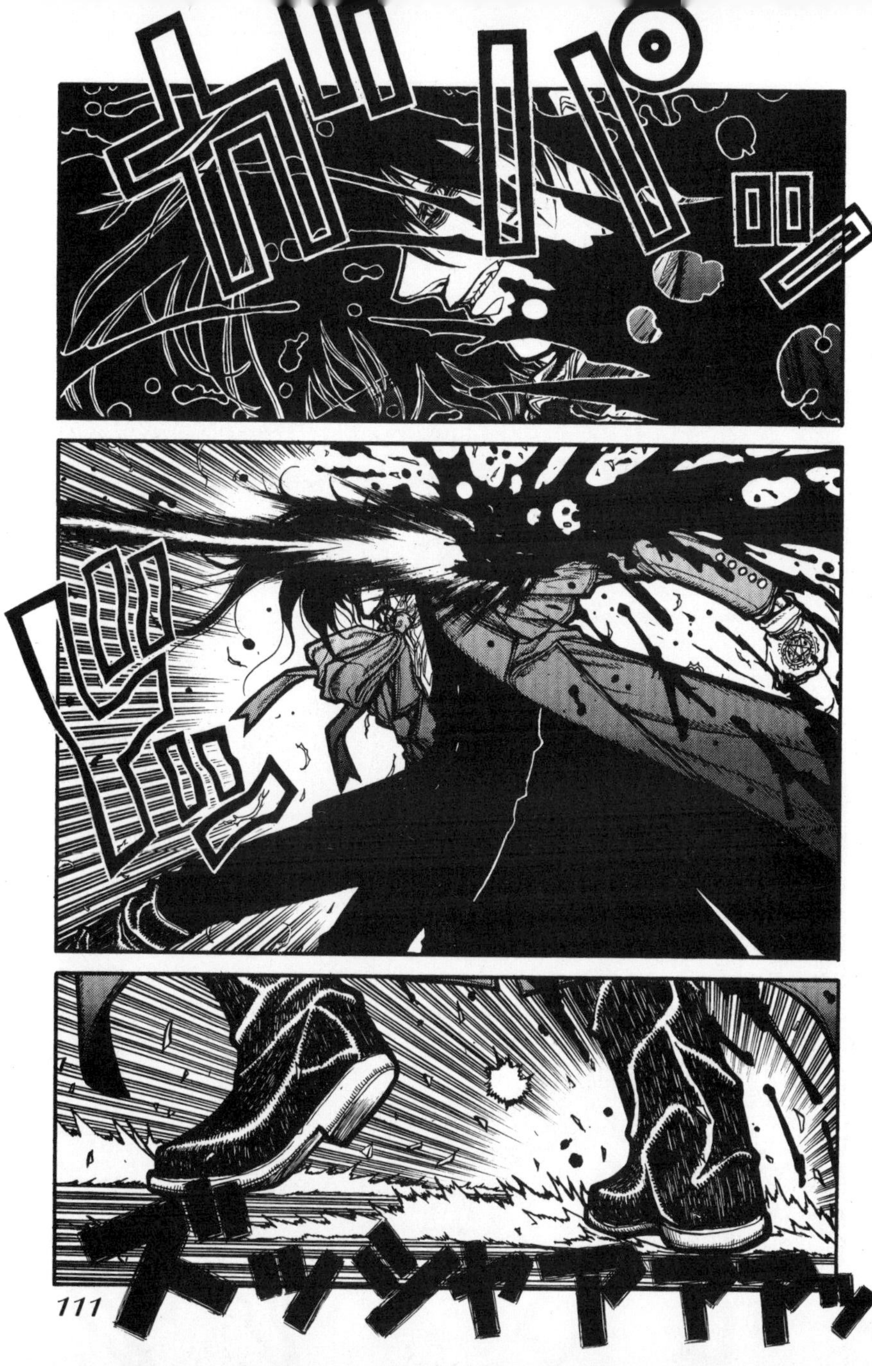

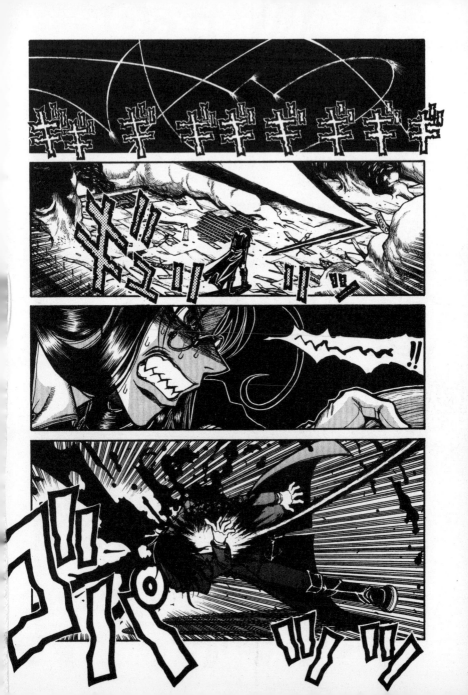

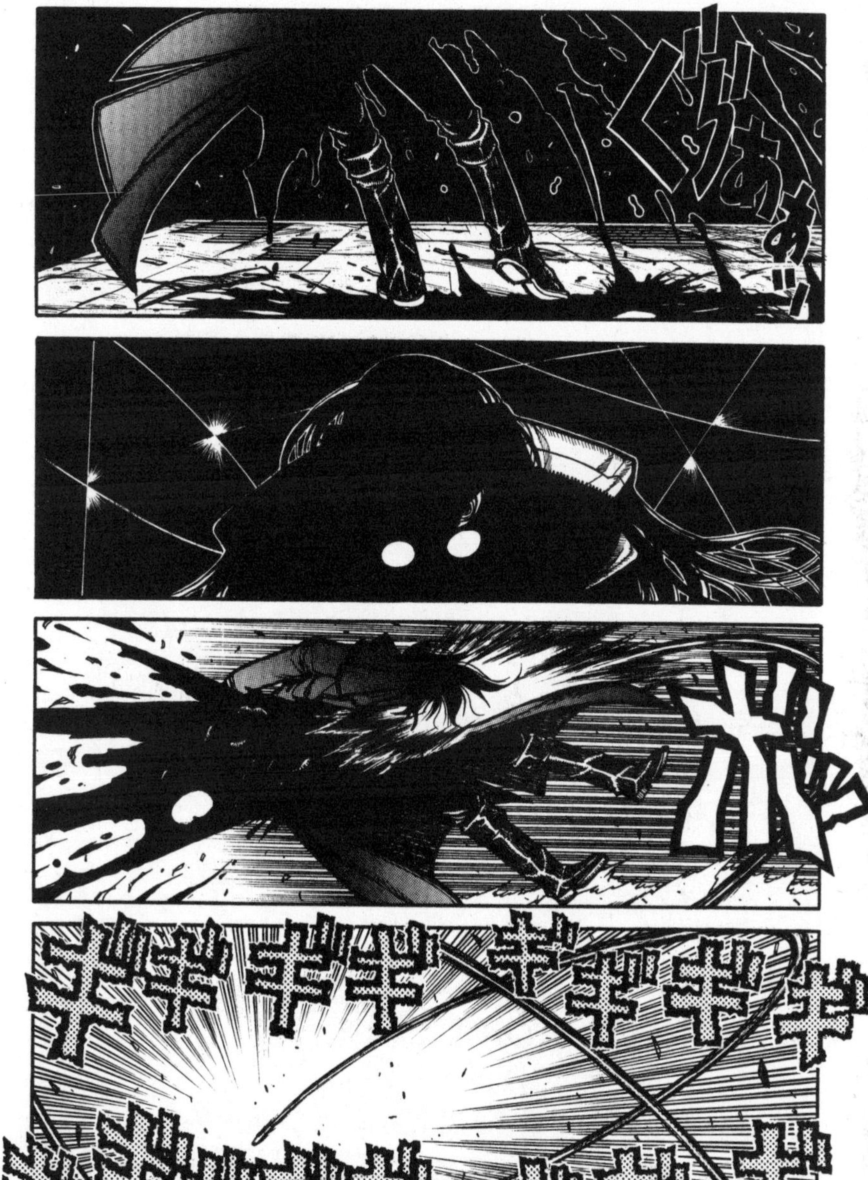
ギギギギギギギギギ
ギギギギギギギギギ

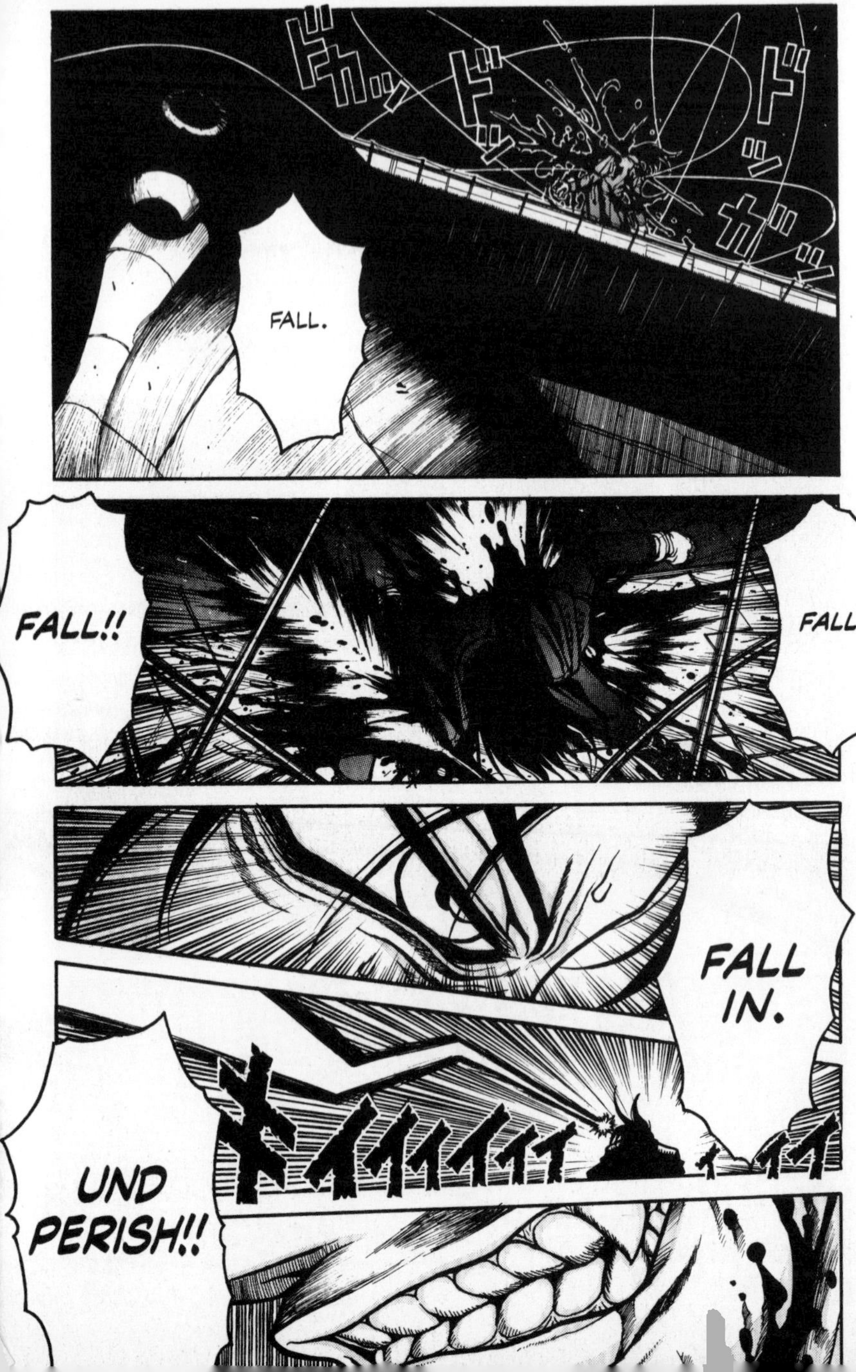
FALL.
FALL.
FALL!!
FALL IN.
UND PERISH!!

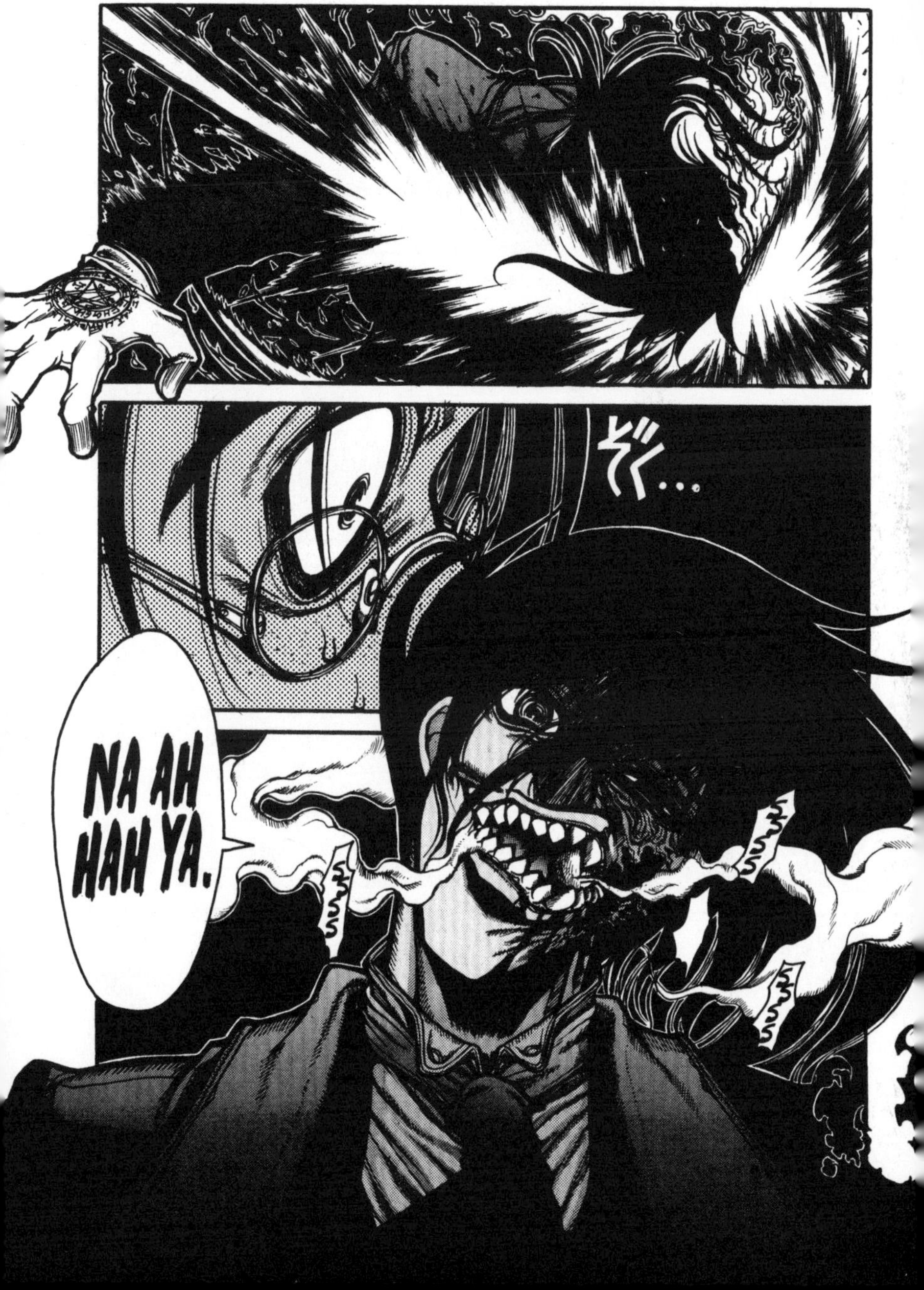
ぞく…
NA AH HAH YA.

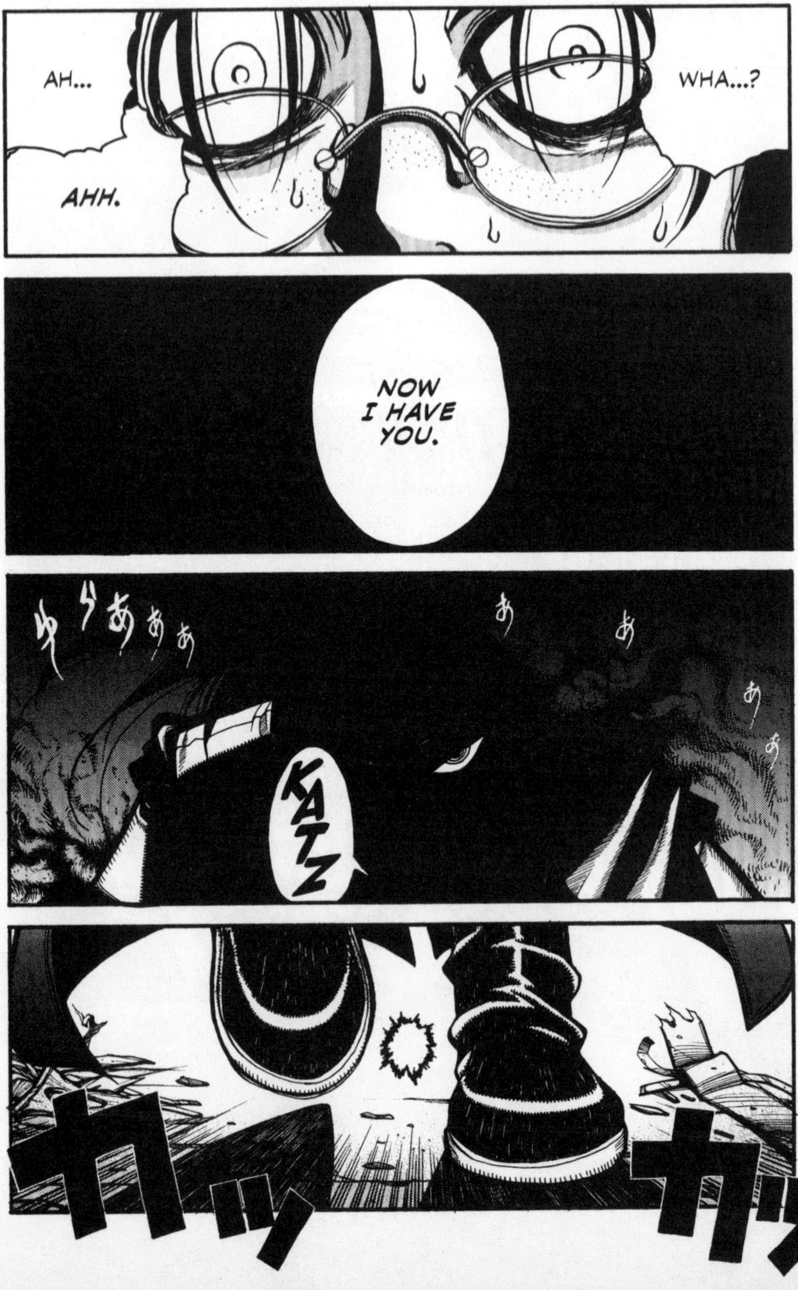
WHA...?
AH...
AHH.
NOW I HAVE YOU.
あ あ あ あ
ゆらあああ
KATZ

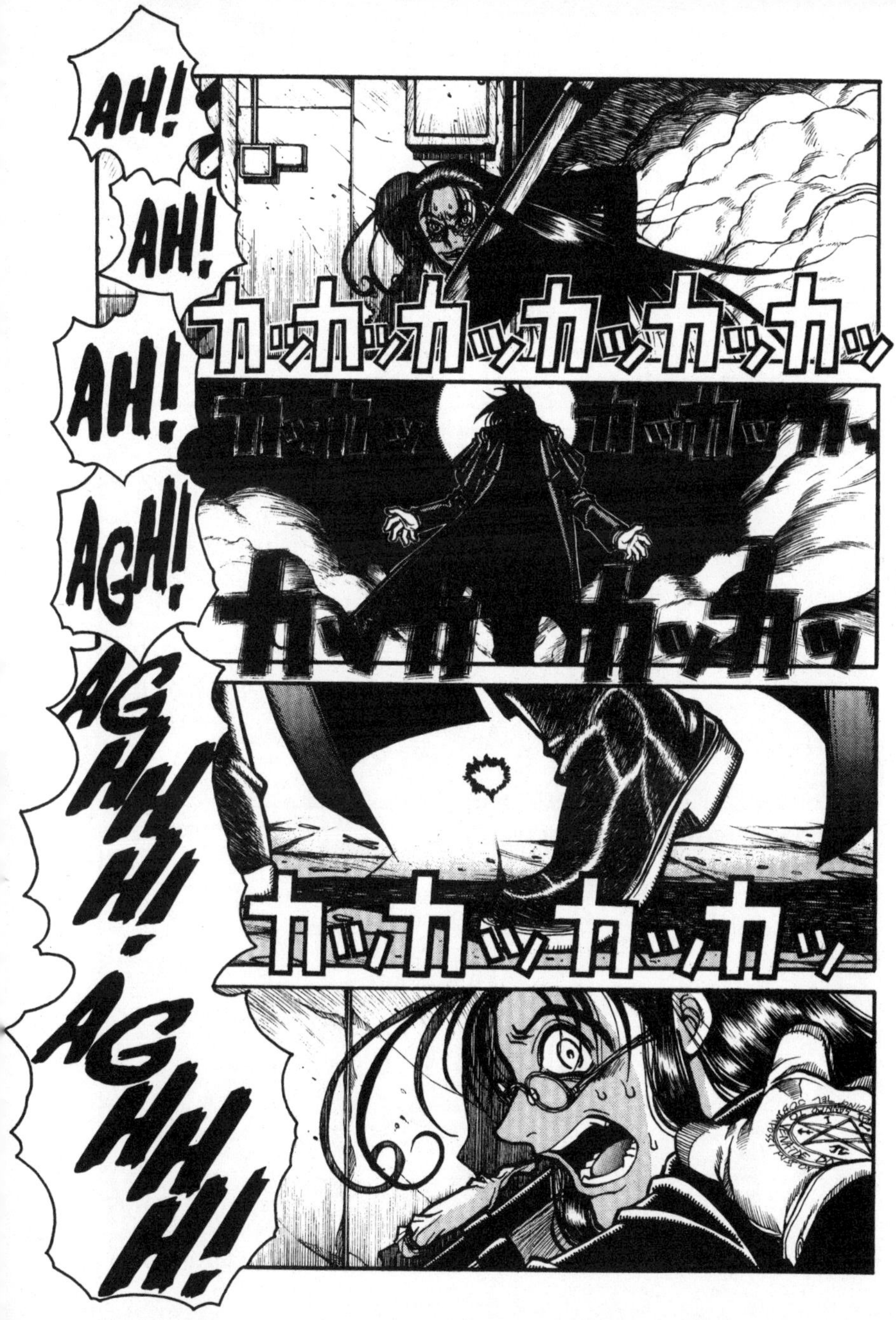
AH!
AH!
AH!
AGH!
AGHHHHH!
AGHHHHH!
カッカッカッカッカッカッ
カッカッカッカッカッ
カッカッカッカッ
カッカッカッカッ

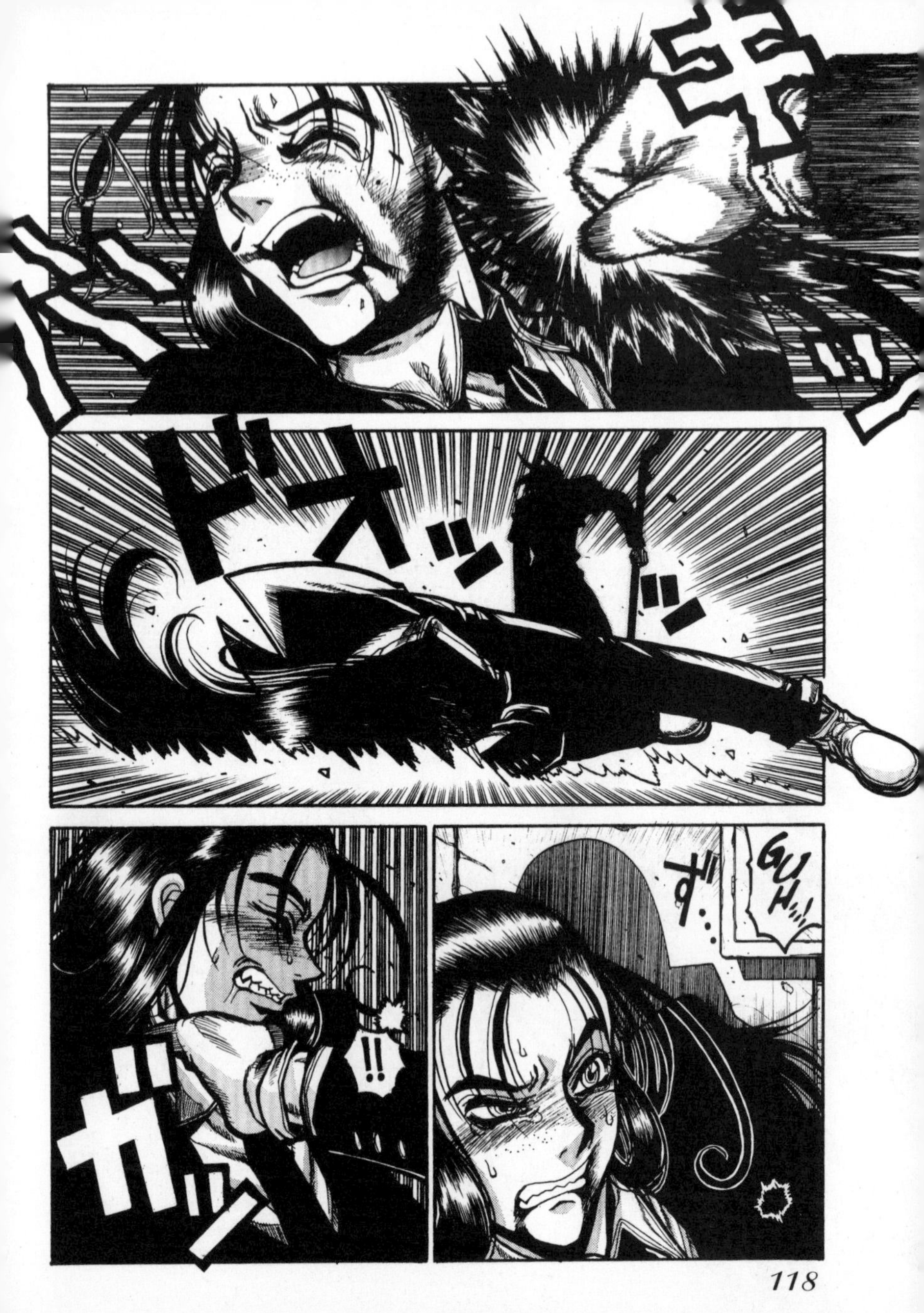
ドスッ
ッ
ず…
GUH…!
ガッ
!!
…

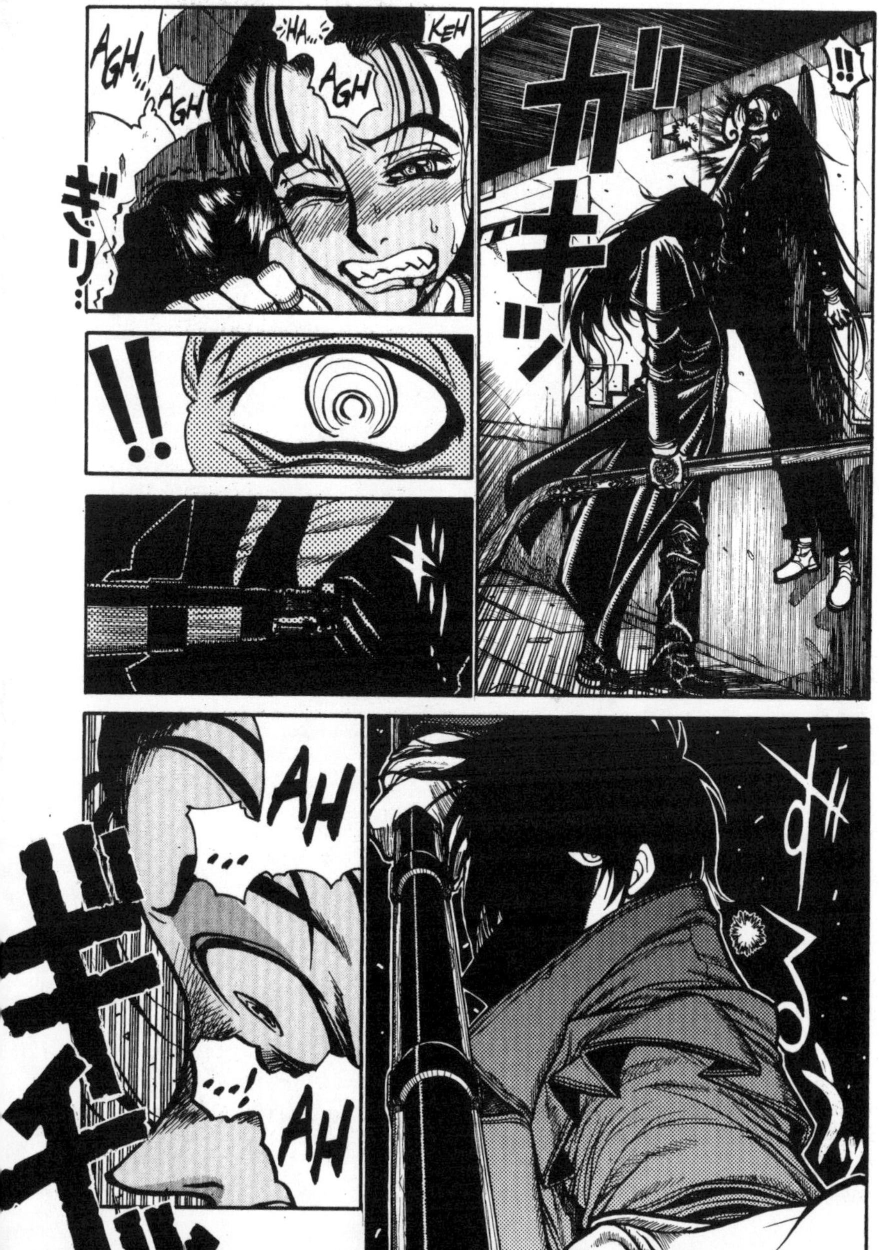

!!
KEH
HA...
AGH
AGH
AGH...!
!!
AH
...
...!
AH

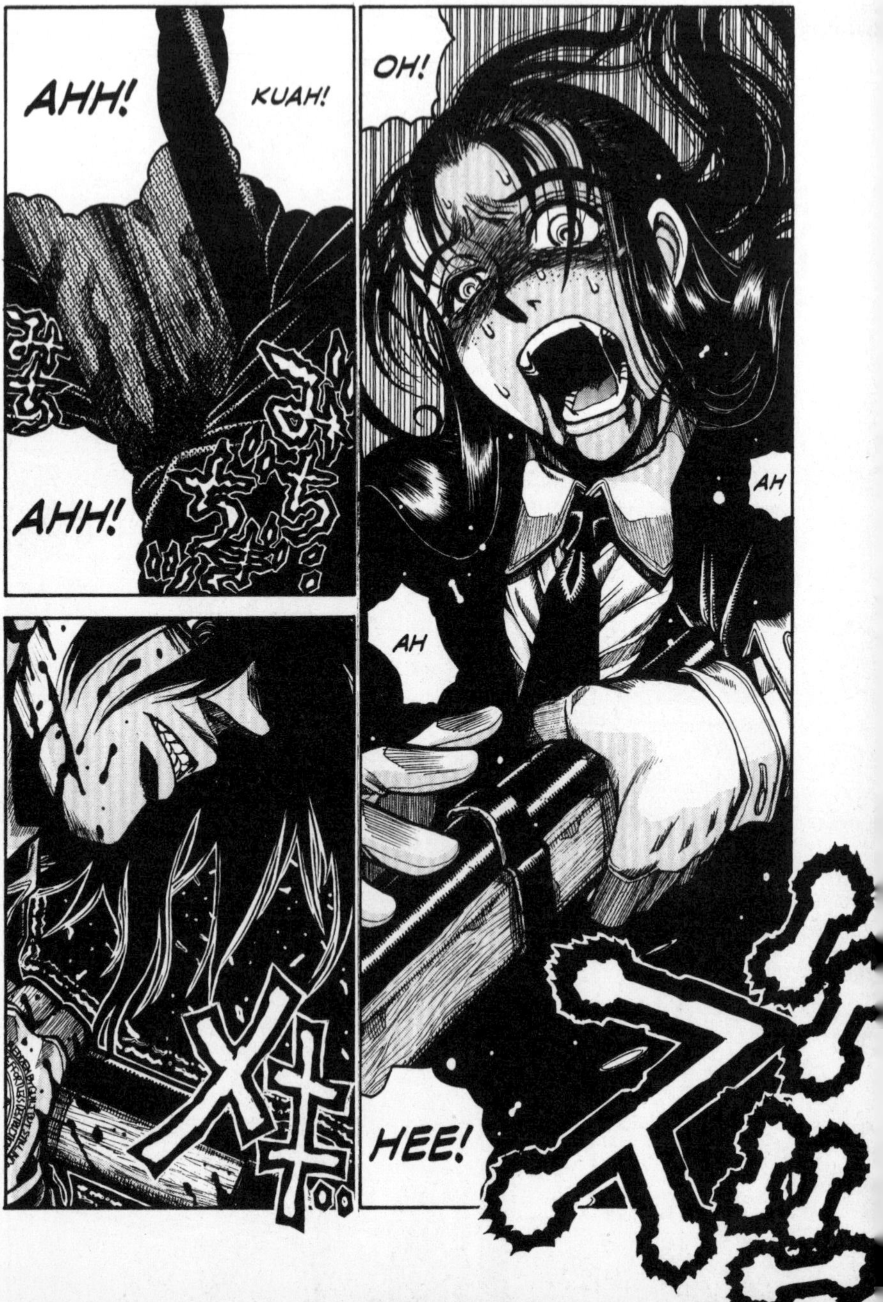
OH!
AH
AH
HEE!
KUAH!
AHH!
AHH!

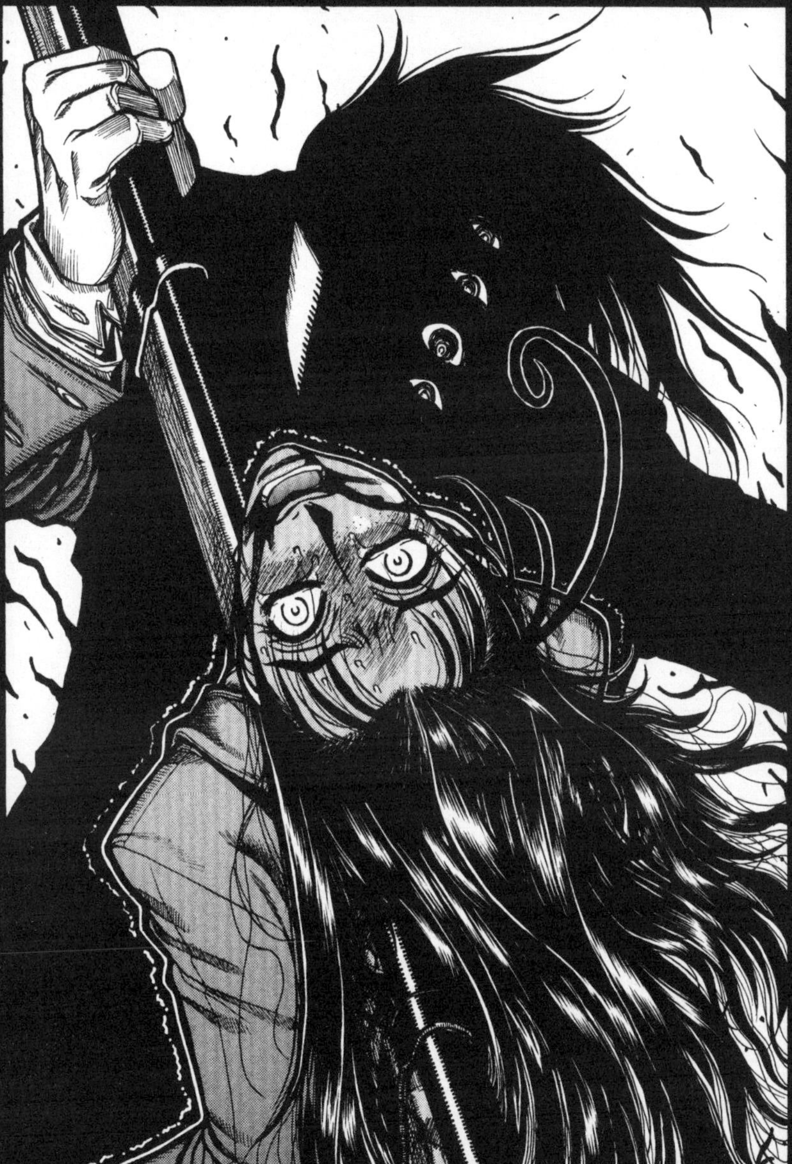

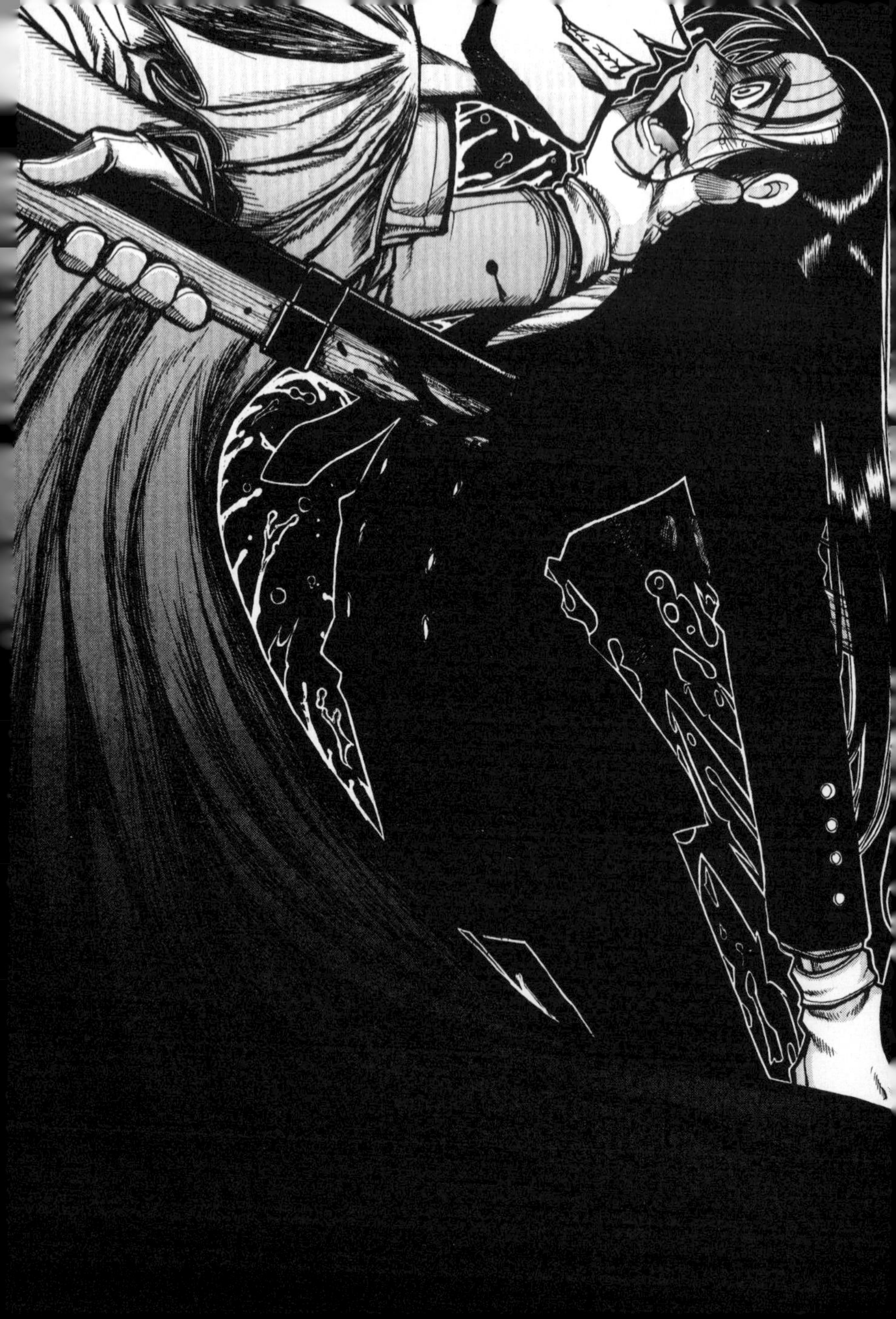

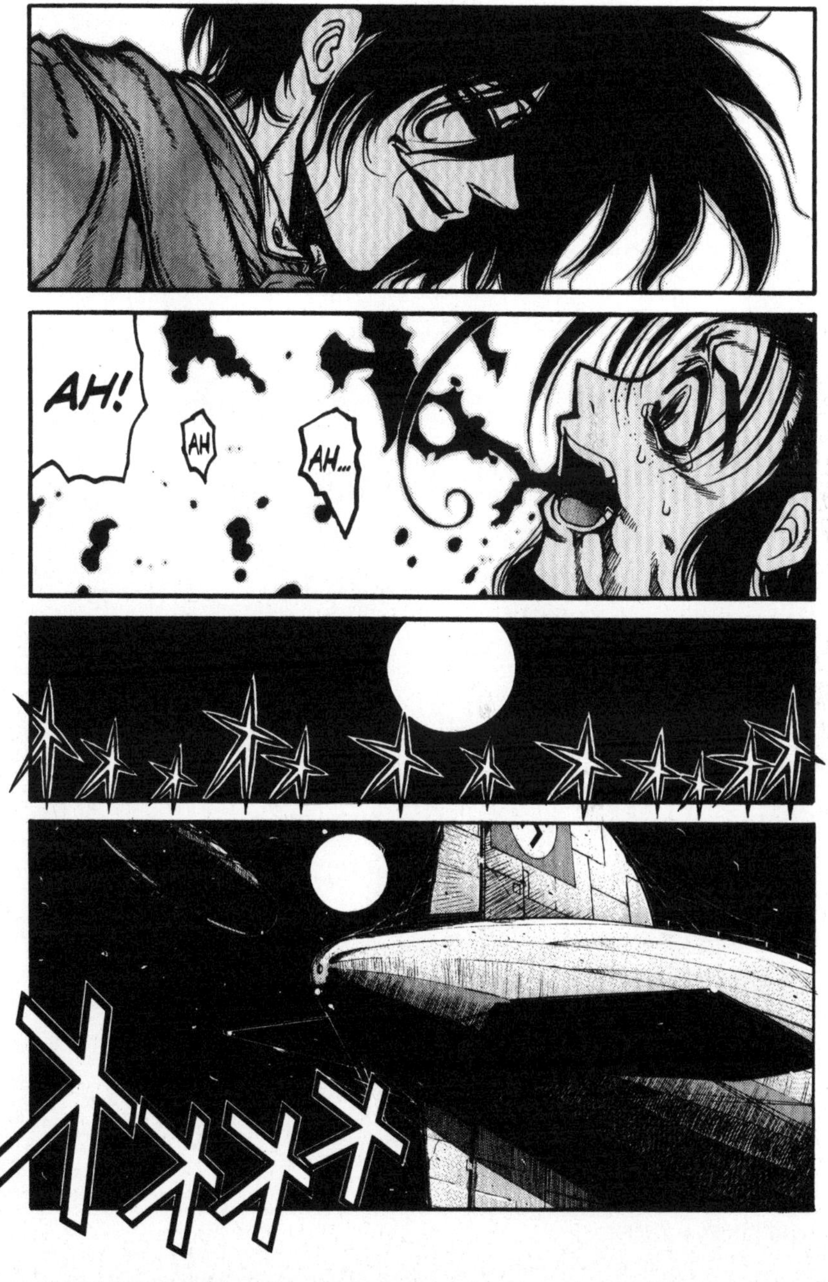
AH...
AH
AH!
オォォォ

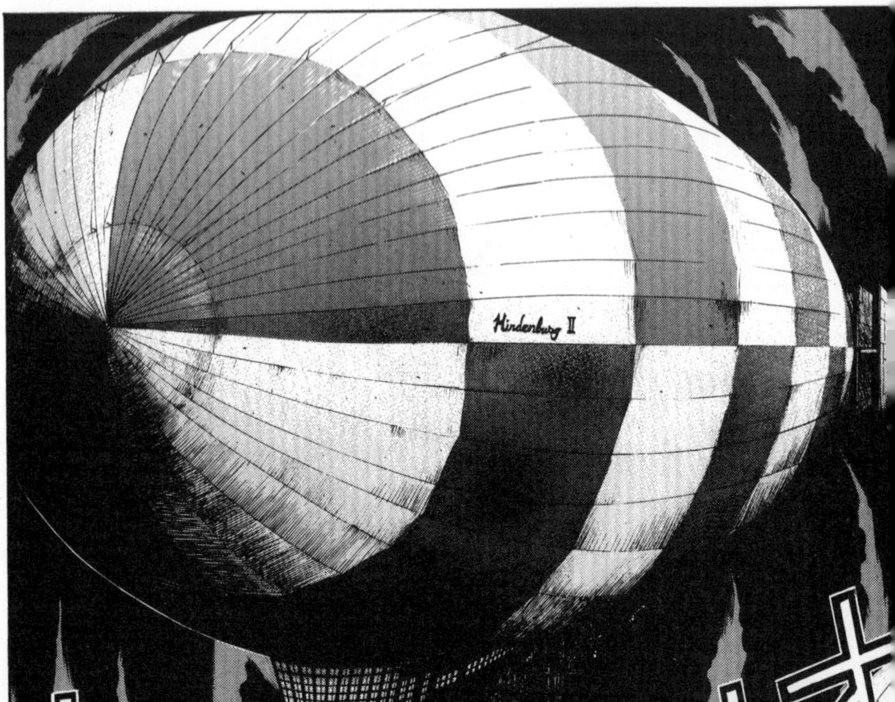
Hindenburg II
オオオオオオオオオ

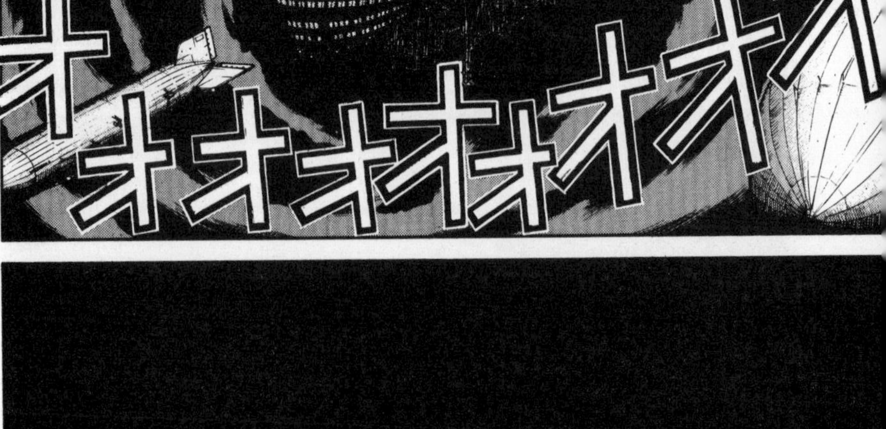
TO BE CONTINUED

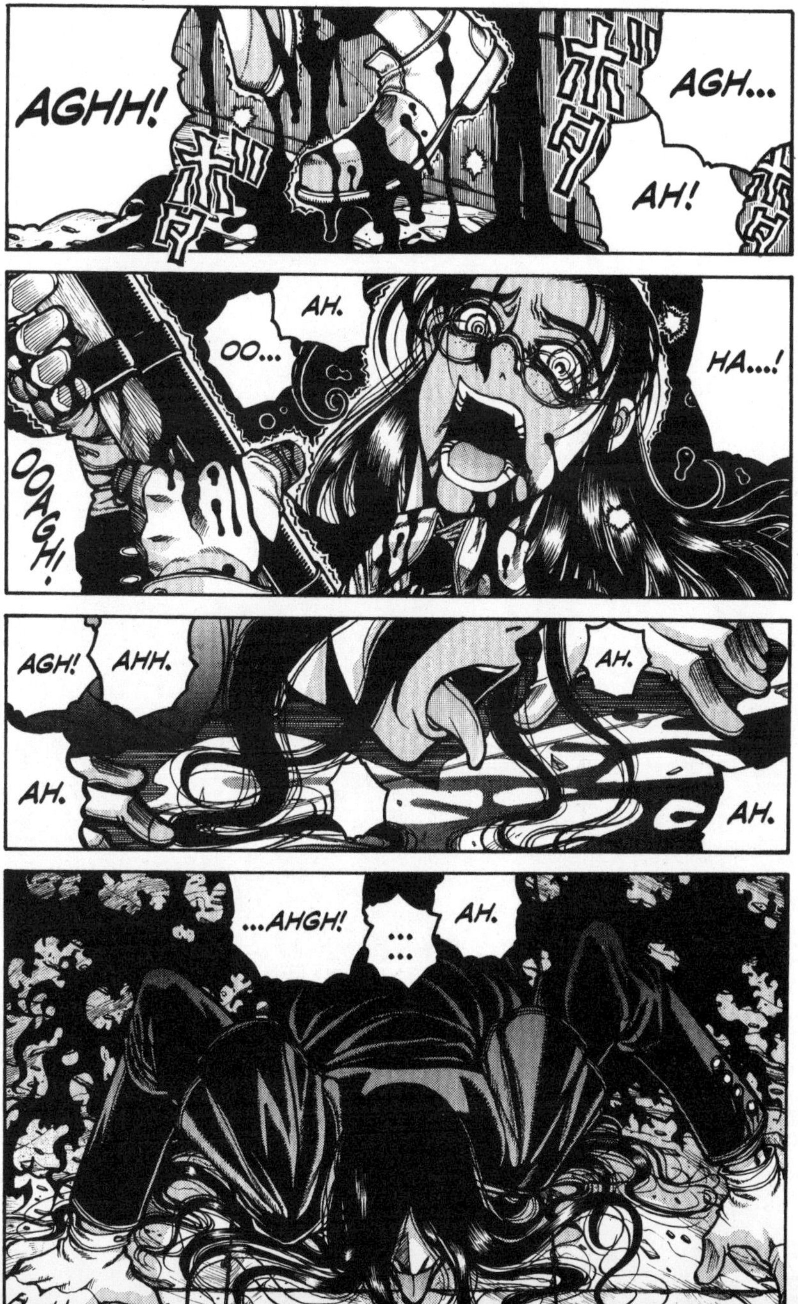
AGH...
AH!
AGHH!
HA...!
AH.
OO...
OOAGH!
AH.
AH.
AHH.
AGH!
AH.
AH.
...
...
...AHGH!

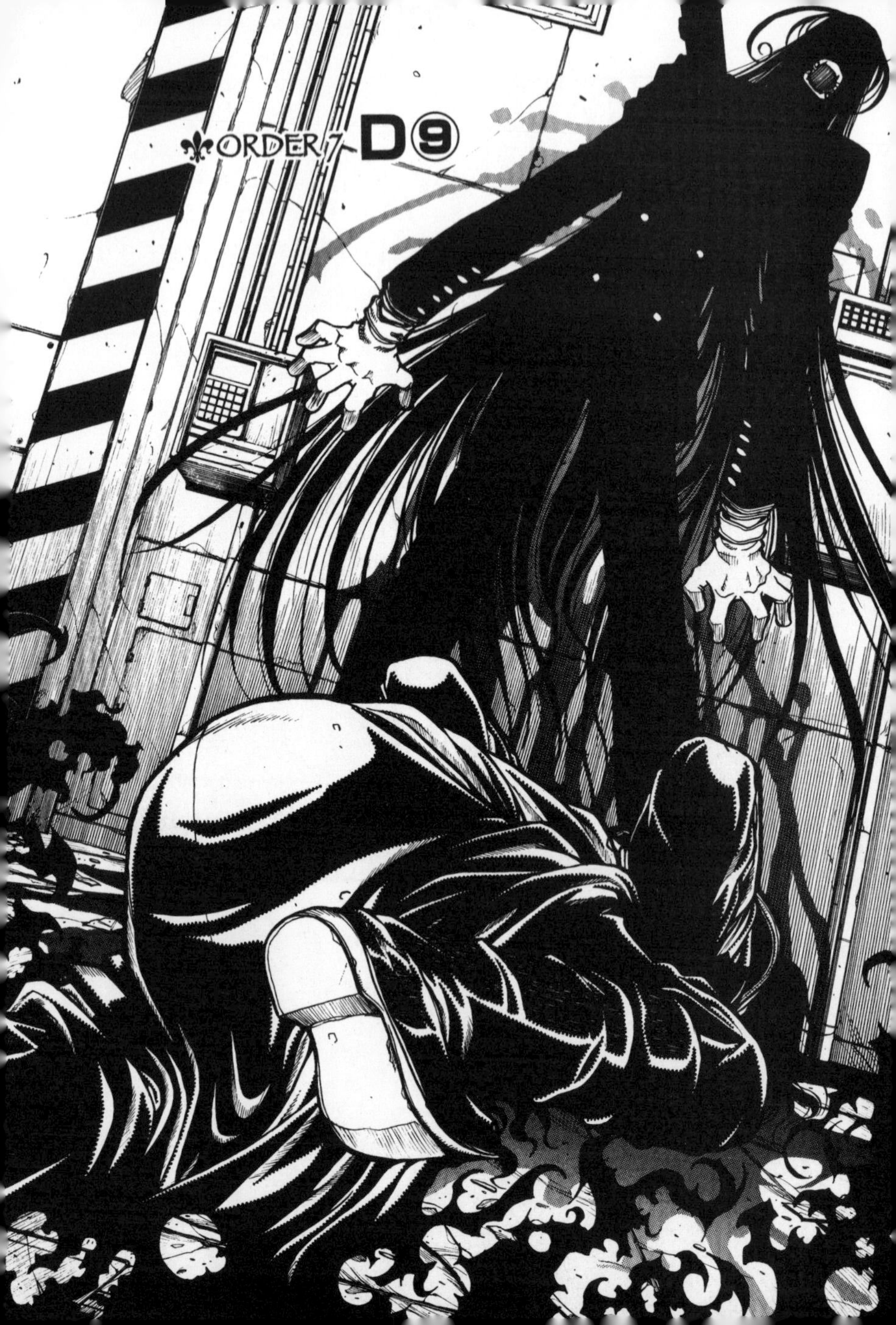
ORDER 7 D⑨

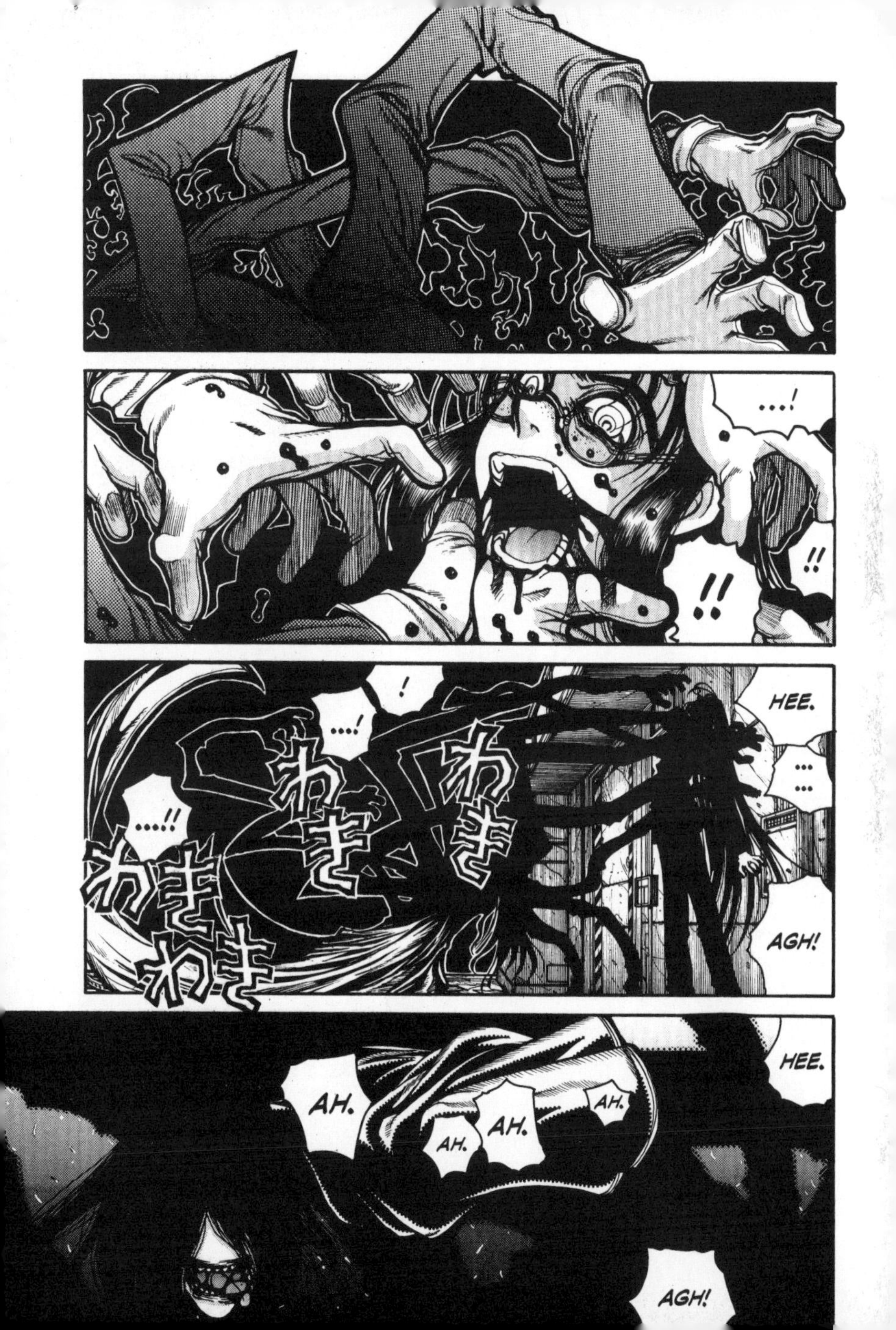

...!
!!
!!
HEE.
......
AGH!
!
...!
わき
わき
...!!
わきわき
HEE.
AH.
AH.
AH.
AH.
AGH!

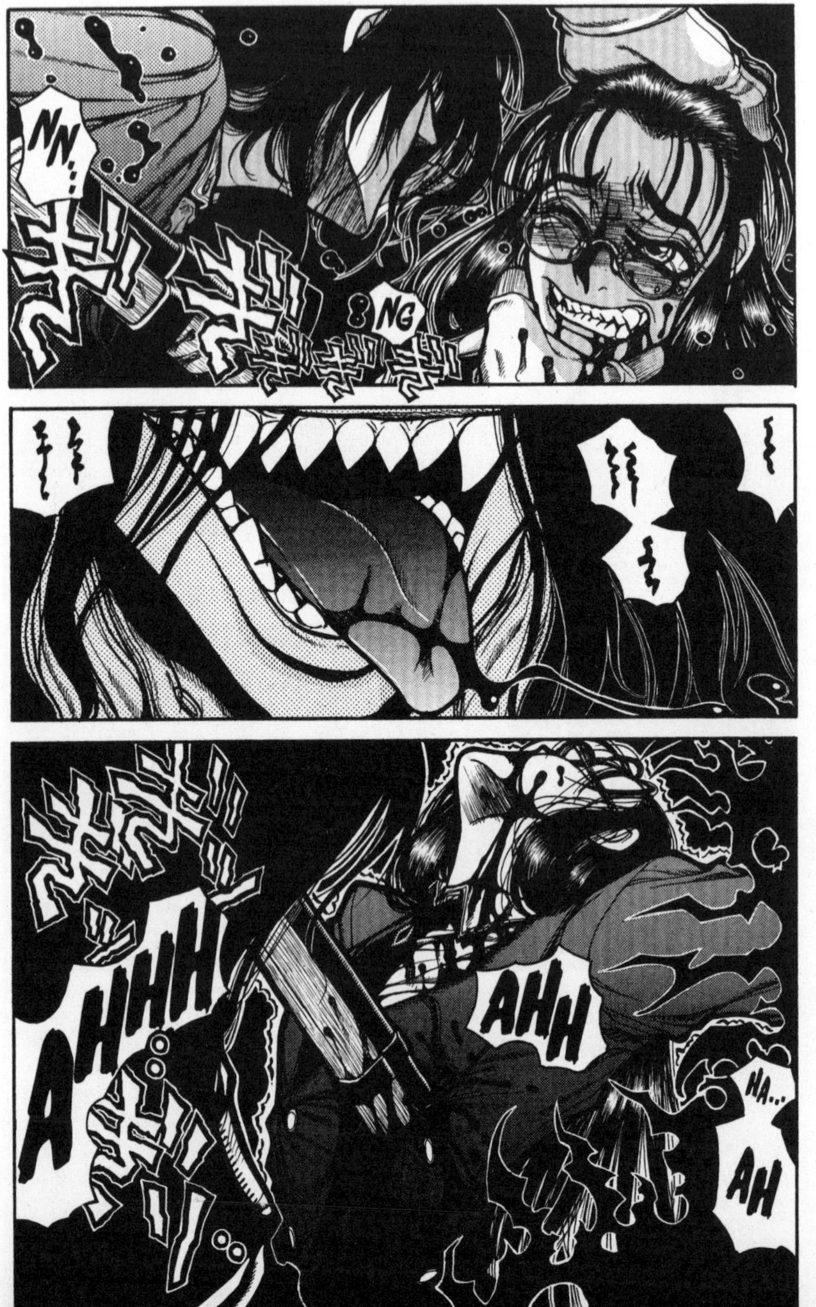
NN..
NG
AHH
NA...
AH
AHHHH

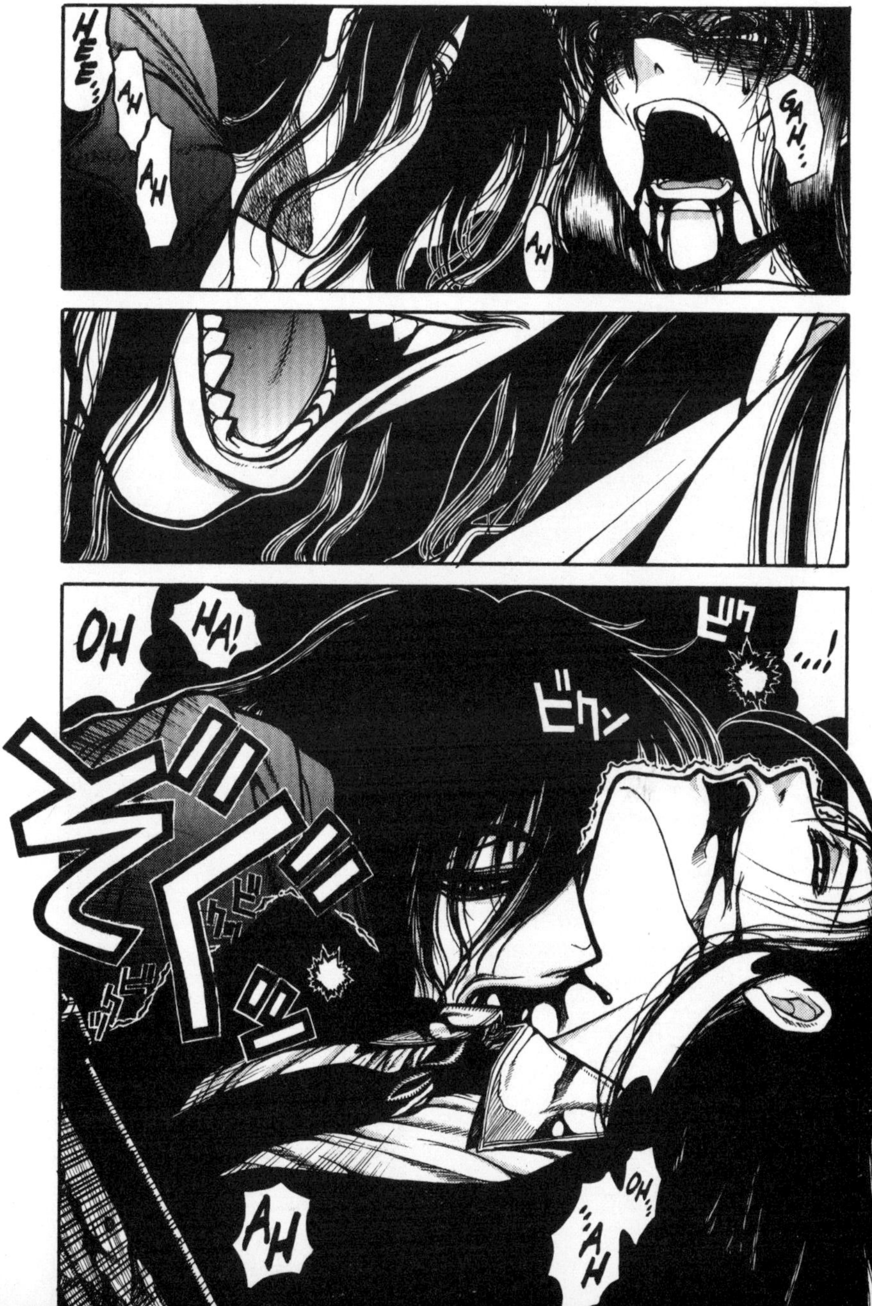
GAH...
AH
HEEE...
AH
AH
...!
ビク
ビクン
HA!
OH
OH... ...AH
AH

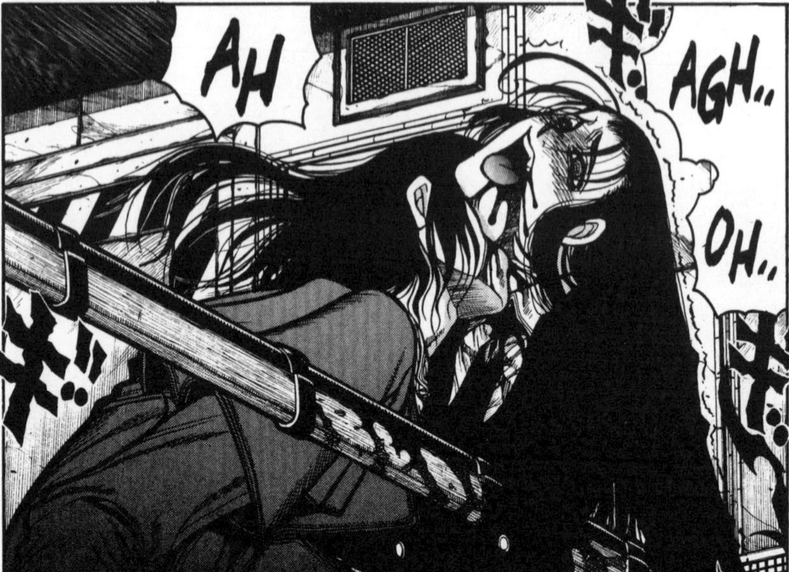
ギ
AGH..
AH
OH..
ギ
ギ!!

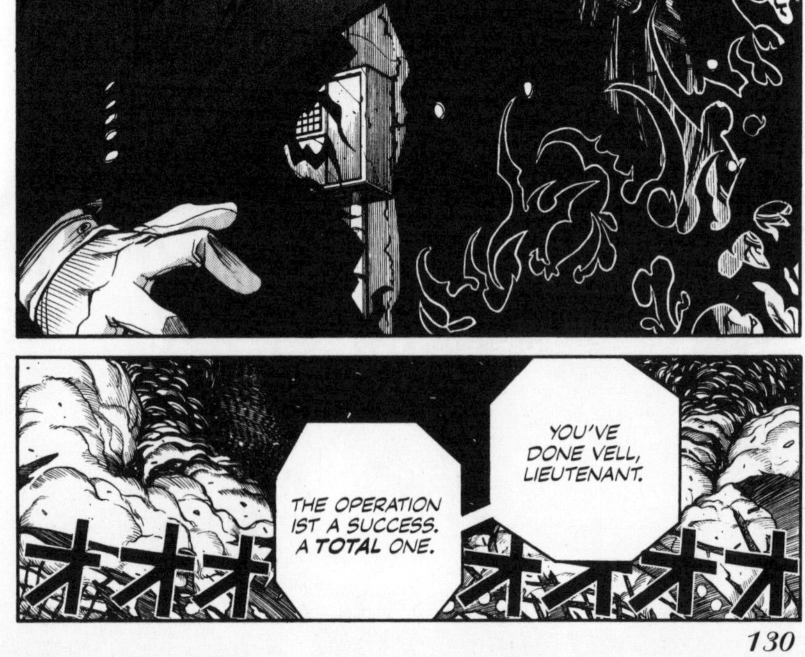
オオオオ
YOU'VE DONE VELL, LIEUTENANT.
THE OPERATION IST A SUCCESS. A **TOTAL** ONE.
オオオ

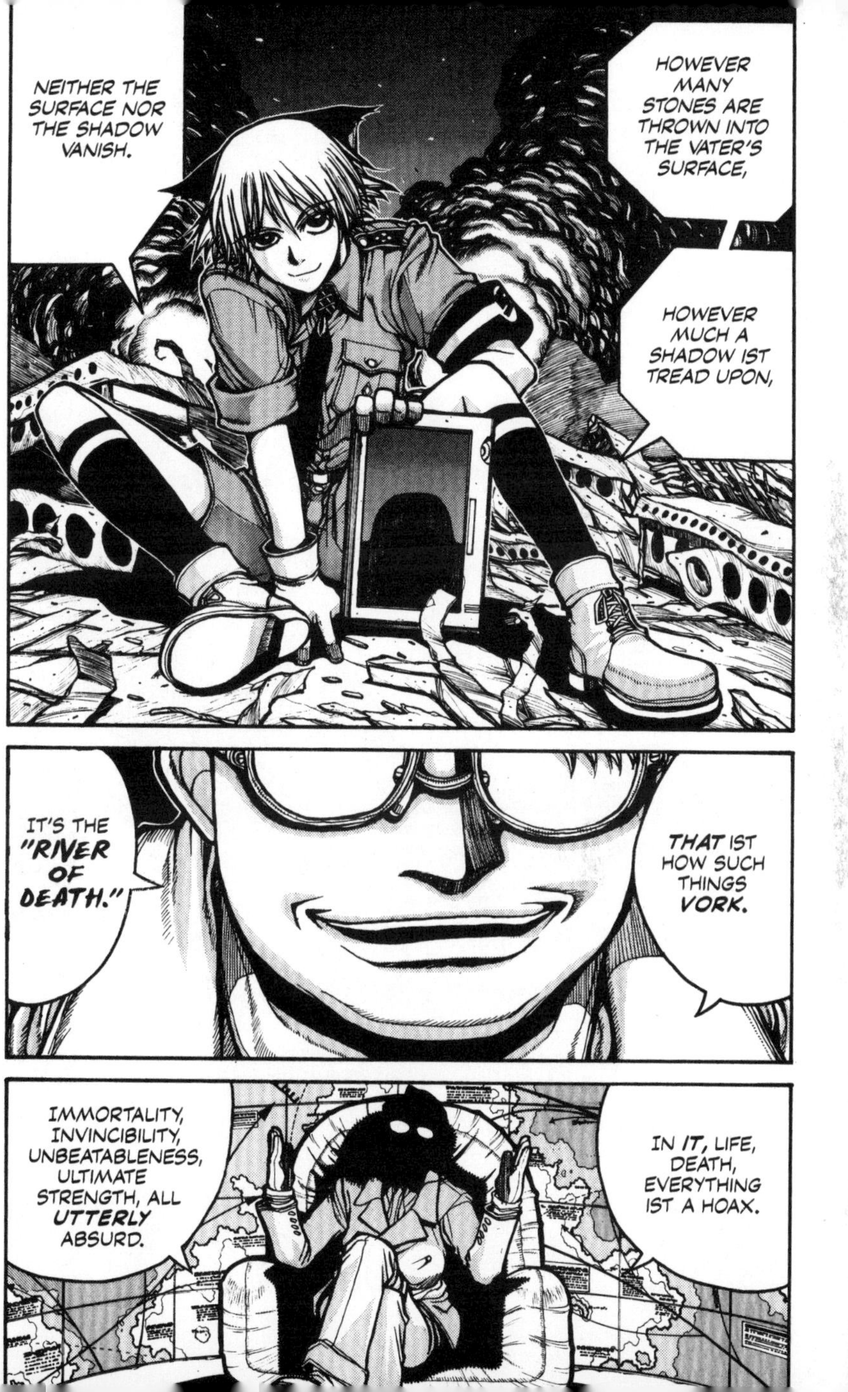
HOWEVER MANY STONES ARE THROWN INTO THE VATER'S SURFACE,
HOWEVER MUCH A SHADOW IST TREAD UPON,
NEITHER THE SURFACE NOR THE SHADOW VANISH.
THAT IST HOW SUCH THINGS *VORK.*
IT'S THE *"RIVER OF DEATH."*
IN *IT*, LIFE, DEATH, EVERYTHING IST A HOAX.
IMMORTALITY, INVINCIBILITY, UNBEATABLENESS, ULTIMATE STRENGTH, ALL *UTTERLY* ABSURD.

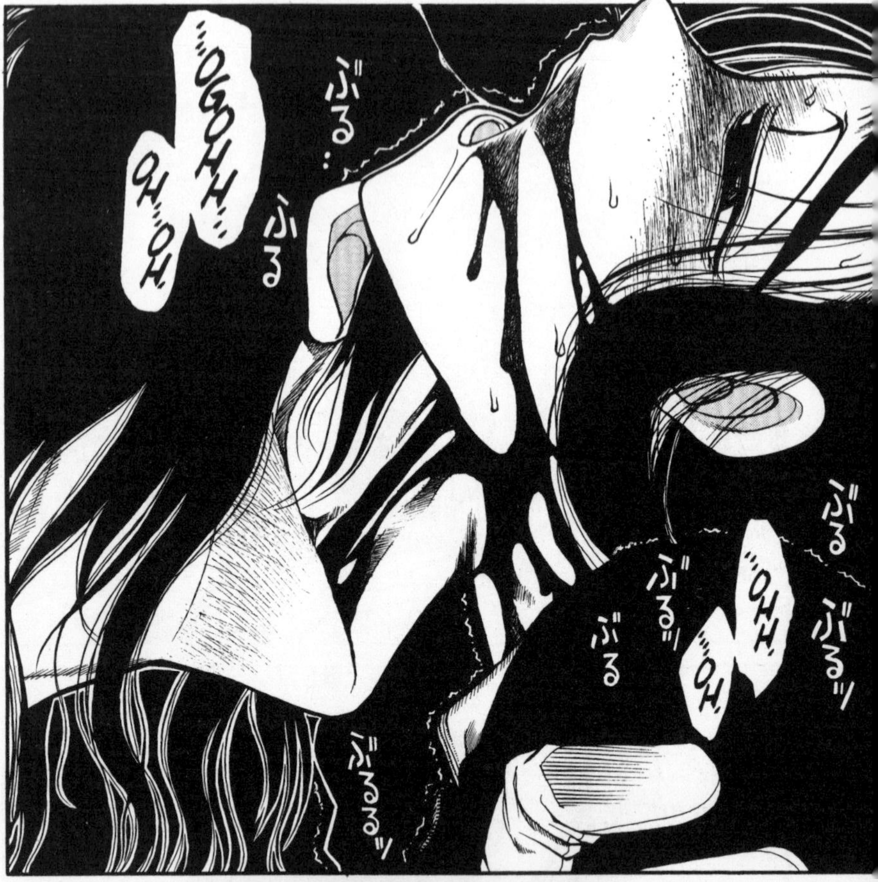
...OHH...
...OH...
ぶる ぶるッ
ぶるぶるッ
ぶる ぶる
...OGOHH...
OH...OH...
ぶる.. ぶる

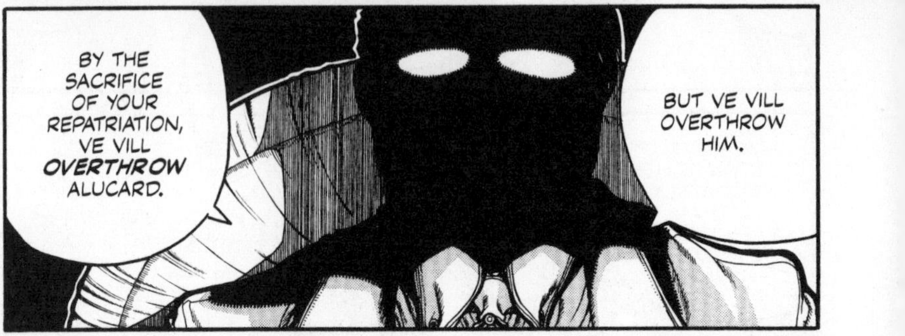
BUT VE VILL OVERTHROW HIM.
BY THE SACRIFICE OF YOUR REPATRIATION, VE VILL **OVERTHROW** ALUCARD.

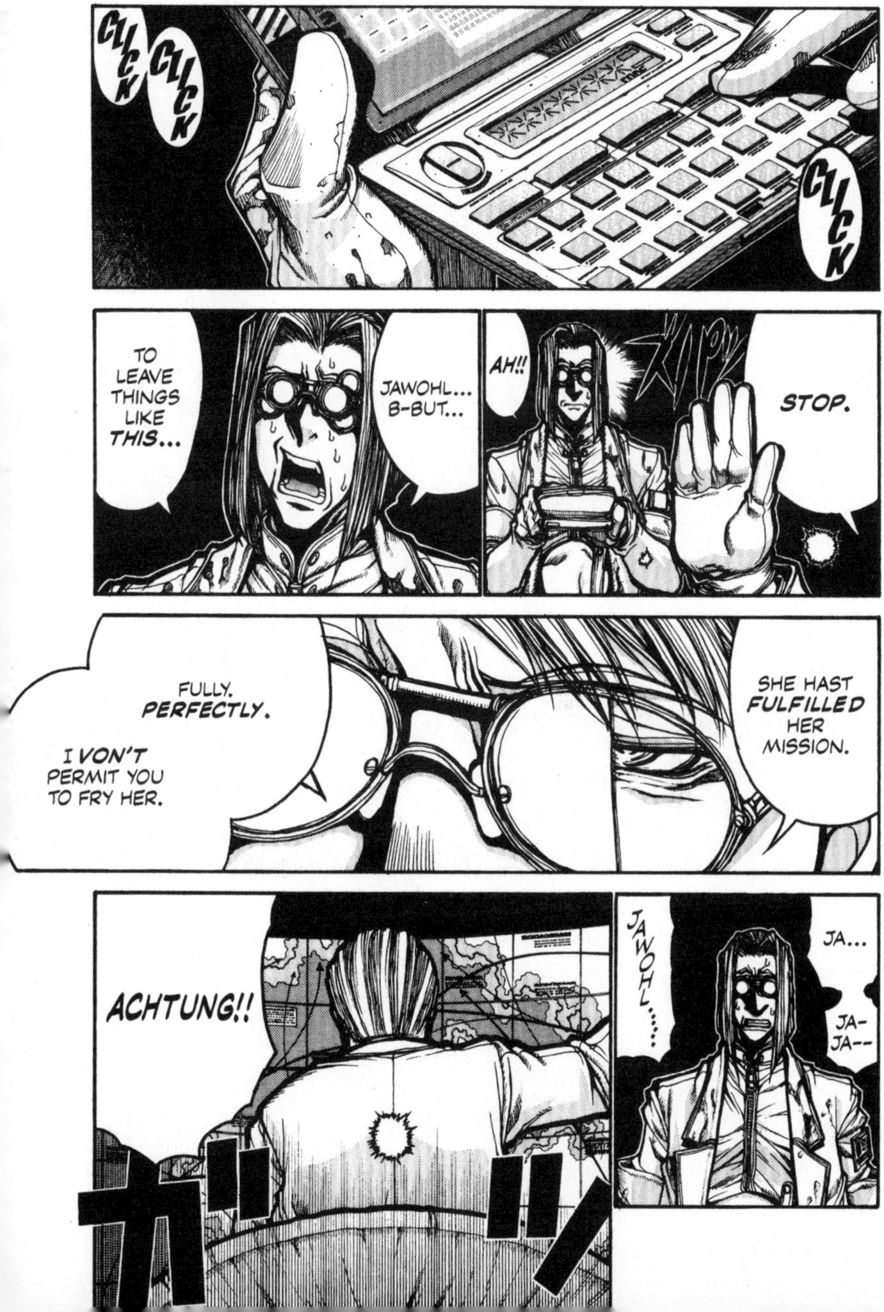
CLICK
CLICK
CLICK
STOP.
AH!!
JAWOHL... B-BUT...
TO LEAVE THINGS LIKE THIS...
SHE HAST FULFILLED HER MISSION.
FULLY. PERFECTLY.
I VON'T PERMIT YOU TO FRY HER.
JA...
JA- JA--
JAWOHL......
ACHTUNG!!

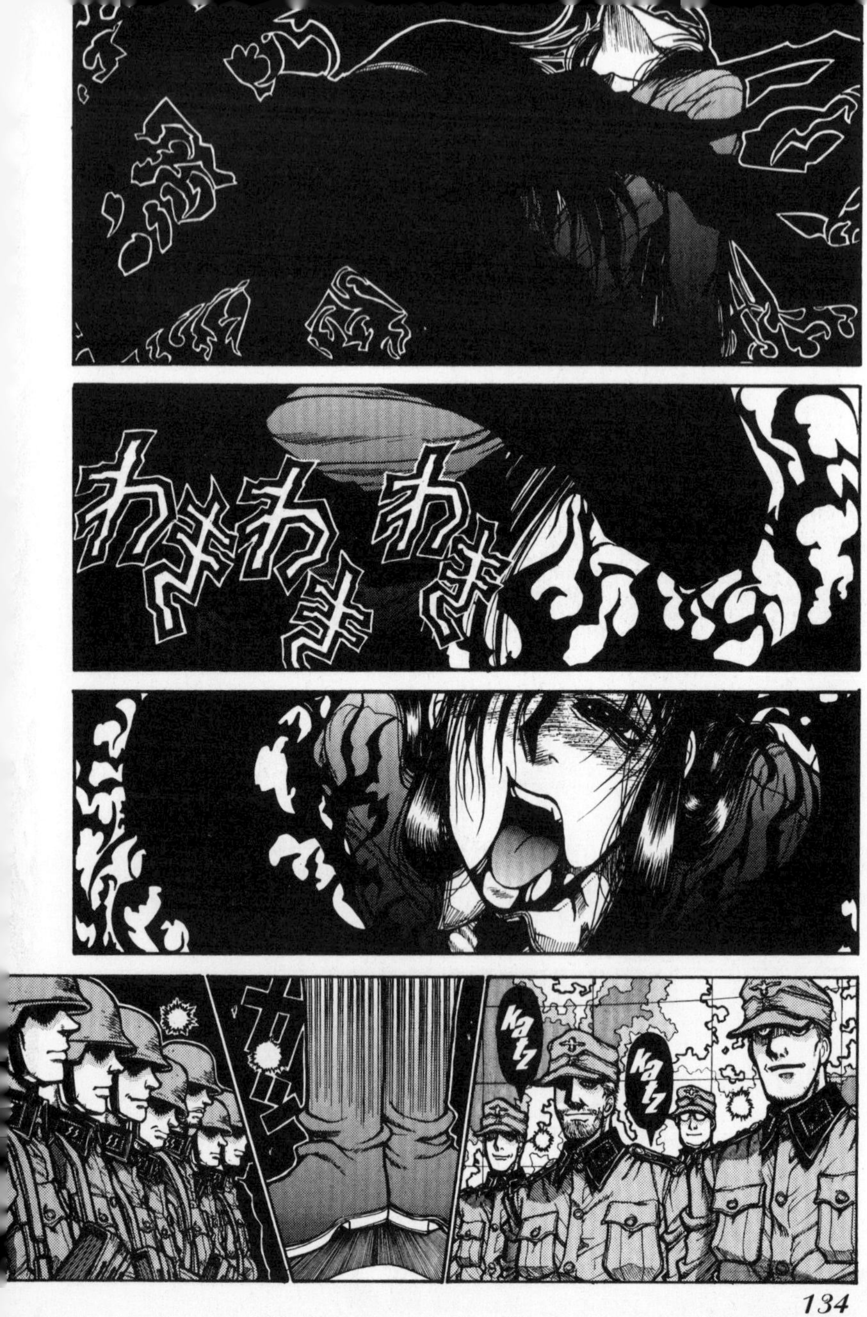
わきわき
わき
Katz
Katz
カッ

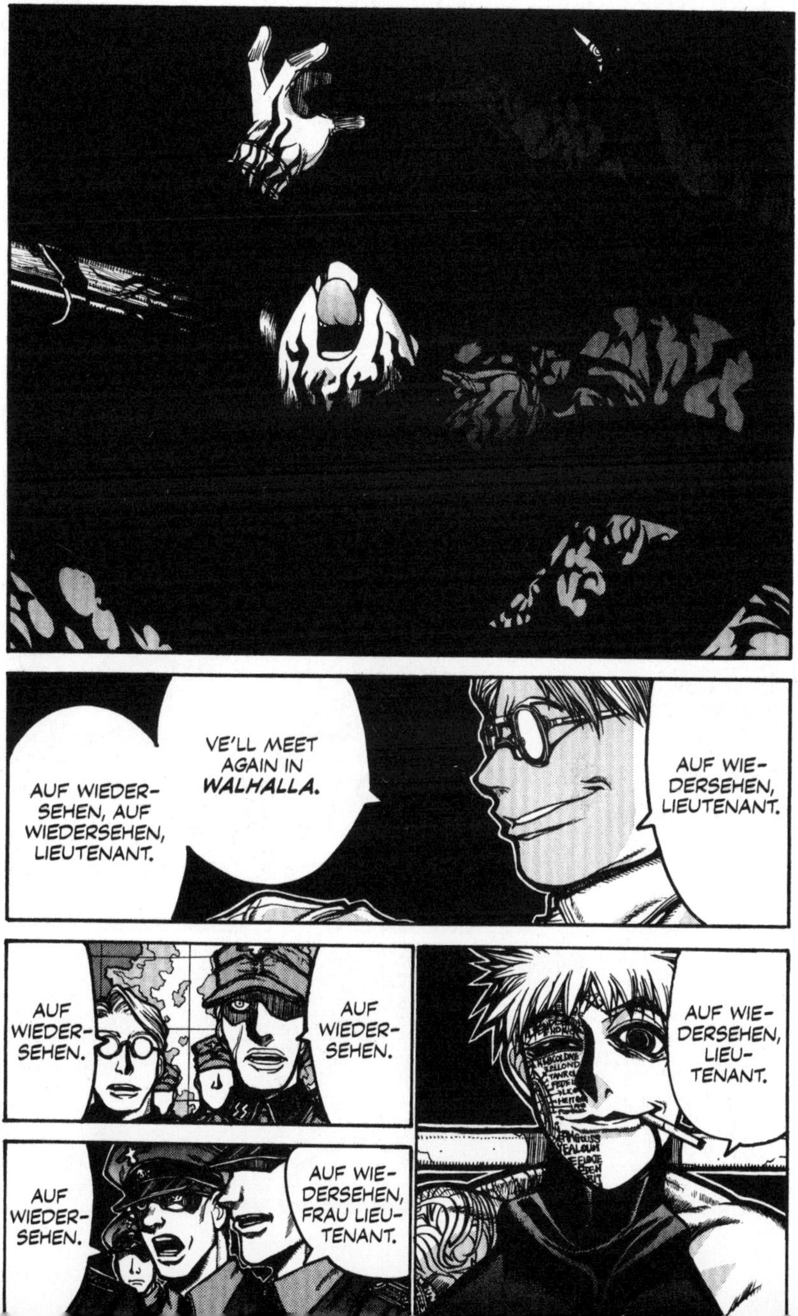
AUF WIEDERSEHEN, LIEUTENANT.
VE'LL MEET AGAIN IN WALHALLA.
AUF WIEDERSEHEN, AUF WIEDERSEHEN, LIEUTENANT.
AUF WIEDERSEHEN, LIEUTENANT.
AUF WIEDERSEHEN.
AUF WIEDERSEHEN.
AUF WIEDERSEHEN, FRAU LIEUTENANT.
AUF WIEDERSEHEN.

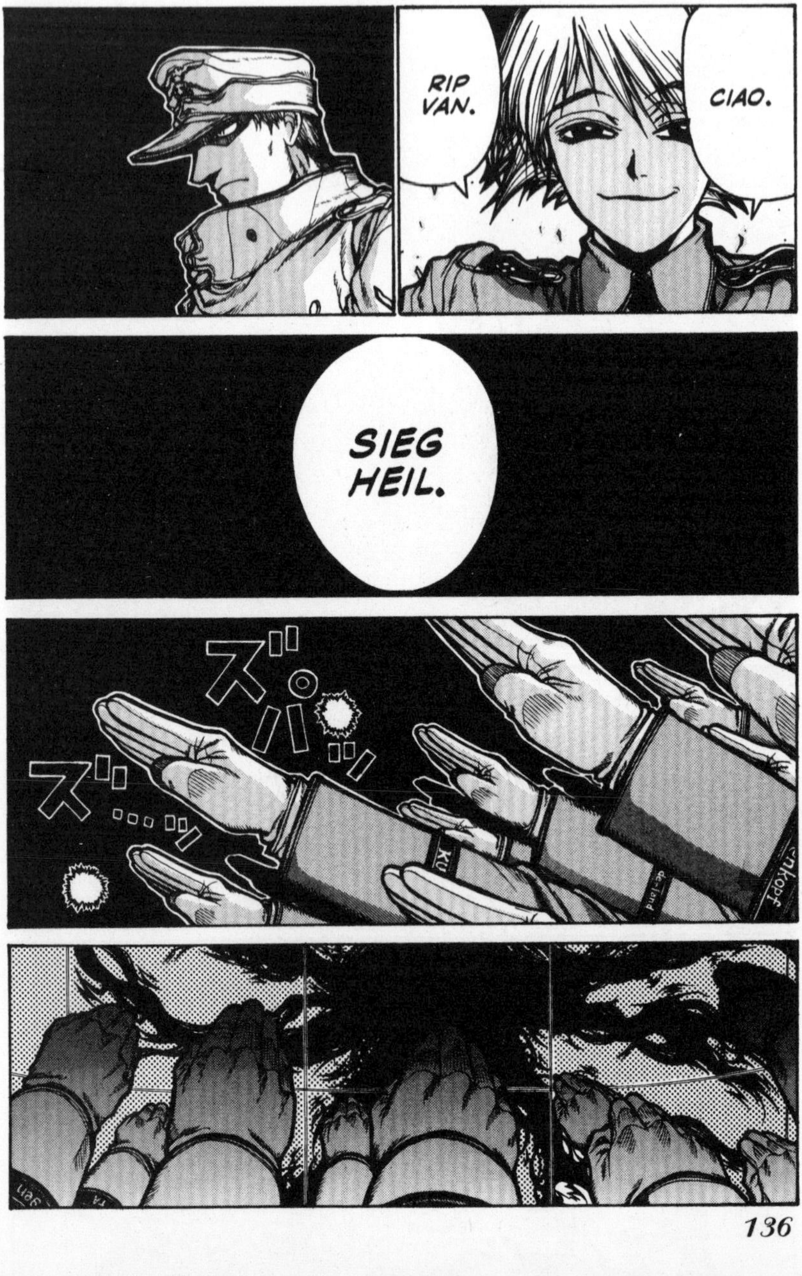
CIAO.
RIP VAN.
SIEG HEIL.
ズパッ
ズ…ッ

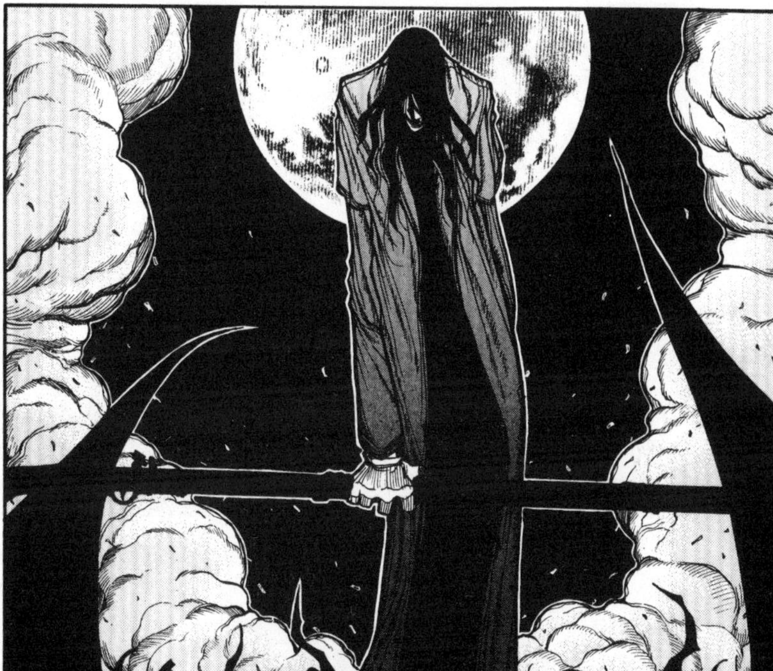

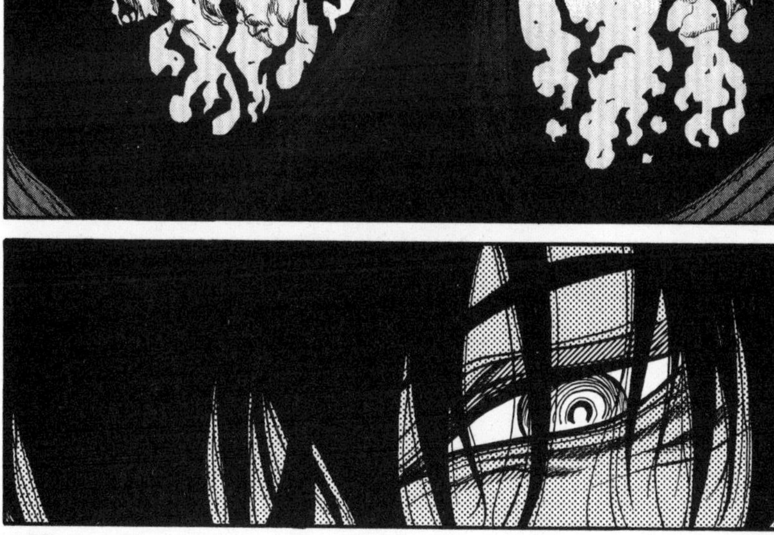

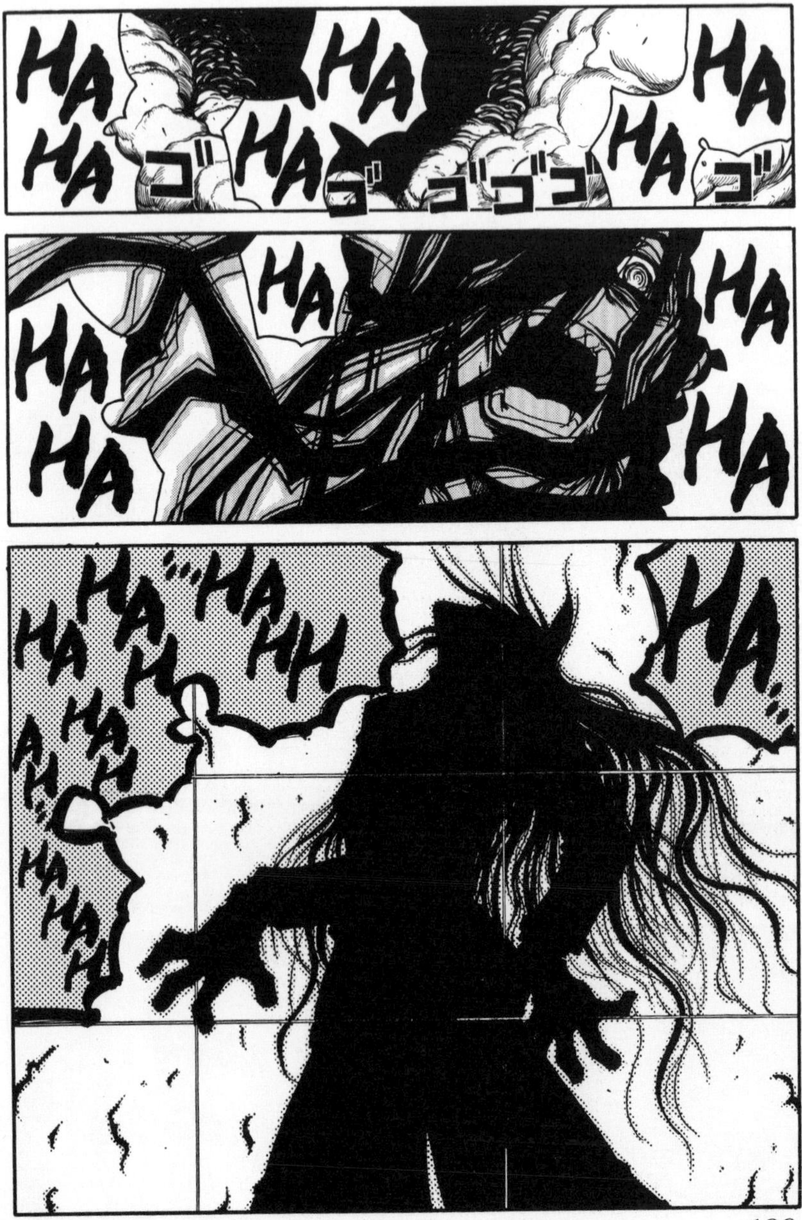
HA HA HA
ゴ
ゴゴゴ
HA HA
ゴ
HA HA
ゴ
HA HA
HA
HA HA
HA...
HA...HAHH
HA HA HAH
HAH
AH...
HA HAH

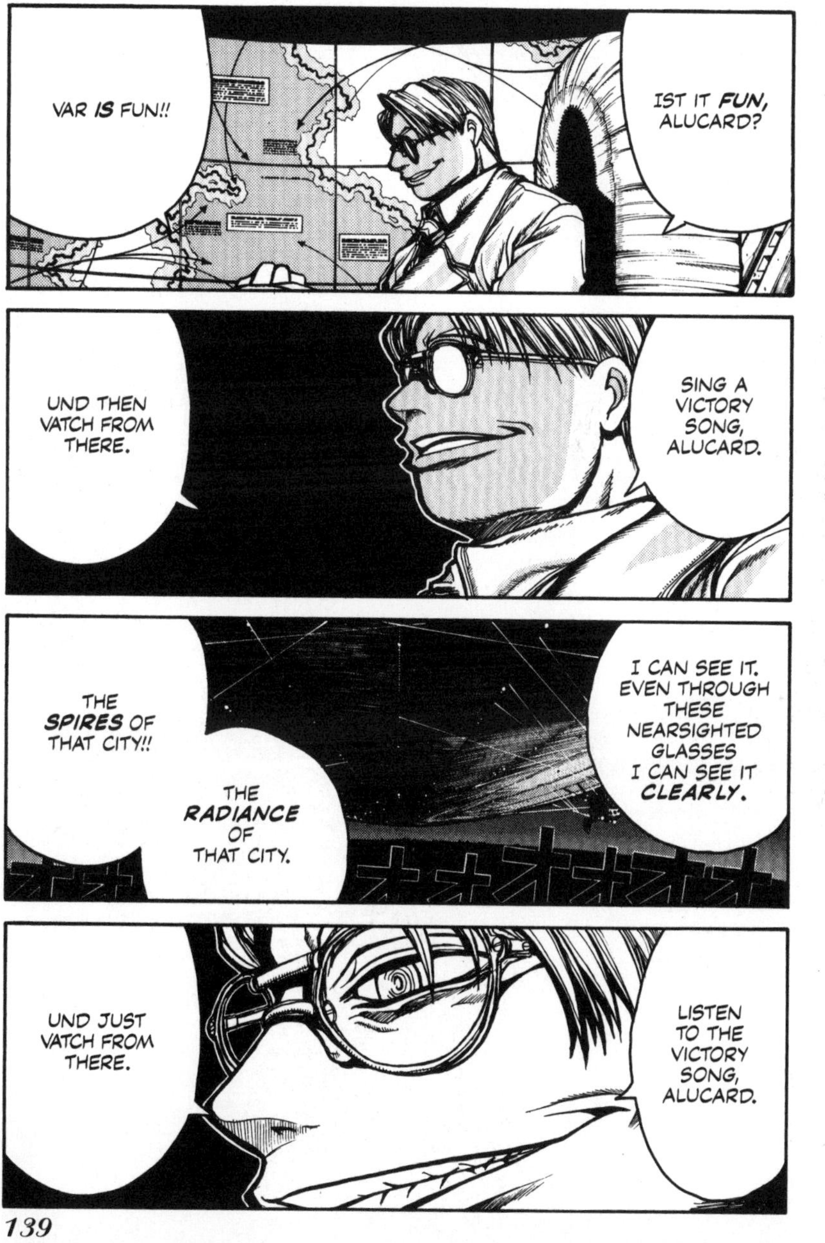
IST IT FUN, ALUCARD?
VAR IS FUN!!
SING A VICTORY SONG, ALUCARD.
UND THEN VATCH FROM THERE.
I CAN SEE IT. EVEN THROUGH THESE NEARSIGHTED GLASSES I CAN SEE IT CLEARLY.
THE SPIRES OF THAT CITY!!
THE RADIANCE OF THAT CITY.
LISTEN TO THE VICTORY SONG, ALUCARD.
UND JUST VATCH FROM THERE.

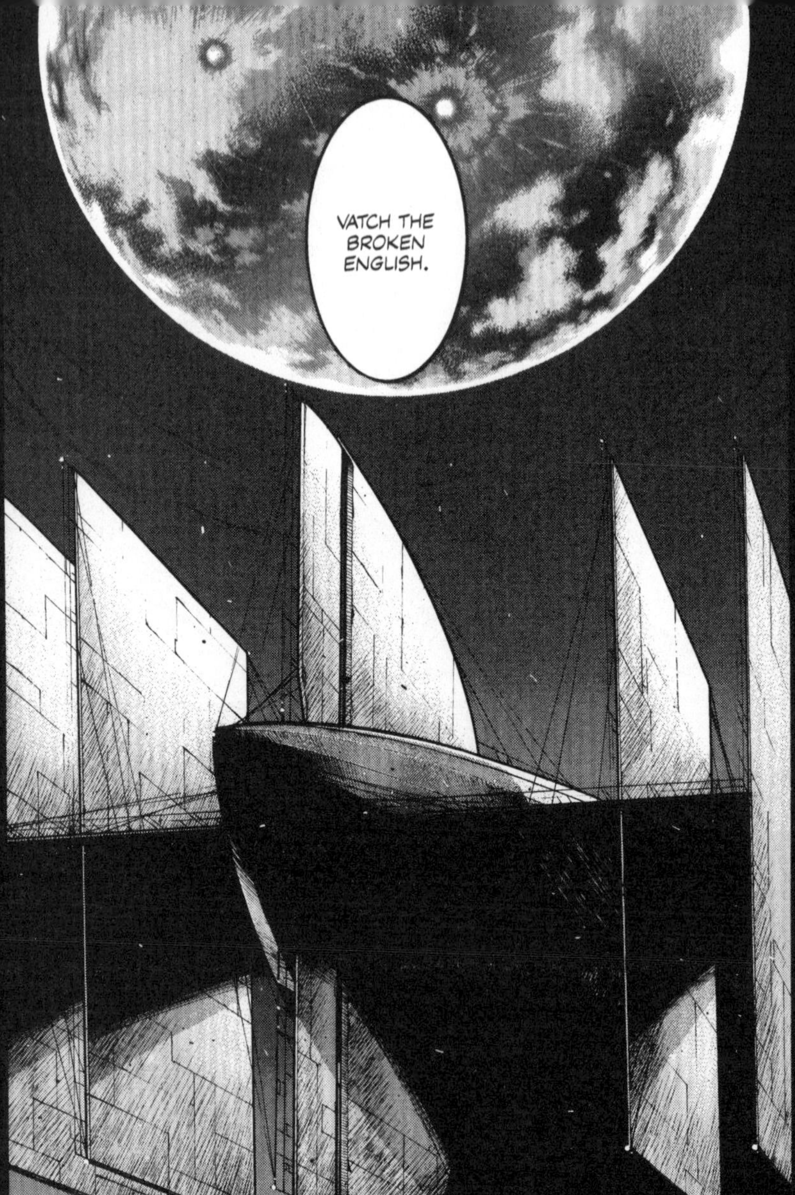
VATCH THE BROKEN ENGLISH.

ORDER 7 / END TO BE CONTINUED

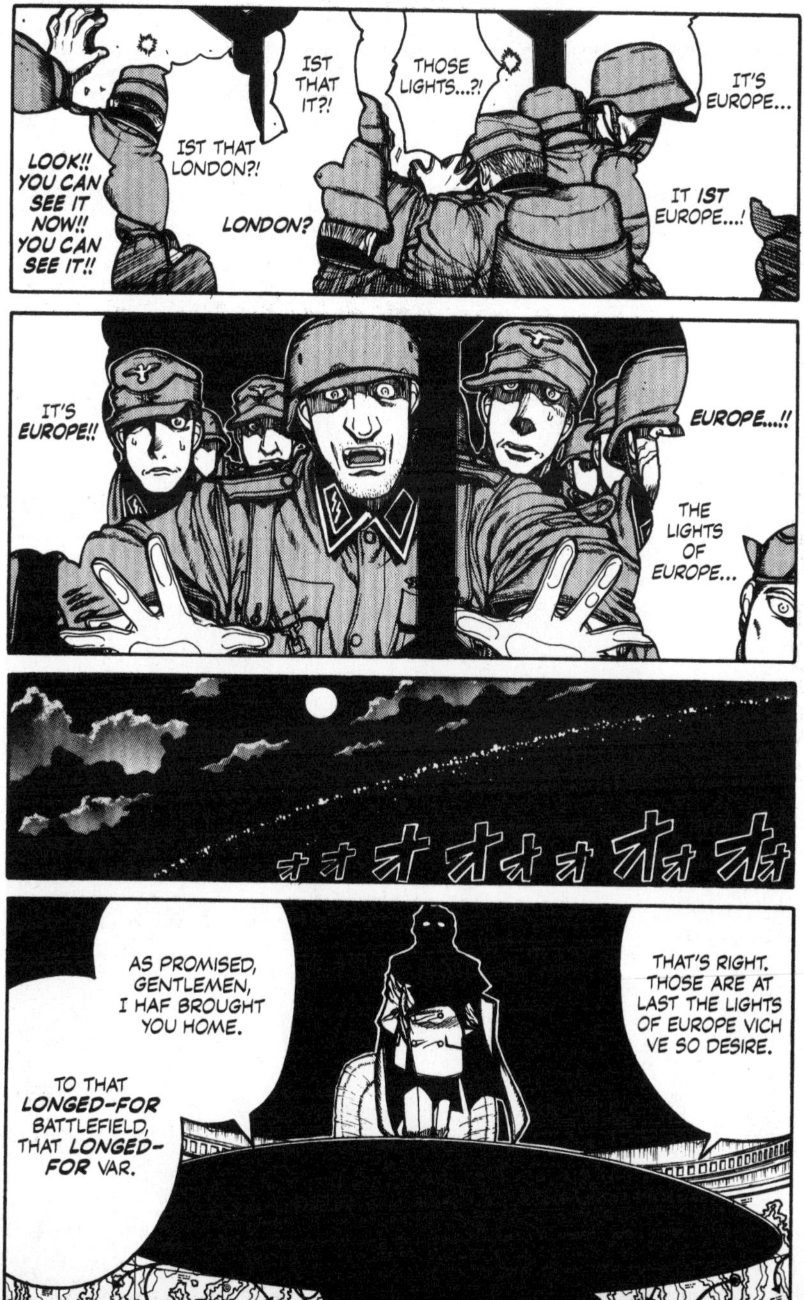
IT'S EUROPE...
IT IST EUROPE...!
THOSE LIGHTS...?!
IST THAT IT?!
IST THAT LONDON?!
LONDON?
LOOK!! YOU CAN SEE IT NOW!! YOU CAN SEE IT!!
EUROPE...!!
THE LIGHTS OF EUROPE...
IT'S EUROPE!!
ォォオオォォオォオォ
THAT'S RIGHT. THOSE ARE AT LAST THE LIGHTS OF EUROPE VICH VE SO DESIRE.
AS PROMISED, GENTLEMEN, I HAF BROUGHT YOU HOME.
TO THAT LONGED-FOR BATTLEFIELD, THAT LONGED-FOR VAR.

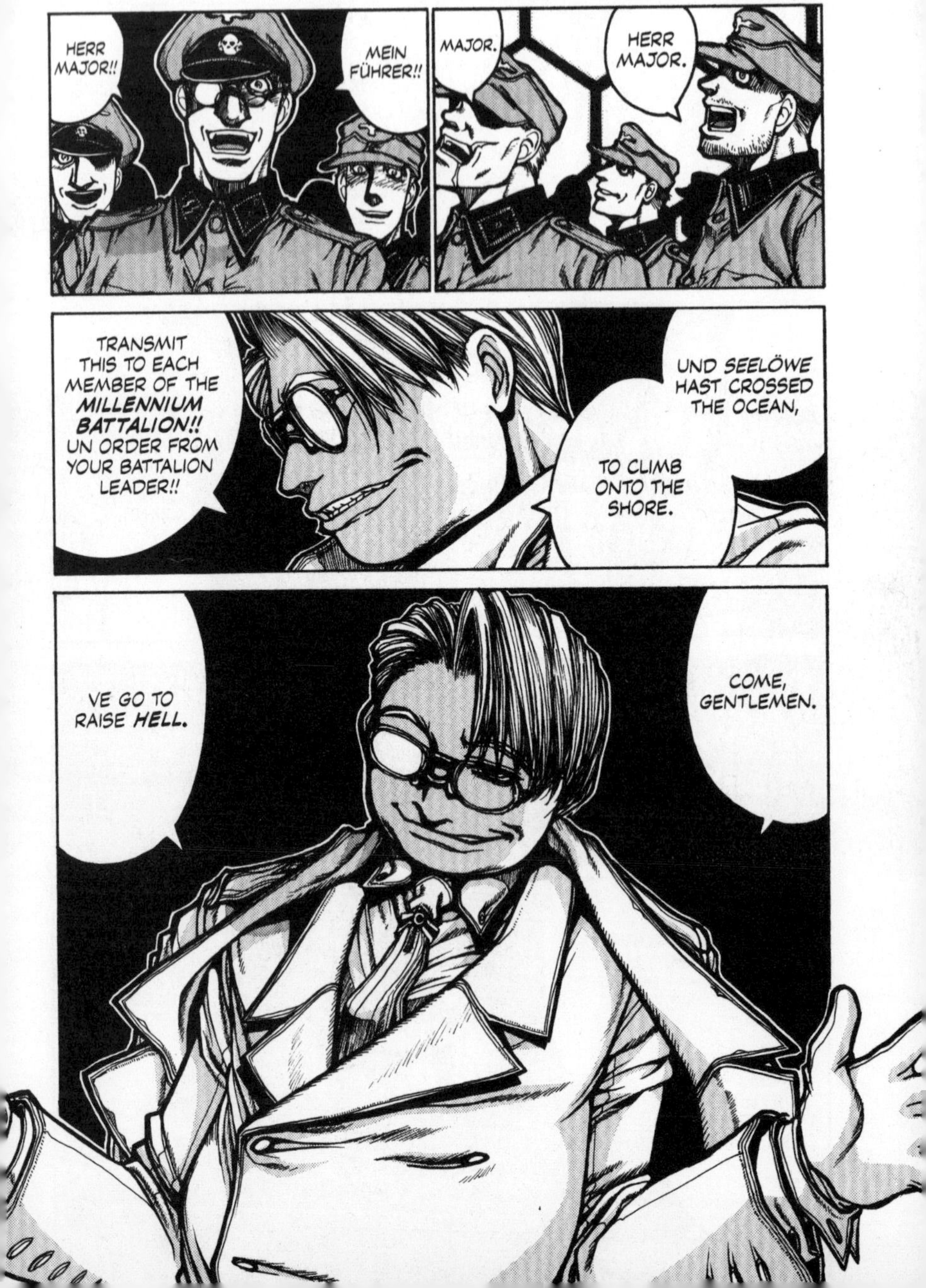
HERR MAJOR.
MAJOR.
MEIN FÜHRER!!
HERR MAJOR!!
UND SEELÖWE HAST CROSSED THE OCEAN,
TO CLIMB ONTO THE SHORE.
TRANSMIT THIS TO EACH MEMBER OF THE MILLENNIUM BATTALION!! UN ORDER FROM YOUR BATTALION LEADER!!
COME, GENTLEMEN.
VE GO TO RAISE HELL.

✤ ORDER 8
ザナドゥ
XANADO

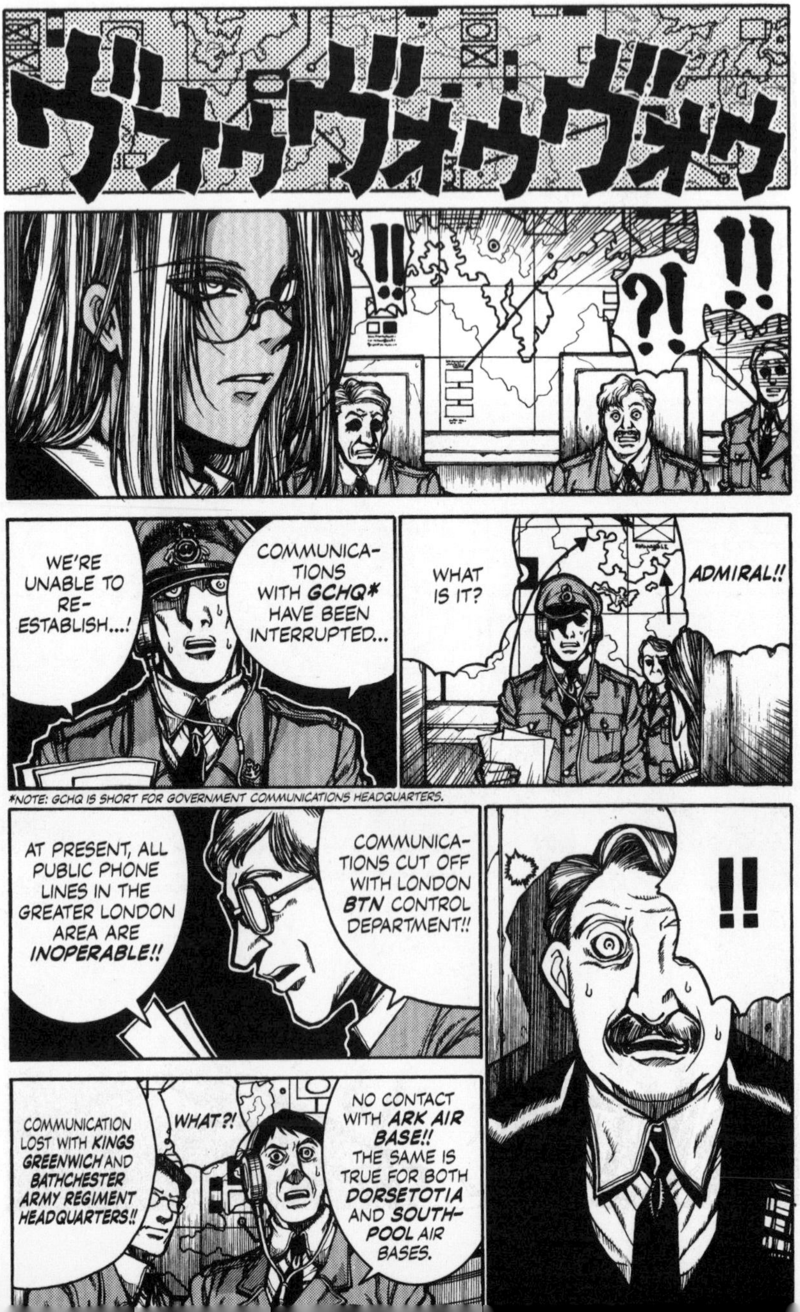
ヴォゥヴォゥヴォゥ
!!
?!
!!
ADMIRAL!!
WHAT IS IT?
COMMUNICATIONS WITH GCHQ* HAVE BEEN INTERRUPTED...
WE'RE UNABLE TO RE-ESTABLISH...!
*NOTE: GCHQ IS SHORT FOR GOVERNMENT COMMUNICATIONS HEADQUARTERS.
!!
COMMUNICATIONS CUT OFF WITH LONDON BTN CONTROL DEPARTMENT!!
AT PRESENT, ALL PUBLIC PHONE LINES IN THE GREATER LONDON AREA ARE INOPERABLE!!
NO CONTACT WITH ARK AIR BASE!! THE SAME IS TRUE FOR BOTH DORSETOTIA AND SOUTH-POOL AIR BASES.
WHAT?!
COMMUNICATION LOST WITH KINGS GREENWICH AND BATHCHESTER ARMY REGIMENT HEADQUARTERS!!

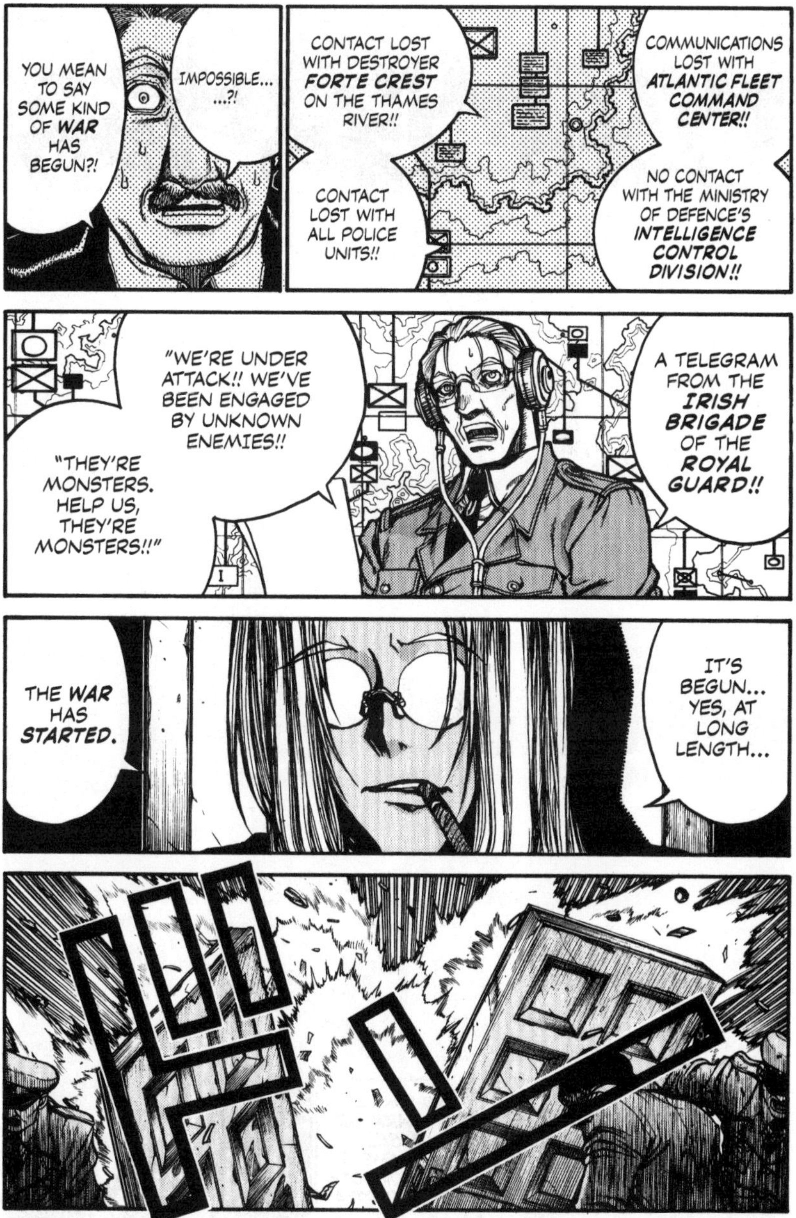
COMMUNICATIONS LOST WITH ATLANTIC FLEET COMMAND CENTER!!
CONTACT LOST WITH DESTROYER FORTE CREST ON THE THAMES RIVER!!
NO CONTACT WITH THE MINISTRY OF DEFENCE'S INTELLIGENCE CONTROL DIVISION!!
CONTACT LOST WITH ALL POLICE UNITS!!
IMPOSSIBLE... ...?!
YOU MEAN TO SAY SOME KIND OF WAR HAS BEGUN?!
A TELEGRAM FROM THE IRISH BRIGADE OF THE ROYAL GUARD!!
"WE'RE UNDER ATTACK!! WE'VE BEEN ENGAGED BY UNKNOWN ENEMIES!!
"THEY'RE MONSTERS. HELP US, THEY'RE MONSTERS!!"
IT'S BEGUN... YES, AT LONG LENGTH...
THE WAR HAS STARTED.

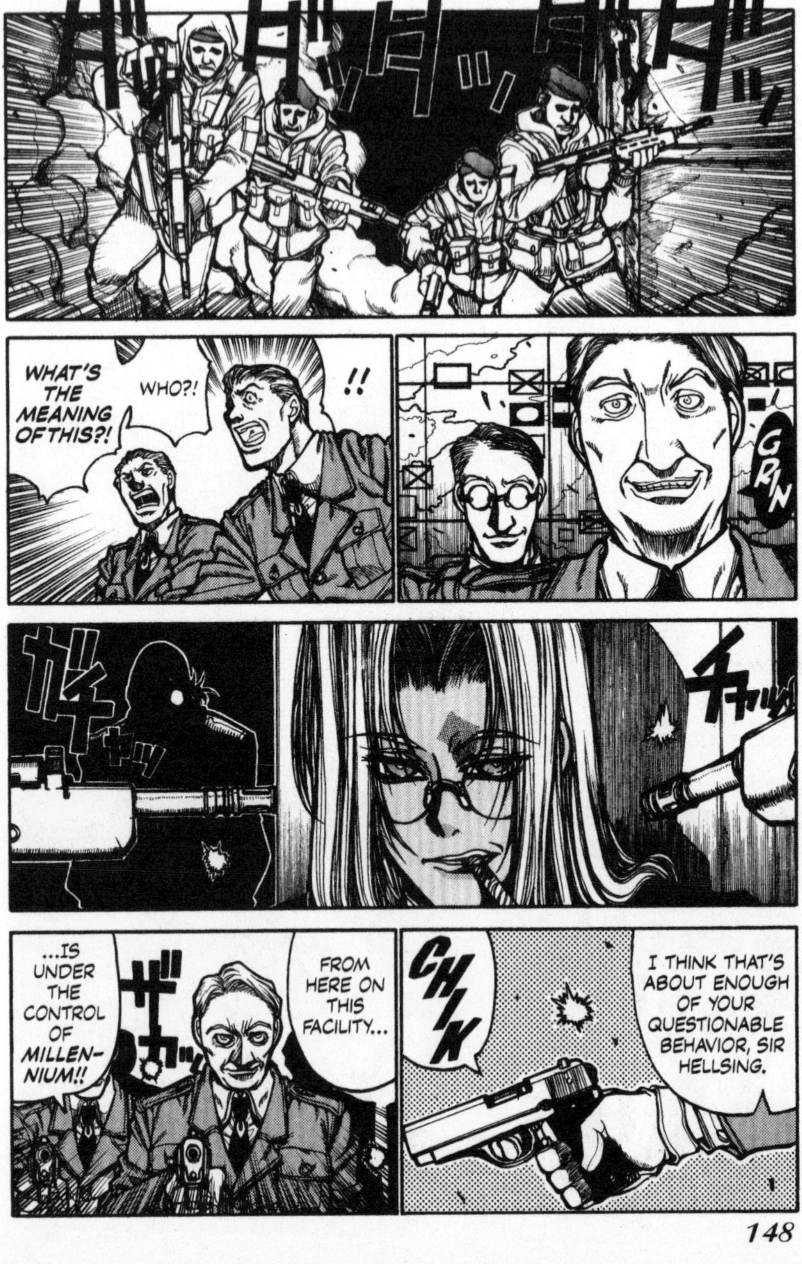
GRIN
!!
WHO?!
WHAT'S THE MEANING OF THIS?!
I THINK THAT'S ABOUT ENOUGH OF YOUR QUESTIONABLE BEHAVIOR, SIR HELLSING.
CHIK
FROM HERE ON THIS FACILITY...
...IS UNDER THE CONTROL OF MILLENNIUM!!

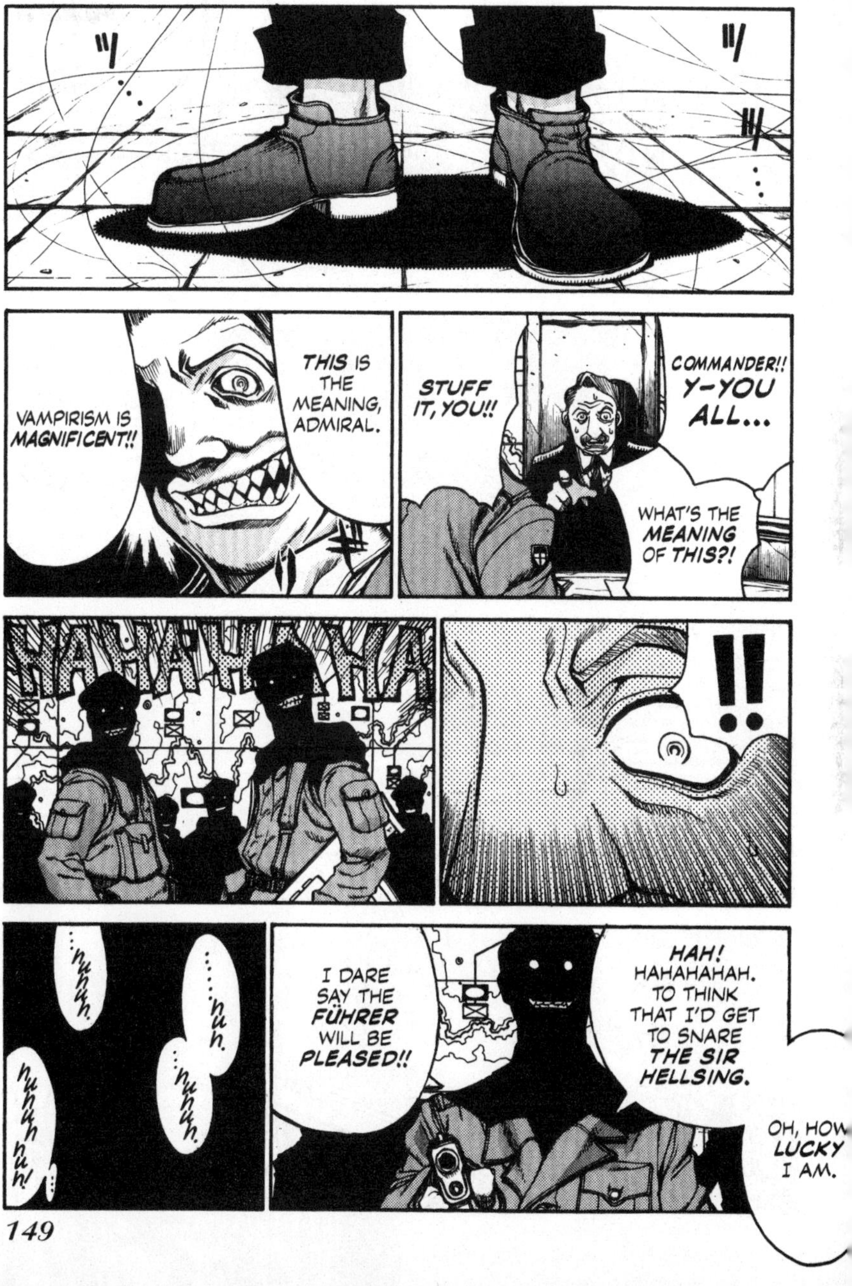

COMMANDER!! Y-YOU ALL...
WHAT'S THE MEANING OF THIS?!
STUFF IT, YOU!!
THIS IS THE MEANING, ADMIRAL.
VAMPIRISM IS MAGNIFICENT!!
!!
HAH! HAHAHAHAH. TO THINK THAT I'D GET TO SNARE THE SIR HELLSING.
OH, HOW LUCKY I AM.
I DARE SAY THE FÜHRER WILL BE PLEASED!!
...nun nun.
.....nun.
...nun nun.
nun nun nun nun!...

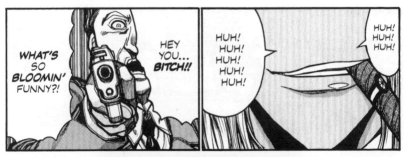

HUH! HUH! HUH!
HUH! HUH! HUH! HUH! HUH!
HEY YOU... BITCH!!
WHAT'S SO BLOOMIN' FUNNY?!
AS VAMPIRES, YOU LOT ARE ALIKE TO NEW-BORN BABES, AND WE ARE AN ORGANIZATION DEVOTED TO EXTERMINATING VAMPIRES.
A BABY FROG, STILL WITH ITS TAIL, SAYS "I'M LUCKY" IN THE FACE OF A SERPENT.
THAT WAS AN AMUSING JOKE, TRAITOR.
MAY YOU RECEIVE YOUR IRON CROSS FROM YOUR CORPORAL IN THE AFTERLIFE.
YOU...
...BLOODY WHORRRRE!
チキッ
ピ
ッ

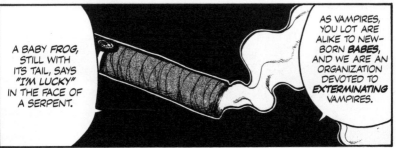

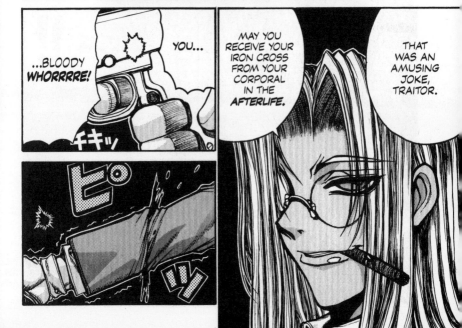

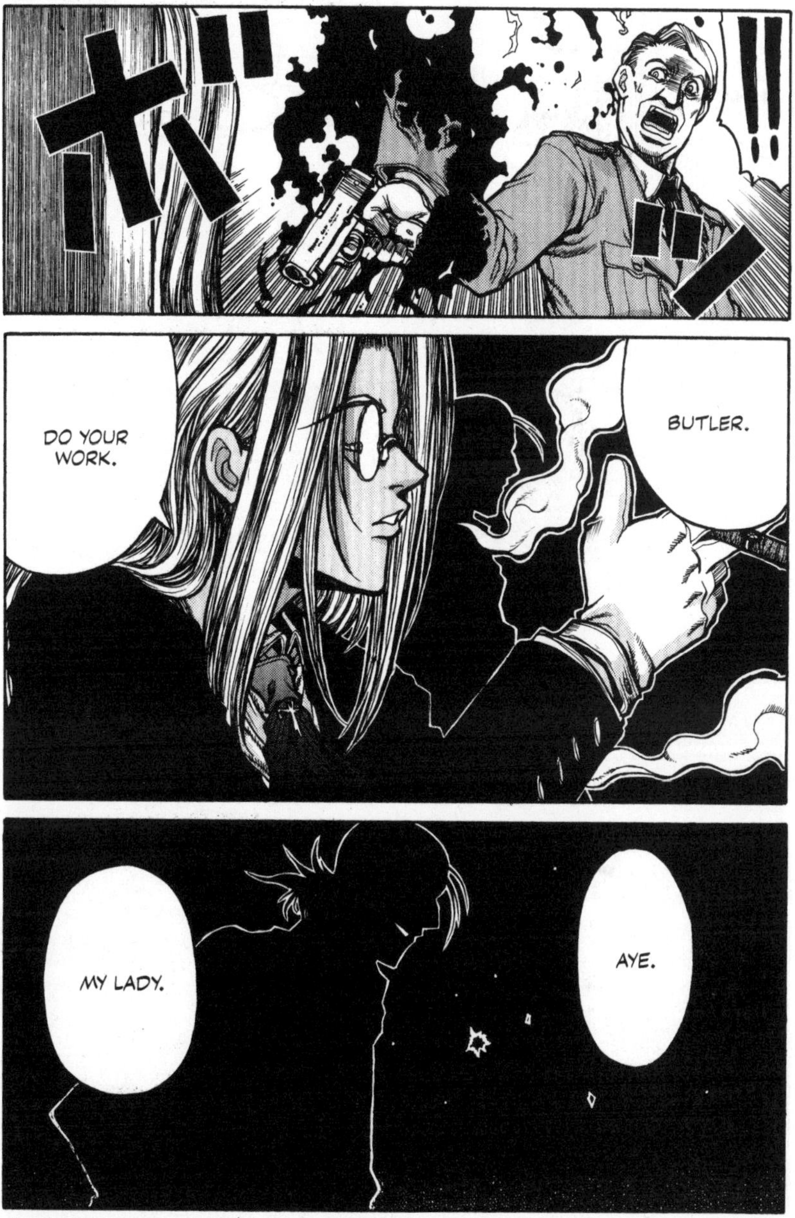
!!
BUTLER.
DO YOUR WORK.
AYE.
MY LADY.

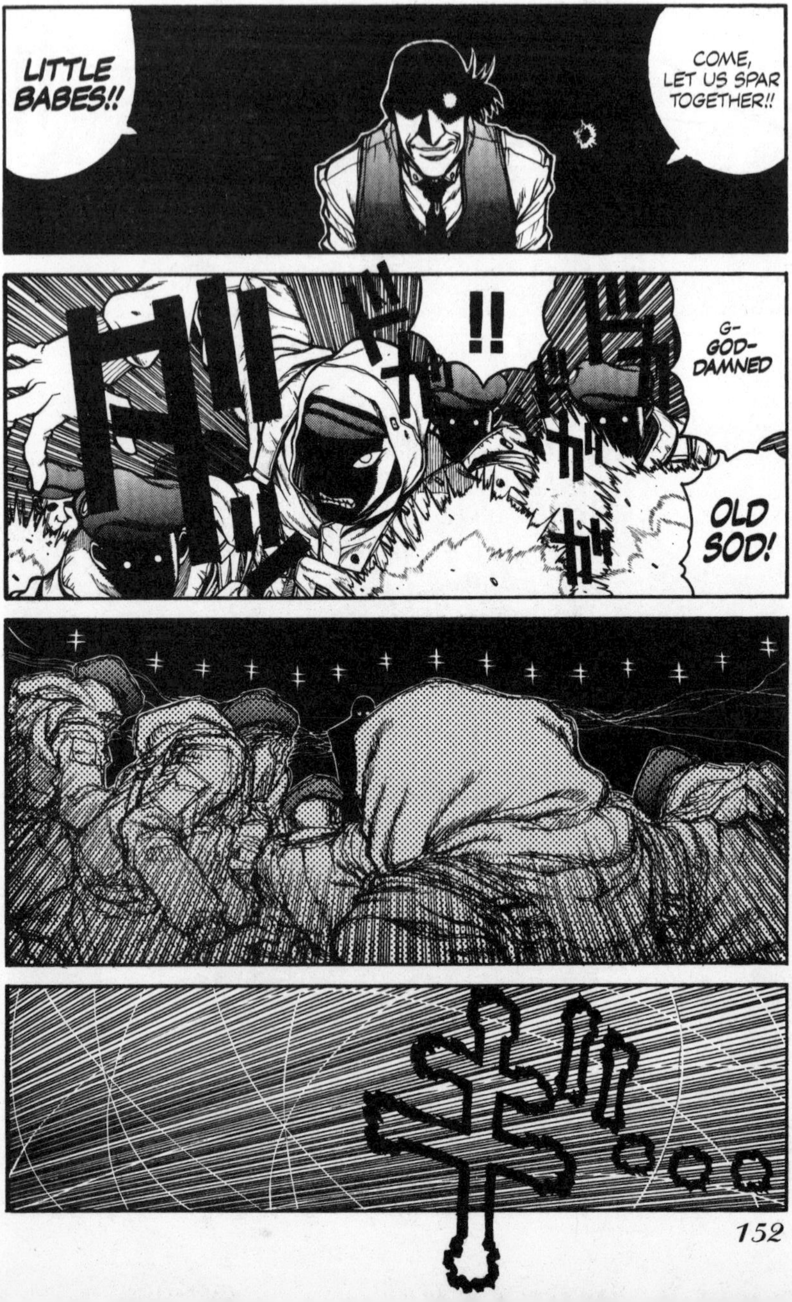
COME, LET US SPAR TOGETHER!!
LITTLE BABES!!
!!
G-GOD-DAMNED
OLD SOD!

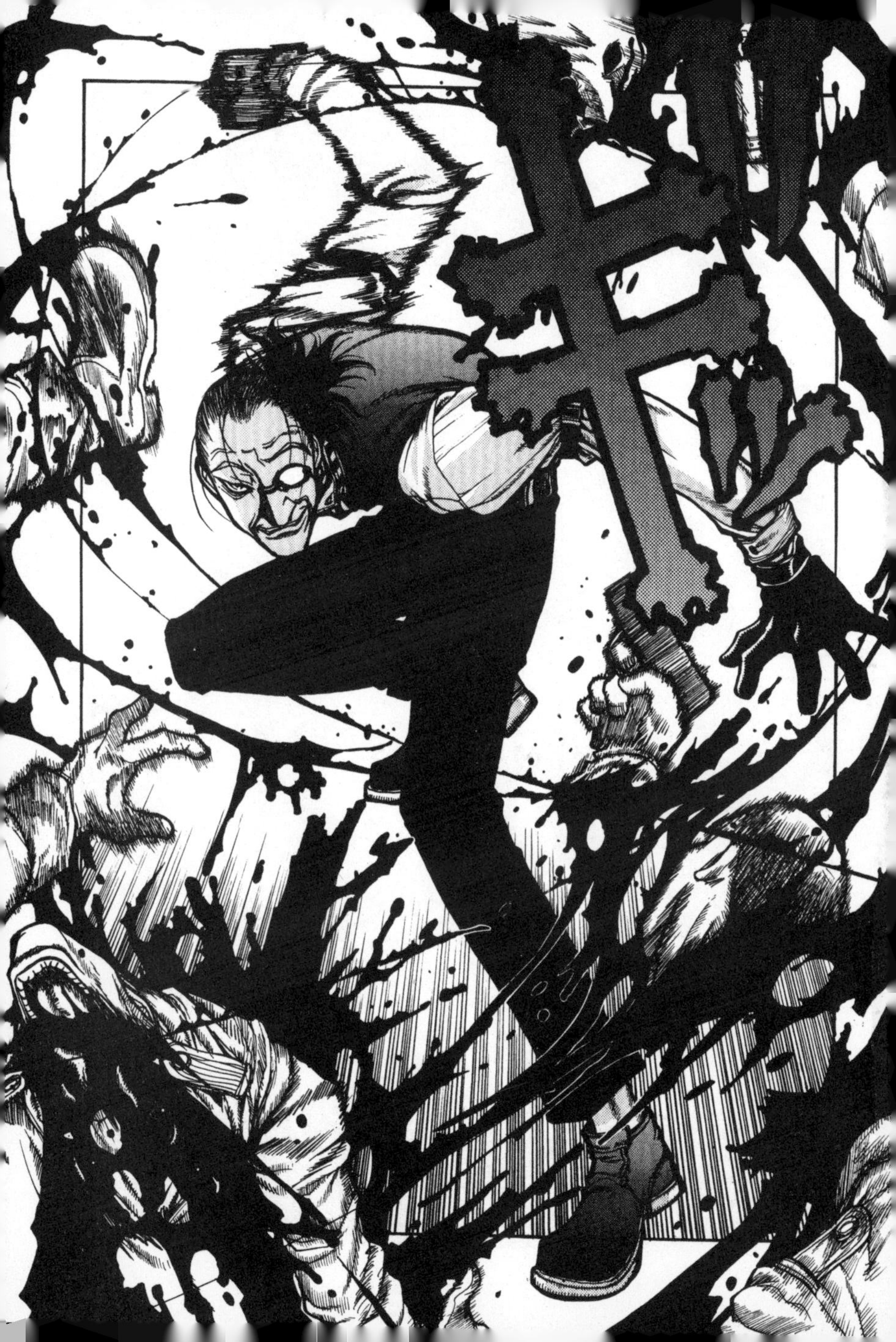

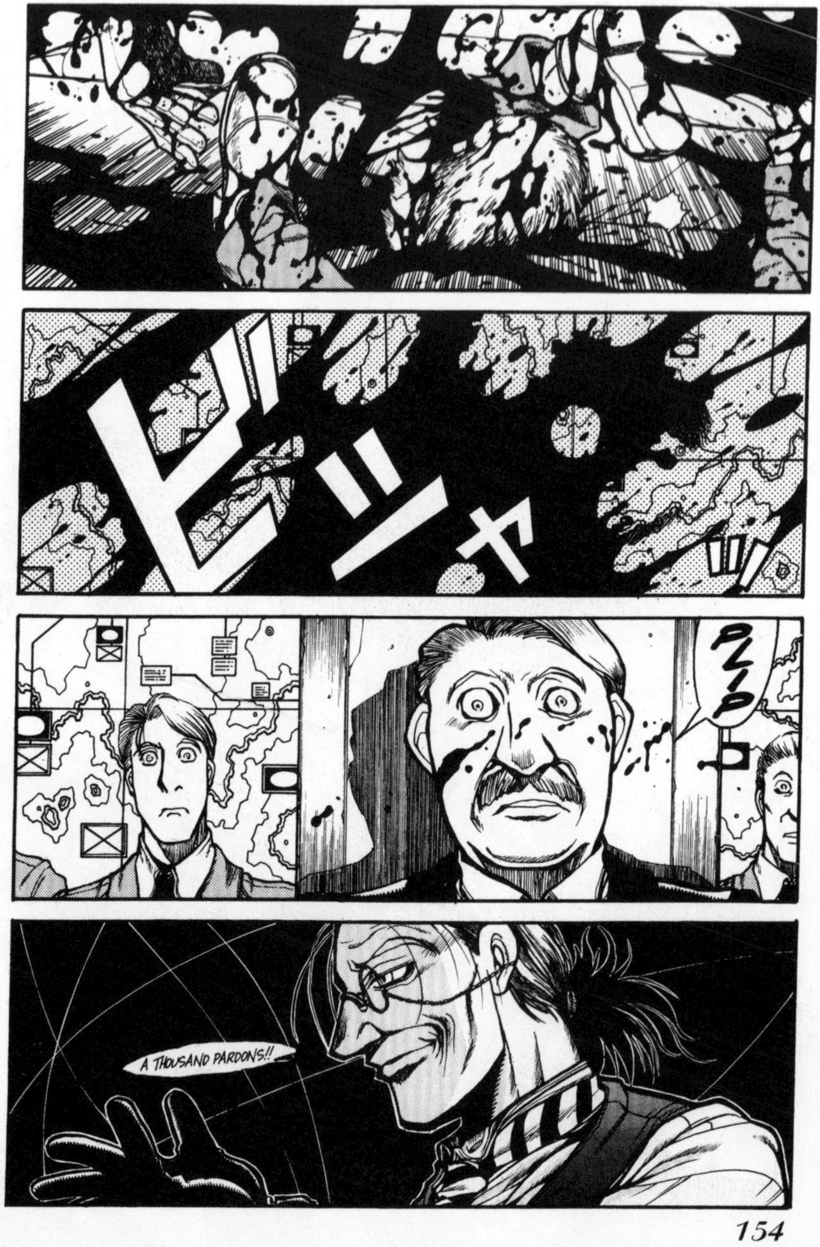
ビシャ!!
PLIP
A THOUSAND PARDONS!!

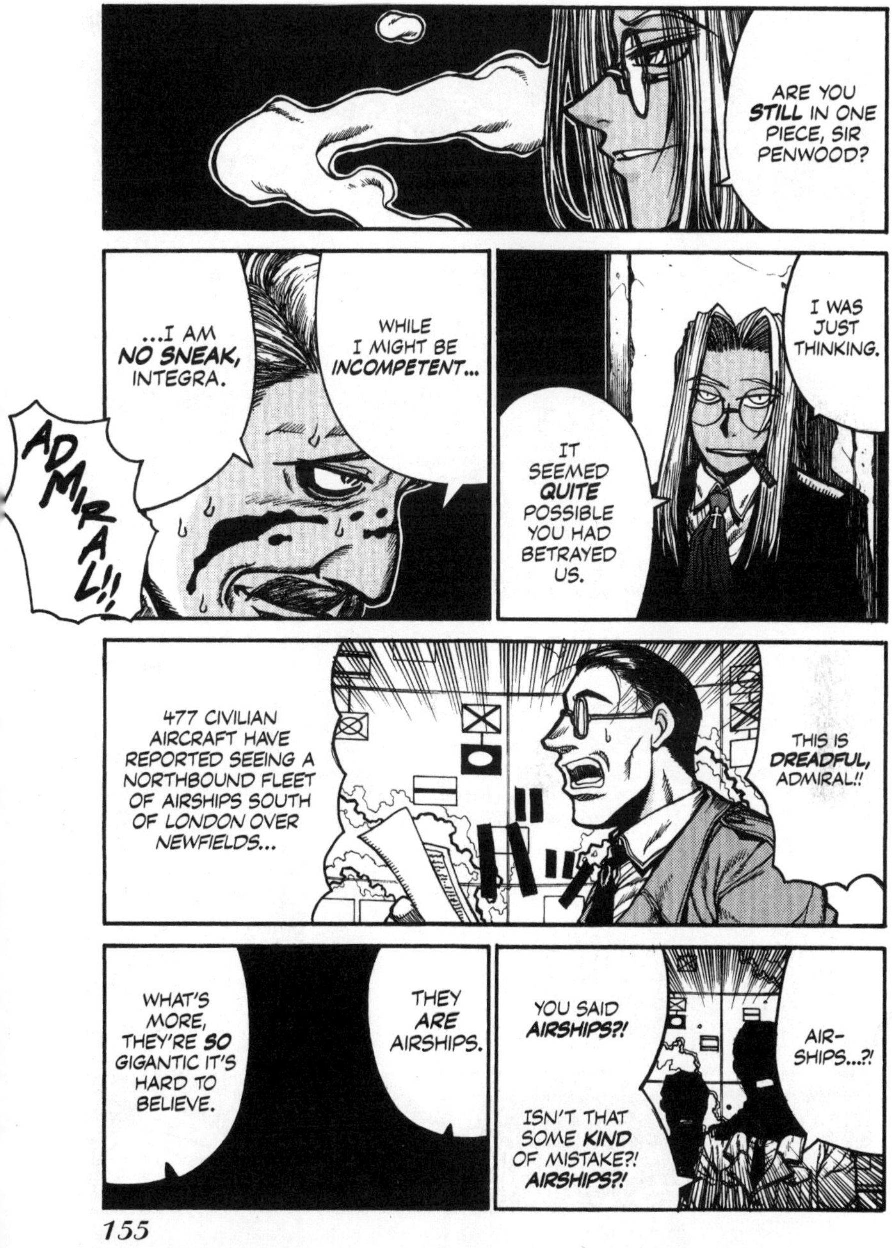
ARE YOU STILL IN ONE PIECE, SIR PENWOOD?
I WAS JUST THINKING.
IT SEEMED QUITE POSSIBLE YOU HAD BETRAYED US.
WHILE I MIGHT BE INCOMPETENT...
...I AM NO SNEAK, INTEGRA.
ADMIRAL!!
THIS IS DREADFUL, ADMIRAL!!
477 CIVILIAN AIRCRAFT HAVE REPORTED SEEING A NORTHBOUND FLEET OF AIRSHIPS SOUTH OF LONDON OVER NEWFIELDS...
AIR-SHIPS...?!
YOU SAID AIRSHIPS?!
ISN'T THAT SOME KIND OF MISTAKE?! AIRSHIPS?!
THEY ARE AIRSHIPS.
WHAT'S MORE, THEY'RE SO GIGANTIC IT'S HARD TO BELIEVE.

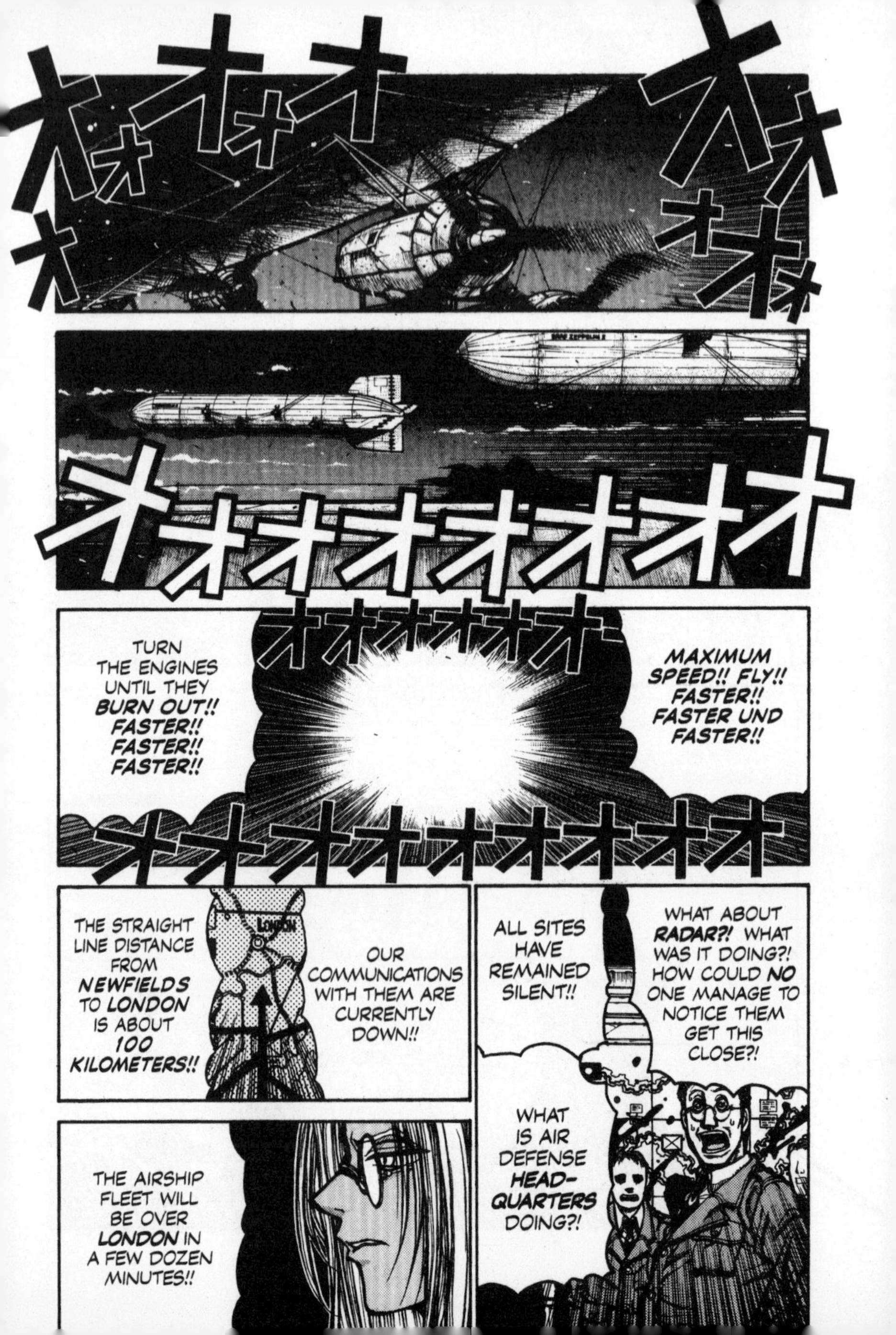
オォォォ
オォォォオ
オォオオオオオオ
オオオオオオオ
MAXIMUM SPEED!! FLY!! FASTER!! FASTER UND FASTER!!
TURN THE ENGINES UNTIL THEY BURN OUT!! FASTER!! FASTER!! FASTER!!
オオオオオオオオオオ
WHAT ABOUT RADAR?! WHAT WAS IT DOING?! HOW COULD NO ONE MANAGE TO NOTICE THEM GET THIS CLOSE?!
ALL SITES HAVE REMAINED SILENT!!
WHAT IS AIR DEFENSE HEAD-QUARTERS DOING?!
OUR COMMUNICATIONS WITH THEM ARE CURRENTLY DOWN!!
LONDON
THE STRAIGHT LINE DISTANCE FROM NEWFIELDS TO LONDON IS ABOUT 100 KILOMETERS!!
THE AIRSHIP FLEET WILL BE OVER LONDON IN A FEW DOZEN MINUTES!!

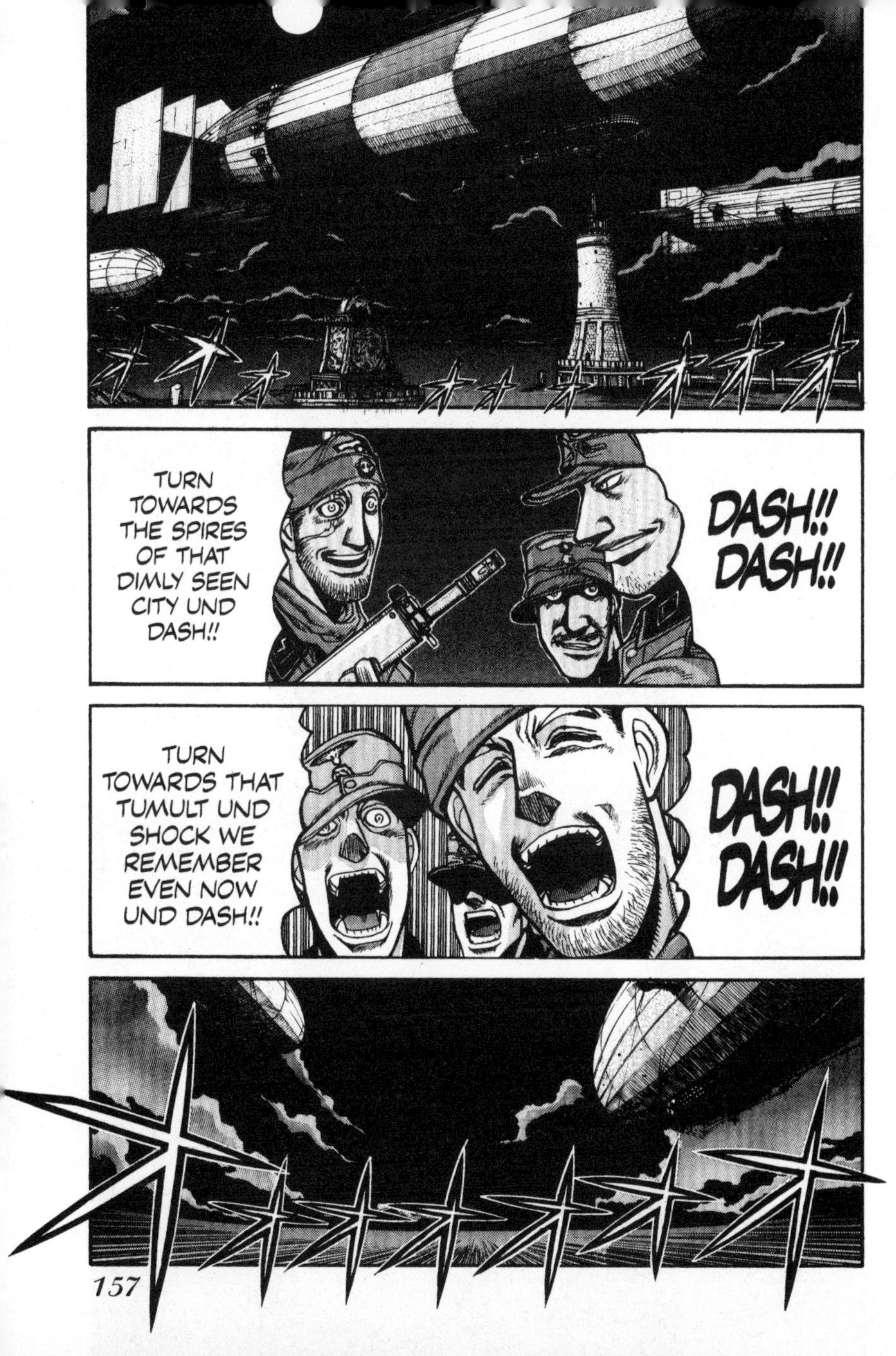
TURN TOWARDS THE SPIRES OF THAT DIMLY SEEN CITY UND DASH!!
DASH!! DASH!!
TURN TOWARDS THAT TUMULT UND SHOCK WE REMEMBER EVEN NOW UND DASH!!
DASH!! DASH!!

オオオオオオオ
All flesh is as grass, and all the glory of man as the flower of the grass. Because
The grass withers, and its flower fall away
Amen!!

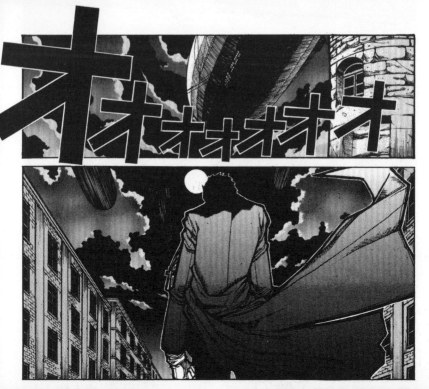

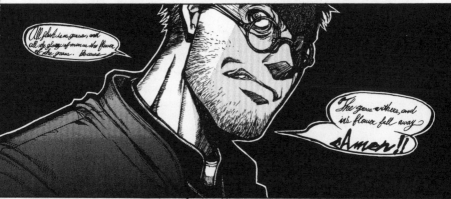

TO BE CONTINUED

ORDER 8 / END

ORDER 9

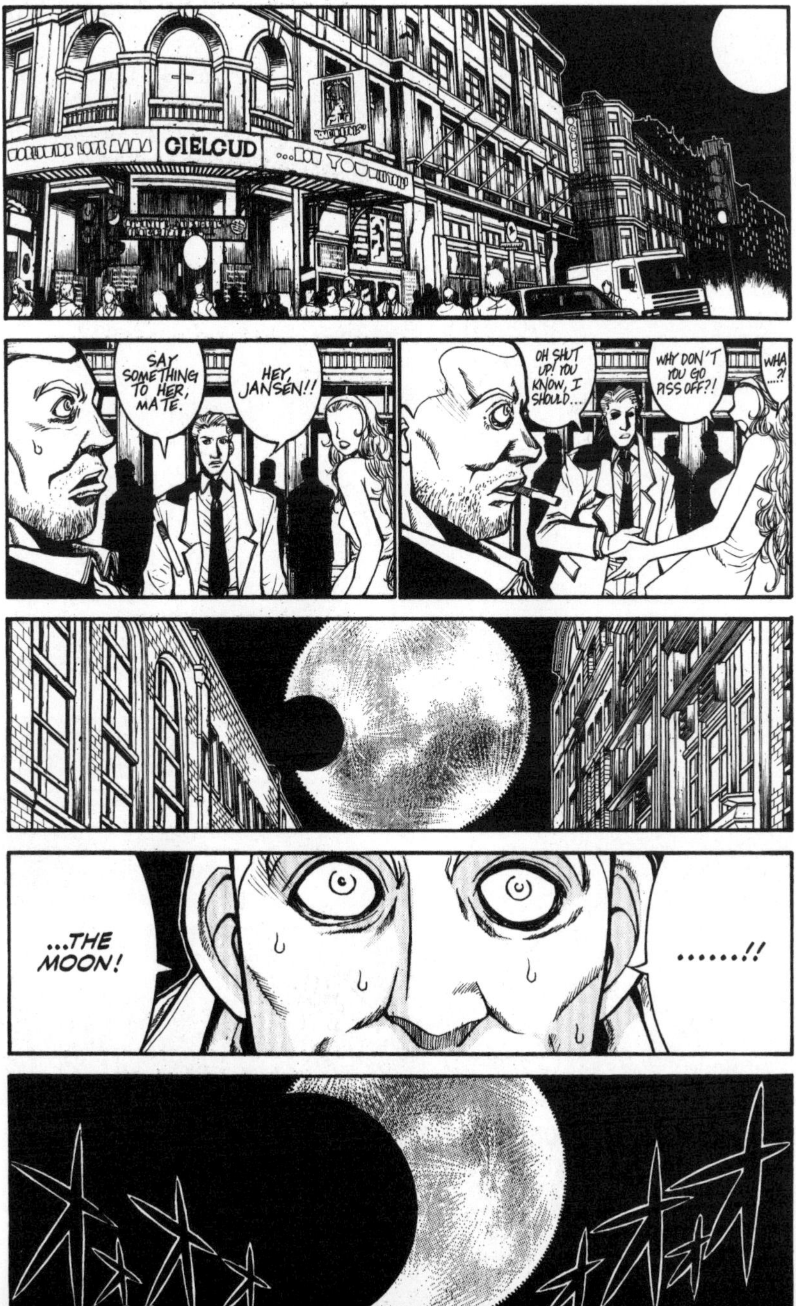
GIELGUD
SAY SOMETHING TO HER, MATE.
HEY, JANSEN!!
OH SHUT UP! YOU KNOW, I SHOULD...
WHY DON'T YOU GO PISS OFF?!
WHA...?!
...THE MOON!
......!!

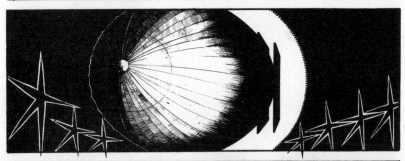

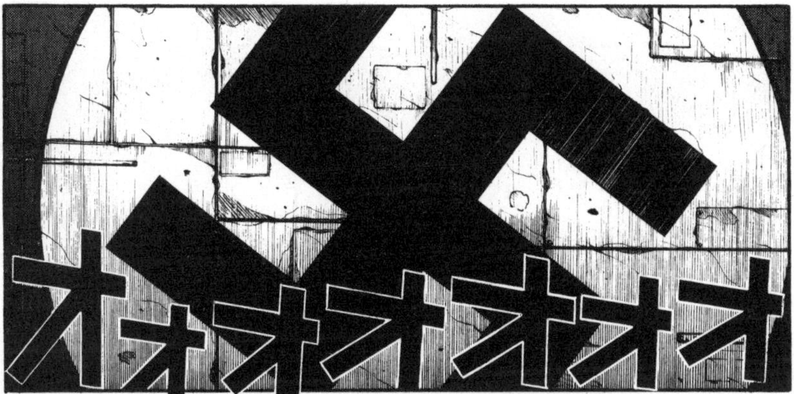
オォオオオオ
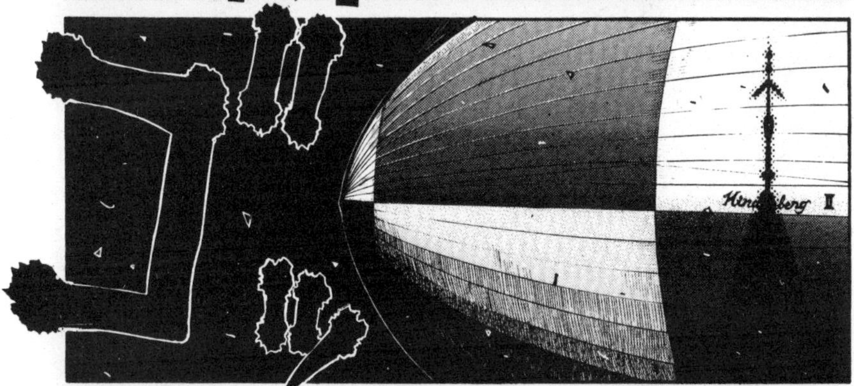
ゴ
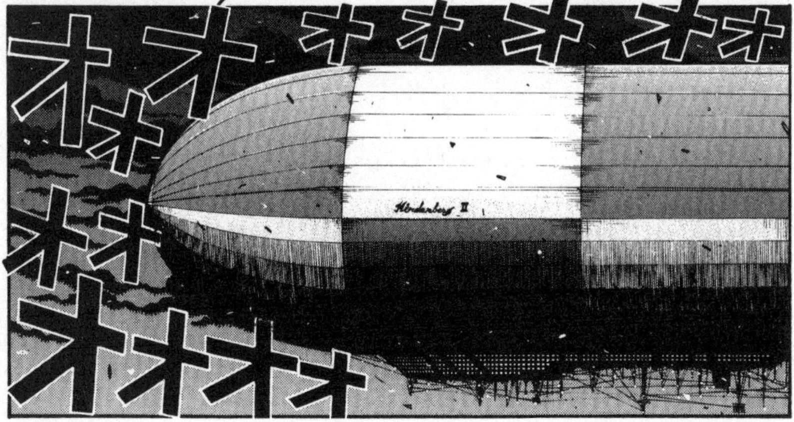
オオォォオオオォ
オォオオオオオォ
Hindenberg II

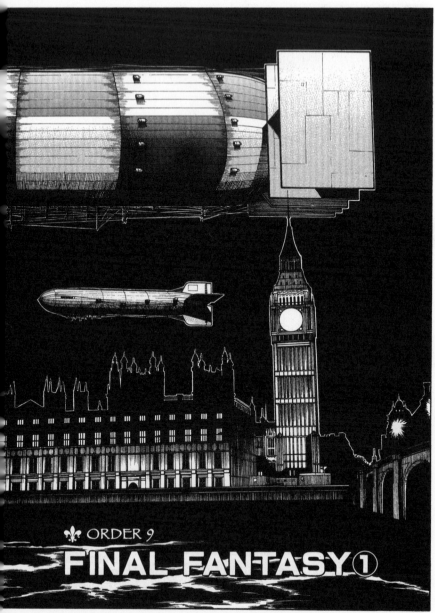

ORDER 9
FINAL FANTASY ①

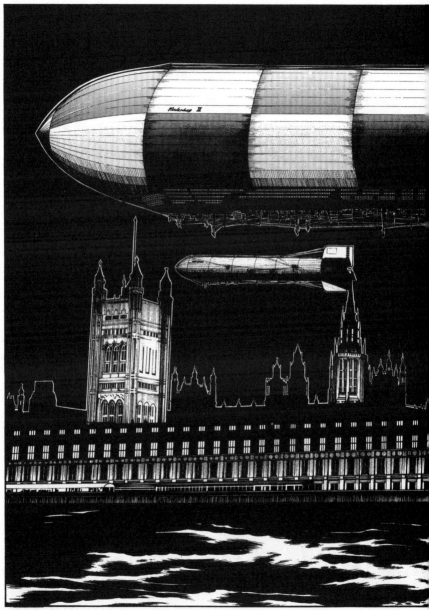

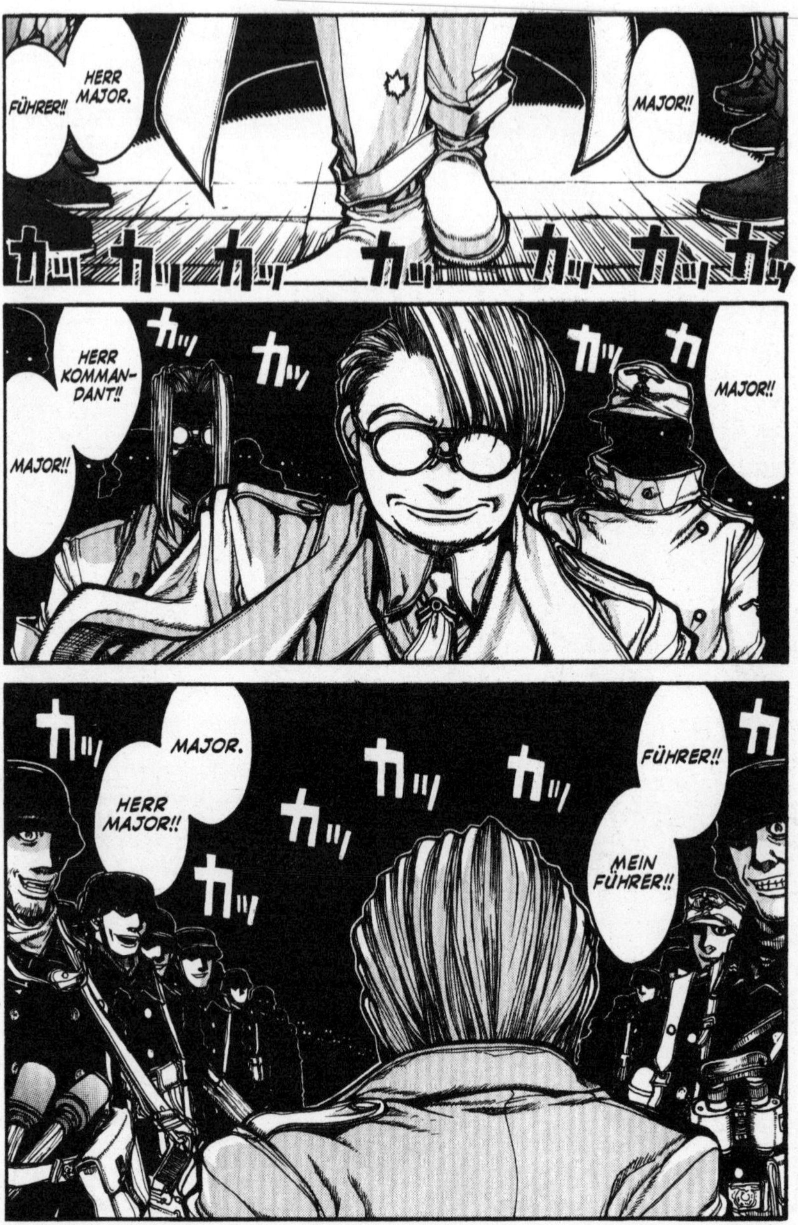
MAJOR!!
HERR MAJOR.
FÜHRER!!
カッ カッ カッ カッ カッ カッ カッ
カ
カッ
MAJOR!!
カッ
カッ
HERR KOMMAN-DANT!!
MAJOR!!
カ
FÜHRER!!
MEIN FÜHRER!!
カッ
カッ
カッ
MAJOR.
HERR MAJOR!!
カッ
カッ

ACHTUNG!!

ALL BATTALION MEMBERS!

NIGHT HAST COME.

GENTLEMEN.

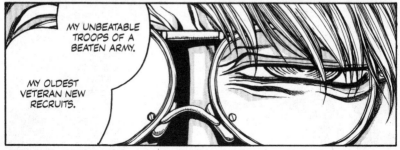

MY UNBEATABLE TROOPS OF A BEATEN ARMY.

MY OLDEST VETERAN NEW RECRUITS.

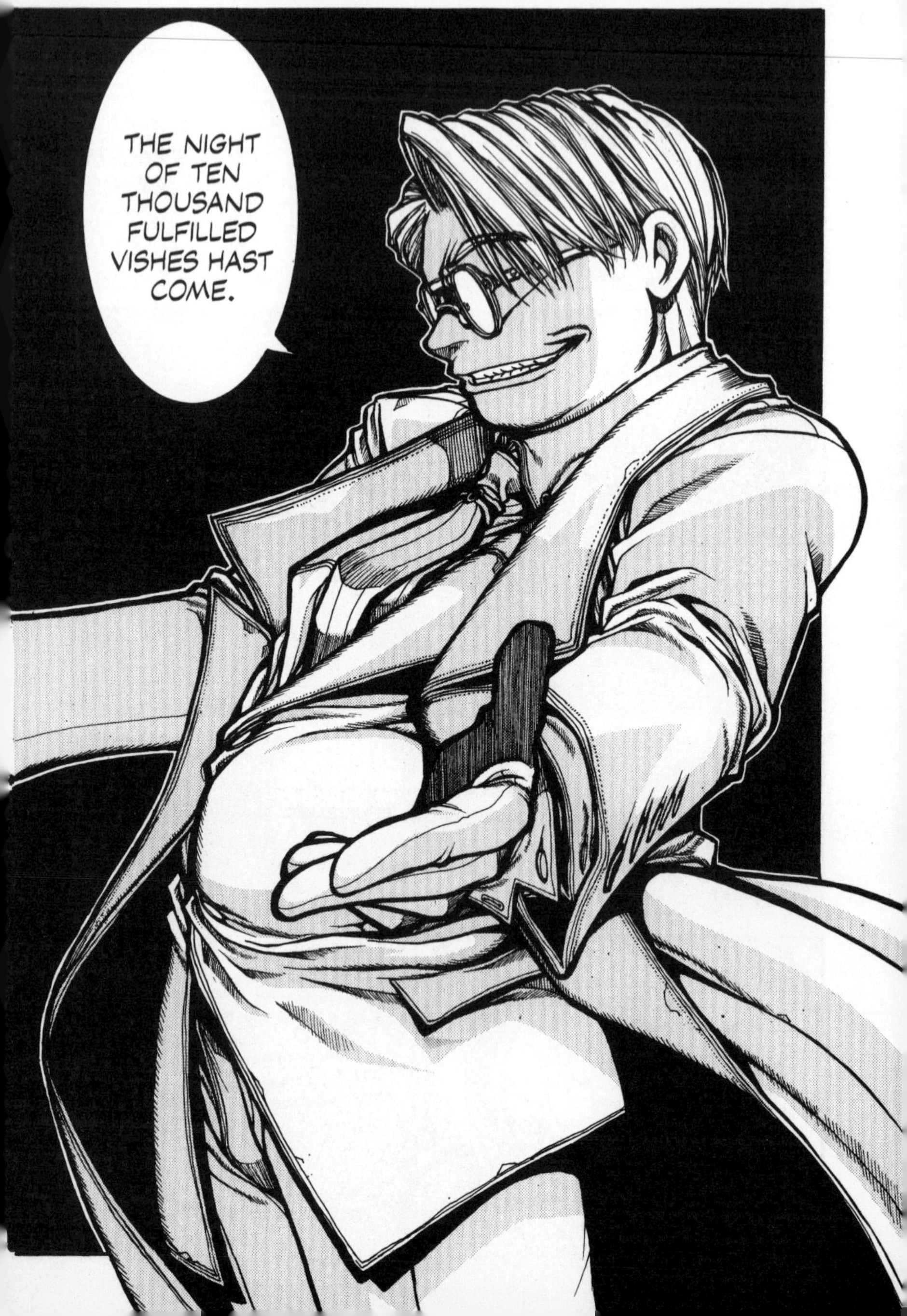
THE NIGHT OF TEN THOUSAND FULFILLED VISHES HAST COME.

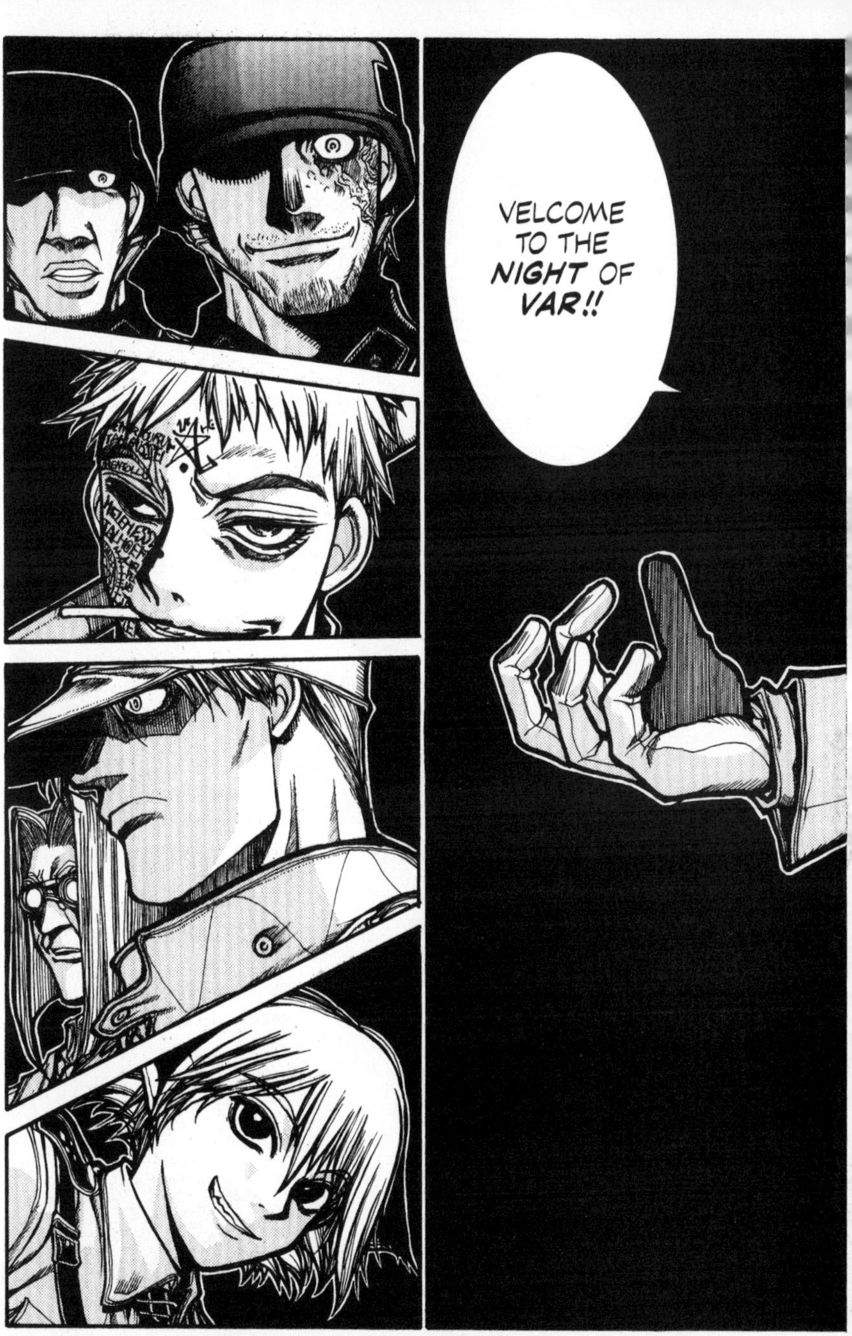
VELCOME TO THE NIGHT OF VAR!!

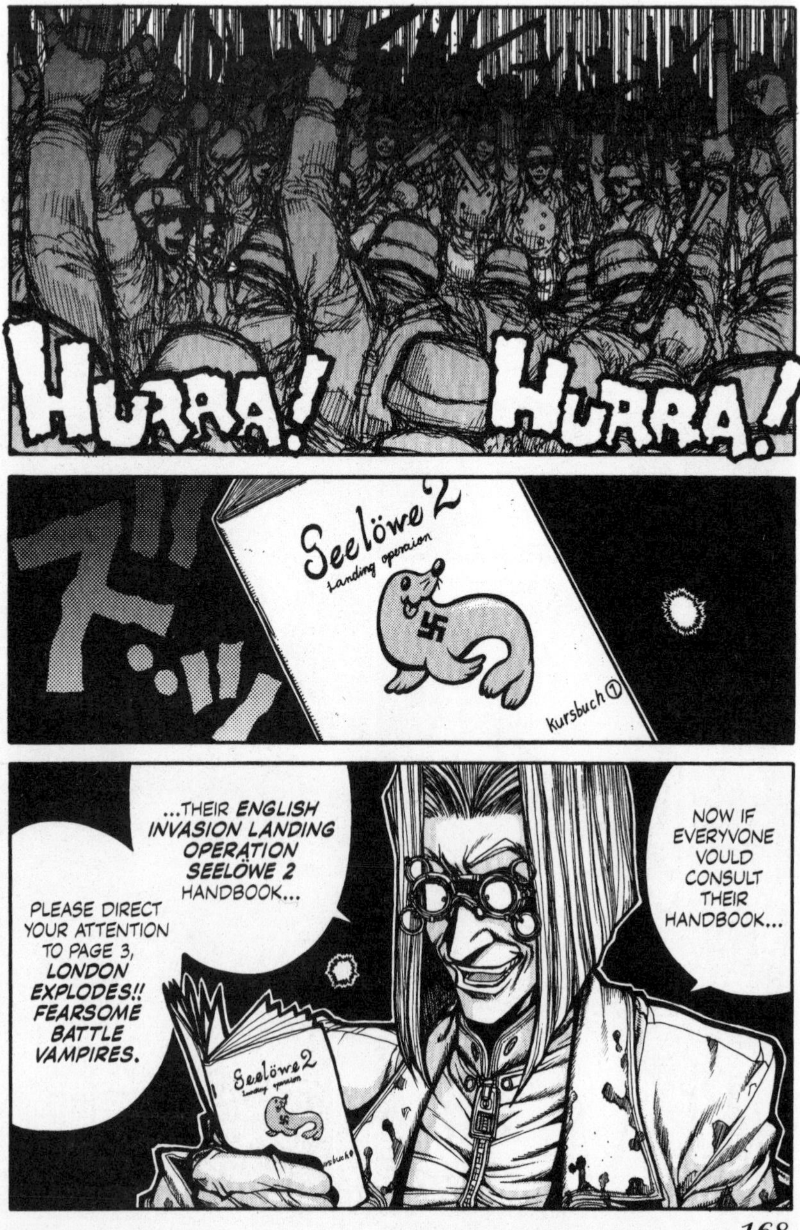
HURRA! HURRA!
Seelöwe 2
landing operation
Kursbuch ①
NOW IF EVERYVONE VOULD CONSULT THEIR HANDBOOK...
...THEIR ENGLISH INVASION LANDING OPERATION SEELÖWE 2 HANDBOOK...
PLEASE DIRECT YOUR ATTENTION TO PAGE 3, LONDON EXPLODES!! FEARSOME BATTLE VAMPIRES.

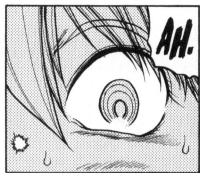

ごそ ごそ ごそごそ
AH.
UH... UMMM.
OHHH DEAR, VATEVER **IS** THE MATTER, SCHRÖ-DINGER?
UH OHHH.
VAT ARE YOU DOING...?
I'M SORRY.
I LOST MY HANDBOOK...
ANGH!! AH, FINE THEN. THERE'S NO FIXING IT NOW.
HAF THE CAPTAIN SHOW YOU HIS.
そ～～ッ
WOWWW.

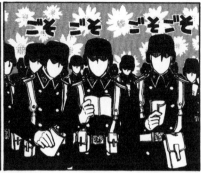

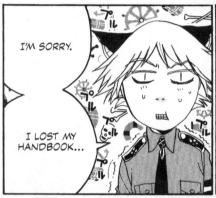

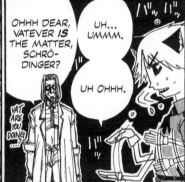

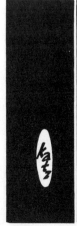

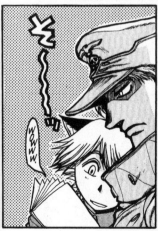

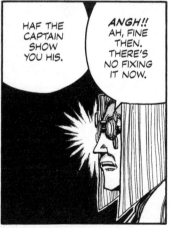

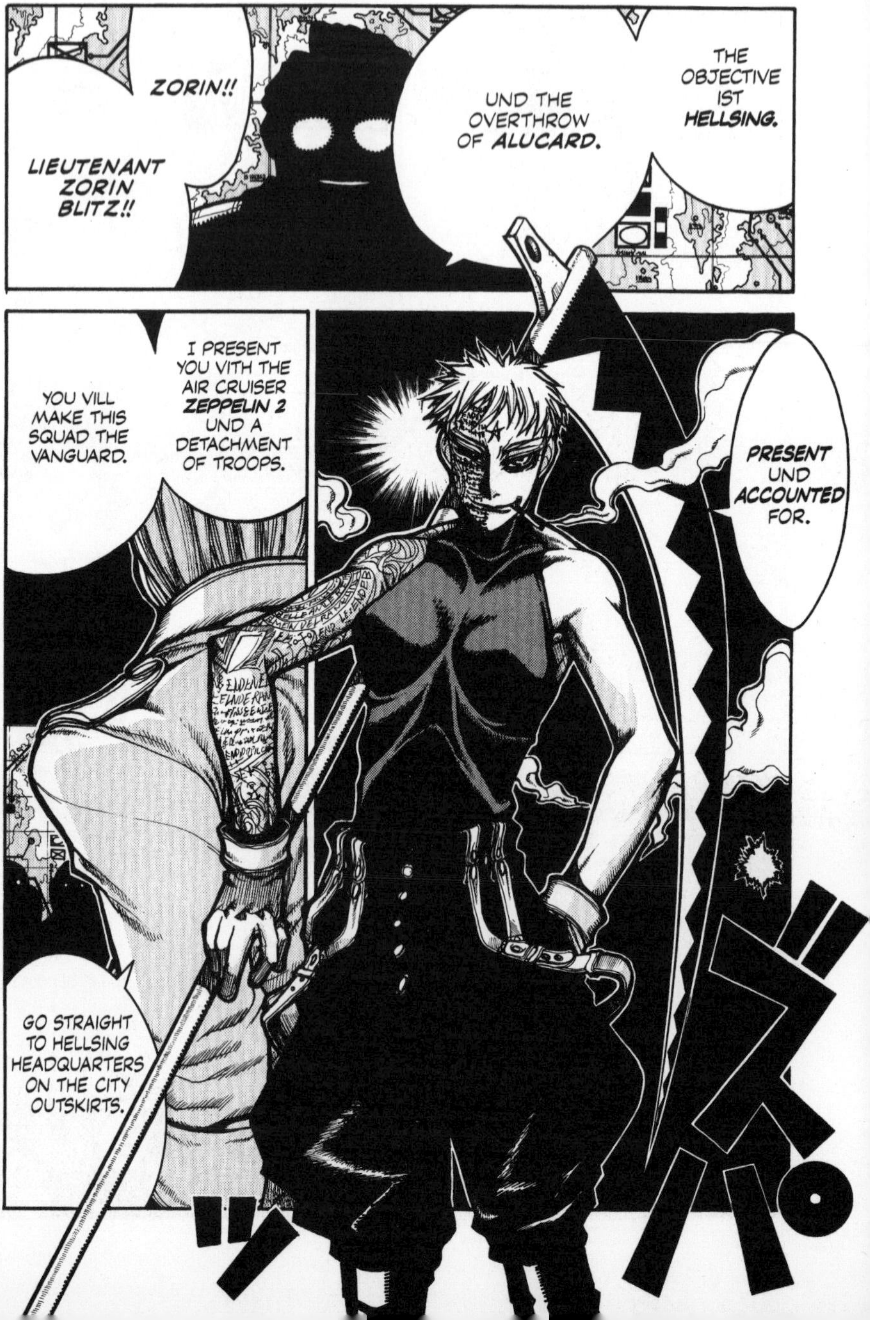
THE OBJECTIVE IST HELLSING.
UND THE OVERTHROW OF ALUCARD.
ZORIN!!
LIEUTENANT ZORIN BLITZ!!
PRESENT UND ACCOUNTED FOR.
I PRESENT YOU VITH THE AIR CRUISER ZEPPELIN 2 UND A DETACHMENT OF TROOPS.
YOU VILL MAKE THIS SQUAD THE VANGUARD.
GO STRAIGHT TO HELLSING HEADQUARTERS ON THE CITY OUTSKIRTS.

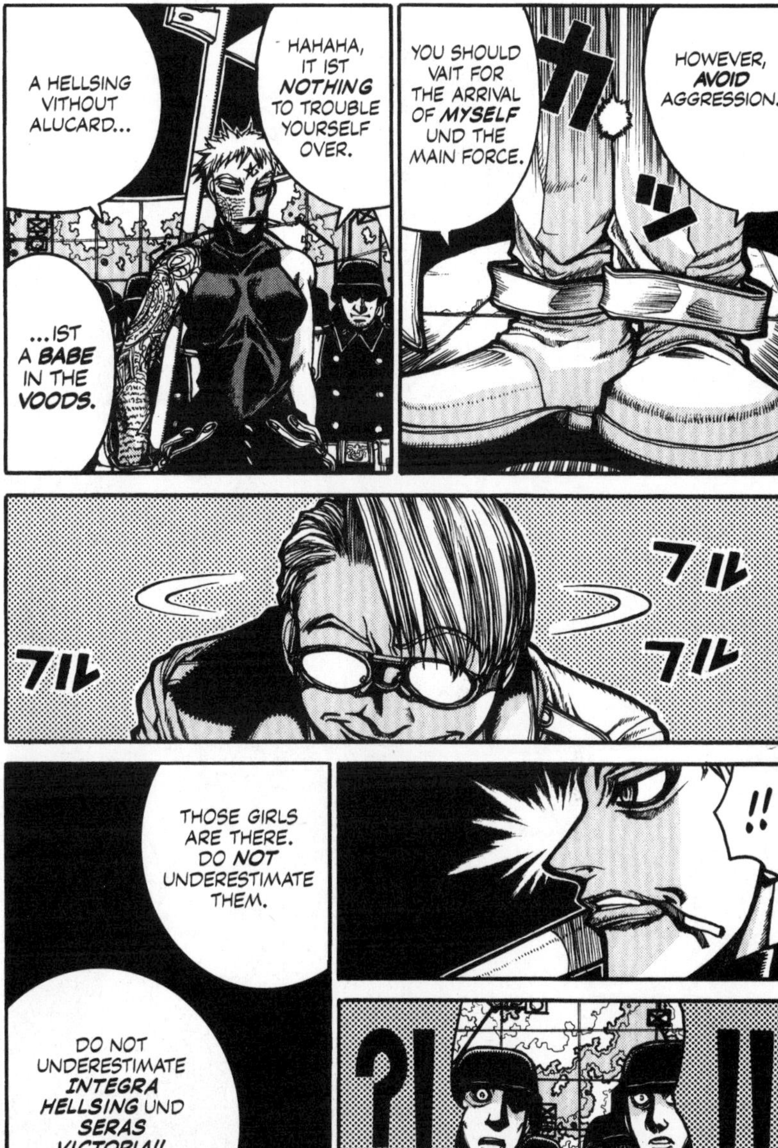
HOWEVER, **AVOID** AGGRESSION.
カッ
YOU SHOULD VAIT FOR THE ARRIVAL OF **MYSELF** UND THE MAIN FORCE.
HAHAHA, IT IST **NOTHING** TO TROUBLE YOURSELF OVER.
A HELLSING VITHOUT ALUCARD...
...IST A **BABE** IN THE **VOODS.**
フル
フル
フル
!!
?!
!!
THOSE GIRLS ARE THERE. DO **NOT** UNDERESTIMATE THEM.
DO NOT UNDERESTIMATE **INTEGRA HELLSING** UND **SERAS VICTORIA!!**

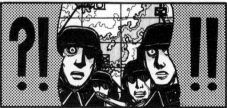

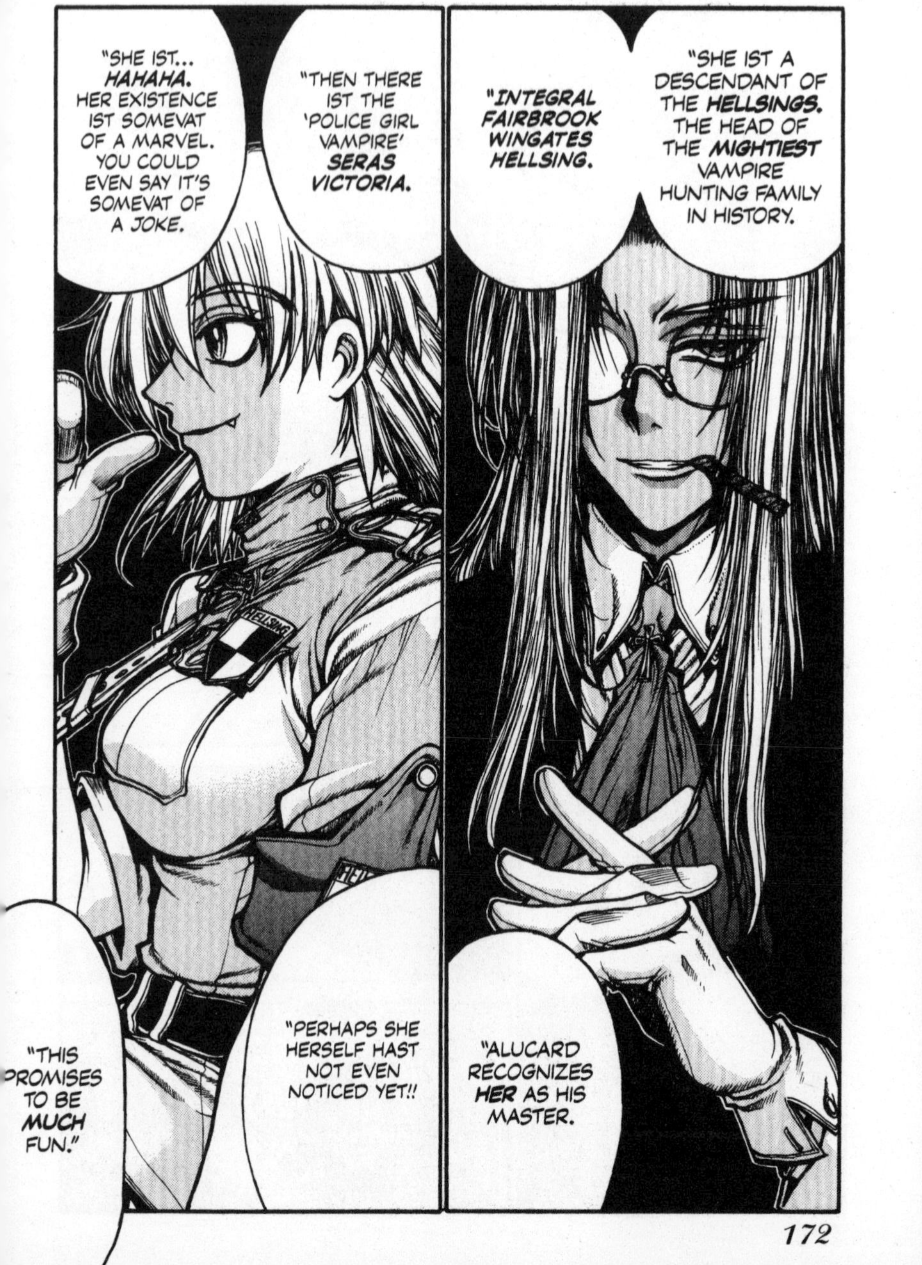
"SHE IST A DESCENDANT OF THE HELLSINGS. THE HEAD OF THE MIGHTIEST VAMPIRE HUNTING FAMILY IN HISTORY.
"INTEGRAL FAIRBROOK WINGATES HELLSING.
"ALUCARD RECOGNIZES HER AS HIS MASTER.
"THEN THERE IST THE 'POLICE GIRL VAMPIRE' SERAS VICTORIA.
"SHE IST... HAHAHA. HER EXISTENCE IST SOMEVAT OF A MARVEL. YOU COULD EVEN SAY IT'S SOMEVAT OF A JOKE.
"PERHAPS SHE HERSELF HAST NOT EVEN NOTICED YET!!
"THIS PROMISES TO BE MUCH FUN."

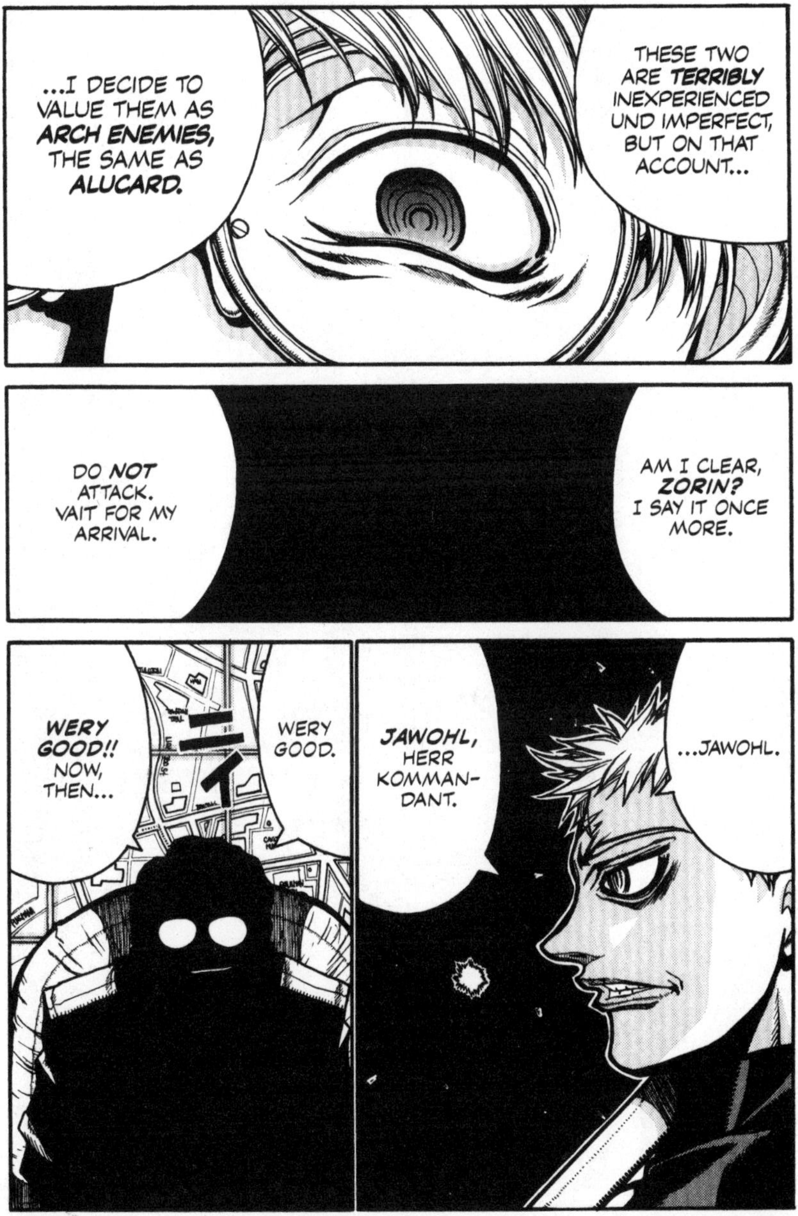
THESE TWO ARE TERRIBLY INEXPERIENCED UND IMPERFECT, BUT ON THAT ACCOUNT...
...I DECIDE TO VALUE THEM AS ARCH ENEMIES, THE SAME AS ALUCARD.
AM I CLEAR, ZORIN? I SAY IT ONCE MORE.
DO NOT ATTACK. VAIT FOR MY ARRIVAL.
...JAWOHL.
JAWOHL, HERR KOMMAN-DANT.
WERY GOOD.
WERY GOOD!! NOW, THEN...

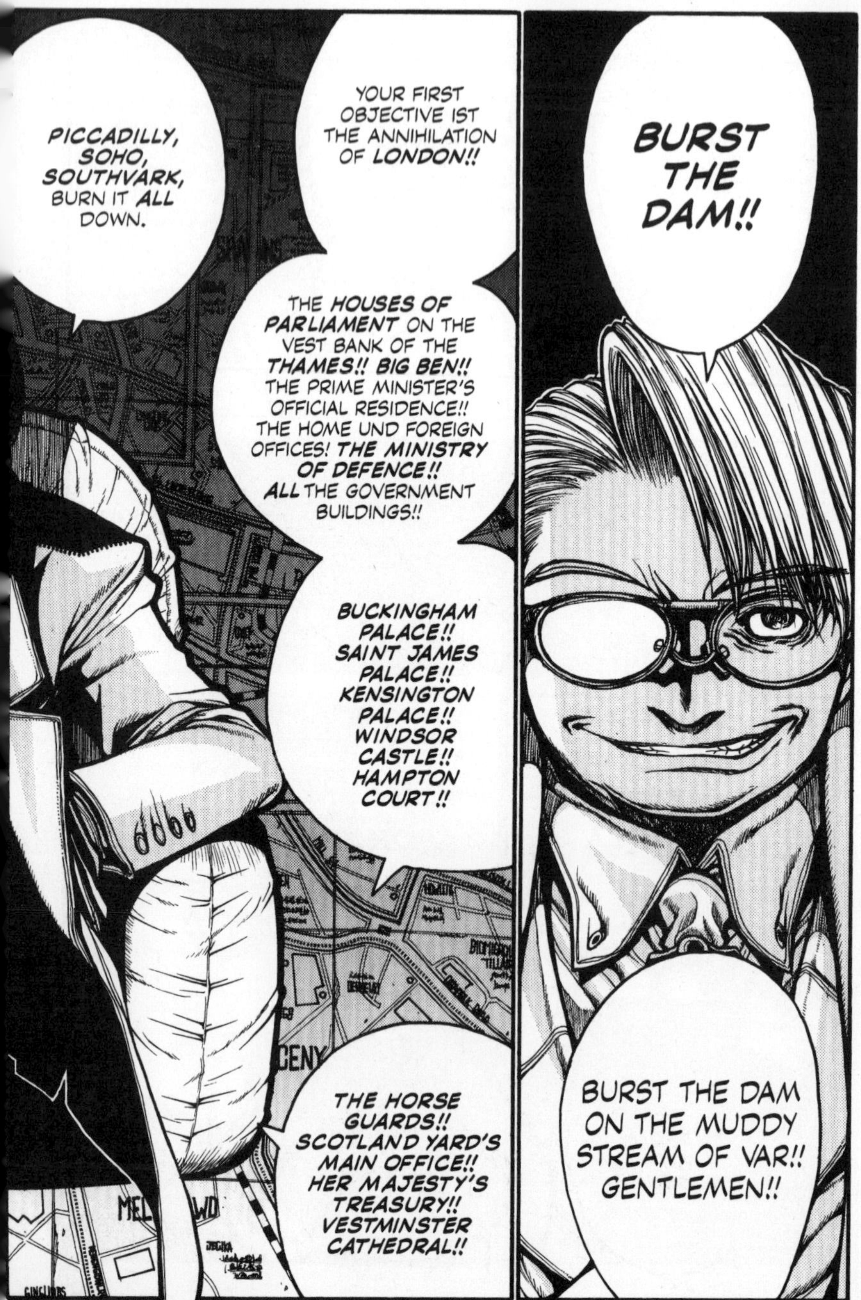
BURST THE DAM!!
BURST THE DAM ON THE MUDDY STREAM OF VAR!! GENTLEMEN!!
YOUR FIRST OBJECTIVE IST THE ANNIHILATION OF LONDON!!
PICCADILLY, SOHO, SOUTHVARK, BURN IT ALL DOWN.
THE HOUSES OF PARLIAMENT ON THE VEST BANK OF THE THAMES!! BIG BEN!! THE PRIME MINISTER'S OFFICIAL RESIDENCE!! THE HOME UND FOREIGN OFFICES! THE MINISTRY OF DEFENCE!! ALL THE GOVERNMENT BUILDINGS!!
BUCKINGHAM PALACE!! SAINT JAMES PALACE!! KENSINGTON PALACE!! WINDSOR CASTLE!! HAMPTON COURT!!
THE HORSE GUARDS!! SCOTLAND YARD'S MAIN OFFICE!! HER MAJESTY'S TREASURY!! VESTMINSTER CATHEDRAL!!

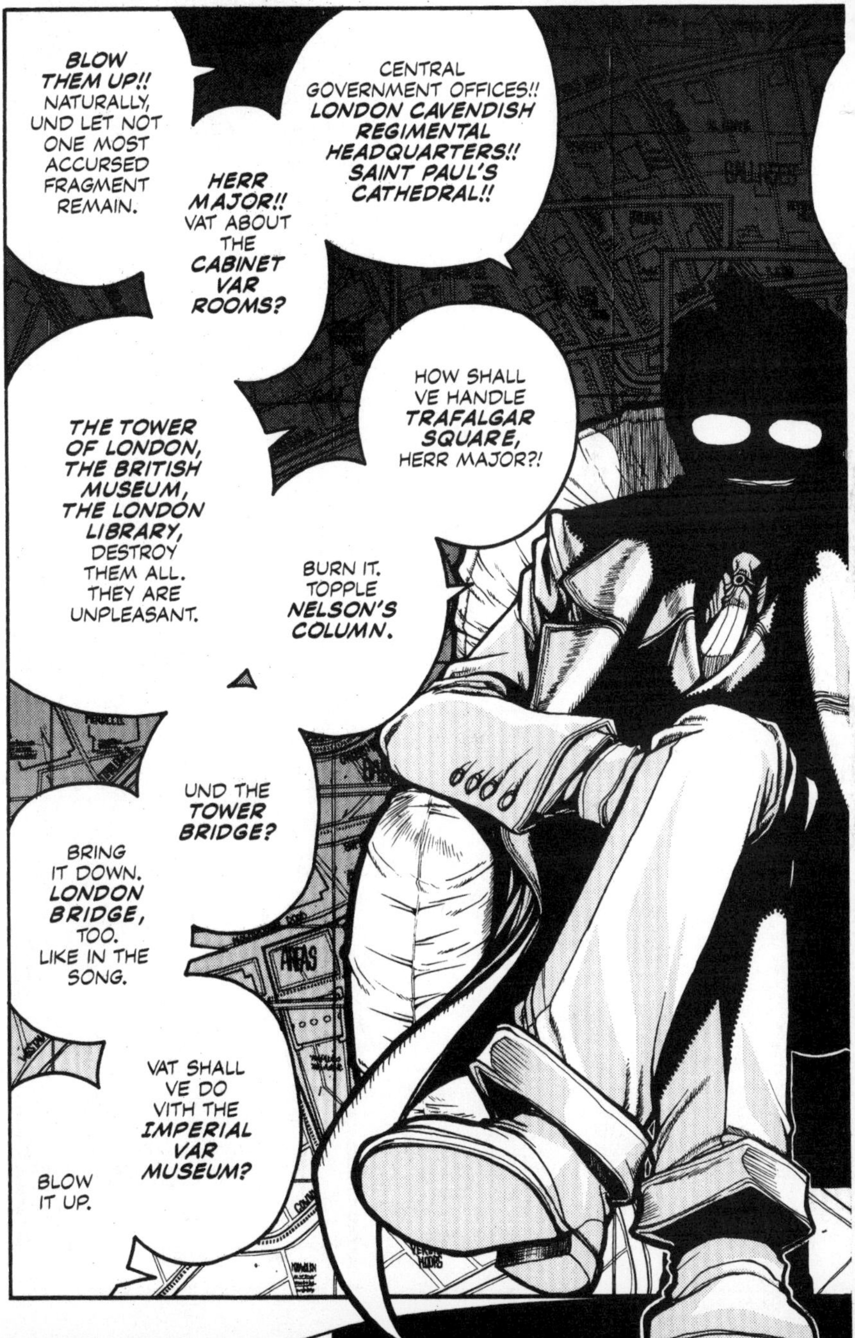
CENTRAL GOVERNMENT OFFICES!! LONDON CAVENDISH REGIMENTAL HEADQUARTERS!! SAINT PAUL'S CATHEDRAL!!
HERR MAJOR!! VAT ABOUT THE CABINET VAR ROOMS?
BLOW THEM UP!! NATURALLY, UND LET NOT ONE MOST ACCURSED FRAGMENT REMAIN.
HOW SHALL VE HANDLE TRAFALGAR SQUARE, HERR MAJOR?!
BURN IT. TOPPLE NELSON'S COLUMN.
THE TOWER OF LONDON, THE BRITISH MUSEUM, THE LONDON LIBRARY, DESTROY THEM ALL. THEY ARE UNPLEASANT.
UND THE TOWER BRIDGE?
BRING IT DOWN. LONDON BRIDGE, TOO. LIKE IN THE SONG.
VAT SHALL VE DO VITH THE IMPERIAL VAR MUSEUM?
BLOW IT UP.

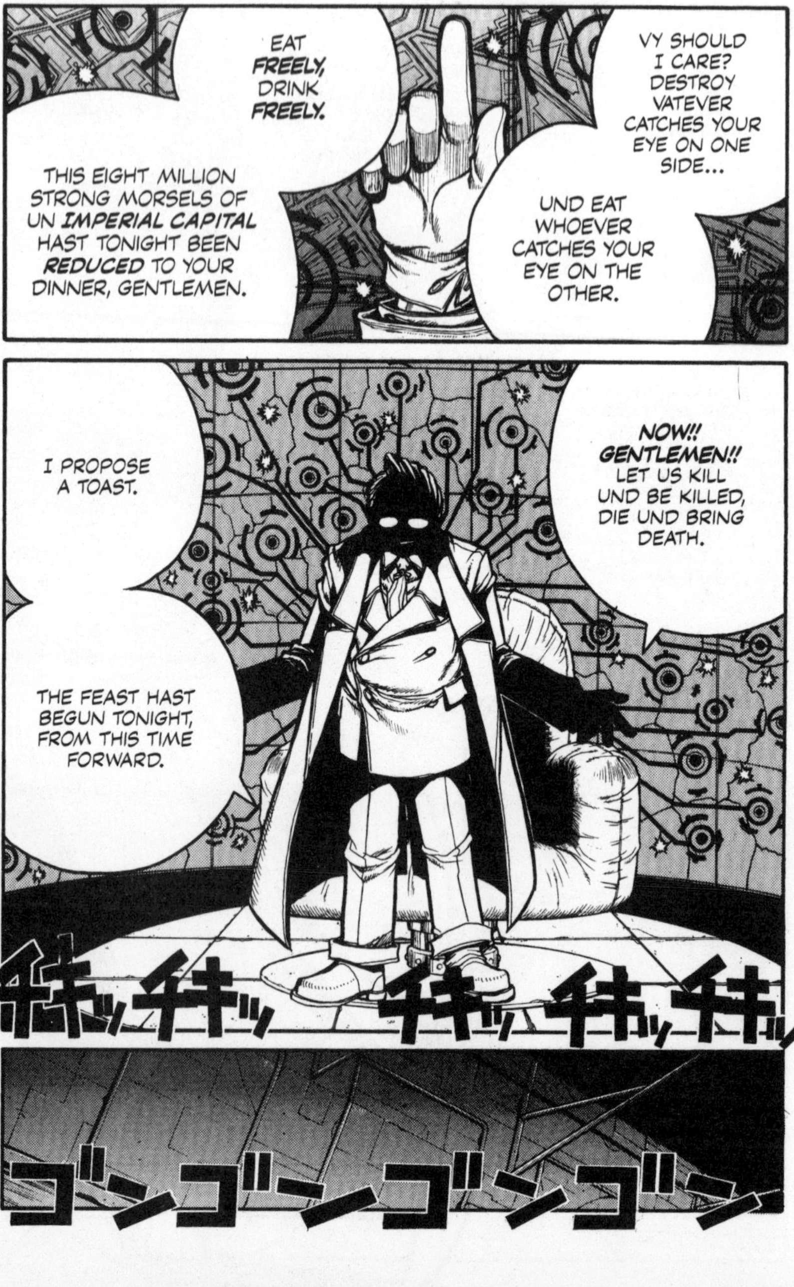
VY SHOULD I CARE? DESTROY VATEVER CATCHES YOUR EYE ON ONE SIDE...
UND EAT WHOEVER CATCHES YOUR EYE ON THE OTHER.
EAT FREELY, DRINK FREELY.
THIS EIGHT MILLION STRONG MORSELS OF UN IMPERIAL CAPITAL HAST TONIGHT BEEN REDUCED TO YOUR DINNER, GENTLEMEN.
NOW!! GENTLEMEN!! LET US KILL UND BE KILLED, DIE UND BRING DEATH.
I PROPOSE A TOAST.
THE FEAST HAST BEGUN TONIGHT, FROM THIS TIME FORWARD.
チキッ チキッ チキッ チキッ チキッ
ゴン ゴン ゴン ゴン

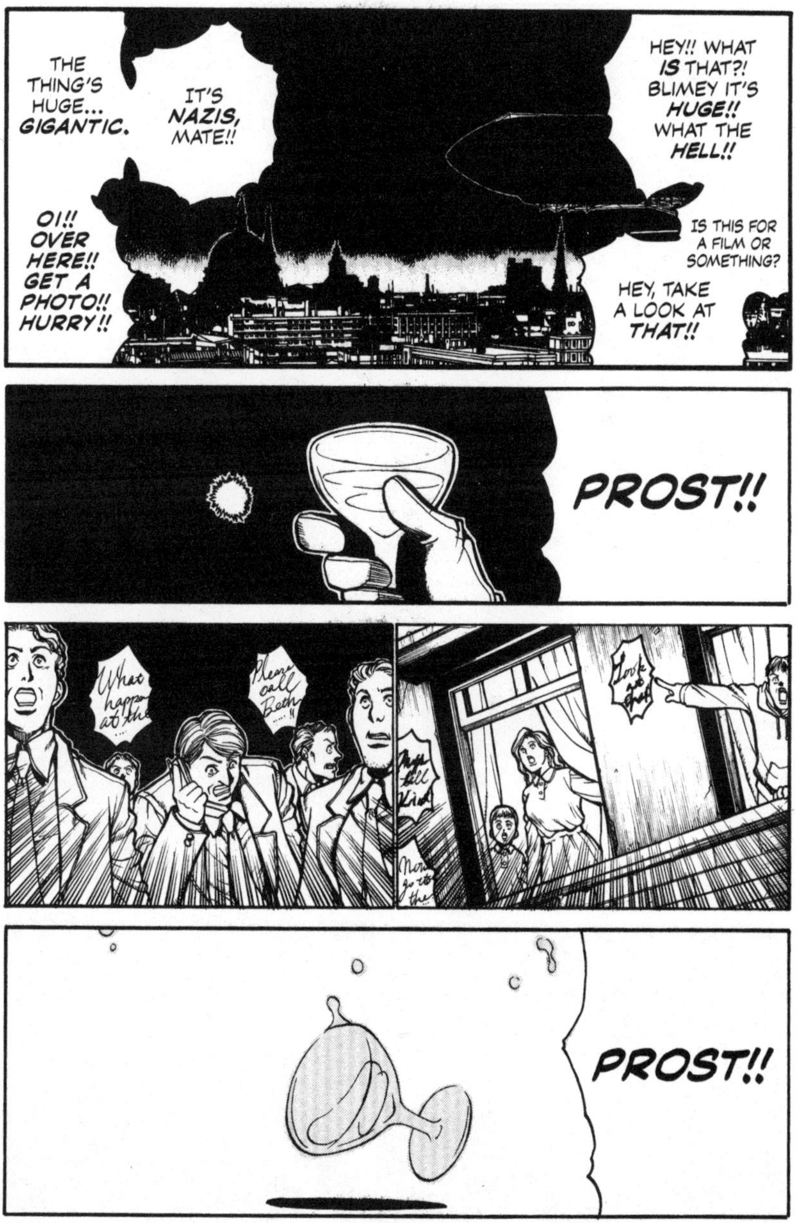
HEY!! WHAT IS THAT?! BLIMEY IT'S HUGE!! WHAT THE HELL!!
IS THIS FOR A FILM OR SOMETHING?
HEY, TAKE A LOOK AT THAT!!
IT'S NAZIS, MATE!!
THE THING'S HUGE... GIGANTIC.
OI!! OVER HERE!! GET A PHOTO!! HURRY!!
PROST!!
PROST!!

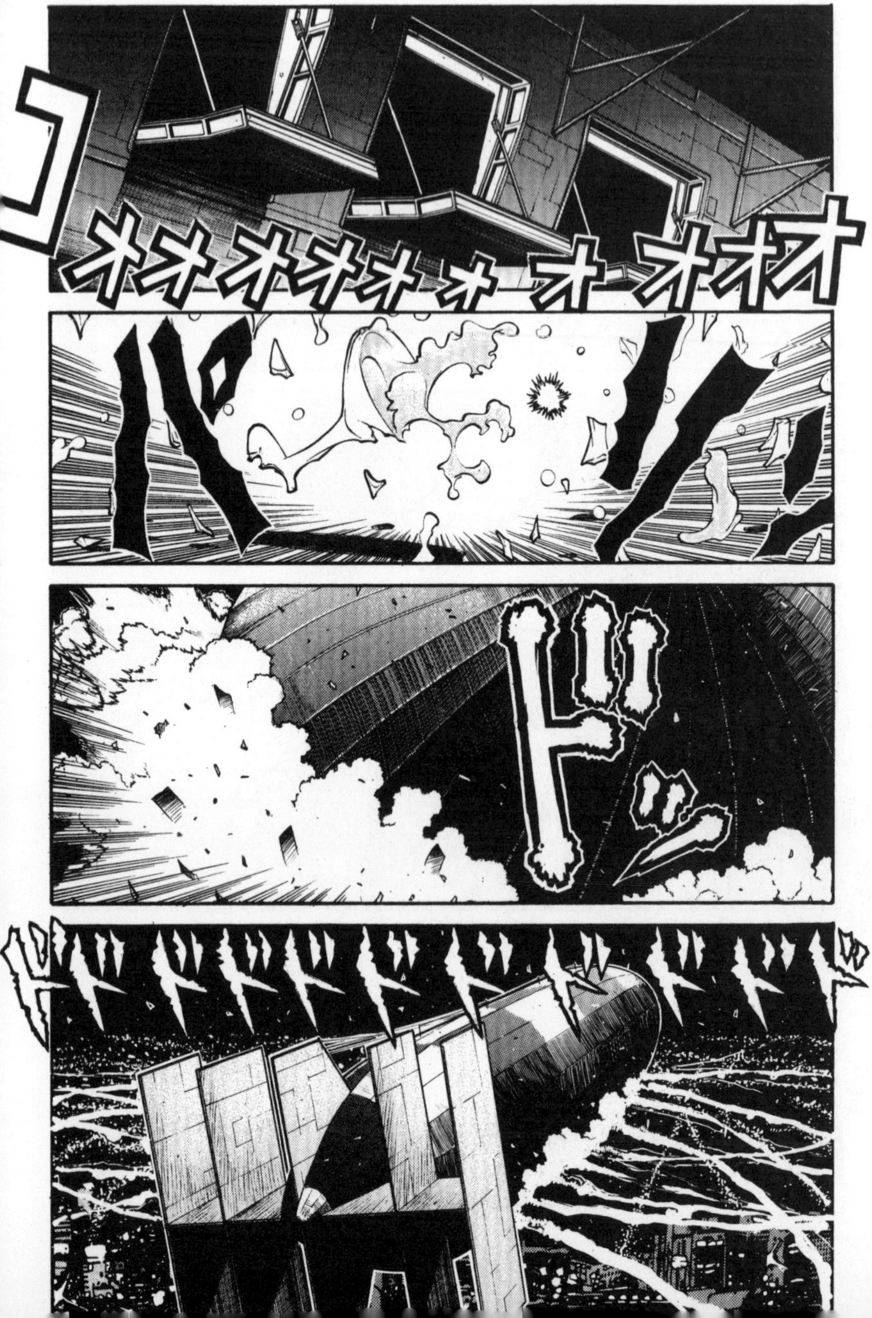
コオオオオオォオーオオオ
パリン
ドッ
ドドドドドドドドドドド

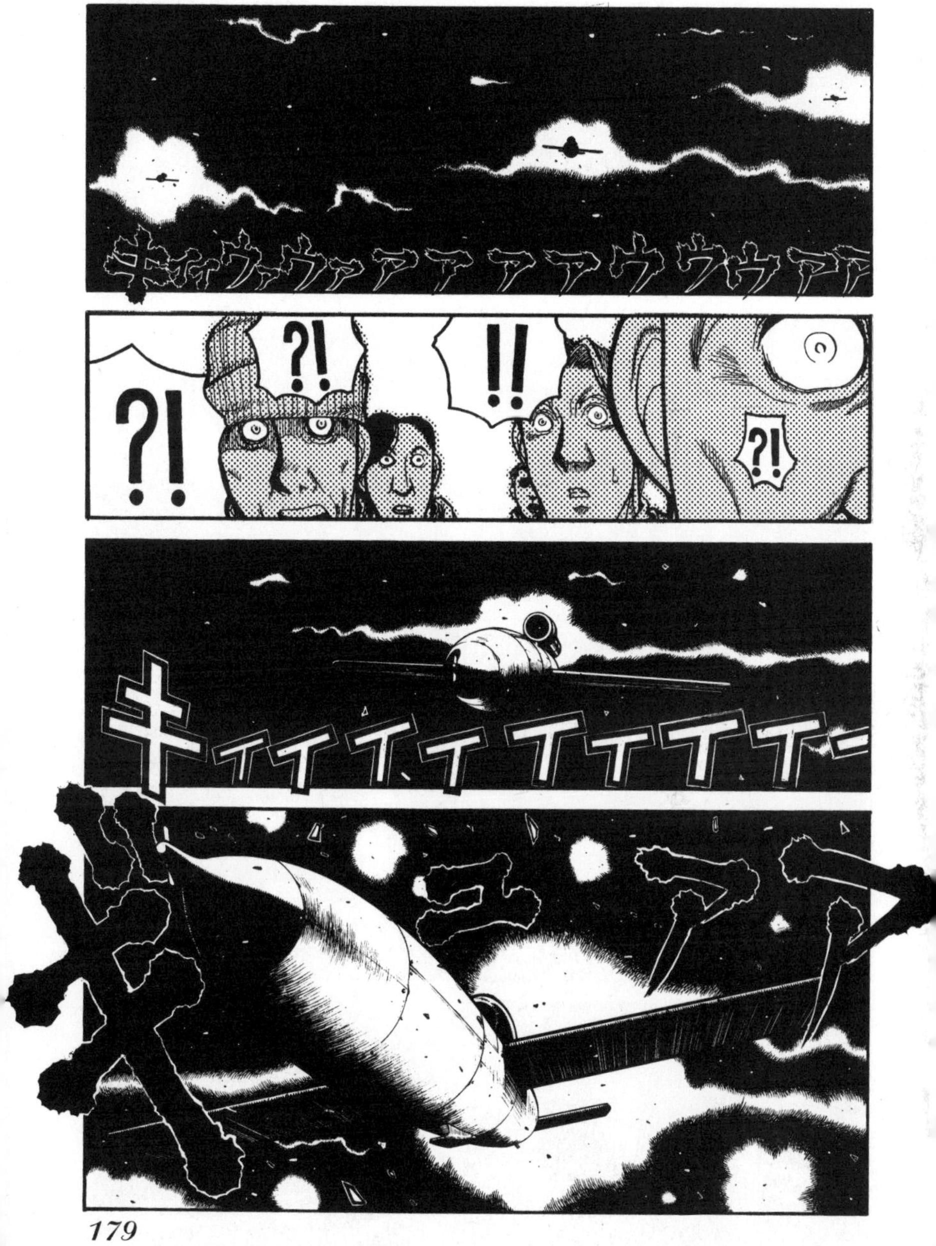
キィヴァウァアアアアウウウアア
?!
!!
?!
?!
キイイイイイイイイー
ズュアア

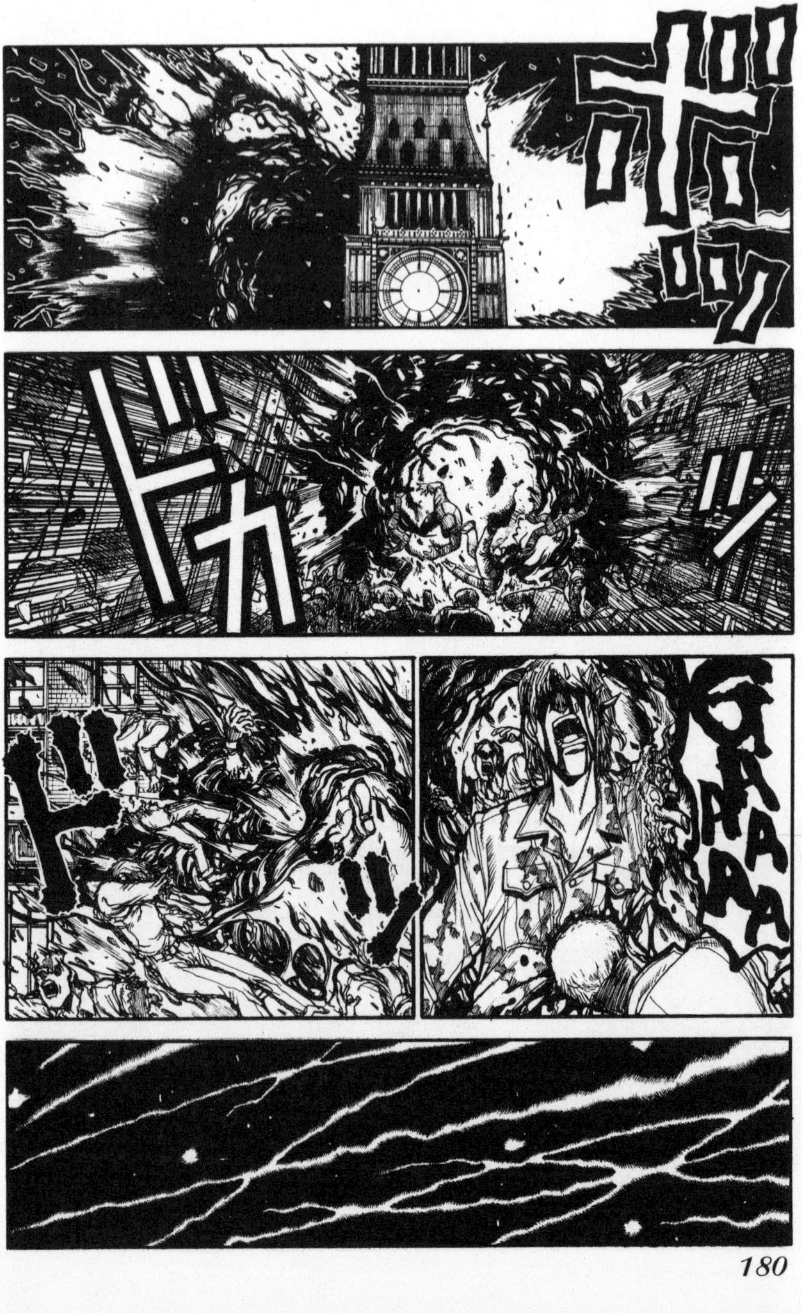
ドカッ
GAAAAA
ドドッ

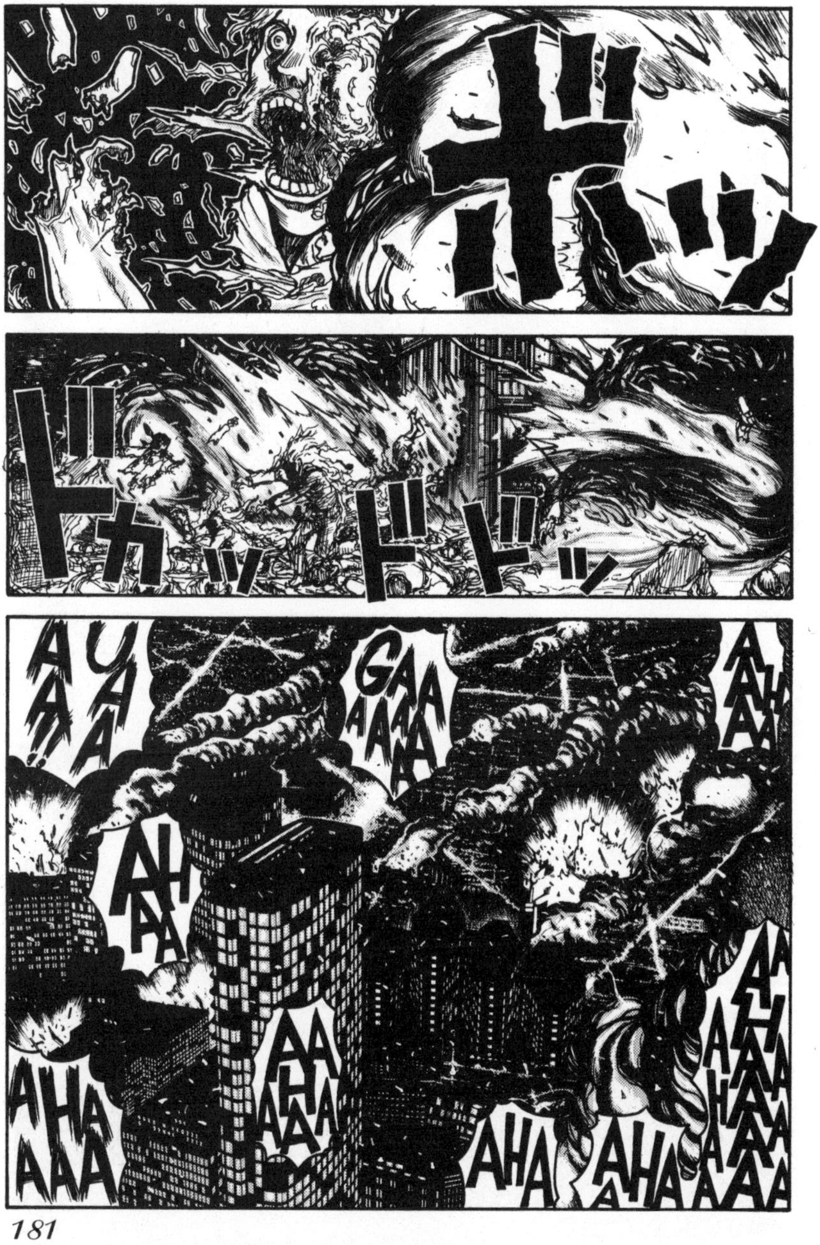
ボハッ
ドカッ
ドドッ
GAAAAAAAA
AUAA
AHAHAAA
AHAHAAA
AHA
AHA

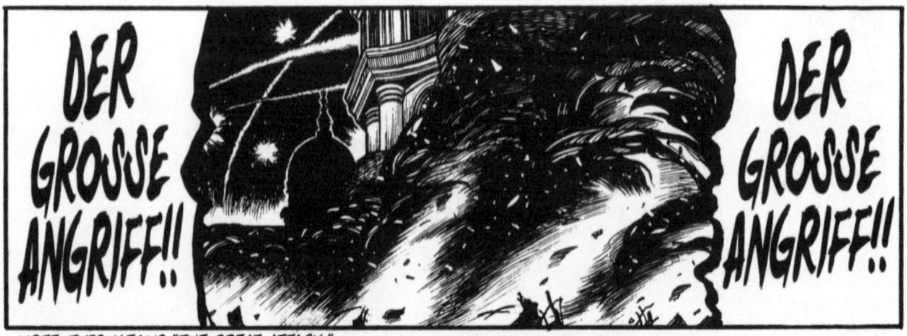
DER GROSSE ANGRIFF!!
DER GROSSE ANGRIFF!!
NOTE: THIS MEANS "THE GREAT ATTACK."

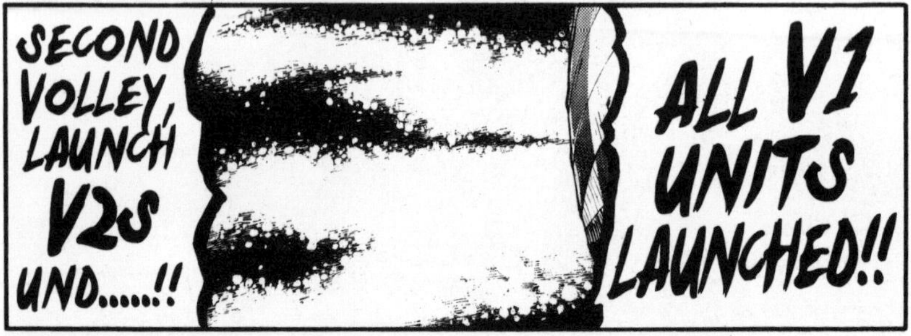
ALL V1 UNITS LAUNCHED!!
SECOND VOLLEY, LAUNCH V2S UND......!!

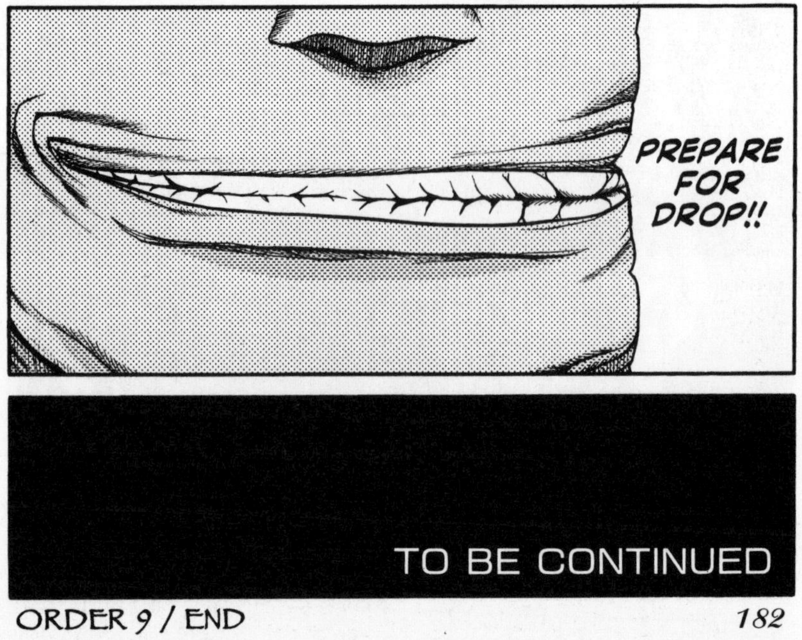
PREPARE FOR DROP!!

TO BE CONTINUED

ORDER 10

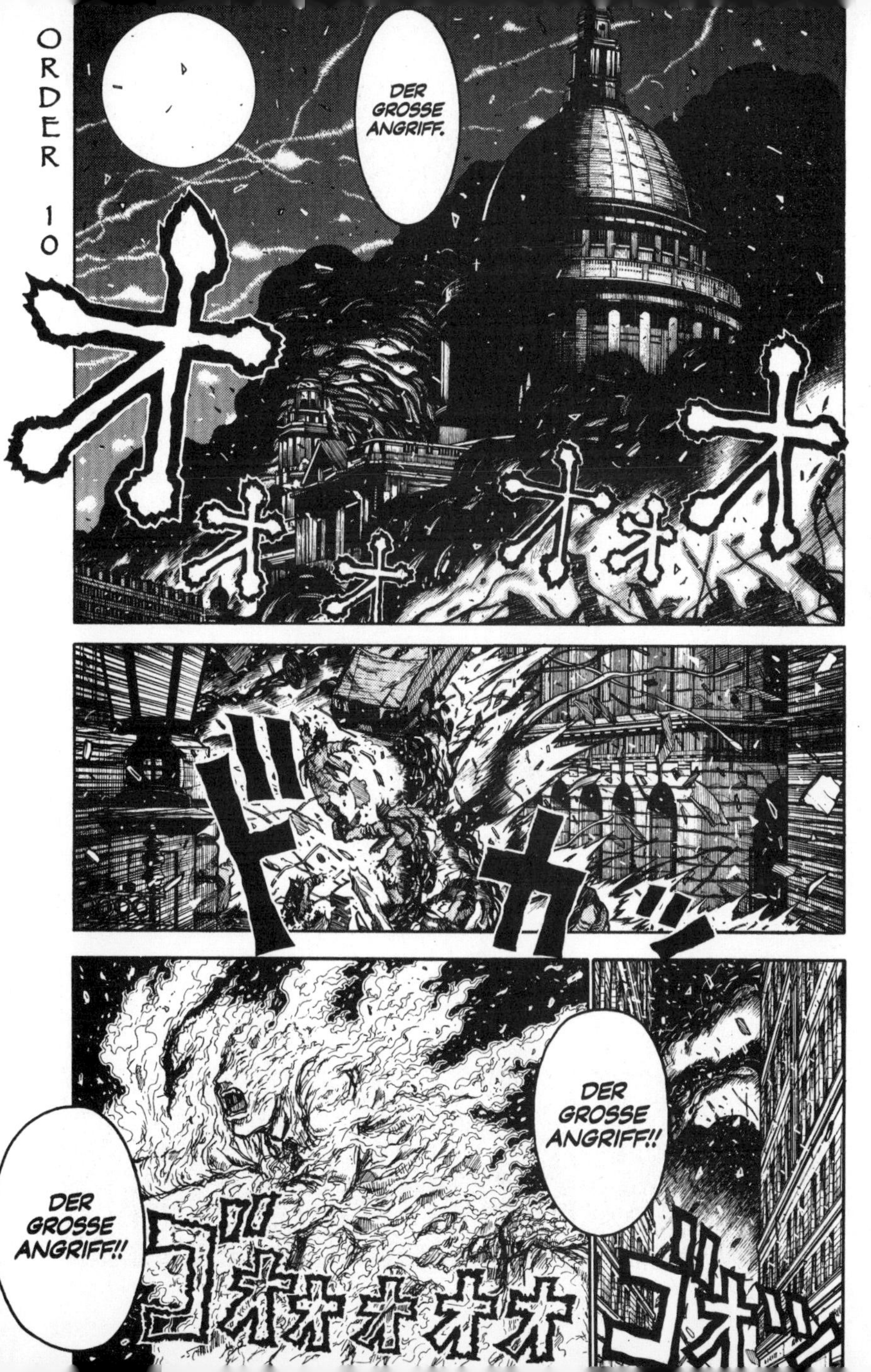
DER GROSSE ANGRIFF.
DER GROSSE ANGRIFF!!
DER GROSSE ANGRIFF!!

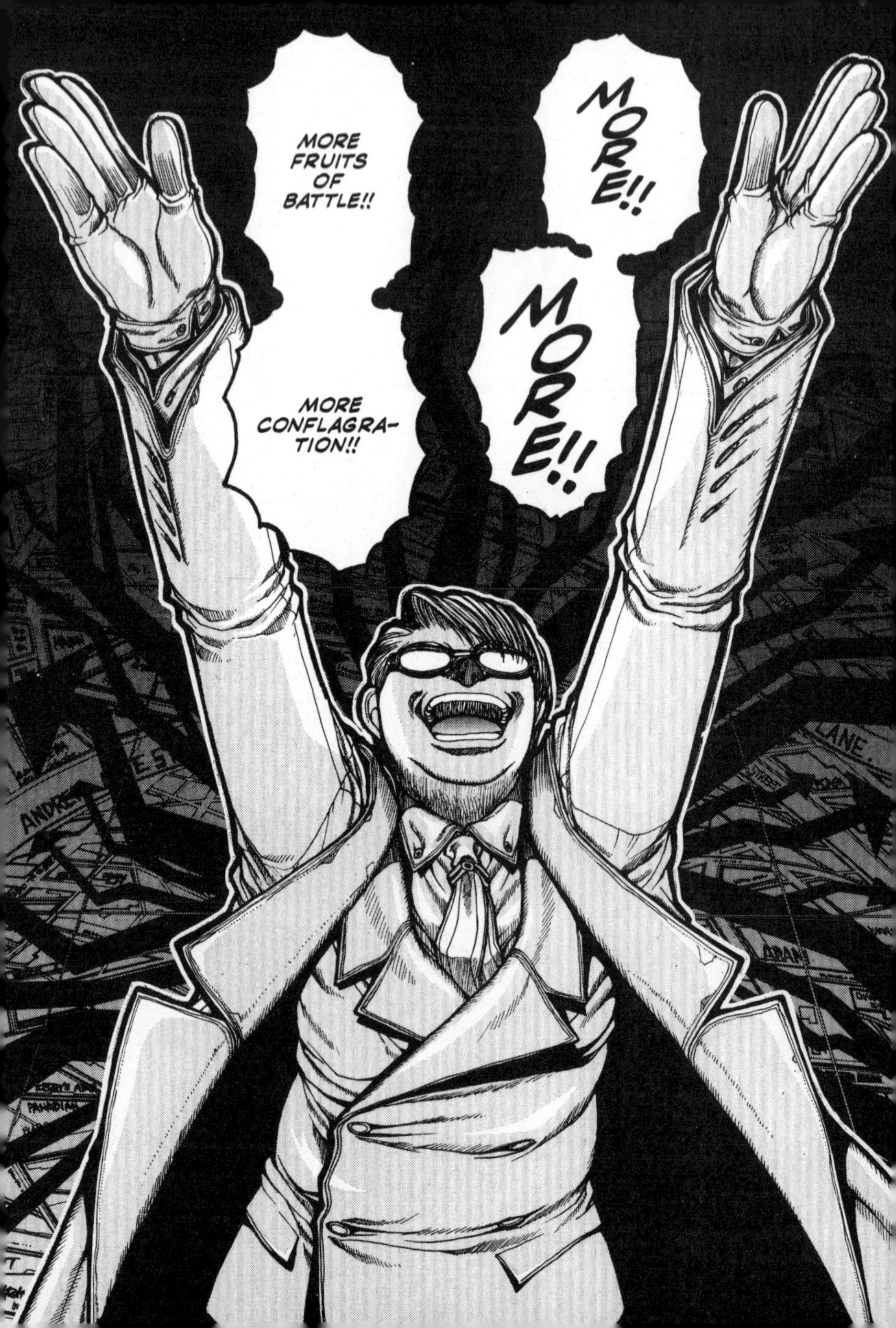
MORE!!
MORE!!
MORE FRUITS OF BATTLE!!
MORE CONFLAGRATION!!

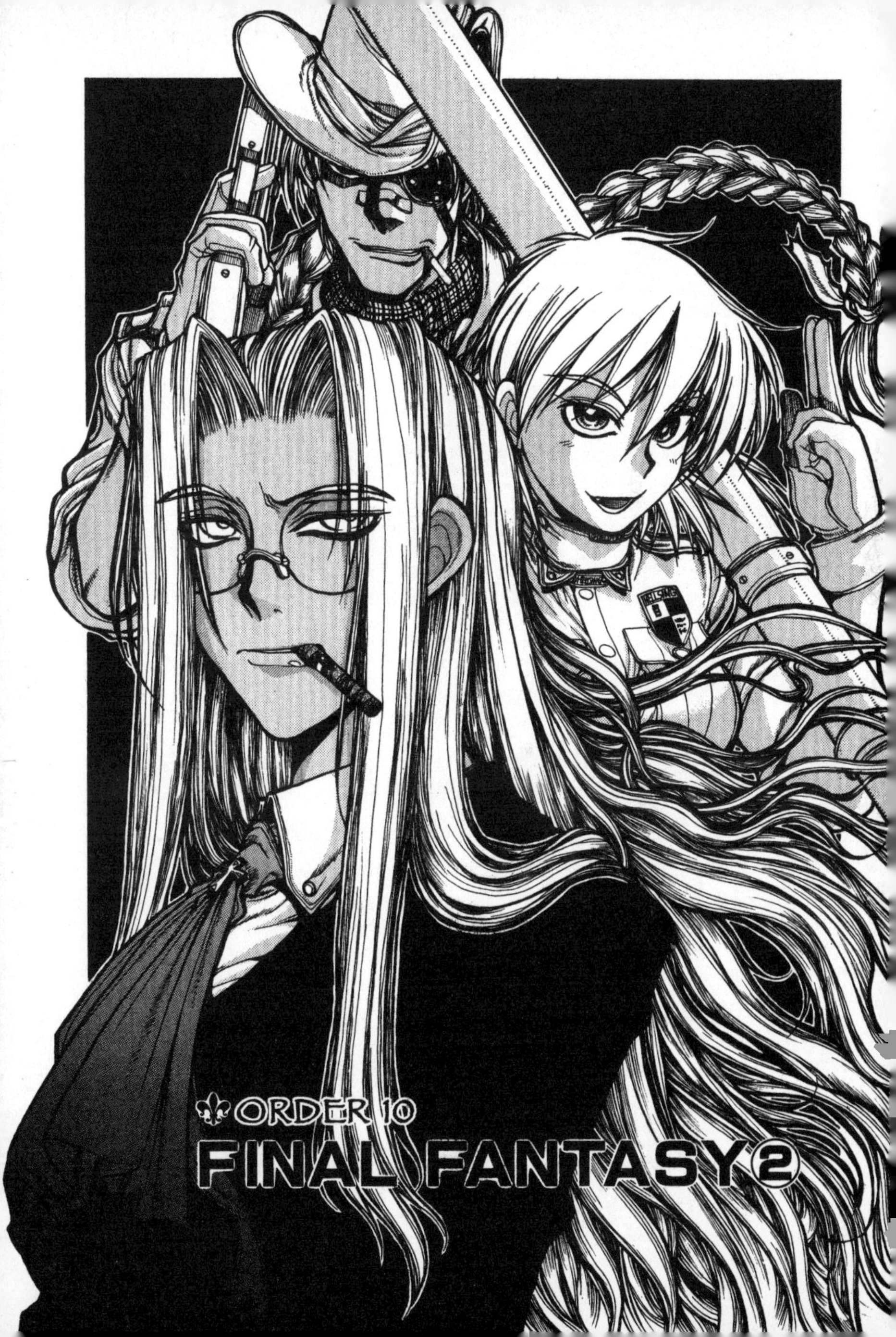
ORDER 10
FINAL FANTASY 2

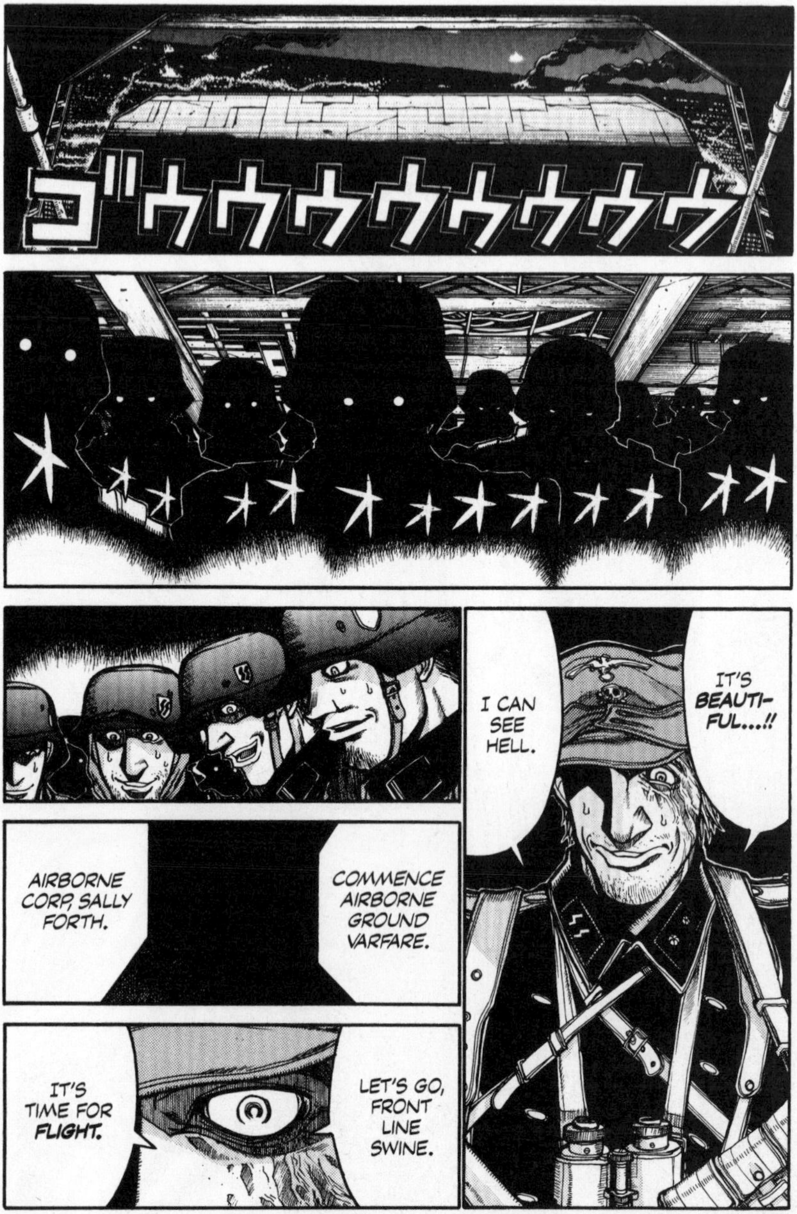
ゴウウウウウウウウウ
IT'S BEAUTIFUL...!!
I CAN SEE HELL.
COMMENCE AIRBORNE GROUND VARFARE.
AIRBORNE CORP, SALLY FORTH.
LET'S GO, FRONT LINE SWINE.
IT'S TIME FOR FLIGHT.

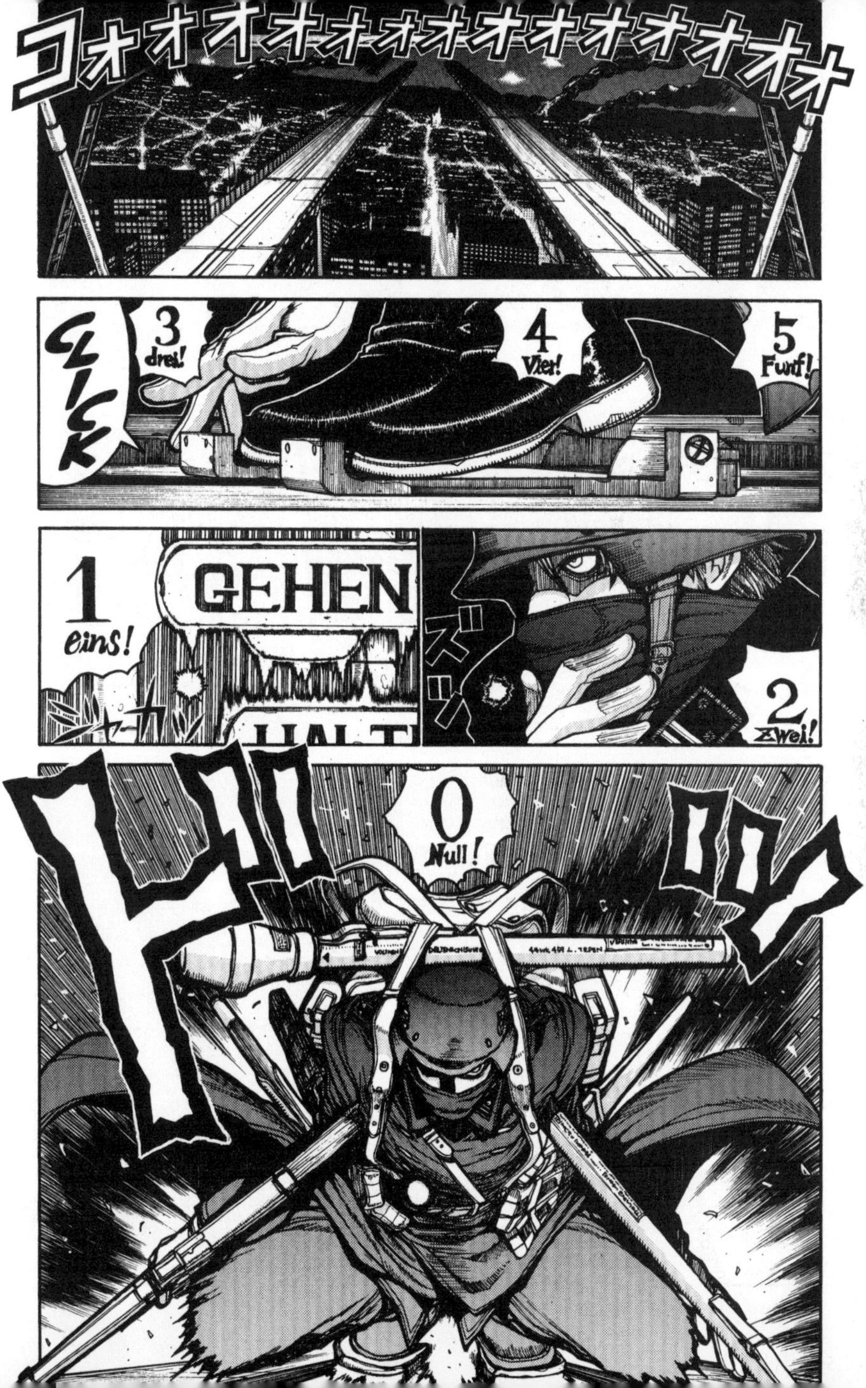

コォオオオオオオオオオオオオ
5 Funf!
4 Vier!
3 drei!
CLICK
2 Zwei!
ズッ
1 eins!
GEHEN
0 Null!

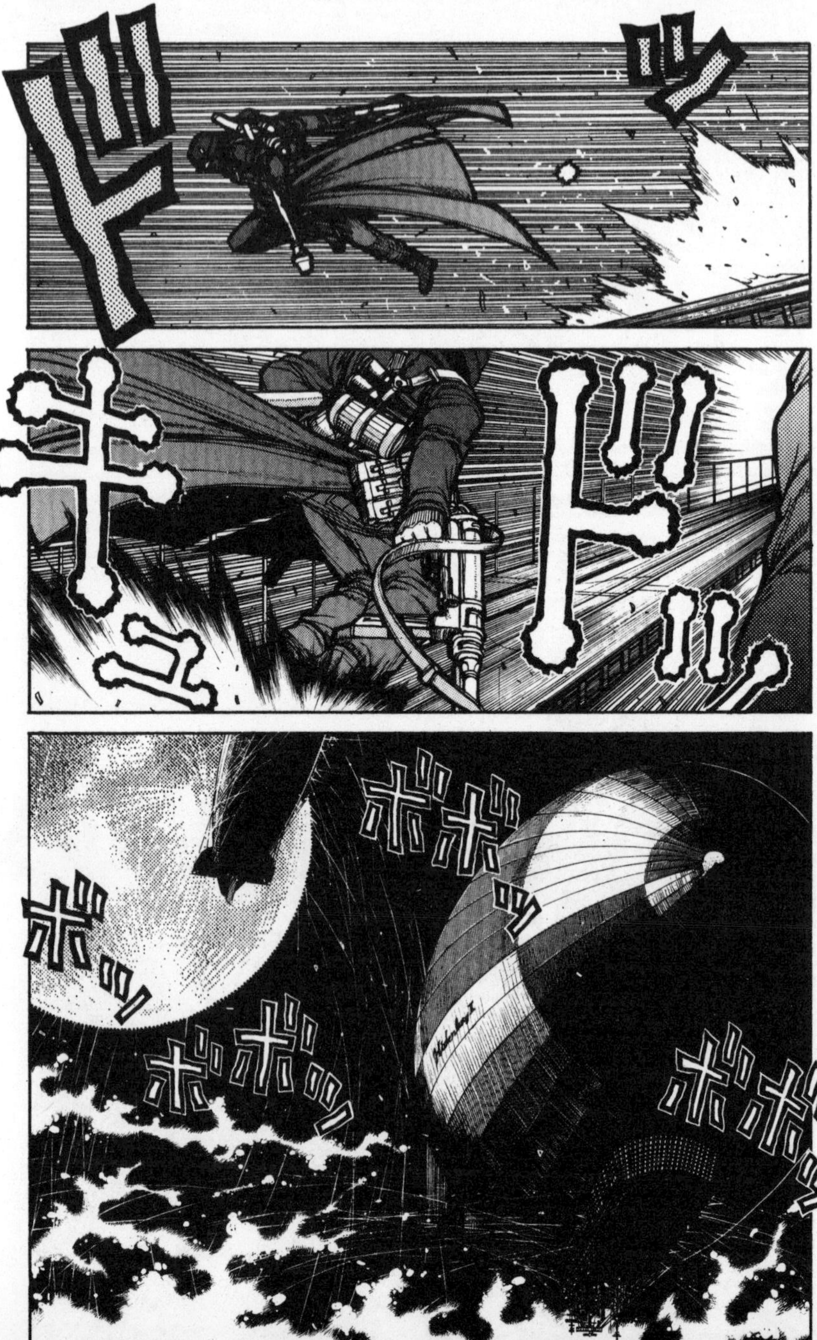
ドッ
ドッ
キュ
ボボッ
ボボッ
ボッ
ボボッ

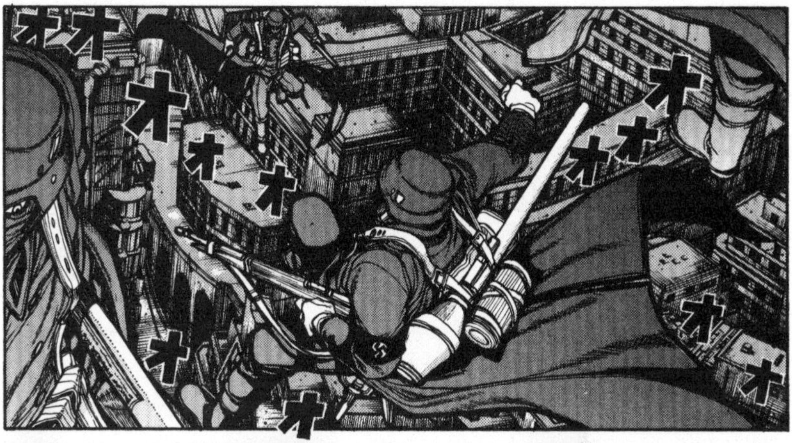

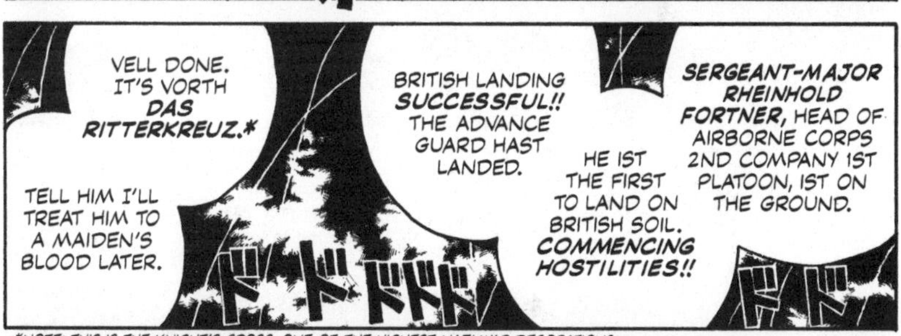
SERGEANT-MAJOR RHEINHOLD FORTNER, HEAD OF AIRBORNE CORPS 2ND COMPANY 1ST PLATOON, IST ON THE GROUND.
HE IST THE FIRST TO LAND ON BRITISH SOIL. COMMENCING HOSTILITIES!!
BRITISH LANDING SUCCESSFUL!! THE ADVANCE GUARD HAST LANDED.
VELL DONE. IT'S VORTH DAS RITTERKREUZ.*
TELL HIM I'LL TREAT HIM TO A MAIDEN'S BLOOD LATER.
ドド
ドドドドド

*NOTE: THIS IS THE KNIGHT'S CROSS, ONE OF THE HIGHEST NAZI WAR DECORATIONS.

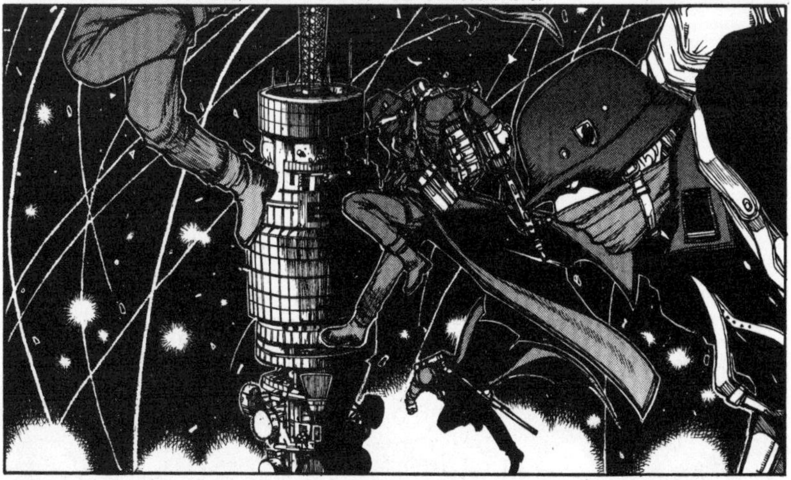

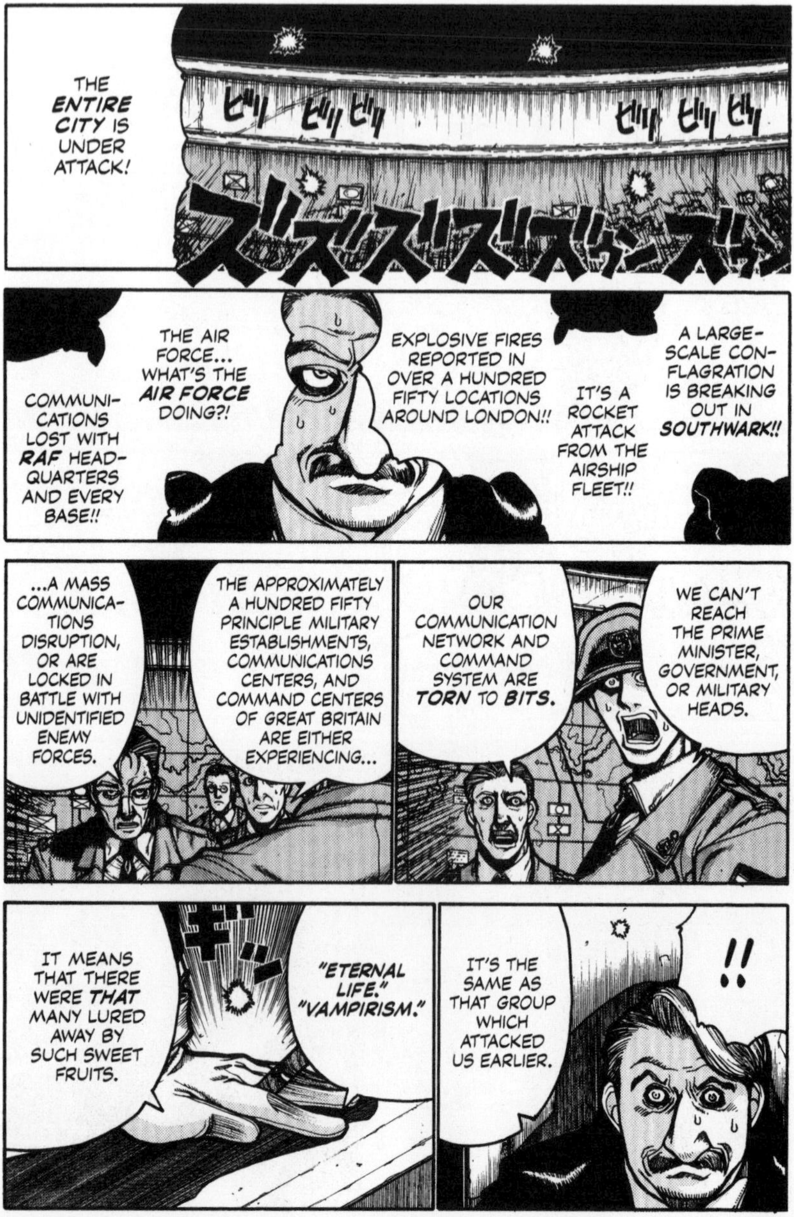
THE ENTIRE CITY IS UNDER ATTACK!
A LARGE-SCALE CONFLAGRATION IS BREAKING OUT IN SOUTHWARK!!
IT'S A ROCKET ATTACK FROM THE AIRSHIP FLEET!!
EXPLOSIVE FIRES REPORTED IN OVER A HUNDRED FIFTY LOCATIONS AROUND LONDON!!
THE AIR FORCE... WHAT'S THE AIR FORCE DOING?!
COMMUNICATIONS LOST WITH RAF HEADQUARTERS AND EVERY BASE!!
WE CAN'T REACH THE PRIME MINISTER, GOVERNMENT, OR MILITARY HEADS.
OUR COMMUNICATION NETWORK AND COMMAND SYSTEM ARE TORN TO BITS.
THE APPROXIMATELY A HUNDRED FIFTY PRINCIPLE MILITARY ESTABLISHMENTS, COMMUNICATIONS CENTERS, AND COMMAND CENTERS OF GREAT BRITAIN ARE EITHER EXPERIENCING...
...A MASS COMMUNICATIONS DISRUPTION, OR ARE LOCKED IN BATTLE WITH UNIDENTIFIED ENEMY FORCES.
!!
IT'S THE SAME AS THAT GROUP WHICH ATTACKED US EARLIER.
"ETERNAL LIFE." "VAMPIRISM."
IT MEANS THAT THERE WERE THAT MANY LURED AWAY BY SUCH SWEET FRUITS.

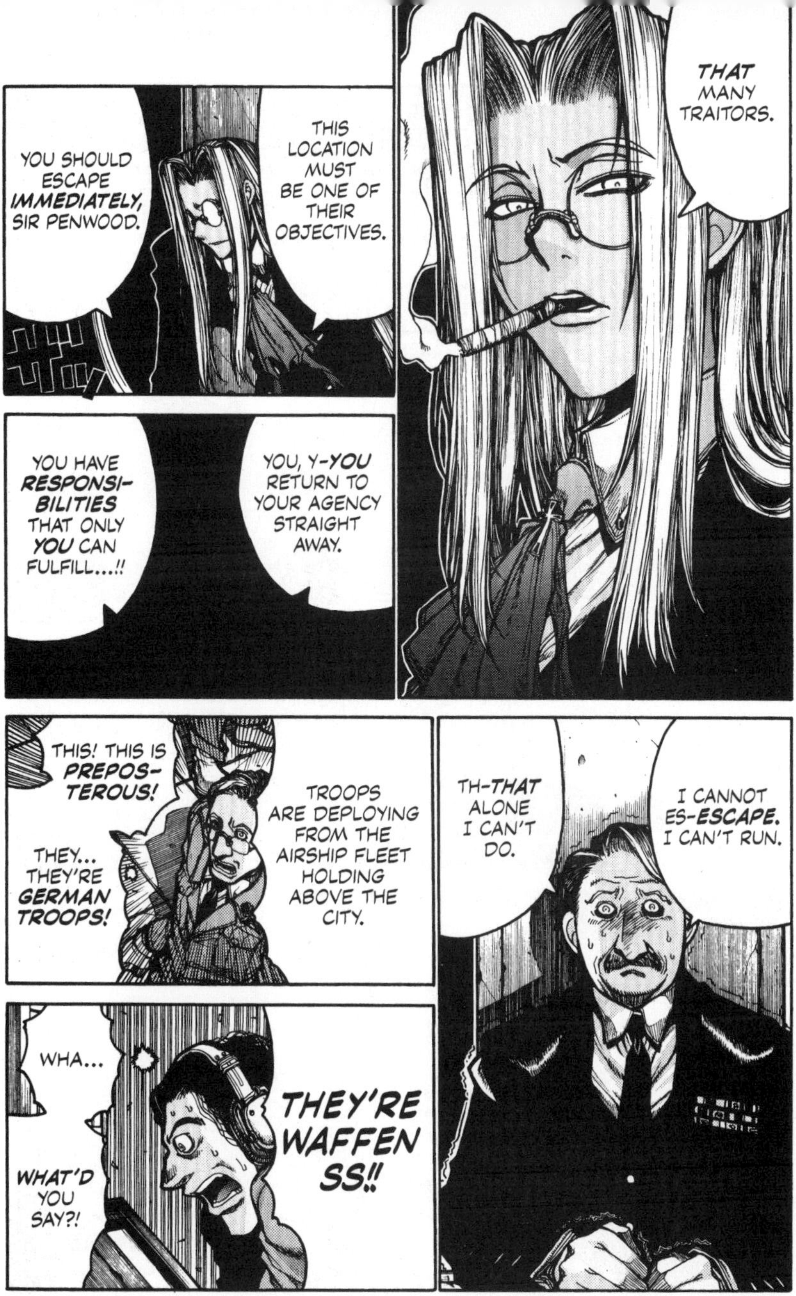
THAT MANY TRAITORS.
THIS LOCATION MUST BE ONE OF THEIR OBJECTIVES.
YOU SHOULD ESCAPE IMMEDIATELY, SIR PENWOOD.
YOU, Y-YOU RETURN TO YOUR AGENCY STRAIGHT AWAY.
YOU HAVE RESPONSIBILITIES THAT ONLY YOU CAN FULFILL...!!
I CANNOT ES-ESCAPE. I CAN'T RUN.
TH-THAT ALONE I CAN'T DO.
TROOPS ARE DEPLOYING FROM THE AIRSHIP FLEET HOLDING ABOVE THE CITY.
THIS! THIS IS PREPOSTEROUS!
THEY... THEY'RE GERMAN TROOPS!
THEY'RE WAFFEN SS!!
WHA...
WHAT'D YOU SAY?!

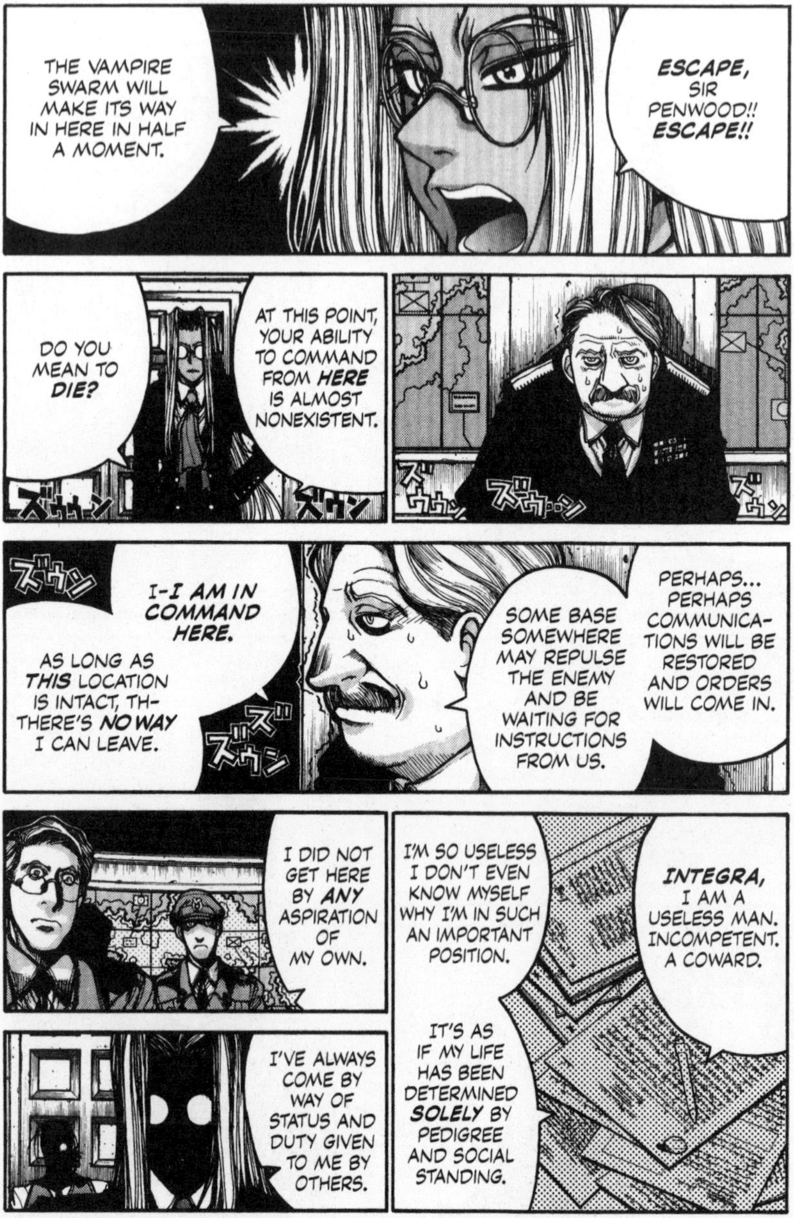
ESCAPE, SIR PENWOOD!! ESCAPE!!
THE VAMPIRE SWARM WILL MAKE ITS WAY IN HERE IN HALF A MOMENT.
AT THIS POINT, YOUR ABILITY TO COMMAND FROM HERE IS ALMOST NONEXISTENT.
DO YOU MEAN TO DIE?
PERHAPS... PERHAPS COMMUNICATIONS WILL BE RESTORED AND ORDERS WILL COME IN.
SOME BASE SOMEWHERE MAY REPULSE THE ENEMY AND BE WAITING FOR INSTRUCTIONS FROM US.
I-I AM IN COMMAND HERE.
AS LONG AS THIS LOCATION IS INTACT, TH-THERE'S NO WAY I CAN LEAVE.
INTEGRA, I AM A USELESS MAN. INCOMPETENT. A COWARD.
I'M SO USELESS I DON'T EVEN KNOW MYSELF WHY I'M IN SUCH AN IMPORTANT POSITION.
IT'S AS IF MY LIFE HAS BEEN DETERMINED SOLELY BY PEDIGREE AND SOCIAL STANDING.
I DID NOT GET HERE BY ANY ASPIRATION OF MY OWN.
I'VE ALWAYS COME BY WAY OF STATUS AND DUTY GIVEN TO ME BY OTHERS.

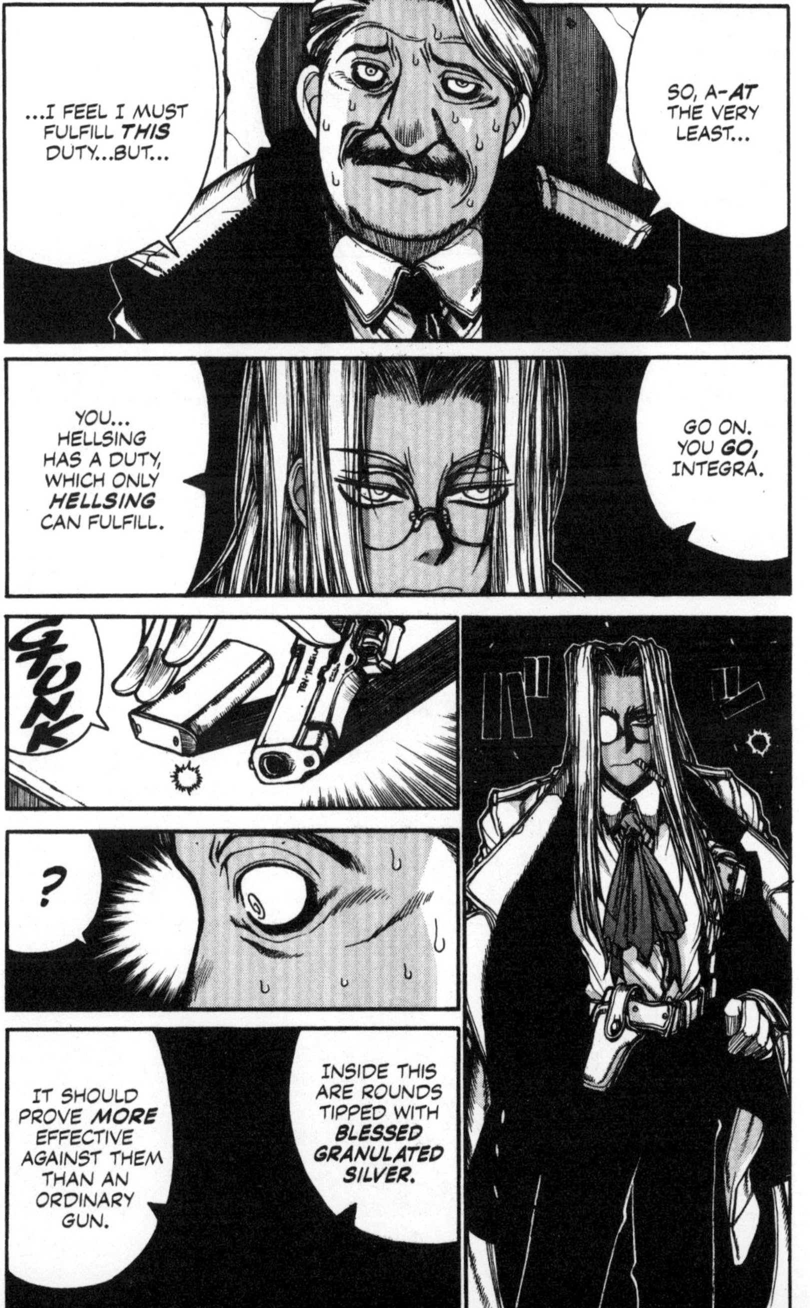
SO, A-AT THE VERY LEAST...
...I FEEL I MUST FULFILL THIS DUTY...BUT...
GO ON. YOU GO, INTEGRA.
YOU... HELLSING HAS A DUTY, WHICH ONLY HELLSING CAN FULFILL.
GUNK
?
INSIDE THIS ARE ROUNDS TIPPED WITH BLESSED GRANULATED SILVER.
IT SHOULD PROVE MORE EFFECTIVE AGAINST THEM THAN AN ORDINARY GUN.

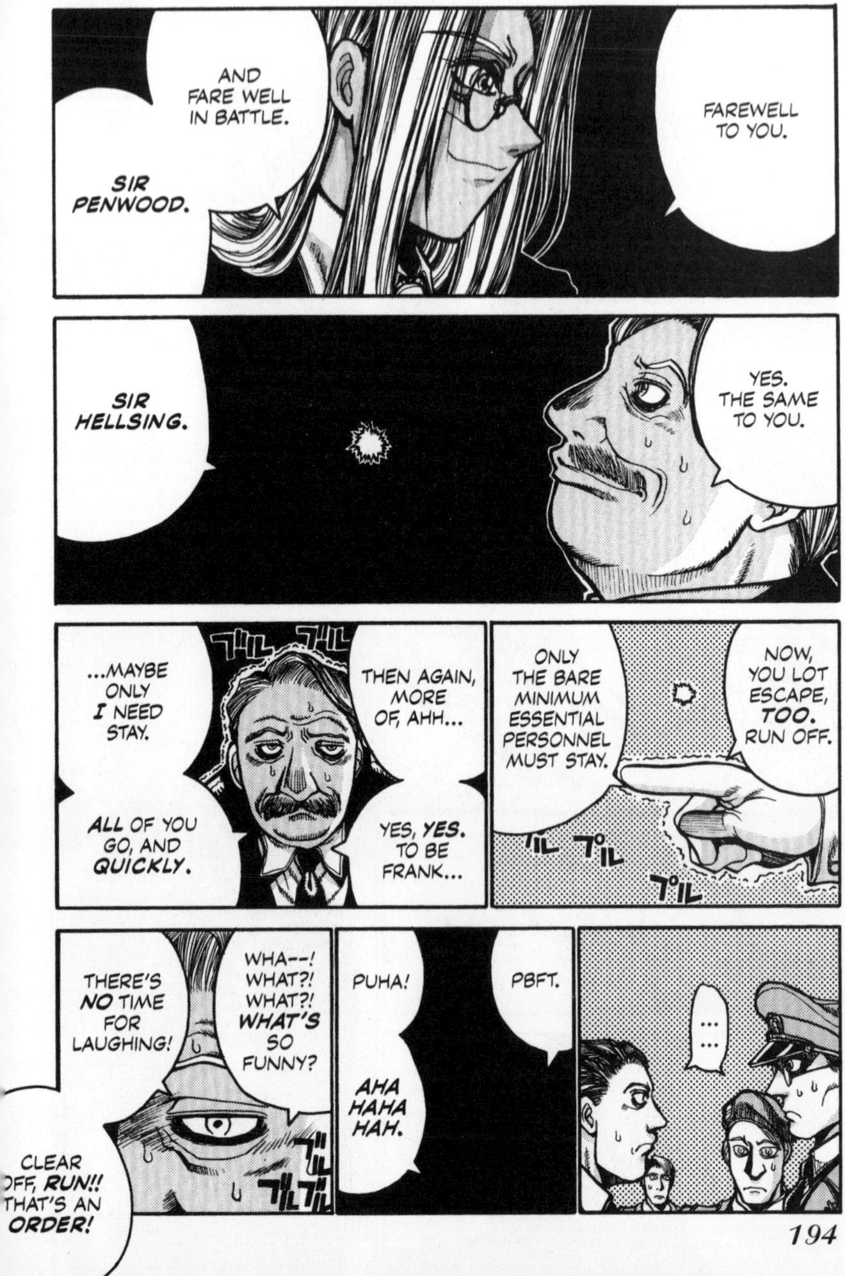
FAREWELL TO YOU.
AND FARE WELL IN BATTLE.
SIR PENWOOD.
YES. THE SAME TO YOU.
SIR HELLSING.
NOW, YOU LOT ESCAPE, TOO. RUN OFF.
ONLY THE BARE MINIMUM ESSENTIAL PERSONNEL MUST STAY.
プル プル
プル
ブル ブル
THEN AGAIN, MORE OF, AHH...
...MAYBE ONLY I NEED STAY.
YES, YES. TO BE FRANK...
ALL OF YOU GO, AND QUICKLY.
......
PBFT.
PUHA!
AHA HAHA HAH.
WHA--! WHAT?! WHAT?! WHAT'S SO FUNNY?
THERE'S NO TIME FOR LAUGHING!
CLEAR OFF, RUN!! THAT'S AN ORDER!

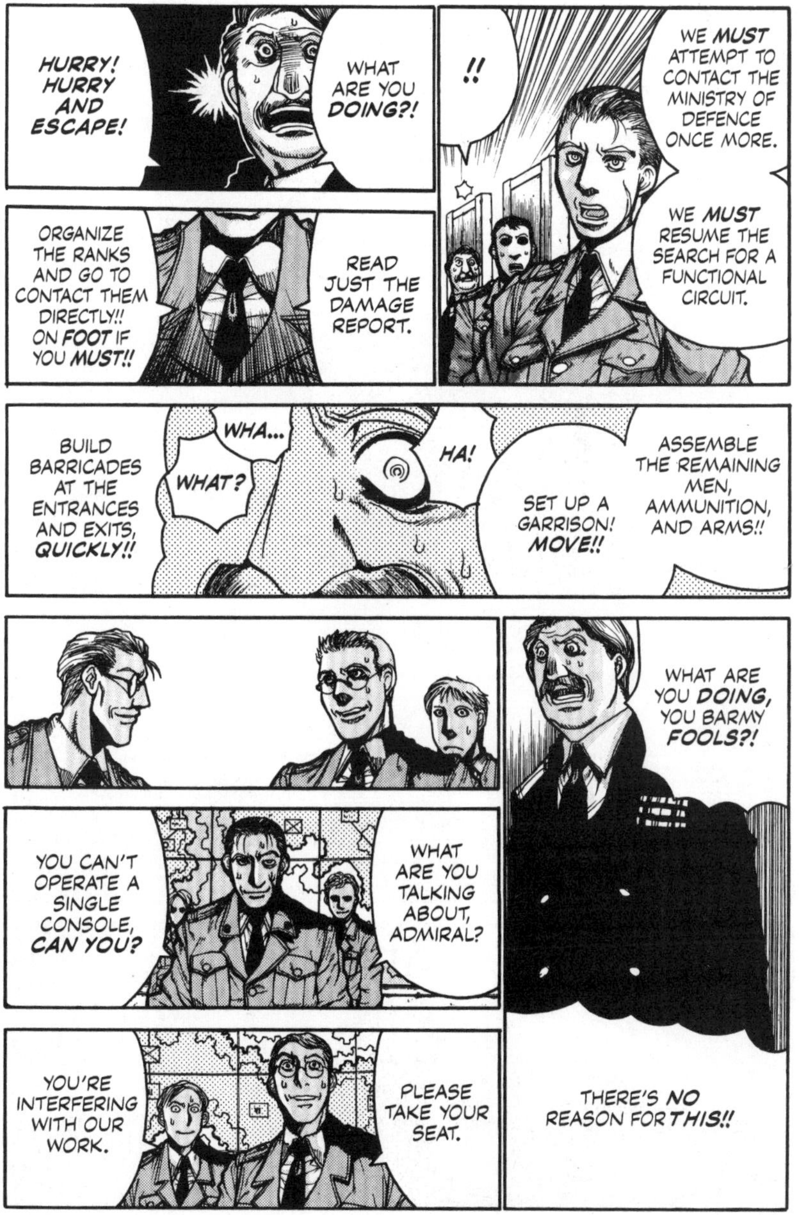
!!
WE MUST ATTEMPT TO CONTACT THE MINISTRY OF DEFENCE ONCE MORE.
WE MUST RESUME THE SEARCH FOR A FUNCTIONAL CIRCUIT.
WHAT ARE YOU DOING?!
HURRY! HURRY AND ESCAPE!
READ JUST THE DAMAGE REPORT.
ORGANIZE THE RANKS AND GO TO CONTACT THEM DIRECTLY!! ON FOOT IF YOU MUST!!
ASSEMBLE THE REMAINING MEN, AMMUNITION, AND ARMS!!
SET UP A GARRISON! MOVE!!
HA!
WHA...
WHAT?
BUILD BARRICADES AT THE ENTRANCES AND EXITS, QUICKLY!!
WHAT ARE YOU DOING, YOU BARMY FOOLS?!
THERE'S NO REASON FOR THIS!!
WHAT ARE YOU TALKING ABOUT, ADMIRAL?
YOU CAN'T OPERATE A SINGLE CONSOLE, CAN YOU?
PLEASE TAKE YOUR SEAT.
YOU'RE INTERFERING WITH OUR WORK.

AND *THANKS.*

I'M SORRY, EVERYONE.

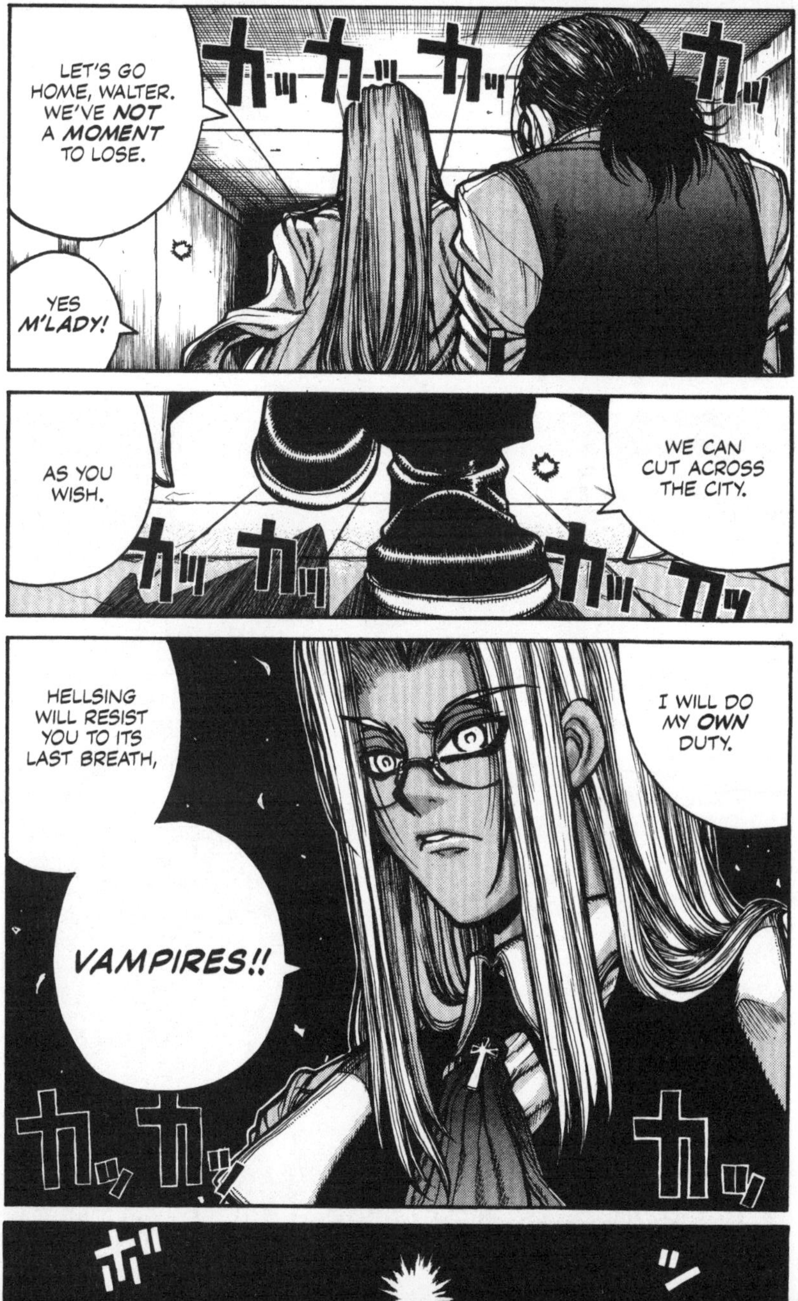
カッ カッ カッ カッ
LET'S GO HOME, WALTER. WE'VE **NOT** A **MOMENT** TO LOSE.
YES **M'LADY!**
WE CAN CUT ACROSS THE CITY.
AS YOU WISH.
カッ カッ カッ カッ
I WILL DO MY **OWN** DUTY.
HELLSING WILL RESIST YOU TO ITS LAST BREATH,
VAMPIRES!!
カッ カッ カッ
ボッ

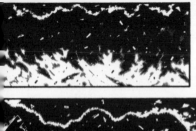

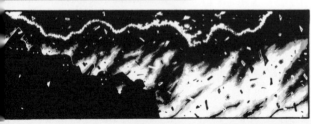

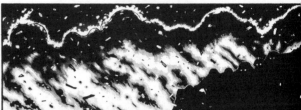

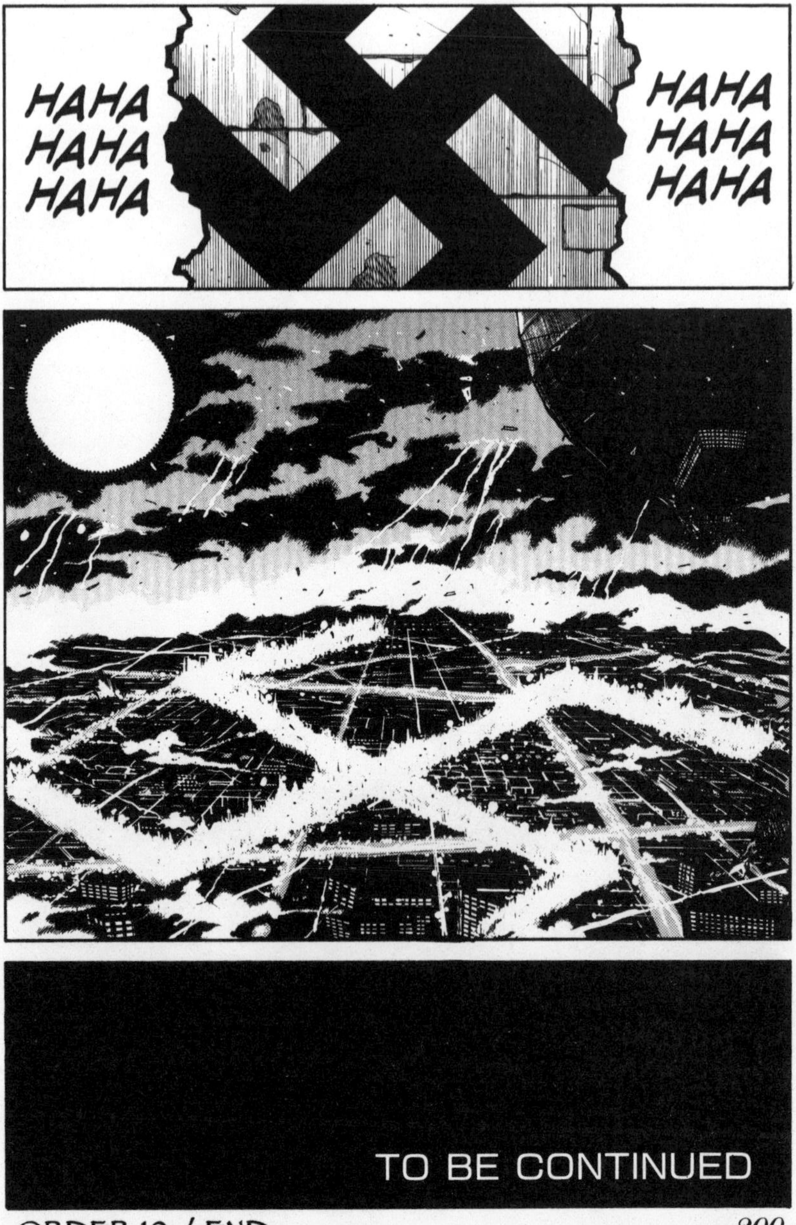
HAHA
HAHA
HAHA
HAHA
HAHA
HAHA
TO BE CONTINUED

KOHTA HIRANO

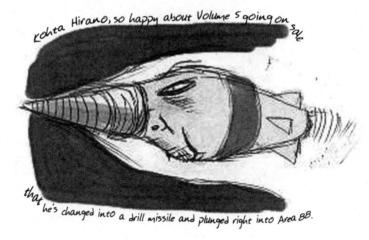

Kohta Hirano, so happy about Volume 5 going on sale that he's changed into a drill missile and plunged right into Area 88.

HAILING FROM ADACHI WARD, TOKYO

HOBBIES
+BEING OBNOXIOUS, BEATING OFF.

FAVORITE KILLER
+THE PRIEST KILLER NAOJIROU NIU.

THE ONE PIRATE WHO MUSN'T BE ALLOWED TO LIVE
+ARLONG

THE PIRATE YOU WANT TO BE IN YOUR NEXT LIFE
+ARLONG

WHAT YOU'D LIKE TO DO ONCE YOU'VE BECOME ARLONG?
+COP A FEEL ON NAMI'S BOOBS, FORGET ABOUT THE
 WHOLE VILLAGE THING, THEN RUN OFF AND LIVE OUT
 MY REMAINING YEARS SOMEWHERE.

PAPER WAR HUMANITY GOD EAT GOD CORNER

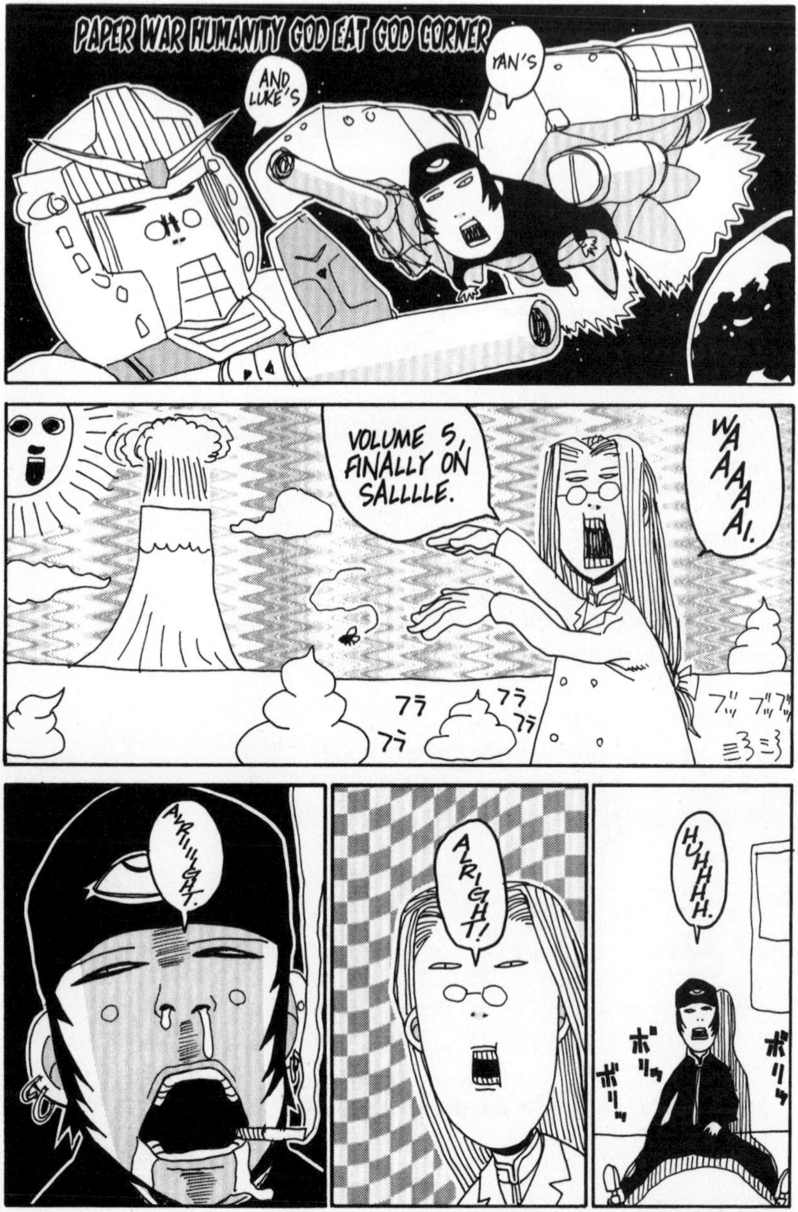
PAPER WAR HUMANITY GOD EAT GOD CORNER
YAN'S
AND LUKE'S
WAAAAAAI.
VOLUME 5, FINALLY ON SALLLLE.
ブッ ブッ ブッ
フラ フラ フラ フラ
HUHHHHH.
ボリッ ボリッ ボリッ ボリッ
ALRIGHT!
ALRIIIIGHT.

SOOOO, MOVING ON, HERE'S ANOTHER TANKOBON AFTER A YEAR AND A HALF'S GONE BY.
HE WAS DRAWING A SIDE STORY OR SOMETHING, AND IT TOOK A LONG TIME.
TSUMO.
ALL TILES CHUN. 1,000,000 POINTS.
YEAH, SOMETHING LIKE THAT. SO ANYWAY, FROM HERE ON HE'LL DO HIS BEST, OR NOT, OR JUST BE LAZY.
SO, PATIENCE.
HEY, LISTEN.
YOU TOTALLY IGNORIN' ME?
TCH!
SO THIS'S GOT NOTHIN' TO DO WITH ANYTHIN', BUT TAKE "GOKAN"*...
...AND STRETCH IT TO "GO--KAN," AND IT'S LIKE "GOUKAN" AS IN "RAPE."
ユラー
*NOTE: "GOKAN" MEANS "VOLUME 5."
LIKE RAPEMAN, YOU DIG?
I RAPE BAD WOMEN AND TEACH THEM A LESSON!!
THAT IS MY IDENTITYYYYY!!
NOW FOR MY DEATHBLOW, YOKOHACHI INFINITY!!
AND THEN THE .44 MAGNUM!!
GYAHHHH!!
OH SHIT!! THE PACIFIC!!
AND FINISH YOU OFF WITH HAKENCROSS!!

*NOTE: "YOKOHACHI" MEANS "SIDEWAYS EIGHT," HENCE THE INFINITY SYMBOL.

ASCENSION

ERECT.

Hiranokouta

● HELLO AFTER SO LONG. EVERYONE. THIS IS
KOHTA HIRANO. HERE'S A TANKOBON AFTER A
YEAR AND A HALF. LAAAG. LOTS OF THINGS
HAVE HAPPENED AROUND THE WORLD THIS PAST
YEAR AND A HALF.
LIKE GUNDAM.
AND KING GAINER.
AND A BUNCH OF SPINELESS PEOPLE DOING
SOME KIND OF EXODUS.
ALSO OJAMAJO DOREMI HAD ITS FINAL SEASON.
NADJA.
IT'S EROTIC, ISN'T IT?
HOW 'BOUT KAMEN RIDER 555?
IN ABARANGER, (THE US VERSION IS POWER
RANGERS: DINO THUNDER), THE GIRL WITH
GLASSES SHOULD'VE TRANSFORMED.
OH GEEZ, I SPEND HALF THE DAY SUNDAY IN
FRONT OF THE TV AT HALF MAST.

● NOW REGARDING THE MANGA, HOW ABOUT IT?
AM I GOING TOO FAR OUT ON A LIMB? AM I?
GUESS SO.

● UHHH, WELL, THERE'S NO REAL POINT TO ANYTHING
ELSE HERE.

● SINCE THERE'S SPACE LEFT OVER, I WILL
SING A SONG.

♪ "THE BOOB SONG"   ♫
YESTERDAY---- ON GOLDEN FOREIGN FILM THEATRE----- THEY WERE PLAYING
UNDER SIEGE----- AND THAT HUGE BREASTED GIRL----- (OH! GIRL! GIRL!
GIRL GIRL GIRL GIRL GIRL-----) WAS SHE MISS JULY OR MISS OCTOBER-----
SUPER HUGE BOOBS SUPER WICKED BOOBS ♪ (HUGE!!)
WE'RE ON A QUEST, A QUEST FOR BOOBS......

CHARACTER
INTRODUCTIONS

ZORIN BLITZ
ALIAS BIG SIS ZORIN.
ASYMMETRICAL LEFT & RIGHT.
ARMED WITH A SICKLE.
HAVING TO DRAW THE TATOOS ON HER
FACE AND WHATNOT EACH AND EVERY
TIME IS SUCH A MONUMENTAL PAIN THAT
SHE DIES IN THE NEXT INSTALLMENT.

HEINKEL WULF
ALIAS WUUUU. (ABOMINABLE SNOWMAN) (SHAGGY)
ARMED WITH PISTOLS. BDANNNG BDANNNG
HAVING TO DRAW PISTOLS AND WHATNOT EVERY
TIME IS SUCH A MONUMENTAL PAIN THAT SHE
DIES NEXT INSTALLMENT.

YUMIKO TAKAGI (YUMIE)
ALIAS BOOOOO. (BECAUSE SHE'S A TAKAGI) (MR. BOO)
                    (LOVES THE UKULELE)
SPLIT PERSONALITY. TOUGH AS NAILS.
ARMED WITH A JAPANESE SWORD.
            SHNK. "GYAHHH!" SHNK. "GYAHHH!"
HAVING TO DRAW THE SWORD AND WHATNOT EVERY
TIME IS SUCH A MONUMENTAL PAIN THAT SHE DIES
NEXT INSTALLMENT.

YOSHIO YAMAMORI
ALIAS FOUNDING HEAD OF THE TENMASA CORPORATION
"BRING IT ON!! FIGHT ME!! C'MON! I'LL GIVE YA WHAT FOR!"
THE FOUNDING HEAD OF THE TENMASA CORPORATION,
WHICH WENT FROM BEING THE HIROSHIMA YAMAMORI GANG
TO BECOME A POLITICAL ORGANIZATION, HE MORE OR
LESS RETIRED FROM PUBLIC LIFE AFTER COMPLETING HIS
DUTIES. TAKING ADVANTAGE OF TENMASA CORPORATION
INFIGHTING, HE HATCHES PLOTS WITH HIS CLOSE FRIENDS
MAKIHARA AND HAYAKAWA.

Created by Kentaro Miura, *Berserk* is manga mayhem to the extreme—violent, horrifying, and mercilessly funny—and the wellspring for the internationally popular anime series. Not for the squeamish or the easily offended, *Berserk* asks for no quarter—and offers none!

Presented uncensored in the original Japanese format!

VOLUME 1
ISBN 978-1-59307-020-5

VOLUME 2
ISBN 978-1-59307-021-2

VOLUME 3
ISBN 978-1-59307-022-9

VOLUME 4
ISBN 978-1-59307-203-2

VOLUME 5
ISBN 978-1-59307-251-3

VOLUME 6
ISBN 978-1-59307-252-0

VOLUME 7
ISBN 978-1-59307-328-2

VOLUME 8
ISBN 978-1-59307-329-9

VOLUME 9
ISBN 978-1-59307-330-5

VOLUME 10
ISBN 978-1-59307-331-2

VOLUME 11
ISBN 978-1-59307-470-8

VOLUME 12
ISBN 978-1-59307-484-5

VOLUME 13
ISBN 978-1-59307-500-2

VOLUME 14
ISBN 978-1-59307-501-9

VOLUME 15
ISBN 978-1-59307-577-4

VOLUME 16
ISBN 978-1-59307-706-8

VOLUME 17
ISBN 978-1-59307-742-6

VOLUME 18
ISBN 978-1-59307-743-3

VOLUME 19
ISBN 978-1-59307-744-0

VOLUME 20
ISBN 978-1-59307-745-7

VOLUME 21
ISBN 978-1-59307-746-4

VOLUME 22
ISBN 978-1-59307-863-8

VOLUME 23
ISBN 978-1-59307-864-5

VOLUME 24
ISBN 978-1-59307-865-2

VOLUME 25
ISBN 978-1-59307-921-5

VOLUME 26
ISBN 978-1-59307-922-2

VOLUME 27
ISBN 978-1-59307-923-9

VOLUME 28
ISBN 978-1-59582-209-3

VOLUME 29
ISBN 978-1-59582-210-9

VOLUME 30
ISBN 978-1-59582-211-6

VOLUME 31
ISBN 978-1-59582-366-3

VOLUME 32
ISBN 978-1-59582-367-0

VOLUME 33
ISBN 978-1-59582-372-4

VOLUME 34
ISBN 978-1-59582-532-2

VOLUME 35
ISBN 978-1-59582-695-4

$14.99 each!

dmpbooks.com   DarkHorse.com

BERSERK by Kentaro Miura ©1989 Kentaro Miura. All rights reserved. First published in Japan in 1990 by HAKUSENSHA, INC., Tokyo. English text translation rights in the United States of America and Canada arranged with HAKUSENSHA, INC., Tokyo through TOHAN CORPORATION, Tokyo. English text translation © Digital Manga, Inc. & Dark Horse Comics, Inc. Dark Horse Manga™ is a trademark of Dark Horse Comics, Inc. All rights reserved. (BL7623)